The Treason of Betsy Ross

A Woman of the Revolution Novel

Wendy Long Stanley

Carmenta Publishing via Ingram Spark T 1 2

Prologue

Philadelphia
March 31, 1777

My father shook me awake with a large hand on my shoulder. I blinked uncertainly, the morning still heavy with shadows so dark it could have been the middle of the night, lightened only by the soft arc of a crescent moon. His hand reached out again, a gentle weight.

"What is it?" I asked. It was very early. Rachel was snoring next to me, puffs of breath soft as a dreaming puppy, and in the bed across from us lay the inert form of Rebecca.

He motioned to the door with a lift of his chin. I saw a lit lantern perched on the table in the hall, a sway of yellow flame. In the shadows, I saw my father was dressed. I nodded and climbed over my sister.

"Meet me downstairs," he said, disappearing into the hall.

I dressed quickly in my work clothes, my hands deft from years of getting dressed in half-light. It was cold, the embers burning low in the hearth, my breath sharp in the room when it passed my lips. Layers of wool in place, I slipped down the stairs, as I had as a girl, my hand barely touching the balustrade, my feet light and sure on the narrow steps my father had painstakingly built thirteen years before. I still loved the place where the stairs curved sharply and continued their steep descent, the dark wood worn and shiny, my head narrowly close to the ceiling.

Father was pulling on his boots in the pine chair by the front door, Mulberry Street still quiet outside. Sometimes we called it Arch Street, for the large arch that ended the street at the river. The arch was put there as an afterthought to provide easy access to riverside shipping, but they'd had to cut Front Street to put it in place, putting the arch up over the cut road. That was in my grandfather's time.

"Where are we going?" I asked, blowing into my cupped hands. "Why did you wake me?" I reached for my boots, slipped them on.

"Help me pick up supplies, dear?" There was a short silence while he waited for me to fix my bonnet. My father's leather carpenter's apron was tied around the slight roundness of his belly, his coat open. I reached for my winter cloak and shrugged it on my shoulders.

"At the docks?"

He nodded. "And up High Street after."

I blinked, shaking off deep sleep. High Street? Today was Monday. Market days were Wednesday and Saturday. Perhaps a boat had come in with fresh lobster and eel. Or maybe he needed nails from Stockton's. I took my basket from its resting spot by the bottom of the stairs. What a treat—a few hours away from my needle, with my father all to myself.

We exited the house to a crisp winter morning and headed south toward the river. The noise level rose as we got closer to the docks: the rumble of wheels on cobblestones, a low drone of voices punctured by the occasional shout, the rugged sound of masts being drawn up ropes. I could smell the baking from the widow O'Brien's boardinghouse as we passed.

"James had best fix that gate," my father grunted as we passed one of the Dunbar cows standing outside its grassy pen, a fresh cow patty steaming nearby. He pushed the cow back into its yard and slid the wire back over the post. Aimless youths sometimes let livestock out as a lark, much to the owners' ire, but in Dunbar's case, the wire was old and loose, the metal latch not quite catching. We continued on to the warehouses lining the wharves, the sun rising before us. A few sheep stared at us from an open field.

"Nice morning," my father said conversationally. "Didn't think you'd mind. I fancied your company."

My empty basket bounced lightly on my arm. I glanced sideways at my father. He was sixty now, the father of seventeen children, although eight of my brothers and sisters had died before the age of five. By birth order, I was eighth in line. Three of my siblings remained in the house that I had just awoken in, too early on a cold morn for my liking, when I'd been cozy and comfortable nestled next to my sister's warmth. Although, none of them were children anymore. Rachel, the youngest in our family, was turning fifteen. George, the only brother left, was sixteen. My older sister Rebecca had never married and still lived at home. I lived next door and had just stayed there last night to help my sisters care for Mama, who had been ill.

"I don't mind," I said easily, smiling up at him. I appreciated time alone with my parents more now that I was older, especially after the enforced solitude of my husband's death. I could go into my workshop a few hours later than usual. Sadly, my time was spoken for by no one other than myself now. I would work as late as I needed to.

We passed the morning in easy companionship, retrieving my father's bag of supplies—mainly nails in different sizes and a new awl—and warmed up over a breakfast of bread and cheese and chutney at McGregor's Inn, watching the boats bob in the water in the morning light, the sky the color of thin gruel. My father stopped to speak at length with some carpenters working on a ship being constructed at Manuel Eyre's place while I watched a flock of crows gather around the carcass of a deer. I was snug in my woolens and cloak, content to observe the flurry of workers along the docks until I overheard someone mention an execution. Excitement laced their voice. Philadelphia hanged a few men a year, but not many. Maybe two or three, sometimes a few more, for thievery, burglary, and murder. Hangings were reserved for the most heinous of crimes. *Poor man*, I thought. While we were running errands, he was waking up to face his death. Or maybe he hadn't slept at all last night.

After a few hours by the river, we made our way up High Street, past the long line of market stalls, the morning full-bodied and growing louder. A lot of people were walking with us—men, women, children—a tide of movement, some surging by. There was an eagerness in the air, anticipation rising up like mist. Realization dawned, and my good mood turned sour.

My father was taking us to a hanging.

"Where are we headed?" I asked him, hoping I was wrong.

"They are executing a *spy*," a woman hissed, as if my question had been directed to her, her face self-righteous and indignant.

"I thought you should see," my father said as we entered Centre Square, "what they do to traitors."

I set my jaw. I could feel my lips press together in a thin line. I could leave. I was a grown woman. Dare I leave?

Centre Square was large, spacious, flat. One of William Penn's designs. We drew closer to the middle and stopped. The gallows were being erected. I looked uncertainly at my father. "Why must I see this?"

He didn't meet my gaze, standing there with one hand in his pocket, the other holding the sack over his shoulder.

The crowd was gathering, increasing in size rapidly, burgeoning like the steady swell of a creek rising with April rains. We waited, watching the gruesome scene unfold.

Someone was crying. I looked around. The sobbing came from a woman trying to make her way through the sea of people to get closer to the gallows. She looked to be about my age, red-eyed and splotchy-faced.

"You shouldn't be here, Lydia," another woman said, holding her tightly. "Please come away. He wouldn't want you here." The woman tried to pull her away unsuccessfully.

"Leave me," Lydia wailed. "James! James! Leave me be, I said!" The distressed young woman attempted to shake off her friend.

My heart sank as I watched the workmen complete the wooden structure and rest the ladder against the top beam.

James who? There had been talk in town, hadn't there? Ah yes. A quick trial, a detailed confession from him once caught. I didn't read the newspapers—I was too busy and at the end of each day my eyes were tired—but facts clicked in my mind from what I'd heard. James Molesworth, yes, that was it. He had been accused by congress of being a spy for the British. Pennsylvania had been hanging men on this site for many years, but today they were hanging a man for treason. Or at least espionage. It was coming back to me in bits. He had been a mayor's clerk who began spying for the British. Apparently, British General Howe had hired Molesworth. Yes, that was it.

When I turned to my father, he was looking at me with the same impassive expression he'd worn all morning.

"I don't want to stay," I said. "I will not stay."

"We'll stay," my father answered. His tone brooked no argument, even though I was a widow of twenty-five and had my own business, my own trade, my own house.

Tears spiked my eyes, frustration. He had no right to force me to witness this. I thought of turning on my heel and striding away, but that would only satisfy him. He wished me to be afraid. If I left, he would think I was frightened of seeing a man die for his country.

"This is not a Patriot being hanged," I said. "This is the execution of a man loyal to the British. His sentence comes from the American Congress. You're trying to get me to be a Tory, like you. But you're on the wrong side."

My father shook his head. "The tides of war can change," he said simply, his tone matter-of-fact. "And for us, they will change soon. In a short time, the British will take back Philadelphia and restore the rightful government. Traitors and Patriots will be hunted in droves." *Including me.* He swallowed. "Daughter, do not let me see you hang."

There was no malice in my father's words. The British *were* trying to occupy Philadelphia, just as they had invaded and controlled Boston and New York. Many went so far as to warn that Philadelphia was going to be *attacked*, not merely taken, as punishment for our city being the clear leader, by a mile, of the revolution. We had watched hysteria grow within the streets at an alarming rate, particularly in the last year or so since the British navy had begun attacking coastal towns that were largely undefended, cannoning them from the water.

I stood there, frozen to the spot and seething. I knew I should leave, but I could not get my feet to obey me.

I didn't know how long we waited while the crowd continued to grow to an immense number, the large square filling. Merrymakers were dancing about as if they were welcoming a bountiful harvest.

"I heard they shite themselves," a boy in front of us said eagerly. His head barely reached my shoulder.

"Nah, they piss," his companion said cheerfully. "And their tongues go black and swell like cooked liver."

"And their legs go like this," the first boy said, doing a grotesque dance, his legs jerking like a marionette being manhandled.

It was a gray day; the sun could not part the clouds. My father's timing, our early arrival, had given us a spot close to the front of the gallows, fulfilling his intention. They brought poor James Molesworth into the square on a cart from the Walnut Street Prison, hunched and wig-less, with visible sores on his shins. His hands were so dirty he looked to be wearing gloves. The sight of the man elicited a wail from the distressed Lydia, followed by her scream of, "I'm here. James, I'm here!" The convicted man did not indicate that he heard her, but he must have. He did not look up; his eyes avoided the crowds.

A short time later the spy was dragged to the bottom of the ladder. As they put the noose around his neck, a great cheer rang out and the crowd stomped and whistled. "Traitor, traitor," they chanted into the morning. Lydia's screams were lost under shrieks of delight. Who was she to him? I wondered.

I stole a look at my father, who was tight-lipped now, his face grim. I had the feeling he would rather not be here at all.

I would not watch, I told myself. I would look away and pray for the soul of this James Molesworth. Were we not all flawed in some way? Yet I could not drop my eyes. There were some murmurs from the clergyman to the condemned man, who shook his head. They pulled James's cap low over his eyes and forced him up the ladder. People in the taverns and coffeehouses said that James had been an inept spy, loose-lipped and trusting, his crime as obvious as the nose on his face. Espionage. Treason. He was working for the British, trying to find men who knew the Delaware River, men who knew the exact location of the *chevaux de frise* buried in the water, the hidden bombs, the obstructions, the natural shoals and shallows. He was going to pay these men a handsome sum to guide British warships up the river and into the waterfront so they could turn their guns to Philadelphia and take the rebel seat. It would have been a tremendous triumph. Two widows who ran inns on the docks had advised Molesworth on which river pilots to approach. The women had also been caught and punished.

"Wait," James Molesworth said at the top of the ladder. He turned his head to speak to the men below him, blind from the cap over his eyes. "Make public the confession I gave last night under court martial. That is my desire."

Without waiting, without another word said to him, the executioners kicked the ladder away without ceremony. He wasn't expecting it.

Molesworth in death did not, in fact, wet himself. The quick end, the sway of his lifeless body, his quiet departure from this earth, seemed to disappoint the crowd, who murmured disgust and quickly dispersed as his confession was being read aloud.

"I am sorry if I upset you with this, Betsy," my father said to me. "I felt it necessary. You must distance yourself from the rebellion. Save yourself."

Rebellion? We had declared ourselves an independent nation last summer, formed a government. This was a war now.

"I am afraid for you, my daughter," he said urgently into my silence. "Please. Think to the future. You must stop."

I wanted to say, *Are you certain they hang women?* but stopped myself from being impudent. There was a time when I had not been so audacious. I wondered what they had done to the two women—Mrs. McKay and Mrs. Bryan—who had aided James Molesworth in his espionage. I chewed my lip, considering my response.

"I know what you're doing," he said again, more insistently, his face an open plea. "I know you're doing business with the navy men. It's not right."

"I cannot simply—"

"I thought when John died," my father interrupted and stopped when he saw my expression. He tried again. "I had hoped, perhaps, you could have a chance to start again. Find a man who—"

"Is a Quaker?"

"Who will take you away from danger."

I took my father's arm and turned him to leave the square, James Molesworth's lifeless body swaying behind us under the leaden sky of this March day.

I nodded to the body. "What will they do with him?"

"They'll make a shallow grave and leave him here."

Like waste. May God bless James Molesworth.

"Perhaps we could talk about . . . what I am doing," I said hesitantly as we walked through the square.

"You must stop," my father said again in a stern tone.

If the last five years had not altered the political loyalties or opinions of Samuel Griscom, nothing I could say would change him, so I would rather not quarrel. *Focus on what's important,* I told myself, trying to quell my anger. *Think of his affection for you. And you for him.*

"Thank you," I said eventually. "I know you are trying to protect me."

My soothing tone and attempt to mollify him fell flat. Instead, my father talked and talked at me, words of caution and retribution and disapproval flowing from him as we walked back down to Mulberry Street.

"Heed my warning, daughter," he urged me again as we stopped outside the house.

"I will be careful," I said sincerely, shifting my basket from one arm to the other. This morning down at the docks, when my father was occupied elsewhere, I had purchased lengths of hemp and silk with a high thread count from one of the importers, materials that would better weather the demands on a ship's standard, tougher fabrics that would withstand wind, sun, and rain on open water. The fabrics were folded and lay at the bottom of my basket, wrapped in paper. Later today, or tomorrow, I would turn them into ensigns for the new American navy. It was paid work that I was pleased to do, and I could easily envision the flags being whipped by the wind on open water, showing a vessel being commandeered for the continental forces.

"I'm going to go finish the McLaren window frames," my father said, striding away. "Tell your mother I plan on stopping by the meetinghouse later, will you? Tell her I'll be home late."

I stopped and watched him go, stretching my back with a sigh by twisting left and right. When my torso twisted to the right, my eyes drifted to Hannah Lithgow's general goods shop, and to the left, my new home next to my parents' house. My display of upholstered goods decorated the window facing the street, a small offering compared to what John and I used to do in our workshop before he died. Missing John was a raw pain, flesh carved open, so I pushed him out of mind and thought of James Molesworth instead. Molesworth's real mistake was working for the British. Why couldn't my parents understand that?

I can't stop, I told my father's retreating form. *I won't.* I had no intention of going backward, even if they tortured me for it. *I have to do this now.*

Chapter 1

September 1767
Ten years earlier

My siblings were squabbling again. George and Rachel, aged six and five, created more noise than two children ever should. You would have thought there was a gang of them, the way they yelled and battled each other in play. My sister Hannah, who knew better at age twelve, egged them on for her amusement and then left to go hide in her bed with her school reader. The youngest two Griscoms wouldn't have been acting like that if my parents were around, that was for certain.

My brother and sister's childish noise, the pitch of it, was banging on my head. Our mother and the house help were occupied in the cellar. These small mischief-makers were left to me to watch.

"When can they go to school?" I had asked longingly the week before. My mother had sent me up the street to the Quaker school when I was six. Surely these two were old enough now?

"If I send George, Rachel will be left with no one," my mother had said. "One more year. Then they will both go."

Like animals, they could smell the freedom of not having adults nearby who would censure their conduct. They weren't afraid of me—that was the problem. I'd have to make them afraid of me. How many hours had I wrestled these children today already? I cursed my older sisters for having the sense to be born first and leaving the house already.

I'd be tougher on them; that's what I'd do. If I took Rachel's doll, I could make her listen. I considered this, but then she would squawk and my mother might come running and I'd be in trouble.

"George, Rachel, come," I called. "Let's do your letters. Think how big you'll be when you can make your own words!" They ignored me. Why learn their letters on the writing tablet I held in my lap if they could attack each other with swords made from dry reeds? The reeds were from a tall vase of dried flowers on the side table. I glanced out the window. What a long, long day. The rain fell like slow tears, barely a drizzle, one drop separate from another, but enough to bury the horizon with a thick iron blanket. I tossed the tablet aside and rose, watching George and Rachel put down their swords and fight over a set of old wooden soldiers stored in the corner chest. I rose and went to the window. The boredom, this daily torment, was weighing down on me like an iron bar.

How I envied my five older sisters, whose age had freed them from this monotonous child-minding duty, from this busy house. They could come and go as they wished. Deborah, married and the only one of us out of the house completely, held the title of eldest at twenty-seven, with Mary just above me at seventeen. Sarah, Rebecca, and Susannah filled the gap between Mary and Deborah. There had been a brother, William, and the first Sarah, both babies, but they were long gone, deceased, along with six of the brothers and sisters born after me. I think that that's why young Rachel and George (not to mention Hannah, who was downright devilish) got away with so much more than us six oldest girls ever could—they held the coveted position of being the last of Mama's babies. After Rachel was born five years ago, the babies stopped coming. Rachel was a gift, my mother said. She'd thought she was past it: forty-two, her body tired, her back stretched to the limit, her heart scoured rough from too many dead children. Some of the babies who'd died I couldn't remember—I was either not alive yet or too little—but the last four I could. Ann, Samuel, Abigail, Joseph. There was a neat line between the living Griscom children and the dead, a similar number on each side. My poor mother. George and Rachel were the two children who had brought our family back to life after four sibling burials in quick succession.

They were sweet, but I still thought they got away with murder. And Hannah! Hannah needed a smack. She was three years younger than me, but she acted like she was the oldest. High-handed.

"Can you two play quietly for a bit?" I asked George and Rachel, placing my hands on my hips to appear commanding.

Rachel stuck her tongue out at me.

I glared at her. "No, Rachel. If you're rude I'll get the soap," I said, knowing my threat was empty. I could never do that.

She quickly put her tongue away, panic flashing on her little face.

"It's not nice to do that, and you're a good girl," I amended. As well she knew. "Stay here. I'll be right back."

I found my mother in the cellar, her work apron covered in peach juice and tomato pulp. We had a separate kitchen house out back, but it was cooler to work in the cellar in September.

"Can I help?" I asked. "Please let me help down here. Why don't you give me something to do and ask Hannah to watch the little ones? Rachel and George are particularly unsettled today."

My mother smiled at me but shook her head. She pointed to the stairs, merciless. She was sending me back to heed the children. I looked around me. Every surface was taken up by jars, empty and full, and bowls of stewed fruit. The women were hard at work, the cellar warm and moist. Pots were bubbling on the hearth.

I groaned silently. "Please," I tried again, in my nicest voice.

"Hannah doesn't have your touch, dear," my mother said. "She's not yet of an age for patience."

I turned to go back upstairs when Ivy gave me an unexpected gift. "Why not take some peaches up to John Webster at the shop," she said to my mother. My ears perked up.

"He's been good to us," Ivy said, "giving Mary work and all. And a good price on the curtains, as well."

Ivy was our longest serving kitchen help, accepting her position in the Griscom household around the time my mother had my sister Deborah, years ago, when, impossibly, Ivy had been my age. Ivy came in the mornings and returned home at the end of each day. She was a grandmother now, her own children gone.

I turned on my heel and eyed my mother expectantly.

"He has," she agreed, considering. "That would be fine. We've plenty to spare this year, thanks be."

"Oh, let me go, please," I breathed. "I'd love to have a little walk."

My mother couldn't stifle her chuckle, but she turned it into a cough. "Betsy, they're only children," she teased me. "Harmless enough."

I loved children and wanted my own one day. However, when they're your own, you can do what you think is right with them. Brothers and sisters, they hound you and you are burdened by them. Right now, I desperately wanted out of this house. Lucky Mary, out of our home already and learning a trade. And only two years older than me!

"All right, go," my mother said, smiling. "Take three peach, three tomato, and a sourdough loaf. Apples too. Oh, and that squash there."

I reached for a wood crate from a shelf and packed it quickly.

"Mind you're not long," she said. "Put the toy animals out before you go. That will keep them amused. They're new."

"I can go up and mind them if you'd like," young Beatrice offered. She was the most recently arrived help, with a round face and big cheeks. Her eyes always twinkled.

"Not yet," my mother said. "We'll give them a chance to behave. They're not babies anymore."

I almost snorted. Then why was I their jailor?

"Hannah can watch them for just a little while, can she not?" I said. Why was my lazy sister lolling about, invisible? "She's hiding in her chamber, Mama, reading."

My mother nodded her agreement, tightening the lid on another jar of peaches. I hurried upstairs before she had second thoughts about letting me go.

I went to the bedchamber I shared with three sisters and put on a clean apron and smoothed my hair. I wouldn't need a cloak. Even with the halfhearted rain, it was still far too warm for that; the air held summer's heat. My short gown in brown linen would do. I reached for the cream bonnet that I had embroidered with rosebuds of light pink and ivory in fine French knots and stem stitching. Mother thought it was too fancy for a Quaker girl, but I liked it. The stitching was small and unobtrusive—one had to look closely to see the finery of it.

I tiptoed to the bed and peered through the drawn curtains. Hannah was lying on her back with her stockinged feet crossed at the ankles, resting up on a bedpost. She'd left the curtains on the other side of the bed by the window open enough to let the light in to be able to see the page. In one swift attack, taking her off guard, I reached through and yanked her book away.

"Wha—!" She leapt up, bed curtains winding around her as she struggled out.

"I'm going out," I said, backing toward the door with her book. "*You're* to go down and watch George and Rachel. Mother said."

"Give me my book!"

I glanced at the title. *Pamela.* That's why she was hiding. Mother would not tolerate that. That definitely wasn't a school reader. I dropped the book on the floor and kicked it with my toe so that it sailed across the rug and landed under the bed.

"Where did you get that? You know that's not allowed. What if Mama found it? Maybe she should know!"

With my parting shot, I ran out before she could detach herself from the bed curtains and lunge for me. I retrieved the toys—little animals of wood my father had made—checked the children, then dashed out into the drizzle and up the street as fast as my crate of gifts would let me.

In less than a block, I reached my destination. *J. Webster, Upholsterer* was printed in a smart green on a sign hanging by the door. I paused outside and peered in the window. John Webster had caused quite a stir when he arrived from London. He told the women in town that he had all the latest fabrics, from calico to silk, and all the expertise to make the Philadelphia ladies' homes look like Europe's finest. He would still drop names of the London aristocrats who used his services. "Mrs. Soane, the architect's wife, you know . . . Mrs. Henley, the lord chancellor's wife . . . I crafted the most sumptuous chairs for them."

I could see Webster behind the counter, showing a woman in a tall hat—a very puffy hat—several bolts of fabric.

I knocked on the glass once, balancing my crate between my chest and the door frame, and then I reached for the handle, pushing the door open. A brass bell jangled above me. Mr. Webster looked up, and a small furrow appeared between his brows. The woman's ridiculous hat sported a tall set of feathers in blue and green. My timing was impeccable, as usual. In comparison, I looked windblown and young, like an indentured girl stumbling in with wares to hawk.

"Good day," I said and lifted the cloth so Mr. Webster could see the contents of his gift, the crate lined in gingham. He was wearing a beautiful waistcoat, I saw, heavily embroidered with bluebells and white tulips. "A little gift from our mother, Mr. Webster. For you, from our family. I'm Mary's younger sister Elizabeth."

The woman turned. I knew her. Eliza Shippen, the judge's wife. Her eyes were blank, her face polite. I knew she wouldn't recognize me. Why would she? She couldn't know that my father and the other carpenters had built many of the homes she frequented.

"Perhaps I could take it to the back for you?" I said quickly, noting Mr. Webster's displeasure at being distracted from a wealthy customer. "I see you are busy."

He nodded, already turning back to the fabric on the counter—velvets, I thought. "From Belgium," he told Mrs. Shippen, "one of the oldest mills in The Hague. The finest of naps, as you can see, and not a single flaw to be seen. Cut on the bias, it will have a . . ."

The back room was deep and crowded. The showroom was small compared to the workshop. At first it was hard to see where to walk to avoid bolts of stacked fabrics and boxes of feathers, ribbons, and notions. I put Mother's offering on a counter in the back corner near a table with mismatched chairs that I guessed was for the workers to eat at. Dirty cups sat on the table.

"Betsy. What are you doing here?" Mary asked when she looked up. She waved me over to her.

"This is my sister," she said to the room of bent heads. I looked around, intrigued. I counted eight workers: four women and four men. One of the women, older, seemed to be in charge.

There were murmured greetings.

I wanted to linger, to be involved in this hive of activity. Excitement thrummed through me. The bolts of cloth were like an invitation, calling to me. Fabrics of every color and texture, materials from all over the world! Flannels, silks, printed calicos, damasks, Venetian poplins, velvets, wool moreens, Indian taffeta. My hands itched to touch them, to make something, to thread up a needle and add myself to the line of workers creating beautiful items. I peered over Mary's shoulder, watching her work. Mary was a fine sewer, but I knew I had a better hand for more intricate work. Mrs. Jones at school, our sewing and embroidery teacher, had said so.

I heard words of farewell and the bell tinkled on the front door. Mr. Webster appeared.

"So you are a sister of Mary's," he said, eyeing me.

I nodded.

"I cannot work with this, Mr. Webster," the girl next to Mary said in frustration, holding up a piece of satined silk.

"The needle keeps pulling the fabric and causing a run. I'm afraid I will ruin it, if I haven't already."

She was near tears.

"That's the wrong needle," I said. "For that fabric."

Webster raised an eyebrow. "You're good with satins?"

"I am!" I said quickly, feeling Mary's eyes on me. "Perhaps I could help?"

"We have a large order for embroidered valances for several windows in the same home. The lady of the house insists on satin, but the embroidery pattern she has chosen makes the work hard going and pulls at the fabric," Webster explained. "We're having a difficult time of it. A fine cotton would have been the better choice, or even a tightly woven linen, but she insisted on a shiny satined silk."

"I can help with that," I said. "It will take the thinnest needle you have with the smallest eye, and a single thread of thinly spun fine cotton."

"Not silk thread?"

"Cotton is more forgiving. If the thread breaks, it is less likely to cut or damage the fabric. Silk thread is more durable, which means the fabric may give or damage before the thread does. There may be less damage to the fabric with cotton. If one does use silk thread, it's best if it's the same weight as the fabric, which can be tricky."

Webster took a fresh piece of the valance cloth and handed it to me. Someone else handed me the needle and thread. "Do one of the flowers and vines."

I felt the eyes of the workshop on me.

I sat in an empty chair, threaded my needle, and worked the tiny stitches onto the delicate fabric, my eyes carefully following the design on the paper pattern. When I looked up from the work, an hour had passed at least. I had forgotten Mother's instructions to return quickly. Well, Hannah was there. Mother's work would be uninterrupted. I handed my work over to be inspected, feeling the older lady looking at me.

Webster looked up from my stitches. "How old are you?"

"Fifteen."

"Are you seeking work, Elizabeth, sister of Mary?" his tone was slightly mocking.

I flushed. "Only if you are in need of assistance."

"If you wish to work here, I will pay a visit to your father and discuss terms. We have no shortage of work, and you've a skilled hand."

I thought I heard Mary inhale sharply.

"I would like to work here," I said, a thrill coursing through me. "I'd be pleased to learn the upholstery trade."

"We could use another pair of hands like hers," the older woman said, nodding to Webster. To me she said, "I'm Ann King. I run the workshop for Mr. Webster."

She smiled at me and I smiled back.

Mary might be cross with me, but I could manage that. She had never been able to stay angry with me for long. The thought of getting away from the ruckus in the house every day, even for a few hours, filled me with joy. I'd been so restless. And to be able to sew for a real upholstery! It was better than making an excuse to go to the meetinghouse just for somewhere to go and sitting in silence, pretending I was in prayer. Father would have to say yes. I'd beg him! I was old enough now to go out and work. And not just any work—I'd be learning about one of the most lucrative trades in town! Besides, extra shillings were always welcome in our house, even if Father had been doing well for years.

Webster nodded, satisfied, and went back to the front room.

I looked over at Mary, who gave me a look and bent her head over her work.

"Well, jolly good," a man said cheerfully from the back table where he was stuffing cushions. "The more the merrier, Mary's sister. We'll be glad to have you."

Dark eyes in a handsome face were looking at me. Inky blue? Muddy green? He was far enough away that I couldn't tell. The man—boy?—smiled at me, a jaunty little half grin.

He was so forward! Taken aback, I lowered my eyes and murmured goodbye to Mary.

"Tell your mother thank you," John Webster said when I passed him in the front room. I didn't know whether he was referring to the food gift or the work he hoped I could do for him. "I'll be by to see your father this evening."

*

I was in the backyard gathering chestnuts and avoiding Hannah when Mary found me.

"You could have told me," she said without heat, sitting on the bench next to where I was picking up the newly fallen nuts. They'd ripened early this year. There was a sea of them under the tree.

"There was nothing to tell," I retorted, gathering chestnuts into a bag. "I was dropping off food. I didn't plan any of that. All I wanted was an outing."

"You could have asked me. You should have told Webster you'd think about it and then gone back after we spoke."

I sat next to her on the bench, putting my arm around her. "Don't be cross with me. I'm sorry if you feel I barged in on your workplace."

Mary was the sweetest of all my sisters. Although there was only two years between us, she always seemed much steadier and wiser than I would ever be. She had a nature that was calm and quiet. She never lost her patience with Hannah and the littles. Mother was almost sorry when Mary got hired at Webster's and she lost her presence in the house during the day.

Mary sighed and opened her palm. She held a fistful of walnuts. She pulled a nutcracker out of her pocket.

"It's the only place that's ever been all mine," she said, her voice soft, opening a nut and handing me the meat to eat. "Just for me."

Her words had the cadence of a Society Hill lady. How was she so cultured when Hannah and I sounded so plainspoken?

I considered what she'd said. It was true that there was always a crowd of people in our house at any given time. We spilled over from one room into the next, seven sisters and one brother and our parents, a constant milieu of moving bodies, although finally no toddling babies underfoot. There were always relatives coming and going, cousins from New Jersey visiting and staying the night, hired help that came and went. The house was always full and loud, breathing people in and out like wind from a bellows.

"And now Webster knows you are better with a needle," she said worriedly.

"Webster's not going to let you go," I said confidently, chewing the walnut meat, although how would I know? "I'm sure he knows by now what a good worker you are. And that older lady too, Mrs. King. The one who runs things."

We watched the chickens scrabble in the dirt in front of us.

"Were you hungry for chestnuts, or are you hiding from Hannah?" Mary asked, lightening the mood.

"I took her book and then left her with Rachel and George. Of course I'm hiding from her."

Mary laughed. "She'll have it out for you."

"Do you know what I caught her reading? I don't even know where she got it."

"Don't tell me. No seriously, do not. I don't want to know."

I held my hand out for the walnuts and nutcracker and started cracking walnuts myself. There was something satisfying in breaking the shell, how much force it took.

"The boy there," I said. "At the shop. The one who spoke to me. What's he like?"

"John? He's an apprentice. Been there about a year. I think he said he's around my age. He's nice."

"He seemed quite bold."

"Oh, Betsy, no, he's not like that. He's a hard worker. John makes us laugh; he's got the funniest sense of humor. Makes the day go faster, you know? He's kind to me."

Something in Mary's voice, a warmth, made me look up at her. "Mary! You like him."

"No." Mary shook her head. "I hardly know him."

I thought of the boy's flashing eyes, the half grin. "Are you certain?" If I was going to work there, I wanted to know if Mary had affections for someone in the shop.

"Very certain. I think he would find me too meek for his nature. Or perhaps I should say he is too social for mine. Besides, he's not Quaker. I could not court him even if I wanted to."

True. My sister Deborah had already been disowned from meeting for marrying Everard Bolton outside of the faith three years ago. They had taken their vows at First Baptist Church. I can still remember my grandmother's disdain: "Baptist! Of all the churches in town! What was she thinking? It's an embarrassment." I have no idea what she thought was wrong with Baptists, what prompted her scorn. Our mother and father had eloped too, twenty-five years ago, but they expressed regret afterward and their penitence allowed them to stay in the Quaker fold. Not Deborah, though. She said she had no intention of expressing remorse to anyone, let alone the church elders who chased her for months. She and Everard were quite happily living as Baptists on the other side of town.

"Our parents do not harbor any ill will toward Deborah now," I said. "She was over just the other day. I heard her giggling with Mama. So perhaps it is possible to make a choice for love."

Mary shook her head. "I wouldn't want to. The meetinghouse is my home. Don't you feel that way too?"

I nodded. We had been raised in the faith, our ancestors arriving in the New World to sail up the Delaware River and settle on the New Jersey coast as Quakers a hundred years ago. Some of them relocated to Philadelphia, like my grandfather. I loved our meetinghouse and the Society of Friends, the way our faith was one of the only ones to teach equality for all, and how we could connect with God directly.

"I do. I didn't like what Deborah did. I saw how much her actions hurt Mama." As the eldest, Deborah was supposed to set an example for the rest of us girls but hadn't.

"Shocking really," Mary said.

"Perhaps another man will come to work at Webster's who is one of the Friends and will catch your heart," I suggested.

"Perhaps," Mary agreed with a shrug, unconcerned.

I put the nutcracker I'd been toying with in my lap and reached for her hand. "Thank you for not being cross with me."

Mary laughed. "Who says I'm not cross with you? There are many upholsterers in town, and you had to choose mine! I was enjoying being away from you lot. You should beg my forgiveness."

I released her hand and waved the nutcracker. "I just did! Forgive me, darling sister! I beg you! Next time would you have me bring grapes and a fan, as if you are a Roman empress and I your servant?"

"Oooh, yes. That sounds nice. I could use a personal servant for a week," Mary said, standing up. "No, a month." We both laughed. "Instead, I think I'll tell Hannah where to find you."

"Don't you dare!"

Mary ran for the back door. "Hannah!" she called. "Betsy's out here!"

Sweet and calm, yes. Meek? She did herself a disservice.

*

That night Mr. Webster came to the house, as he said he would. My father was out but my mother said she would receive him herself. She invited Webster in for tea, but he declined, standing just inside the door holding his hat. He must have walked; I knew his carriage, and it was not on the street.

My mother listened to Webster's offer, hands folded, face thoughtful. From my spot in the hall, peering around the wall, I could see her, but not Webster. I hovered eagerly, not sure whether I should go in or not. Hannah was listening next to me.

The front door stood open behind Webster. Despite the warmth, the evening carried the first hints of autumn, the air laced with wood smoke and the earthy smell of plants decaying, although the tree in the yard behind the open door had only just started to turn.

"I need someone who can do fine work, you see," Webster said. "Give our competitors a run for their money. Show them we're just as good with the elaborate work."

My mother nodded.

"I can pay Elizabeth a shilling a day," Webster said. "And it would be my pleasure to teach her the trade, like Mary."

Hannah gasped and smacked my arm. I would earn money. I'd never earned my own money before. A wage!

Although I could not hear all that was being said, I knew from the rhythm of the conversation and my mother's congenial tone that a deal had been agreed to. I sighed in relief, warmth flooding through me.

I heard the front door close and my mother laughing, pleased.

A shilling a day! I rushed into the front room and dropped into an easy chair, pulling my knees up to my chest, feeling giddy. Hannah plopped down in the matching chair across from me and glared at me. "I wish it was me," she pouted.

My mother came and sat on the sofa under the window.

"I wish I could work," Hannah said sulkily.

"You will one day," I said.

"Very good for a girl of fifteen, Betsy, very good," Mama said, smiling at me. Her eyes were shining. "Hannah, do you see what can be gained from practicing your needlework? Apply yourself. Perhaps in a year or two John Webster will employ all three of you. Wouldn't that be something!"

I felt as light as air, my body as weightless as a feather, spinning in the breeze.

"To think, I was only going to ask for half what he offered," my mother said, winking. She grinned and got up to get her snuff box from the fireplace mantel, tweaking my cheek on the way. It must be pleasing to them, another child reaching an age where they could learn skills and contribute to the household.

The real reward was freeing myself from this house and the little creatures, even if I wasn't solely responsible for their care all the time. I still missed my days at Rebecca Jones's Quaker school. Unfortunately, by the time I was thirteen I had learned everything she could teach me. I had outgrown the school and had not been enjoying my time at home since then. Webster's upholstery was an unexpected gift. Oh, I couldn't wait! I liked learning, and I loved sewing, the satisfaction of making lovely items from pieces of fabric. I was taken by the beauty and creativity involved in the craftsmanship of creating high quality pieces for people's homes. The work would be no hardship, and I would have companionship. Some of the girls were similar to me in age. Even Mrs. King seemed nice. My heart leaped at the freedom of it. Strange, to think of work as freedom. To me, it was.

"I'm going to go tell Mary," I announced, standing up.

Hannah followed me. "Can I come visit you one day at work?"

"I haven't even started yet. Don't suffocate me."

I took the stairs two at a time, Hannah close behind.

"Did you tell on me about my book?" she asked my back. "You are a wretched girl, you know that? Why are you nice to Mary and not me?"

"You should not be reading Samuel Richardson," I threw over my shoulder. "You know it. Confess in meeting."

"Did you tell?" she persisted.

I didn't really care about what she was reading. I just wanted to annoy her. I laughed without answering.

"You are getting too big for your boots, Miss Betsy Griscom!" Hannah cried. "Pride cometh before a fall!"

She shoved me in the middle of my back. I shook her off like an ant and called for Mary.

I didn't know about pride coming before a fall, but I'd rather that than keel over from the strange exhaustion, the wretched tedium, of daily boredom.

Chapter 2

1769

I was happy working at Webster's with my needle, content with my friends and my life at the meetinghouse, so at first I did not notice the violence seeping into our lives. Perhaps I did not want to.

Two years ago, shortly before I started working at Webster's, parliament decided that duties must be paid by all the colonies on some of the goods we imported from Britain. The taxes, called the Townshend Duties, applied to paper, glass, British china, lead, and tea. Everyone was furious, especially after the Stamp Act four years ago, a tax law which was passed and then repealed a year later after widespread protest erupted across the colonies.

The Townshend Duties were met with the same rebellion. At first many of the troubles seemed to be up north in New England. Towns in Massachusetts, Connecticut, and Rhode Island protested the Townshend Duties so passionately that they told everyone to stop buying and using British goods for one year. Non-importation. That would teach the British to make arbitrary rules, they said, rules that weren't fair and were an abuse of power. New York started to reject British imports as well.

The king didn't like the protests. Or the disruption to his trade. He sent two thousand soldiers to Massachusetts to subdue the biggest troublemakers in his colonies and restore order. Redcoats patrolled the streets in Boston, doing their best to appear imposing and threatening, jostling the people and being combative if need be. Or if the mood struck. All the colonies eyed Boston to see what would happen.

I heard my parents talk about the Townshend Duties but it didn't affect me so I stopped paying attention. I hoped it would blow over quickly and that they'd repeal them the way they'd repealed the Stamp Act. I didn't care for politics, and the level of rage many people expressed frightened me. I tried not to get involved, telling myself it was nothing, until the day I saw them beat the tax man.

At work that day, when Webster was out, disagreement broke out about the wrong and right of what was happening in Boston. It seemed to be an almost daily argument now, and the conversations always made me uncomfortable. My fellow workers were quick to anger. I didn't really know much, but I heard one of the men in the workshop say that John Dickinson had it right when he wrote *Letters from a Farmer in Pennsylvania* and accused the Townshend Duties of being illegal because they were intended to raise direct revenues rather than regulate trade, which is what we were used to. He said we should have a say in the taxes we pay if we're all British subjects, and that our liberty was being taken away. Another worker disagreed and their voices rose.

"Are those chair covers done?" Ann King asked pointedly, walking back to where the men were joining the chair frames. They fell obediently silent and I breathed a sigh of relief. Conflict was ugly. Mary and I exchanged looks.

Ann appeared by our side. "Can I send one of you to the weaver's? They have the new fabric ready for the Presbyterian church pew cushions."

"You go," Mary offered.

"Thank you," I breathed, leaping up.

I took my time walking back to Webster's from the weaver's, made sweeter by the gorgeous October day. I walked past the glass maker on Third Street, noting a trend toward thinner panes, and then stopped briefly to admire a fan in the window of a new shop filled with European goods. *Anything but British,* I thought ruefully. Next to the fan, resplendent with images of Venice, was an equally beautiful case for the fan in midnight blue.

I heard a sharp cry of pain, out of place. I looked up to see a circle of men on the corner across the street creating a cage of legs around a man lying on the ground. I moved to step toward the fracas. What a strange sight this was, on a warm day filled with sunlight.

A hand on my arm stopped me. "That's not for you, lass," a man said. "Best move on."

I shook off the hand. I ignored the stranger, stepping away. I stood watching, puzzled at first, wondering what was happening. My eyes tried to make sense of what I was seeing. They weren't beating him, were they? Who was the fallen man? What was going on?

It happened so fast. In quick succession, one by one, each of the men in the circle stepped in to deliver a kick to the prone form. A glimpse of ginger hair appeared on the stones when legs and boots shifted. The man cried out again, a pitiful sound of anguish.

"Go back to where you came from!" a fat man cried as he gave the fallen man a swift kick. "Tell FitzRoy that one's for him," he yelled as his boot made contact with the man's back. Augustus FitzRoy, the prime minister of Great Britain?

"Go on now," the man next to me encouraged quietly. "Walk on. There's a good girl."

I didn't look up at him, I was still staring at the scene unfolding in front of us.

"Why are they hurting him? Why isn't anyone trying to stop them?" I asked, dumbfounded.

There was a process for trying people who had done something wrong in the courts. This man was being openly beaten in the middle of the day. It was not right, not by anyone's account.

I turned finally to glance up at the man next to me. He was taller than I, his head framed against a startling blue sky. The man was old, upright and proper, rigid as a post, cane in hand. His eyes met mine, bushy eyebrows sticking out in white and black under his hat.

"Can't someone make them stop?" I said again, looking around. I winced at the sounds the ginger-headed man was making.

"That man's a tax collector," the man said, his voice gravelly with age. "No one dares get involved."

I did not understand. You couldn't just thrash a man in the street because you fancied having a go at him. I looked around for other men, younger men who could stop this. Unfortunately, it was a quiet day, on a corner only lightly frequented by merchants and tradespeople, none of whom seemed to be around at this moment.

"You had best go," the elderly man said again with more conviction. "This has been going on for a time. I was in the coffeehouse and saw it through the window."

"You saw them start beating him? What did he do?"

"Go, miss. I entreat you. This is not for the fairer sex's eyes."

Just then a horse and cart pulled up.

"Took you long enough," one of the attackers yelled to the driver.

"Piss on ya," the driver responded and spat tobacco on the ground.

I watched, stricken, as the man was moved unceremoniously to the road behind the cart. They tied his ankles with rope then secured the rope to the cart.

"No," I said, horrified.

The men stepped back, surveying their work.

"Yaw," yelled the driver, and the cart lunged forward, dragging its victim behind it along the street. *I hope he's unconscious now*, I prayed, but the man cried out again and lifted his head in an attempt to protect it from the hard stones. His captors laughed. That bedeviled man. His suffering would be great.

"Stop," I exclaimed, rushing forward. I put up a hand. "Please! Stop!" No one heard me. There was blood on the stones where the man had been.

I turned and ran toward Webster's.

"Hey now," the old man called after me, but I did not stop. I could barely see where I was going, but I dashed down Third

Street and around the back of the churchyard until I arrived on Mulberry.

I entered Webster's with tears burning in my eyes. I quickly went through to the workshop and dumped the weaver's package on the table, heading for the privy out back.

"Betsy, wait," John was moving toward me. "What's wrong?"

"Come out back," I choked, not wanting to been seen by everyone when I was upset. I pushed open the door to breathe in deep gulps of the October air, hugging myself.

John stood under the sycamore tree with me and waited for me to collect myself, his forehead creased with worry. "Are you unwell? What happened?"

My sister Mary joined us, looking at me anxiously. "Be quick, Betsy, before Ann notices us gone."

I took another deep breath. Geese honked overhead, heading south in a sweeping formation. "I was picking up the order when I saw a group of men harassing a man, a tax collector, someone said. They beat him terribly. For a long time. Then they tied the man to a cart so they could drag him through the streets! I don't mean they put him inside the cart—no, they roped him to it by his ankles and hauled him along the stones. I think they might have killed him."

John exhaled loudly, and Mary made a noise of distress.

"How horrible. You must try to put it from your mind," Mary said, clasping my arm, trying to calm me. "There was nothing you could have done."

"They didn't care who saw! They weren't even trying to hide what they were doing," I cried, my mind replaying the scene. I stared at a patch of brown grass, not seeing it. "It made no sense, to see a man being hurt in broad daylight, in full view of shops and a coffeehouse—anyone could see through the window. There's even a school around the corner! What if the children had come out? I can't get it out of my mind. The satisfaction they took in it."

"How do you know the man was a tax collector?" John asked, his expression concerned, his eyes on my face. I had been wrong that first day I saw him; his eyes were not blue, not green, but a liquid brown so deep they looked black up close.

"A man told me, a passerby. An older man. Too old to stop them."

"There may be more of that, unfortunately," John grimaced. "Townshend was a fool to impart such measures after what happened in '65."

"Try to put it from your mind," Mary said again.

I shook my head to break up the violent images playing repeatedly in my mind.

"I need a moment to recover myself," I said, taking a few steps and resting my back against the tree. I squeezed my hands together. "It was awful. The terrible sounds he was making. . ."

"What a frightful thing for you to have to see," John agreed sympathetically.

"I'll go in," Mary said, "lest they miss us." She looked at me sorrowfully. "I'm sorry for what you saw, Betsy. We'll speak more at home. What a relief you are unharmed."

I barely heard her, hardly noticed when she left.

"I could see his hair flopping when his head banged on the street," I told John. "His yells . . . He was crying out in such pain. He was beaten for doing his job, John. The cruelty."

"You could not have stopped them," John said softly. "I hope you know that. Mary's right, there was nothing to be done. There was another one last week. They tarred the poor bloke to the point where he had no skin left. Burned like bacon cooked to black. Try and forget what you saw."

Surely no king's man would work as a tax collector in town after this. Word would spread. One might be an attack of chance, but two attacks in a month? Two would be a warning of imminent danger.

"Do you think he's dead?" I asked. "The man."

"It would be a blessing if he is."

"If he were alive, where would he be?"

"No, Betsy, don't do that. This does not concern you. Let's go back to work." Concern was spread across John's face. He had been a good friend to me over the past two years here at Webster's. I had come to be very fond of him, and our friendship.

"Would he be at the hospital?" I asked. I needed to know the man's fate. Had I witnessed a murder? I needed to know.

Something shifted in John's face, a slight tensing of his features, at the mention of the hospital.

"Maybe, if he's alive," John agreed. "They may have dumped him by the road, and perhaps someone took him to the hospital. If he's still being dragged through town at the end of a rope, it's unlikely that he'll be alive."

"Oh," I said and felt tears spring hot into my eyes again.

"I am truly sorry that you had to see that. No girl should. You've a kind heart to care so much."

I brushed at my tears with a brusque fist. "Enough of this. I'll go in."

"I'll ask Ann if one of the men can do the pickups for a while," John said. "Just in case."

I nodded. "Thank you."

I felt so sad. Philadelphia was changing. My home since middle childhood, it had always been a thriving city, bursting with commerce and people and growing so quickly that my father was kept busy building houses, one after the other, many of them more elaborate than the one before. People seemed happy here. At community gatherings, the Friends would talk about how fortunate we were to live here, in a place that was rapidly expanding, bursting with advances in medicine, science, social justice. How lucky we were to be in a place concerned with public welfare, they said, and in a province mostly ruled by Quakers. The Society of Friends held power in Pennsylvania and let God's light shine through us, for the betterment of all people. It was a wonderful time to be alive, the elders said, to see better times for rich and poor alike. I liked that. I wanted to believe that all people could be treated well.

It didn't feel like that now though. Now the city was seething with anger over the duties and how Britain was taking advantage of us. Blood was being shed on our streets. I'd seen it with my own eyes.

*

I hounded my parents for news of the tax collector's fate, but they didn't know. They hadn't heard anything. They didn't understand why it mattered to me. The following night, in the parlor around our fire, I tried again.

"Mrs. Shippen is a regular client at the shop," I said. "Her husband is a judge. I could tell them what I saw. Will you let me do that? Surely this crime is not above the law? Those men shouldn't just walk away scot-free, no matter their politics. Mrs. Shippen holds calling hours every Saturday. Will you take me?"

My father sighed, and my mother busied herself with Rachel's music lesson.

"Tell me we cannot just attack anyone we wish?" I asked. "He was the king's man, not a street thief."

"You should discuss this in meeting with the elders," my father answered. "You may find solace."

"I do not want solace," I snapped, "I want to know if the man survived." I softened my eyes at him in apology, hoping he would not chastise my impertinence.

My father raised an eyebrow at me as Rachel began a choppy violin sonata. Mother reached up to adjust her hand placement on the bow.

"Father, Betsy saw this man's suffering firsthand," Mary said, glancing up from the sampler she was stitching. "Surely you cannot begrudge her the need to know how he fares, if he's alive. If he *is* alive, perhaps we can we provide help in some way? Wouldn't it be the right thing to do? The godly thing to do?"

I knew my family did not want to get involved. That was not our way, or any Quaker's way for that matter, but I was haunted by the man's head slapping against the street, his neck bouncing about, his face twisted in agony. The Society of Friends eschewed all violence, but couldn't we offer charity after someone else had been a victim?

"Who's suffering?" George asked, looking up from where he was playing a game of backgammon with Hannah on the rug. Rebecca was at the corner table, making a picture out of tiny seashells.

"Someone was hurt," I said. He shrugged and went back to moving his game piece.

"Can we play chess, Hannah?" George asked.

"No. It's tiresome," Hannah retorted.

"Do you even *know* how to play chess?" George shot back.

"Why do you care about that man, anyway?" Hannah asked me, rolling her eyes at George. "You didn't know him at all."

"Should we not *all* care?" Mary retorted, pushing the cat away from her needle. Clumpy, the family cat, would not comply and began to try and catch the moving thread, batting it more aggressively with a quick paw whenever Mary pushed the needle down and up and then down again. Mary stopped and put the embroidery ring behind her back until the cat gave up and wandered off. Mary picked it up again and returned to the letter *E*.

I looked over at Mary with gratitude. At least I had one sister left at home with common sense. At nineteen, she would soon find a suitor and leave the house, and I dreaded that day. I needed her here. I still believed she was sweet on John at work, but if her heart was guarded and it was a secret, it had nothing to do with me. She had resisted all my attempts to put them together.

"I think we should try and find out," I said again. "If he died, then someone could tell the magistrate. We'll know he was killed."

"Yet if he's alive . . ." Mary said, letting her voice trail off with the possibility.

My father sighed again and reached a big work-reddened hand up to rub his face. I saw he had fresh scrapes and scratches from his work at the Carpenters' Hall site. His guild was building their own trade quarters.

"All right," he said finally.

Mary and I exchanged glances, eyes widening. "Yes?" I asked hopefully.

"Go ask at the hospital, if you must. Tomorrow, after you both finish at the shop. Don't go inside, girls, mind you, ask at the front. Then be done with it."

I did not know the man's name, but that bright ginger hair—that would identify him quickly, along with the extent of his injuries. I didn't think they'd have many men who'd been dragged through town tied to a cart.

*

I believed the day would seem long, but Webster's was busier than ever and my hands were never idle, which meant my mind was also forced to pay close attention to complicated needlework. Even with all the other upholsterers to choose from, Philadelphia was growing so rapidly, and becoming so wealthy, that Webster's had no shortage of work. I expected the normal requests for bed curtains, pillows, and mattresses, but what surprised me were all the orders for expensive furniture upholstery, tasseled lamps, and decorative home pieces heavy with fringe and brocaded damasks from the orient.

Webster lapped it up, his energy never flagging, and talked daily of becoming more successful than Plunket Fleeson, who still held, from what I could tell, the coveted position of being the most lucrative upholsterer in town. We had outgrown our Mulberry Street location, and Webster was looking to move the shop closer to the river and the source of incoming materials.

I had been enthusiastically learning the upholsterer's craft at Webster's for two years. I really enjoyed the trade, which had long stopped being an escape and an interest unto itself for me. I felt grateful that Webster had taken me under his wing and into the fold of his team of skilled workers. We constantly tried to produce the best and most current of all textiles in the city. Webster did his best to import the finest fabrics, designs, and influences from all over the world, always hustling and making deals down at the docks to get the most beautiful cloth and embellishments from incoming ships. In many ways, I had grown up here, going from fifteen to seventeen under the eyes of customers and the other shop workers, some of whom had been in the upholstery business for years. And of course, under the especially watchful eyes of Ann King, who'd become like a second mother to me. It was rewarding work, all of it, no matter whether I was sewing, piecing, stuffing, or doing lacework or tassels. Webster was constantly trying new designs in draperies and bed hangings, or attempting to reproduce the finest furniture fashions of Europe. The shop bustled with life and artistry. It didn't feel like a job to me, it felt like a privileged education.

I was busy sewing fringe onto a cushion when I heard the front door open and then close with a hard bang. Webster's irate voice followed, muttering to himself. I imagined the ladies in the front were looking up in surprise. Webster had hired two well-spoken women, Mrs. Mercer and Mrs. Hollingsworth, both recently arrived from England, to serve customers in order to free him to tend to the more pressing matters of growing the business. Webster was an ambitious man who had conquest on his mind. He wanted to be Philadelphia's largest upholsterer. He had been out all morning but strode back in a foul mood. We braced ourselves: we'd all worked here long enough to know when his temper was short.

"Hello, Mr. Webster," Mary said mildly, cutting lengths of fabric to be sewn into chair backs.

"Good afternoon, dear," he responded. He climbed onto a low stool and put his hands on his hips, chin thrust forward, and heaved a sigh. His belly seemed to be growing each year, along with his income, and stood out from his jacket, solid and round as a stuffed Turkish ottoman.

We stole glances at him from our work. Webster had a tendency toward the theatrical, but this was a bit much even for him, standing over us on the stool.

"I have bad news, I'm afraid," he intoned in a dour voice. "Very bad news. There is no point in piddling about. You have no idea how difficult this is for me. I may have to let some of you go."

He had our attention now, and all scissors, needles, pressers, and hands stopped as ten heads swiveled toward him, including the heads of Mrs. Mercer and Mrs. Hollingsworth, who were framed in the doorway.

"Well, not right away, of course. But in due time. Due to the troubles, you see."

"What troubles, Mr. Webster?" Agatha asked. She was older and had been here the longest. Her eyesight wasn't what it used to be. She squinted as she stitched now, holding her work farther away. She no longer was asked to do any embellishments, no fringe or braid or small buttons or fussy work.

"On account of Townshend's bloody duties," Webster huffed. "I had thought to avoid this since we seemed to be keeping afloat after Philadelphia joined the non-importation movement on goods from Britain earlier this year. But alas, no."

"Oh dear," Mrs. King said.

"Six months in, and we are already pinched," Webster announced with a scowl. "I must warn you that your positions here are not secure. As much as it pains me." He heaved a sigh.

"Charles Townshend is dead now," Levi muttered under his breath. "Yet I'd like to curse him. Is that wrong of me?" Levi was the most recent worker to be hired at Webster's, replacing another boy who moved south to Charlestown. He was a little younger than me, with no shortage of energy or jokes. I think Webster hired him for his brawn. He was good at hauling furniture around as if it were dominoes.

"Going forward this will impact the fabric we can use," Webster said, "especially the specialty English cottons that are still in demand. We have very little left. And silks! Oh God, silks! Pennsylvanians are useless with silk worms. We can only hope that parliament will repeal the act, and soon."

The Stamp Act hadn't lasted a year after Britain imposed it on us. British merchants and manufacturers were upset by their lost trade in America and appealed successfully to parliament to reverse it, and here we were trying to push back with non-importation all over again. Since I'd witnessed the tax collector's attack, I felt I should start paying more attention. Be more grown up in the ways of the world.

"Pins too?" Mary asked.

"All of it," Webster grunted. His dreams of flying past upholsterer Plunket Fleeson in sales and prestige were dying in front of his eyes, although all upholsterers in town would be in the same position, including Fleeson. "We can use up the stock we have, of course," he added. "And we shall sincerely hope this all rights itself very soon. I don't have to tell you what this means to business. The lack of goods available for purchase will push up the price of whatever is left. Few people will have enough money for finery. Homespun will be everywhere." He shuddered at the thought. Rough flax, how artless!

There was silence as we turned this over in our minds. How long would it take to work through our stock, and then what? Britain had the mills that were not available here, with specialized equipment to make long lengths of fabrics that we used all the time, not to mention the extraordinary Spitalfield silks.

"If there is no repeal, no new supplies, when the work dries up, the work dries up," he said grimly. It was hard to imagine. We had been rushed off our feet for months.

"The taxes won't last, sir," John said. "Not if all the colonies keep protesting."

"Quite right," Webster said, waving us back to work as he strode out again, one of his shoe buckles clanging on the metal leg of the cutting table as his foot came into contact. He was not a man of easy grace.

We returned to our tasks, trying to absorb the news. I could not imagine the fine ladies of town wanting to use homespun and coarse linen for their fancy drapery, gowns, or settees. Only sumptuous fabrics would do for those. Everyone would be planting more flax next spring, praying for a repeal of the duties.

"I need a hand back here," Levi said, over a mattress that needed more stuffing. John went to help him.

"We could do with two more," John said. "This beast will weigh near on sixty pounds when it's done. Mary? Betsy? A hand?"

I was grateful to stand up, my hips aching from sitting all day in one position. Mary joined me at the mattress, and the four of us, the youngest in Webster's shop, stood stuffing horsehair into the mattress. Someone wealthy had ordered this. Goose feathers would be the final layer.

"Well that was bad news," Levi said in a hushed voice. "I just got here. I'll be the first out."

"Not necessarily," I said, thinking of Levi's physical strength. Poor Agatha might be the first.

"I don't really understand it," Mary whispered. "I thought the protests were just up north. Who decides such things? Won't the king object to more colonies blocking British goods? He'll send soldiers here to sit on us just like in Boston."

John shrugged. "How else will we get our message across if we don't speak with our money?"

I felt certain the Townshend Duties would be revoked and we'd carry on as before. Britain always seemed to wait for a crisis to get to the boiling point before they took the pot off the fire. Made no sense to me.

We worked at the mattress together for a long time, pushing stuffing in and struggling with the size of it, our conversation eventually changing to our usual lighthearted fare as we ran out of things to say about Britain and their love of taxes and soldiers. Levi and John started telling jokes as we whispered together out of earshot of the rest of the workshop.

"You're looking all rosy-cheeked and becoming," John teased Mary, noticing how flushed she was.

Mary did look warm, I noticed. Her color was high, and she was perspiring at her hairline. She kept tugging at her cap.

"Don't tease me, John," Mary said. "This is heavy work, that's all."

"Must you two flirt all the time?" I jested. "Levi and I will be jealous."

"I could flirt with you," Levi offered to me with a wink. "If you would accept my flirtations."

"No thank you," I warned him. Levi played at looking wounded, raising a hand to his heart and fluttering his eyelids at me in mock rejection.

"You really do look ever so fetching like that," John whispered to Mary in jest. I laughed, but when I looked at Mary, she looked as if she was about to cry.

"I must get a glass of water," Mary said suddenly and dropped her corner of the mattress to head to the back where the food was, an area always crowded with pitchers of water and ale and cold coffee. It made me think of the day I had first come to Webster's and put my crate of food on the table back there. At her abrupt departure, Levi reached out a hasty hand to stop the mattress from banging the worktable. We would treat the mattress with bug wash before Webster delivered it to the customer, of course, but no need to give stray vermin a home before we could finish it.

John frowned. "Mary looks annoyed," he said in a low voice. "I was just teasing her."

"She has been tired lately," I said. "Maybe she has a cold starting."

We continued working on the mattress, the three of us. Mary was slow in returning, and when she did, her face was set and unsmiling.

"We're all right here, Mary," John said kindly. "Why don't you go have a sit-down and maybe keep going on the headboard buttons? If you're feeling a little under the weather today?"

Mary nodded and went back to her chair at the sewing table. I noticed John's eyes followed her, and the small tug of emotion in my belly surprised me. It John was sweet on my sister, it was no concern of mine.

"I have some news," I told John and Levi in a low voice, pushing curled hair into a stubborn corner. "Father said Mary and I can drop by the hospital after work and see if they have that man in their care."

"Huh?" Levi juggled the mattress against him as it got heavier. "What man?"

"The tax collector. The man I saw being beaten."

"Do you think that's a good idea?" John said. "If he's alive, I'm not sure seeing him will make you feel any better. He could be in rough shape."

"I'm not going to see *him*, not like that. I just want to know if he's there. I don't know why it concerns me, yet I cannot get him out of my mind."

I thought John would be pleased that I was finally going to find out his fate after two days of wondering how the man fared, but a frown crossed his face. "And then what?" he asked pointedly. "Besides satisfying your curiosity?"

"The hospital is full of sickness," Levi warned, "so take good care. It's been a bad year for yellow fever and malaria. I would tell you not to go if the weather wasn't turning. It's safer now than it was."

"You're always afraid of getting ill," I teased him. "You are like a curmudgeonly old man. All twisted with worry and you're not yet eighteen."

"I don't like hospitals myself," John said.

"Why?" I pressed. "They help sick people."

John shrugged. "I just don't."

"That is not a reason," I countered. "Have you been a patient there?"

He shook his head and kept working on the mattress. His normal agreeable demeanor had disappeared. I studied his closed face, felt the tension in his body. Working together all day with people, day in and day out for years, made you know them as well as family. Maybe better than family. He and Mary were both acting strangely.

"I was going to ask you if you would come with me," I suggested. "Levi, you too. Why don't the four of us go? I'll be quick. We could stop for a sweet after. Marzipan, maybe?"

"Not me," Levi said. "Just got through a dastardly case of the runs. Er, begging your pardon. No, thank you kindly, not me. As much fun as it sounds to go ask about a beaten man, widely hated, perhaps more dead than alive, I must decline. I shall wait for the next jovial invitation. Shall we hope for an amputation next time?"

I ignored his sarcasm. "John?"

"Not me either," he said without looking up. There was hair everywhere, and his fingers reached for the stragglers to add them to the stuffing. He seemed far away in thought.

"Truly?" John was always up for everything.

"Not this time."

I thought John would want to come with me and Mary. He was like a big bear of a brother, interested in everything Mary and I did, always there to protect and tease us. Yet not today. Mary and I would have to go to the hospital on our own.

Chapter 3

Buoyed by our sudden launch into fresh air and freedom from work, I expected Mary to be good company as we walked to the hospital, but she was withdrawn.

"Why so glum, little songbird?" I asked her, trying to draw her out.

"Leave it, Betsy," she said flatly.

We turned onto Fourth Street and walked past the burial grounds, past Market and Chestnut, over Walnut and Locust, then turned onto Spruce Street and headed west toward the outskirts of town, where the hospital was. I was enjoying the weak sunshine and the satisfaction of kicking my feet through the dry leaves scattering the road. We had to hurry; it would be dark soon.

"Are you unwell?" I asked her. I surveyed her pale face. Mary was usually chatty. I always looked forward to her company outside of the upholstery. Today she looked worried, or perhaps just pensive.

"I am fine."

"I caught John looking at you today." I hoped to draw her out, earn a giggle from her.

"*Stop it*," she said with unexpected force, her words a slash in the space between us, and I was taken aback.

"As you wish." She did not have to be so short with me. "I am sorry if I have imposed upon you. You seem unhappy."

"I wanted to come with you." I noticed she didn't say she wasn't unhappy.

I sighed and walked faster, hoping to get the hospital sooner rather than later. I had let the tax collector's beating affect me more than I should have, but this would put the matter to rest. I needed him to be alive, needed to know that townspeople couldn't murder people at will.

We came to the Spruce Street entrance at the east wing, and I stared up at the imposing red brick building, a fence separating it from the lawns that spread to the road. It was an impressive structure, regal and sweeping, its red brick façade invoking grandeur. When it opened almost fifteen years ago, the Pennsylvania Hospital became a haven for the poor and sick, long overdue. The building stretched high and wide, perhaps more beautiful than the State House. Unfortunately, the hospital also had a large population of insane people who were confined on the ground floor and spent years there if they couldn't be healed. Until a couple of years ago, it was common for walkers to wander up on Sundays to try and get a peek at the lunatics before the hospital made sure visibility was obscured.

At the main door, we hesitated before going in. Mary took my hand and we walked through. A man sat behind a desk in the outer vestibule, looking at papers through a monocle.

"Excuse us, sir," I said, feeling nervous. He looked up at me over a hooked nose, his eyes unwelcoming, impatient. He saw young girls and sensed an annoyance coming.

"I'm looking for someone," I began. "Er, I'm trying to find out if a particular man has been admitted."

"We have many patients here in our care," the man said, flipping his papers. Had he even heard me? "A hundred usually, and sometimes double that."

I folded my gloved hands together. "I'm asking after a ginger-haired man who was beaten in the street earlier this week."

The man put down the papers. "Pocked face? He died," he said baldly. "Not long after he arrived. Government man, yes?"

I took a breath. "A tax collector. He died here? Monday?"

"The next morning."

I stood there, uncertain, feeling like our conversation was unfinished but without any idea what I could say next. "His name, may I ask?"

"You're not a relation?" The man's eyes were beady and raven-like, staring at us.

I shook my head. "I came upon him being abused in the street. I wanted to see if I could be of service to him somehow. Or his family, if he had one."

The man shrugged, his suspicions about us being unnecessary work for him now confirmed, and returned to his paperwork.

"Come, Betsy." My sister tugged my elbow. I resisted. The man's shrug irked me. A life too easily dismissed.

"Excuse me sir."

"Yes?" he said, his mouth curling.

"May I know his name?"

"Why should that interest you? I told you the man is dead. You are not family."

Mary pulled me outside, and we stood by the street watching the carriages pull in through the arch on Eighth Street and into the stable area.

"I'm sorry, Betsy," Mary said. "At least now we know."

I nodded, feeling deflated. "Let's go home."

Just then there was a shriek, and a woman ran in front of a carriage exiting the hospital. The driver pulled hard on the reins, and the horses whinnied, skittish and confused. I saw a well-clad couple in the carriage lean forward to peer anxiously out the window at the commotion the woman had caused.

The woman threw herself in front of the agitated horses, raising her arms over her head. "Run me over!" she screamed. "Please!"

A man and two women burst through the door the woman had come through.

"Restrain her!" the man said. They all leaped toward the woman, who had stepped away from the horses and appeared to be trying to rid herself of her clothing.

"Go," the man said to the shorter woman. "Go find the manager in the lunatic ward. They may not know she has escaped. Bring help."

The woman ran back inside. The couple inside the carriage stayed put, staring out the window. Neither of them moved.

The runaway patient was nimble of foot, quick with her slender body. In one fluid move, she ran behind the carriage and out the brick archway toward the street, toward us, escaping the outstretched hands of those trying to catch her.

"What should we do?" I said to Mary. "Should we try and reach her?"

Mary looked around helplessly. "I don't want to frighten her."

"She is already in a state," I offered. "Perhaps we can help."

Fast as a lightning bug, the woman dashed down the side of the building and around the corner. Mary and I ran after her, hearing the hospital workers behind us. When we turned the corner after her, we saw her crouched low by the wall, rocking herself back and forth, head down. We stopped a short distance away.

"There," Mary said, pointing, when the hospital workers caught up.

"Thank God," the man said. "She shouldn't have got out."

The nurse began to hum, approaching the woman slowly.

"No, thank you," the runaway said, soft and childlike, although she was a grown woman. "Not today."

"Let's go inside, Mrs. Ross," the nurse said kindly. Instead of moving closer, she patiently stood a few feet away, engaging the woman with her voice, offering comfort. "Come inside and we shall play a game of cards, shall we? All-Fours?"

"*No.*" The runaway lifted her head and stared for a moment before covering her face with her hands like a child. Her clothes were askew from where she had just tried to remove them by the carriage. She uncovered her face and looked at the nurse. "Let's play hide-and-seek."

Oh God. The woman looked just liked John. The same dark hair and dark eyes. The same sharp chin. The resemblance was extraordinary. Mary and I exchanged a look. They could be twins. *Mrs. Ross*, the nurse had called her. His mother? Was that why John tensed whenever the hospital was mentioned?

"Hide-and-seek it is," the nurse said airily, taking a step toward her patient still crouched by the wall. "It's my turn to hide first, Mrs. Ross, remember?"

"Yes, but call me Sarah," the patient said.

"Come find me, Sarah," the nurse called teasingly over her shoulder, drawing her charge into her make-believe, and skipped back toward the hospital. Sarah ran after her, as giddy as a five-year-old, with the male attendant carefully following in case the patient ran in a different direction.

"Can it be—" I began, staring after them.

"Yes, it has to be. That's John's mother," Mary said. "They look the same, and she's the right age. John's mother is insane?"

"She must live in the apartments in the hospital."

"All this time and he never said a word," Mary said, shaking her head. "A lunatic."

"Maybe we're wrong," I said. "Maybe it's a cousin or an aunt. Another family member."

"John talks about his father all the time," Mary said. "Have you ever heard him mention his mother?"

I shook my head.

That's why John wouldn't come with us today. I was suddenly glad he wasn't here to see this. I would have to find a way to ask him. We were friends. Perhaps it would lighten the burden of a secret.

*

Mary was in no better spirits on the walk home. If anything, she was more morose. I left her to her thoughts and sought sense in mine as I tried to make peace with the death of the tax collector and seeing the woman who looked like

John's mother at the hospital. Two years of working closely together daily and he hadn't breathed a word.

Mary's steps slowed as we neared home. I could smell cooking as we passed a tavern, smells of roasting pork and pungent spices. Was that oregano? I was hungry, I realized. It was well past when we would normally eat supper. Mary was walking slower and slower.

"What's the matter?" I asked her irritably. "Why are you dragging your feet?"

I wanted to get home and eat.

"I have something I need to tell Mother and Father." Her face was pinched and gray.

"Then tell me first now and it might help you with them?" I suggested.

"I am unsure I can." Mary stopped and sat on the low wall in front of a whip maker's shop. *Oh no,* I thought. *Don't stop here. I need food.*

"Unless you murdered someone, how bad can it be?" I said impatiently.

"Like Deborah," she said darkly. "In a way."

Oh good grief. It hit me like a lightning bolt. Mary was going to tell our parents that she planned to marry John! John's father was an Episcopalian minister, just like his grandfather. Mary was going to be exiled from the Friends. She would be disowned by the church. That is what was causing her misery.

"I wish you had told me," I said, forgetting my hunger pangs. "When?"

To have another daughter marry outside the Society of Friends would pain our parents tenfold. Just this summer my sister Susannah, too, had married outside the faith when she took her vows with Ephraim Doane at St. Paul's Church. At least it was a relief for my parents when Deborah and Everard, who had been prepared to leave the Friends for good, made amends and chose to return to the Quaker meetinghouse, pledging obedience. But now Mary? They would be terribly upset.

I had suspected John was sweet on Mary. Had Mary just found out her future mother-in-law was a lunatic?

I swallowed hard. Oh Mary. What an unfortunate circumstance I had unknowingly led her to.

"You suspected, didn't you?" Mary asked, watching my face. "I knew you would find out. You know me so well."

"You must be terribly worried." I sat down next to her on the wall. "Why didn't you say anything? You can trust me, Mary. Always."

"I didn't want you think less of me. My situation is awful," Mary said sadly. She lowered her eyes. "And yet I don't have regrets," she whispered.

"No, you mustn't! We cannot always choose our heart's path." I laid my hand on hers.

"I thought you would feel differently." Mary entwined her fingers with mine.

"How so?"

"I feared your disapproval. Your disgust. I wish I had made different choices, now. But I was not forced."

"No, John's not like that. He would not wish you to feel so—"

"John!" Mary stared at me. "Surely you don't think—" She stood abruptly.

"If you wish to marry John," I said, confused now, "then you must stand up for your—"

"Stop it Betsy! You don't know anything!" Mary's eyes raked my face, and then she turned on her heel and fled down the street to our front door, almost as fast as the hospital patient in her game of hide-and-seek. She slammed it closed before I got there.

I thought of all the times Mary and John had flirted and laughed together at the break table. I thought it harmless at the time. I had been clueless to the depth of her affections and then how troubled Mary had become when she realized her true feelings. I suddenly felt very selfish. I should have paid more attention, been more of a comfort to her.

"What is the matter with her?" Rachel asked from the stairs, violin in hand. Unlike myself, she loved learning music. I always felt I couldn't work any instrument under my fingers, which was odd given what beautiful items my fingers could craft with a needle and thread.

"I wish I knew," I sighed.

Oh, Mary, what are you going to do? What has possessed you?

*

I was sitting by the window in my bedchamber, repairing a hole in my pocket, when my mother came in. Dark had fallen. I had two candles burning so I could better see my task. The threat of losing my key or a coin precipitated this hasty repair.

A commotion had been going on for at least an hour. I heard the faint sound of Mary sobbing under the accusatory tones of my father's angry voice. My father was not a man who was quick to heat, although I have no doubt that Mary's news was upsetting to him. I wondered briefly where Rachel and George were, and Hannah. I knew Rebecca and Sarah were at the meetinghouse.

My mother sank onto the bed and stared out the glass at the darkness over my shoulder. The wind had picked up, and I heard it whistle and slap the glass.

"Mama?"

"I cannot believe it," she said softly. Her eyes looked glazed. The shadows from the candles illuminated her face and left other parts of her body as dark as silt. "I just cannot believe it. Mary! Of *all* my daughters . . ."

I tied off the end of the thread, snipped it, and laid the pocket to one side.

"What did Mary say?" I asked. "She started to speak with me on the way home and then became upset."

My mother shook her head as if to cast off a pall that had come over her.

"What is it?" I asked. "What's the matter? Surely you do not think ill of Mary for wishing to marry?"

My mother let out an unpleasant sound, derisive and choking. "If only that were the case."

"Mama, what did Mary tell you? What's wrong?"

"She really didn't say anything to you?" My mother eyed me closely.

"No."

"Mary is with child," my mother said, her voice as flat as a dull steel blade.

The room tilted. My sister was with child? That wasn't possible. Mary? Sweet, unassuming Mary? She never did anything wrong.

"What? No. How? No, *who*?" I asked, my mind working.

"She will not say." My mother returned her gaze out the window, even though it was dark and she could only see the reflection of my candle flames. Disappointment hardened her features at her daughter's sin. "I thought you might know."

"I didn't know. I swear it." I was trying to understand how I could not have known. Mary and I worked together. We lived together. We were always together. I suddenly thought of all the times in the past few weeks she had been quiet or out of sorts. Mary was expecting a baby? That wasn't possible. I might expect it from one of my other sisters, but not Mary.

I was not forced, she had said earlier. My sister had participated in an act of passion out of wedlock? *Willingly?* How had she found the time to be in circumstances that would lead to that? When was she ever alone with a male?

"Betsy, do you know who took advantage of Mary?"

I hesitated. "No. But there is a boy at the shop," I murmured. "A man, John. They seem to like each other. I am unsure, though, if . . ."

My mother got up and left. I winced. Had John taken my sister's honor? It didn't seem like something John would do, but who else did Mary know that closely? Mary wouldn't look twice at Levi.

I could hear the ladies tutting at meeting. *To think, a minister's son . . .*

I chewed on a cuticle, thinking of my sweet sister and John from work sneaking about. How far along was Mary? How could I have not known this had been going on right under my nose? There had to be a mistake.

Chapter 4

When Mary finally came to bed, she seemed calm.

I raised my head to peer at her through the darkness. "Mary?" I whispered.

She crawled under the covers and turned to the wall, giving my waist a squeeze to let me know her anger with me had passed. Rachel was in the other bed with Hannah. I'd found out that Hannah had taken the littles out at Mary's request. They had walked down to the confectionary and purchased candy.

"Just tell me," I whispered. "Who is the father? Is it John? I'm not upset with you." If it was not John, who else? Was she protecting someone we knew at meeting?

A slight shake of her head, her sleep cap flashing pearl gray in the inky blackness, and then stillness. Mary's body radiated quiet determination. She did not fall asleep sobbing, did not toss and turn. Perhaps it was a relief to not have a secret anymore, after weeks of worry and fear. She had made a decision, I realized, and that decision gave her peace. I remained frustrated, staring at her after she fell asleep. Mary was the most pious of all of us in the Griscom brood. How could she have done this? This wasn't the Mary I knew.

The next day both Mary and John were not at Webster's. I had been sent in with her excuse—a blinding headache that confined her to bed. I didn't know where John was. In the two years I'd been at Webster's, I could count on one hand how many days John had been absent. Three. Each time for illness. His empty chair seemed to speak to his guilt. Mary must have told him my parents knew.

I looked at Mary's unoccupied chair in the workshop all day and felt sorrowful. Her choice would be a painful one. No one would condone her actions. Shame would follow her. I felt sick thinking about it. And where was John? Had my father gone to find him at first light?

I tried to attend to my work, my thoughts filled with concern for John and my sister. It was hard to concentrate. I was tasked with making a wool blanket, heavily embroidered with a seashell motive. As I reached for a bolt of wool, I realized Mary would turn twenty next year, and already be a mother. If both Mary and John left Webster's, I wasn't sure I could stay. The thought was like a wound. To face that emptiness, I couldn't. They were my lifeblood. The other workers were fine, some I liked very much, but they weren't my friends. I counted Mary as a friend. I liked working with her, having her close to me. I needed her.

I managed to work steadily through the day, although I kept looking at the empty chairs belonging to Mary and John. The end of the day came, and I rushed home.

"We're all going to meeting," my mother said when I walked in. She was already out of her work clothes and wearing a simple gown. "Go up and change."

"Where's Mary?" I asked.

"She is not coming. She's fine, Betsy," she added when she saw my face. "She needs a day to rest. Go up and change. I'll get Rachel and George. Tell Hannah to change and remind Sarah and Rebecca to bring a shawl."

And so we went, a large group of Griscom girls plus George and my father, heading to the meetinghouse, as if everything was normal, and yet nothing was. Our lives had changed overnight. Suddenly, Susannah's marriage this past summer to Ephraim seemed trivial compared to Mary expecting a baby out of wedlock, which completely unacceptable.

Father took George with him to the men's meeting room while the rest of us gathered in the women's room. We fell into silence and prayer. This was my favorite part, when there was no talking and I could be alone with my thoughts and my prayers, aligning my spirit. The constant haranguing of the elders with all their rules and opinions, I could do without.

We reached the portion of the meeting where Mother had to confess Mary's disobedience. I squirmed inside, feeling awful. Despite my sister's mistake, Mary was such a good person, so truly kindhearted. Could a woman ever make a mistake and not be damned for it?

My mother stood and calmly announced Mary's pregnancy.

A murmur of sympathy. And then:

"There have been far too many of our youth falling in sin lately," Frances said. She was the oldest of the elders, with a face like cracked meringue. She was petty, I knew, and I had always thought her stern. "How many members have we disciplined this year alone for marrying outside of the faith? How many more will go astray? Our guidelines help form the morals of our children so the young people will come to know our faith as well as we do. The strictures make sure our youth are aware of what is good conduct, provide a moral compass, and yet these young people do as they like." Her voice was laced with distaste.

"I cannot speak for all those young people," my mother said. "I only speak for Mary, and she is pained by her actions. She is truly sorry. My daughter is very attached to the young man in question. I must tell you this was no passing matter. A meeting of the heart first, for a long time, then the body, in a weak moment."

"What is Mary's age?" Valrosa asked. She was the elder I liked the best. She was soft in body and voice, and her eyes were kind.

"Nineteen."

"Who is the young man?"

"I cannot say," my mother admitted softly. "My daughter wishes it so."

"A Quaker?"

"He is not."

There was a wave of sound, clucks and objections, and I felt suddenly pity for my mother, standing here with such strength. First Deborah, then Susannah, and now Mary.

Deborah had made amends, but Mary never could. We were cleaving a hole in our faith family and in my mother's heart.

I struggled with the knowledge that Mary had told my mother who the father of her baby was, but wouldn't tell me. I thought Mary and I were like strands of rope woven together. I looked around at the congregation, a sea of female faces that I had grown up with. Most of the women received Mother's news respectfully, with solemn faces. There had been no shortage of scandals lately, and unfortunately for our community, this was just one more. You would not think it would be so difficult for a young woman to find a nice Quaker man to marry or for youth to obey our laws, and yet every month there was news of someone else being exiled for disobedience.

"Will she express remorse?" Frances asked in a voice thick with judgment.

My mother swallowed. "I believe so. My daughter is struggling, as you can imagine. No one chooses this predicament. It is a regrettable turn of events. Mary is a good woman. And a godly woman."

"We shall come to the house," Valrosa said, "and speak with Mary there."

Frances sniffed. "We cannot have an unmarried mother attending meeting."

My mother nodded her agreement. She understood.

The disciplinary portion of meeting continued to jerk along. The Griscom family would survive another scandal and possibly keep their good name intact. We had influence: My father was a valued member of the Friends and one of the highest-ranking craftsmen in our neighborhood. He liked to tell everyone that his grandfather Griscom had arrived in town long before Ben Franklin, as if that gave him some sort of ancestral bragging rights. Although that was before Franklin got raked over in the House of Commons over the Stamp Act a few years ago. After that, my father wasn't quite as keen to compare his family name to Franklin's.

The meeting moved on.

I whispered to my mother that I wasn't feeling well and slipped out.

*

I had to see him.

The steeple of Christ Church loomed magnificently against the sky as I approached, one of the oldest churches in the colonies. I went around and stood by the main door. I could hear the closing hymn, "Awake, Our Souls." I took a chance that he would be at Thursday evensong.

I paced outside. A few squirrels scampered about, unbothered by my presence. Soon the congregants flowed out, bubbling with color. So much color, and such fine fabrics. Not like the Friends at all. I pushed back my bonnet so I could see better.

"John!"

He turned, breaking away from the man he was with to come over to me. I followed him over to stand under a maple tree.

"Betsy." He lifted his eyebrows, puzzled. "What are you doing here?"

"I've come about Mary. I couldn't stand it any longer. I had to see you."

"Mary? Why? What about Mary?"

"Mary is with child," I stated firmly. "Did you know?"

He blinked at me.

"Where were you today?" I asked.

"What?" He looked confused. "My uncle needed my help. I cleared it with Webster. What's this about Mary? Are you joking?"

"You're not responsible?"

John stared at me like I was brimming with madness. "No, I am not Mary's suitor. Good God, Betsy, what must you think of me?"

"I'm sorry," I said in a rush. "You weren't at work, and then my father was not home, and I guess I—"

"Thought me a pig?"

"I was worried. Sometimes it happens; you know it does. There's always someone who has fallen from grace. I thought maybe she loves you. All I know is Mary is having a baby and she told my parents."

"Good grief. *Mary?*"

"We are all surprised."

"It cannot be so," John said. "Makes no sense."

"I have had a little while to take it in. The shock of it wears off a little."

"I am not courting Mary."

I averted my gaze. There were just a few people left in the churchyard now, small gatherings spotting the walkway.

"Betsy! You didn't. You told your parents it was me?"

"I'm so sorry! I really am. I thought maybe it was true. I see the way you look at her in the shop . . ."

John was frowning. He looked decidedly unhappy.

"I said I'm sorry," I repeated. I suddenly felt very young, no older than little Rachel. I was certainly making as many errors as a child. Was I destined to get everything wrong? I hadn't known about Mary, hadn't had any idea what was going on in Susannah's life before she left with Ephraim, and now John was looking at me as if I did not speak the same language.

His brows drew together in a scowl.

"You imagined me to be dishonorable and then beaten and bleeding," John muttered, "at the hands of your father. And by the sound of it, from your own accusation toward me."

Words left me. I struggled to speak. "When you say it like that, it sounds horrible. I'm here because I care for you. Your friendship means a great deal to me. It all happened so fast. I reacted poorly."

"You're supposed to warn a friend *beforehand*. Not after the confession. Make that *false* confession."

He was furious with me, and I deserved it.

"I snuck out of meeting to come find you," I said, trying to win him back. "No one knows I'm here. Does that count?"

"Brave of you." Sarcasm.

"I was truly worried! Please, John."

John stepped away from me toward Christ Church. Behind him, the red brick walls of the beautiful church climbed upward past two layers of arched windows. He faced the tower which led to the steeple, and up to the spire soaring towards the sky.

My heart banged in my chest. *Don't be cross with me.* I followed him, anxiously trying to think of something I could say that would make him forgive me. Tomorrow we had to be back at work at Webster's. We had to get along. We were friends.

"John, I—"

He turned toward me. "It's all right Betsy." That smile.

The good-natured John that I knew returned and I breathed a sigh of relief. "You've had a shock. What a week it has been."

"I don't know what I was thinking."

"I'm sorry to hear about Mary but it wasn't me."

I took a breath.

"The tax collector?" he asked. Ah yes. I hadn't seen John since then. He didn't know.

"He died."

"I'm sorry."

I suddenly remembered our visit to the hospital after work yesterday and seeing the woman that we thought was John's mother trying to escape. I could see her running across the courtyard in a state of dishabille, hear her childlike laugh ring out across the lawn.

"When we were at the hospital we saw a woman there that looked just like you," I said gently. "They called her Mrs. Ross. Is that your mother, John?"

He nodded. "I wasn't hiding it. I never knew how to bring her up. My mother has never been in my life, Betsy. She was ill from the time I was very young. She's been in the hospital for years. The woman you saw is my mother, yet also a stranger to me. Father used to take us to see her, but she stopped knowing us."

"I'm sorry for your loss. And I'm sorry for your father." It was almost worse than a death, she was gone but had not died.

John nodded, his eyes on mine.

The air was thick between us, not with tension but intimacy.

John hesitated. "Betsy, how could you think I wanted Mary? It's you I care for."

Chapter 5

1770

Mary left Webster's when she started to show in December. It was a relief to Mr. Webster, for he was getting less business now that the strains of non-importation were being felt across town, and Mary's departure took away his need to remove workers from his shop against their will. We managed to keep busy with sundry household items and the upholstery stayed afloat, although it was nowhere near as robust and exciting as in prior years when we'd been bursting with sumptuous fabrics from all corners of the globe.

Mary had her baby in the summer, a boy, and called him George. After the baby was born and was a cuddly, warm, breathing person, Mary's shame faded into the background. The manner in which baby George joined us no longer seemed to matter; we were all just glad he was here. We returned to being the same big old noisy Griscom family we had always been, with one more tiny body in the mix. My father was especially besotted with the newcomer, taking the baby in his big rough hands and cooing down to him like a mother bird to a chick. Not even my sister Sarah's marriage to William Donaldson at Christ Church that summer could dampen my parents' spirits when their infant grandchild was in the house, even though it marked the fourth Griscom daughter to marry outside the faith. I could only imagine what they said about us in the meetinghouse. Come to think of it, I didn't want to imagine that.

"How is Mary's bonny babe?" Mr. Webster asked me one day when he was lugging a barrel of dye from the back door to the sewing area.

"He's a gem," I answered. "Healthy and marvelous. Mary takes naturally to mothering."

"She would be a natural, wouldn't she?" Mrs. King said fondly. "She was always taking care of all of us here. Making everything better."

This got a few murmurs of agreement.

"I miss her," Agatha said, looking up from pressing a curtain. "Such a dear girl. You'll tell her I say hello, won't you, Betsy? Give her my very best wishes."

"I will." I smiled at her. I missed being with Mary all day too.

"I actually have a message," I announced. "Mary is going to marry the father of her baby. She asked me to tell you all. Thomas Morgan. She's been keeping him a secret while he was looking for work in Delaware."

I would never understand my sister's choices and why she hadn't just told me her plans, but all of that was in the past. I couldn't let it come between us. I was happy that she had a family of her own and would be moving to New Castle with Thomas as a married woman. She said she had met him at a harvest dance with friends and tucked the courtship away to herself. It reminded me of the day in the back yard when she told me she'd wanted Webster's to be all hers. Maybe some people needed privacy, invisible walls. In our noisy heaving house, that was understandable.

The girls in the workshop cheered for Mary's news.

*

I had to make my peace with the tax collector's death. My parents would not allow me to report what I'd seen or pursue the matter in any way. After a while, they forbade me even to speak of it.

"You're a young girl, Betsy," my father said. "Leave it alone. The matter doesn't concern you. The government will know what happened. Leave it to them to administer justice." They asked me to pray for the ginger-headed man, and denounce violence.

I wanted to disobey them but I was too nervous. With Mary occupied with motherhood, I had no one to be my ally in pursuing the matter or slipping around town. John and I had maintained a distant truce in the months since he'd revealed his feelings for me. It was safer that way, for me at least. I didn't wish to give him false hope. When the Townshend Duties had finally been repealed in April, I told myself the unrest in Philadelphia would die down. Surely it was all over. No more beating of tax collectors, not more mobs in the streets railing against Britain.

I expected life to feel a little more normal, yet I couldn't find my footing. Deborah, Susannah, and Sarah were married and out of the house now, with Mary almost on her way to Delaware with Thomas and baby George. I sometimes caught my sister Rebecca sneaking spirits and drinking alone, which was unsettling. I found myself strangely lonely, even though I was surrounded by people night and day at home and at the upholstery. I longed for something interesting to happen, but I didn't know what. There were no young men in the meetinghouse who interested me. For a while I tried. I didn't want to end up like Rebecca, who was twenty-six years old and sneaking whiskey at home, believing her prospects slim. At eighteen I still had time, yet all of the boys I spoke with held no interest for me.

I decided I would throw myself into work, but Webster's was no longer the same vibrant upholstery it had been. Mary being gone was only part of it. John and I didn't joke around as much. I couldn't be that easy with him now, and the work was less interesting. Even after the troubles with Britain settled down a bit and imports began flowing back into the colonies, Webster wasn't doing as well as he had been in previous years. Fewer orders were coming in, and the work was less challenging, the pieces less luxurious.

I was reflecting on this sad state of affairs one day at work when Levi came to tell me that John's mother had died.

I was in the corner tidying the ribbons.

"Is that where he is now?" I asked, looking at John's empty workspace. "At the funeral?"

"There's not going to be a funeral, I heard," Levi said. "A quiet burial for the family. I just thought you should know."

"I'm glad you told me. I'll speak with him."

"Do you know he's waiting for you?" Levi said, lowering his voice and looking around to make sure Mrs. King wasn't around. "John. Do you?"

"I don't want that. It's not possible for me," I said. "He's mistaken to wait. Levi, you know my situation."

"Then tell him," Levi interrupted. "But stop punishing him for being fond of you. He may put on a brave face, but the second he leaves work he droops like a lovesick fool and mopes around. You're ruining my fun in the taverns."

I laughed. "I doubt that, Levi. And the conversation is not that simple."

"It is precisely that simple. Try trusting him. What has John done all these years besides care for you? He was never Mary's man, Betsy. He didn't ever have feelings for her. He has done nothing wrong. You forget that, I think. You don't have to return his feelings, but don't let him wallow in false hope thinking you'll change your mind."

I thought about this. I believed I'd made myself clear.

"You don't owe him anything, but you could be less . . . terse," Levi chastised me. "Between his moping and your self-righteous brooding, Webster's has become a hard place to work."

"Self-righteous brooding?" I protested. "That's unkind. Besides, I'm not sure he'll want my friendship now."

"You are not going to find out by asking the ribbons and buttons, are you? Speak with him."

Why was it so complicated? Deborah. Susannah. Mary. Sarah. My sisters and their romantic crimes were stacked up against me. I couldn't be number five to cause a scandal in our Quaker world. Why were there so many rules?

"Preferably today," he added with a wink.

"Self-righteous?" I said, stung by his comment. "Really? I'm making it hard for you? Truly?"

Levi laughed.

"Levi. Betsy." Webster's voice rang out and we jumped.

"Yes sir?" We said in unison.

"I sent John to pick up the buckram. Can I send you two to get the order of canvas that's come in? Down at Blyth's warehouse. It'll need two sets of hands."

"Consider us already gone," Levi said, and Webster waved us away.

Levi and I headed east to the river when we spotted John slide into the backyard of a blacksmith's ahead of us.

"Let's see if we can catch up with him," I said. I wanted to give John my condolences about his mother, and, if I was honest, try to mend the rift between us after Levi's confession.

Levi and I stopped outside the blacksmith's and stood out back waiting for him. We watched John walked through the forge and spoke to the smithy. They seemed to have a lot to say to each other. The smithy kept looking over his shoulder at the front of his shop while they talked. We couldn't hear much, though I thought I heard a name: Charles Thomson.

"What were you doing?" Levi asked John when he came out the back. John jumped. "That doesn't look like buckram to me."

John walked over to us.

"Nothing," John said. "Saying hello to a mate."

It didn't look like that to me. The smithy had been looking cautiously over his shoulder while they spoke. He was much older than John. Something seemed off.

"Why did you follow me?" John asked.

"Webster sent us to get something from Blyth's warehouse," Levi said. "We saw you duck in here."

"You two are like flies on a horse's rump. I'll see you back at the shop," John said cheerfully and loped off.

"A mystery," Levi said drily as we set off again.

I shrugged, feeling another twinge of loneliness. I missed John. I'd shut him out because I couldn't bear what he was offering, but I missed him. We'd been so close and had barely spoken for the last few months.

I was still annoyed that John had feelings for me. I wouldn't have let our friendship deepen if I had known. Perhaps it was my fault for being too familiar. I had no choice but to distance myself when I saw tenderness crinkle across John's face when he looked at me in the workshop, affection changing his eyes, softening his expression. John knew my sisters had hurt our parents by marrying outside the faith. I did not want to have feelings for John, didn't want to add my name to the disowned Griscom sisters before me. I could not choose that path.

I wasn't brave, and I didn't wish to be. I was the hardworking Griscom girl, the diligent one. I kept my head down, didn't cause trouble. I wasn't going to hurt my parents or our meetinghouse by adding another rejection and exile to the growing list of badly behaved Griscom girls. I knew what people were saying: *What is wrong with those girls? Poor Samuel. Poor Rebecca! How* embarrassing. *Those girls had every advantage, and look. Shameful. Who would have thought. Appalling!*

"What are you thinking about?" Levi asked. "You're far away."

"Sorry. Dreaming of cake. Can we stop on the way back?"

*

We popped in to Pryor's Bakery, packages of canvas under our arms, and I bought three cream cakes. I always kept a few coins for myself from the week's pay and gave the rest to my mother towards the upkeep of our household. Levi and I scarfed our cakes down before we picked the packages back up and headed back.

"Make sure there's no trace on my face," I said, jutting my jaw out. I couldn't go back to the fabrics and jobs in progress covered in sugar dust.

"Clear. Me?"

"Not a crumb."

At Webster's, there was a cart outside, and Webster was busy loading in eight chairs with newly upholstered seats. There was also a matching sofa waiting to be loaded. Finally, a large order.

No sign of John. I hid his cream cake at the back of the shop near the cups and got back to work.

We worked in silence for an hour until the arrival of the day's newspapers led to a conversation about the troubles in Boston. Again. Honestly, did we speak of anything else?

"What has happened now?" I asked, shaking off my reverie. I was sewing lace onto a curtain and had been half-listening.

"Mind your work, please," Mrs. King said firmly to the workshop. "We'll have none of that talk today."

"The British troops shouldn't be there in the first place," John said, removing his gloves and unbuttoning his coat. I hadn't heard him come in. "They're supposed to be restoring order but that's a pretense. They're really there to stop anyone from protesting. No one's allowed to rebel."

"Enough, John, please," Mrs. King said. "To work."

I went to the back where he was hanging up his coat and handed him the cake I'd brought him.

"Peace offering," I said tentatively.

"I could walk you home later?"

I nodded.

*

John and I stood outside my house watching the sky streak with orange as the sun began to set. Inside I could hear my brother George on the violin and Mary's baby wailing and my sisters Rebecca and Hannah singing. The chimney was smoking, and the smell of braised rabbit stew wafted onto the street heavy with onions and thyme. Through the window, I could see Rachel dancing, twirling with her hands outstretched and her skirts flying out. Mary walked past her with the baby in her arms, jiggling little George to the music. My mother was in the corner, bent over the loom. My family often came together like this, waiting for my father to come home for supper, enjoying that brief time between the end of the day's toil and the subdued evening hours by the hearth.

I tried to think of what to say to John that would let him know I was not going to ever return his affections. I suddenly, after being without his company for these few months, didn't want to lose his friendship. I scrolled through my mind.

"John," I blurted out. "I know it can't go back to the way it was between us, and yet I miss—"

"I know you don't return my feelings," John said. "It's fine."

"I've been acting poorly toward you all these months. I want to apologize."

"No, Betsy. We're all right."

"I wish I could feel for you the way you want me to."

John grinned. "Your loss. I'm a catch. Son of a minister. Heck, grandson of a minister, too! Holy through and through. Not to mention a talented upholsterer, gainfully employed. So unless you change your mind. . ."

I snorted and laughed at the same time, unladylike. I appreciated his humor and how generously he forgave me. His kindness diffused the tension.

"Come inside? Mama will want to see you."

"Is it safe?" he asked mockingly. "Do they still think me a scoundrel?"

"Don't worry, I told everyone my error." I opened the door on the revelry.

The house was bright and warm, the candles and parlor fire lit. I inhaled the scents of my home, pine wood in the fire and the smell of fresh coffee. Rachel was laughing as she danced, a light bubbly sound next to my brother George's squeaky violin playing.

"Mama, look who I've brought," I said over the din. I was allowed to walk alone with John because I had known him for so long and we worked together. Mama's friends who attended Christ Church remembered when John's father was assistant rector there years back before relocating to his own father's old parish in Delaware. The family was well respected in town, and folks knew that John's great-grandfather had come from Scotland as a minister in 1684. Family ties went far in this town.

My mother looked up from her loom and smiled. "Let me finish this row and I'll join you."

John and I sat. I had to push Rebecca's knitting off one of the chairs to sit, and John moved Rachel's paper dolls off the other. She was using an old copy of the *Gentleman's Magazine* to cut out the bodies. I'd have to remember to ask Mr. Webster if he had some leftover piecing paper scraps at the shop that Rachel could have.

Mama came and sat across from us, stretching her back before she sat. I had not told anyone that John was sweet on me. I wasn't going to add that to her worries. John and I would both just forget that ever happened and continue on.

"How is your father?" my mother asked him.

"Very well," John answered. "Thank you. He's enjoying his congregation in Delaware."

"I was very sorry to hear of your mother's passing," Mama said. "Betsy told me. Please accept our condolences."

"Thank you. A relief for my father. He is free to marry again now."

Just then my father arrived home, and my mother rose to greet him and begin preparations for serving the meal.

Curiosity got the better of me. "Why did you go the blacksmith's?" I asked John. "It seemed strange. You were acting a bit odd."

John reached down and picked up the dice from where someone had left them on the floor. George, probably. He tossed them in his hands, juggling. George squeaked his way into a new tune, in his own world, as Rachel stopped dancing and wandered off to find the cat.

"I shouldn't say," he finally said, watching the dice flip into the air and then catching them again. "He actually isn't a friend of mine. I don't want to place you in a difficult position."

"You don't have to tell me if you don't want to."

John stilled the dice, which disappeared into the palm of one of his strong hands. He leaned forward. "Do you remember the day you saw them beat the tax collector?" he asked in a low voice under the scraping of George's violin bow against the horsehair strings.

I nodded. Not a scene I could forget. Sometimes the tax collector's cries echoed in my dreams. What a terrible way to die.

"First off, I would never condone the killing of an innocent man. But that attack represents what's happening, Betsy, on a larger scale. A resistance is forming, especially after the shootings in Boston in March when British soldiers killed those men in the town square. The British want to suppress us, continue to tax us for their own profit, while making sure we don't have a say. Our future is at stake. A good friend of one of my uncles' is one of the men that organized the non-importation efforts last year. I couldn't risk saying anything in front of Webster, knowing how it may affect his business."

I thought about what he was telling me, that men were joining together to resist Britain, and that somehow John was involved.

"What has this to do with you being at the smithy when we saw you?" I asked.

"I told my uncle I'll help protest against the British," John said. His voice was so soft I had to lean in to hear him. "I joined the Sons. There are many of us now, and the blacksmith is part of that group. I won't tell you his name. I normally don't do any of this on the clock, I'm true to Webster. You know I am. But I had a good reason. And no one was supposed to see me."

Philadelphia now had its own Sons of Liberty group to oppose Britain's policies? In Boston they were known as a radical group who would use violence when necessary to intimidate colonial leaders over dealings with the crown. They were agitators, instigating change.

"Who is Charles Thomson?" I asked. "I heard the smithy say his name."

"A name I ask you not to repeat. Charles Thomson is a merchant who has invested in an iron foundry in New Jersey that can produce munitions." He paused. "And now, a friend. I met him at the philosophical society meetings. He is someone who is very invested in changing the order of things."

"Munitions? You mean weapons?" I asked, my brows knitting together. "Please tell me you're not going to do anything dangerous, John. Or against the law. Or foolish."

"It would be shortsighted for Pennsylvania to not be prepared," John said. "Five years have passed since the troubles began, and it's not getting any better. If anything, the gap between Britain and the colonies is widening. Repealed or not, the Townshend Duties were meant to choke us and remind us that Britain can make money off us and we are expected to suffer in silence, cowed and obedient." He paused, shaking the dice in one fist. This was a new side of John being revealed to me. He was either always joking or focused on his upholstery work. I had not pegged him for a rebel.

"I don't know what to say," I said, thinking, *Don't tell my father.* Quakers couldn't agree with going against the government. My parents would have a fit to hear this.

"If I've said too much, I apologize. I hope I haven't frightened you." John's eyes searched mine.

Perhaps if we had not been estranged for a while, John may not have told me any of this. I knew the information was an extension of missing me, a vote for our friendship, a nod of confidence in my discretion.

"Don't apologize. I asked you." I crossed my arms over my chest, feeling uneasy. What he was describing was damning for all involved, even if the weapons were never used. The intention alone was ominous. He made it sound like there were many of them in Philadelphia, like a surging tide.

"I know you won't say anything," John said, asking for reassurance.

"I will not."

John knew he could trust me. But I was still a Quaker. We could do no acts of violence. My father held important positions in our meetinghouse and in the carpenters' union and within the greater Quaker community of Philadelphia. My whole life I had been taught the values of peace and non-violence. This news felt unsettling, uncomfortable, as if I was attempting to climb a flight of stairs with my shoes on the wrong feet. His words made me nervous.

George put the violin down and went in search of food, paying us no mind at all. The silence was a balm to my ears. At least Rachel had musical talent.

John's dark eyes were glinting in the light from the wall sconces. "I'm just one cog in a wheel, but we are working at being organized at a greater level. Men in the Sons are talking about stockpiling weapons and gunpowder. Charles Thomson is planning to help, with his foundry. He's a leader in the Philadelphia effort, if not the leader. You should hear him speak."

"I confess I don't really see the need for rebellion," I said uneasily. "And where is the stockpile? At the foundry in New Jersey?"

John shook his head. "For your safety, I won't tell you exactly where. But it's here in Philadelphia, near the Delaware River. The iron forge itself is at Batsto. I can explain more to you, if you want. But let's talk together another time, when we can't be overheard. I've already said too much."

John tossed the dice he'd been playing with down on the table next to his chair. If the colonies were forming groups to oppose the British, that meant there would be growing hostilities. The British wouldn't put up with that.

"John."

He looked up.

"You must be so very careful."

"I will. Don't tell Levi," John cautioned. "He's a friend, but he's loose-lipped."

In my mind, I saw the tax collector being tied to the cart, his life being so casually taken. The man I had seen attacked worked for the king, that was true. Yet I knew from what John was saying and the reports from Boston that it could have easily been the other way around. Five men had died in the shooting incident that had happened there in March. The papers called it a massacre. To think they died from the bullets of the soldiers stationed there, and for what purpose? Temper? We were all British subjects.

"I hope this rebellion comes to naught," I told him. "That we return to peace."

I had so many questions. I knew John had three or four uncles in law and government. Which uncle was a leader in this? I would save my questions for the next time we talked.

"I should go," John said, standing.

I stood too. "You could stay and eat with us."

I heard baby George crying again upstairs.

"Thank you, but I'd best be going. See you tomorrow," John said awkwardly. I ignored the tender expression on his face as he looked at me and walked him to the door.

I closed the door behind John and almost bumped into Hannah when I turned around. My least favorite sister, although she was starting to soften the older she got.

"What's the sour puss for?" she asked. "You've got a face on like a squished eel. Did he upset you again?"

"That's just the way I look when I know I have to sit next to you at supper," I shot back, tweaking her nose. "It's going to be a long meal."

I picked up Clumpy, who was winding herself between my legs like a figure of eight, and kissed her furry face. "I think Rachel was looking for you, kitty," I told the cat.

"Give her to me," Hannah said. "She doesn't like that."

"It's you she doesn't like," I retorted.

Chapter 6

1770

"I would like you to meet my uncle," John said to me at the Indian King tavern as we walked into the backyard. "George Ross, esquire."

I smiled in greeting.

"You must be the Betsy I've heard so much about," Mr. Ross said.

John had the decency to look slightly embarrassed. "A friend," he muttered to his uncle.

"Are you participating in the wood-chopping contest too?" I asked.

"Good Lord no." George Ross grinned. "At my age, I'd break. I prefer to exercise my muscle in the courtroom or the assembly room. I'm leaving the physical prowess to my young nephew here."

John's uncle didn't look much older than forty to me. He was handsome, with a long face and a high forehead and perfectly arched eyebrows over expressive brown eyes. He was a lawyer who represented Lancaster, a town about eighty miles west of Philadelphia, in the assembly.

"What brings you from Lancaster?" John asked.

"Ann wanted to visit a friend. Although I'm sure a hearty visit to the shops is in order as well. Lancaster shops can't compare, I'm afraid, when you've got Ann's tastes."

Although he spoke teasingly of his wife, I noticed George's eyes lit up when he spoke of her. John had told me his aunt was a great beauty and the two were well matched and very devoted.

"We brought our daughter with us," George said to me, "who's five. I'm afraid there will be many shopping trips in our future now that our little Mary's of an age to be indulged."

I smiled. "I'm from a family of mostly girls, so I can appreciate that. Girls need lovely things."

"Good grief, the owner of this tavern is no fool," George said, looking around at the setup for the wood-chopping contest. "He's going to get a winter's supply of chopped wood and the winner gets what? A pint of ale? He'll be in business forever."

John laughed. "And a few shillings. The egos of men. What we won't do to show our strength."

"Boys," George corrected. "The egos of boys. Men spend their time on land and money."

"I almost won last year," John said, flexing his muscles. "This time I'm going for victory."

We sat at one of the tables in the sun overlooking the wood-chopping area and ordered ciders. The owner was happily selling drinks and waiting for the rest of the male contestants to arrive.

"John tells me you work together," George said, "and you still tolerate him."

"For a few years now," I agreed. "He's good company. We're still at Webster's upholstery."

We chatted and laughed, enjoying the warmth of the late afternoon. George Ross was quick witted and intense. John had told me that being in the assembly, George had been able to see firsthand the strain and growing rift between Britain and the colonies. I thought of what John had told me about the Sons of Liberty and his uncle's contribution to the rising conflict. George Ross was definitely on the side of the colonial struggle and desire to protect liberty, although all of that seemed far away sitting outside on this gorgeous day while the birds twittered.

"Good day, all," Levi said, arriving with two girls. I recognized them from the quilting bee the Philadelphia Ladies Society had held in the spring, although I couldn't remember their names. I seemed to remember they were friends of Levi's. I thought they were silly, and I wasn't keen to get to know them further. They were like Levi, young and giddy and rather unrestrained.

"This is Charlotte and Edith," Levi made the introductions. They sat at the table with us, and we exchanged greetings.

"Are you prepared to lose, Ross?" Levi boasted, filling out his chest.

"I sincerely hope you're not talking about me," George quipped.

"No, sir," Levi laughed. "Just your pathetic nephew."

"Hey now," John said, flexing his arm muscles again, which made Charlotte tinkle with laughter and gaze at John with interest. Edith, I noticed, had her gaze set on Levi.

"Go ahead and drink more of that cider, mate," Levi said to John. "Give me an advantage. Seal my win."

"Oh, I don't know," Charlotte trilled, looking at John. "He looks strong."

John grinned at her. "I almost won last year. Levi is crushed by the memory."

"I came with Levi, but I'll cheer for you both," Charlotte offered, fluttering her eyes. "Consider me a friend."

"Me too," Edith chimed in.

I pressed my lips together, annoyed.

"My church is having a picnic after this, down by the river," Charlotte said. "We could all go. I made fig candies. Shall we?"

"I'll leave you all to it," George said. "This old man has to get back to his wife and child after I watch this gollumpus chop some wood."

"Please," John said. "Clumsy I'm not. Picnic, eh?"

The girls tittered.

"John, have you forgotten?" I blurted out, not knowing what I was going to say. "We're going to tea after this."

John looked surprised, but I was more surprised.

His uncle caught my eye and winked at me. George Ross, I realized, could see right through me.

John grinned at me, and I looked away, annoyed at his cheek.

I took a sip of cider to hide my smile. Well then. So be it. There was no way I was letting Charlotte sink her dainty little white uncalloused fingers into John.

As it turned out, neither John nor Levi won the wood-chopping contest. The winner was a Swede who made rope for a living. John said he won something better that day: me.

"Who knew you were the jealous type?" He teased me for the rest of the afternoon. "I guess we're courting, Miss Griscom. You have affections for me after all!"

I guessed he was right.

*

1772

How could time pass so quickly? A couple of years evaporated before me in a happy blur. I turned nineteen, then twenty without many people any the wiser that I had fallen in love with John. The exception was John's uncle, who was safely contained to Lancaster and had more serious matters of governing to attend to.

I felt no hurry to change our lives. All around me, my older sisters were in a whirlwind of marrying and having babies and keeping my parents on their toes by falling out of favor with the Society of Friends. My sister Rebecca, the only sister older than me to remain unmarried, was unlucky in love; she had one suitor after another who let her down and broke her heart—all Quaker men. I found comfort in the anonymity of John and I, in the lack of expectation and planning. My private relationship was as soothing to me as wrapping in a warm quilt after being caught in the rain.

I was also very much a coward. I asked John to keep our romance between the two of us, and I kept my parents in the dark. They were busy with our large family and their grandchildren, so it was easy to slip in and out without lying.

I could be with John all day at work and then see him a few evenings a week with friends and be open about where I was and who I was with without raising suspicions. I was also afraid to make plans. I could not see my way out of my current life. I liked being an upholsterer at Webster's, and I loved John, but next month, next year? It was all a worrisome blur. How could I marry him? I had no stomach for disobedience. I seemed to be the coward in the family.

John had been content with this arrangement too, for a while, but the last few weeks he had been more serious, and I could feel the tension rise between us at the workshop and outside of Webster's too.

"I'd like to show you something tomorrow," he whispered to me as I was stitching the hem of a blanket. "Can you come?"

Saturday. "In the afternoon," I agreed. "After the market."

We met outside the bespoke tailor on Walnut Street. He led me down toward the docks, to an old storehouse that looked run-down. John led me to the side door and through a few dim rooms, lit only by the light coming in the dirty windows, toward the back of the building.

"This is what I wanted you to see," John said, opening a door and motioning me inside. I looked around, my mind working to take in what I was seeing. The room smelled of must and iron. There was a flag in the corner. An assortment of empty tables, piecemeal, and a variety of hard-backed chairs, scratched and worn.

"This is where the Sons meet."

That was a name I had not heard in a long time. John was vigilant in protecting me from his work in the resistance; he kept his work quiet when it came to the cause. After all this time, I was looking at some sort of meeting room for the Sons of Liberty?

I wondered if the threat was still there. In Rhode Island, they had burned a British cutter called the Gaspee in June. King George may have been livid about it, but nothing came of it. In Philadelphia, the men had a good guffaw and applauded the rebels who'd rowed out to set the fire and had gotten away with it.

Perhaps what he was doing was more like a diversion for him, like the club that Ben Franklin started, Junto. It seemed hard to imagine that John and the Philadelphia Sons of Liberty were going to be called to pick up arms any time soon. When John had mentioned an armory, I imagined one of the old cave homes on the Delaware River, long abandoned, with a few muskets propped up against the dirt wall and a couple of crates containing ammunition on a dirt floor. I pictured a boys' treehouse rather than an extensive stockpile of weapons and artillery. Seeing this room was unexpected. This was no dirt cave.

"This is where you go for the cause?" I asked.

John nodded. "Yes. Remember that outside these walls, this doesn't exist."

"I know. You keep telling me."

We stood in silence for a moment.

I needed to pay more attention. After the Townshend Duties had been repealed two years ago, it seemed like the tension had passed, and I was glad. John had been honest with me about his intention to take action to ensure that any unreasonable conflict with the British would not be tolerated, but he wasn't seeking out trouble for the sake of it.

Apart from the odd mention about the Sons of Liberty agitating the governor in Massachusetts, the fervor had died down. In fact, there hadn't been much news other than an article that was published in New York. The article had been critical of the New York government for enforcing the quartering of British troops after the assembly had refused to pass it as a directive for the prior two years. The author had signed his name, *A Son of Liberty*. When the man who wrote the article had been revealed as a New York City merchant, an Alexander McDougall, he had been tried and thrown in prison for a few months.

"I know you're with the Sons of Liberty, John," I said quietly, as if someone could hear me. "You told me, and I'm grateful that there are no secrets between us. But why did you bring me here?"

"I have made less of it the last while, Betsy." He reached for my hand.

"How so?"

"I haven't said much, so you probably think we haven't been doing anything. I wanted to show you this so you know what's really happening. Do you see the flag in the corner? The red-and-white-striped one?"

I nodded.

"That's our flag. The Sons of Liberty. And do you remember I told you about Charles Thomson and the iron forge at Batsto? We're producing munitions there. For Philadelphia, Charles is to us what Samuel Adams is to our brothers in Boston."

I'd heard my father refer to the Boston Sons as agents of terror.

"I want to ask you to marry me but to enter marriage without you knowing what I truly am would be a disservice to you," John said earnestly. "I can't pretend or lie to you. That would be unconscionable."

I had known he would ask me eventually. We loved each other. I had hoped for more time, but to what end? I took a breath, my chest tight.

I searched his eyes. "What do you want to tell me?"

John cleared his throat. "That's it. Now I have no secrets from you. Betsy, there is no one else for me. You are my heart."

Silence fell between us.

"Betsy?"

"Yes?"

"Will you be my wife?"

There was a long pause.

"Yes." I laughed when I saw John's expression. He had expected me to refuse him the way I had outside Christ Church. So long ago now, it felt like that day had happened to two other people.

"I thought you'd say no."

"Me too." I laughed, suddenly giddy. What on earth was I doing? Me, here, with an Anglican boy, in this dingy back room belonging to a group of surreptitious rebels. None of it made sense, and yet I felt tremendously happy.

"You're laughing at me?"

"No." I smiled. "I'm laughing at us. At myself. What a crooked ladder we have climbed together since we met."

John grinned. "You've certainly given me a hard time."

"It was never my intention to mislead you."

His eyes started to spark, dark and suggestive. "Oh please, mislead me. Shall I continue? I adore you. No other girl—"

"I would be honored to be your wife," I said firmly, and a little primly.

Hadn't I already been at his side for five years? I knew his heart. I had seen him in good times and in bad. I knew his strength, his humor, his faith. His intense sense of right and wrong. His vehement need for justice.

I felt a strong sense of all the years of my life staring back at me with my acceptance of him. I had just agreed to cross the invisible line that would take me from Quaker to Church of England. For twenty years, my family, my being, had been wrapped in the Quaker world, closely entwined with the meetinghouse and our Quaker ways. And now I was willing to break from my heritage, my faith, my family's history. The meetinghouse women would walk along Fourth Street to our house on Mulberry to try and chastise me, I knew. Despite years of me trying to actively avoid this moment, I would now embarrass my parents just as all of my sisters had before me. I regretted that already, but what choice did I have when I loved this man? I tried to run from fate only to have it stare me in the face.

In truth, I was glad I had the misadventures of Deborah and Susannah and Mary and Sarah before me, for I was not brave. I certainly would never have had the courage to be the first to leave the fold if my sisters had not broken away first.

An advantage, perhaps, to being a middle child. I could ride the coattails of their defiance.

Yet, standing there looking at John's sweet face, I had no desire to choose another path. I had long felt cuckolded by the harsh press of rules upheld by the Quaker elders that I found outdated. Even if I had not developed feelings for John, my heart had long questioned the strictness of my faith. Surely all those old tenants of behavior could be updated? The meetinghouse was keeping to the rules of our parents and grandparents, and the ancestors before them, but the world was changing.

I knew from watching what my parents had gone through with my four older sisters that they had an infinite capacity for forgiveness—eventually. With time, they would come to accept John and my decision to marry him. I was certain I could make good with them after the fact. If I had a choice, it would be my preference not to have to leave my faith. But I was not permitted to marry a man outside the faith, even if my husband was a good man. Surely that was one of the reasons the Quakers were losing the youth of the congregation in vast numbers. I would rather stay in the Society of Friends, but what choice had I been given?

"I remember that day you walked into Webster's shop," John said. "Your cheeks were all red, as if you had raced someone down the street. And your hair was sticking out. You had come to deliver something, I recall. I think I fell in love with you when I saw your face glow when Webster offered you the job."

"Your description of me is alarming."

"You were lovely to look at. Apart from that little line of snot under your nose from the wind—"

"That's not true! Stop it!"

John laughed. "Webster certainly did not find you lacking." He leaned forward and kissed me. "Nor did I."

Had I ever been that windblown girl? I was already twenty. So much had changed since that day.

"There is another matter," John added suddenly. He played with the buttons on his jacket. "I wish to leave Webster's and set up my own shop. An upholstery of our own. Hopefully for our family, one day."

"Our own upholstery! Oh, John!" Exhilaration flooded through me. The waves were breaking over us now. There would be no going back. Soon I would leave home for the first time, a woman grown and married. I could set up my own home. Decide what I would make in our upholstery! Choose my own things. Have a child.

"We will have to elope," I told him abruptly, sobering. I did not wish to repeat the drama of my sisters, all the pleading and crying and hysterics. My parents had no choice than to oppose our marriage. That was the way it was. The Friends would not accept our union. John was an Episcopalian; firmly Church of England and from a family of clergymen, he would never convert to Quakerism.

"I have a friend in New Jersey who can help us," John said. "I'll talk to him. Are you sure you want to elope? We could marry at Christ Church, ask my father to come and officiate."

"No." I threw my arms around his neck. "That would cause me too much worry. And after all these years, I don't want to wait any longer."

"But you'll have to be twenty-one," John reminded me. Was that why he'd been so patient these past two years? "In order to post the marriage bond, we'll have to wait until next year whether we want to or not."

I had forgotten that. I drooped. I still wanted to elope, though. I would need time to ease into the world of John's church, all the shiny ostentatious metal memorials on the walls, the stark red cushions, the men who preached. The overwhelming loudness of it all.

"It's a good thing, Betsy. It will give me time to set up our shop and save money for our union. You'll see. Let's leave this place. Let's go celebrate."

Chapter 7

Winter 1773

I had never felt such cold. The frigid temperatures clogged the Delaware with ice so thick no ships came in, the mercury often nine below zero or more. The river pilots gave up on trying to lead even the smallest schooners up into the Philadelphia docks by the middle of January. We scurried like mice to be indoors, waiting for the deep freeze to lessen.

I ran from home to Webster's and back again, loathing the way the icy wind clawed at me and chilled me to the bone. The small distance was a blessing. On Sundays, the extended trek along Fourth Street to our meetinghouse on Chestnut Street felt like an hour's walk instead of fifteen minutes.

I may have been frozen on the outside, but on the inside I was warmed by my secret intent to marry. My thoughts were seldom far from our plans to elope and open our own upholstery shop. I longed to tell my sisters, especially my sweet eleven-year-old Rachel, who would find joy in my news, but I couldn't. Half of me hoped my father would say, "Why are you smiling like that, Betsy?" and I then could spill my news. I wanted him to rest a gentle hand on my head as he had when I was little, offer to stand with me when the day came. I wanted my mother there, wishing me well, at peace with my decision to choose John. Even pleased. Ah, but that was fantasy. Would any of us marry a Quaker man? It remained to be seen. Maybe Hannah or Rachel? Or, God willing, Rebecca. None of us had yet.

For now, John and I whispered and beamed at each other. John said he thought it best if he set up the shop and sorted out how finances would work so we were secure in our marriage before I joined him. I could not disagree. We had to take it a day at a time.

With the frigid temperatures of January came my birthday. At last, I was twenty-one. My mother said the weather was the same as the day I came into the world. She said that year people lost in a snowstorm died frozen where they stood, trying to get their bearings as they were blinded by wind and whiteness. Winter seemed a punishment for the soul. How ironic that the cold temperatures took away so many fevers and sicknesses but brought with it a different type of suffering.

How had it been six years since I first walked into Webster's with that crate of food? I had been so proud of my stitching, that girl of fifteen, which was laughable now, having spent six years mastering advanced stitchery and working different types of fabric for many well-to-do families in Philadelphia. I could create lace so fine now that wealthy men would pay to have me put it on their shirts.

One day in late January I arrived at work a little late after trudging through snow up to my knees. Mother had a cold that had gotten into her chest and had barked throughout the night. I had helped her steam over a bowl of boiling water under a towel before I left for work.

There was a new girl stuffing feathers into a bolster. I was surprised to see a new face. Webster wasn't doing as well as he had in earlier years and hadn't mentioned he was bringing in new help. He'd never really recovered from the import rules when the Townshend Duties were in place, before they were repealed. He blamed the government, but I couldn't help thinking it was his lax bookkeeping and attention to detail that caused his problems. Philadelphia was still growing rapidly—there were many new upholsterers to choose from, perhaps even a dozen or more. No one had time for a man that frequently put down other upholsterers or was late to deliver promised goods.

I heard John and Mr. Webster in the front, and I could tell by the cadence of the conversation that John was giving his notice. I nodded at the new girl before going to retrieve a bolt of broadcloth by the door.

"If I find you at Fleeson's, I'll have your bollocks boiled," growled Webster. Fleeson, always Fleeson, his imaginary competition. Plunket Fleeson had been in business for more than thirty years, his sign with the easy chair a landmark in the city. I don't think any of us was brave enough to suggest to Webster that he couldn't hold a candle to him.

"No, sir," I heard John say. "I'm going to make a go of it on my own and open up my own shop."

"Well good, then," came the absentminded reply. I could hear the sound of coins chinking as Webster set up for the day. "You're a hardworking fellow, right enough. You've been a help to me. You've certainly put in your time here. And your sweat."

"Blood too," joked John. "Remember when I sliced the top of my finger cutting the ticking?"

Webster laughed. "Hazard of the trade."

"We might be able to help each other out," John ventured. "Share jobs, if need be, or fabric and notion shipments. We trust each other; there's something in that."

Webster grunted but did not object.

I took my fabric and walked back to my worktable. John and I had worked together at this shop for years, day in and day out, and then just like that, he and I would be working our own upholstery business away from here, the place where we'd spent six years. How strange life could be.

I stopped by the girl stuffing the bolster. "Hello. You're new?"

She nodded. Her hair under her cap was the color of a crow's wing, black with a faint violet underneath, her eyes a pretty blue when she looked up.

"I'm Betsy."

"Emily."

"Welcome," I said warmly. "I'm over there if you need anything. I've been here for a while."

She smiled and returned to her work, but her eyes flashed a warmth before she lowered her head. "I've come from the

Chair and Crown," she offered. Not a novice, then. Perhaps Webster had lured her with a few more pennies in pay.

"I wish him luck," she said with a nod to the front room. She'd heard.

Webster was good-natured about John's desire to leave and open his own shop, although I suspected his generous spirit was rooted in his lack of confidence that John's business would ever pose a threat to him. He spent several minutes satisfying himself that John did not plan to flee to the clutches of Plunket Fleeson. Webster was still moaning the fact that Fleeson had made all the curtains for the State House and claimed that Plunket had stolen the job right out from under him. We smiled and nodded, knowing that Webster had still been in London when they finished the State House twenty years ago. I didn't know why Webster was so envious of Fleeson, everyone knew that Plunket Fleeson had been in business for almost twenty-five years. He had earned his success.

Fleeson was known for his aggression on chasing trends. Despite the fact that he was aging and had been in Philadelphia for so long, his understanding of changing tastes made him more in demand, not less. He sold and hung the latest fashions in wallpaper in drawing rooms across town, as well as invested in the local manufacturing of papier-mâché moldings before they were truly in vogue. The other upholsterers said Fleeson seemed fearless: he was just as happy to have fabric and fashions shipped in from Europe as he was to bolster the local economy and grow his concern in local manufactures here. My father called him astute. In comparison, John Webster seemed to be a man perpetually looking over his shoulder instead of ahead.

I caught John's eye when he walked past, and he winked at me. I wasn't looking forward to the days here after he left. I hoped it wouldn't be too long before I could join him in our own place.

That evening John walked me home as a vicious wind whipped our scarves and snow fell sideways, wetting our faces.

"Webster is being quite good about you leaving," I shouted. Webster would miss John more than he knew. John was a hard worker, and he helped Webster with the brunt of the heavier furniture being upholstered.

John shrugged. "I am no threat to him. He won't lose trade. He can easily replace me."

"Still. It is good of him to be gracious. It's not easy to lose a worker who's been there as long as you have." I raised my voice over the wind. I hoped the fire was high in the parlor when I got home. My bones were frozen to the marrow. It might take until April or May to thaw me out.

"My father is worried that there are already too many upholsterers in town," John said. "He would rather I be a clergyman. Like him and his father."

I could barely hear him. We passed the door to a laundress that was closed, and I pulled him into the alcove around the door so I could adjust my scarf and pull my winter hat back over my face. The opening gave us temporary shelter from the wind and I didn't have to shout.

"He only wants what's best for you," I said, circling my throat with my scarf once, twice, thrice. I was glad I had knitted it extra long. "The city is sprouting like a weed. You will have no shortage of work. We kept busy even during the ban on British goods, didn't we? I suppose it would be admirable to follow in the footsteps of your father and grandfather, although if you are worried about excess, there seems to be a great many clergymen in this city already."

John laughed at my wry comment, ducking his face into his collar. "The religious life is not for me. As well you know."

"I heard him talking about Plunket Fleeson again when you were giving your notice," I said. "He can't seem to leave it alone."

"Fleeson will always be a thorn in his side," John agreed, bouncing on his toes. "He's jealous that's all. It seems

Webster's fortunes are waning, but Fleeson's empire just keeps growing, and Webster knows it. The fact that he even considers himself in the same league is laughable. I heard at the coffeehouse that Webster is buying on credit now. He's been thin before, but this time it seems like he's dug a hole by investing in the new range of paduasoys from China. Hurry up, Betsy, please, I'm freezing."

I grabbed his arm, and we headed back into the wind.

"Then maybe he won't replace you," I yelled. Which also explained why Webster was not upset at John's departure. One less worker to pay, and if John opened his own upholstery, it would only make Webster look good as a mentor. Levi would be hard-pressed to manage on his own as the only man left in the shop. The other men had taken other jobs.

"Have you seen Fleeson's wallpapers? They're beautiful," I said.

"You wait. We'll give him a run for his money," John said, head down. "With your needle and my business savvy, we'll be at the top of the heap. I don't know about wallpaper though."

"Have you found a location for your shop yet?"

"Our shop, love. I keep looking. It takes time. I figured it'll be a few weeks at the least. I need to be close to the wharves, but not so close that customers are put off by the smell of the tanneries or the stockyard."

We finally reached my house and almost tumbled through the front door in our eagerness to get out of the icy wind. Thankfully, the fire blazed. John didn't need convincing to come in and warm up.

*

As luck would have it, John found just the right place three days later, and by week's end he had finalized the location for our business: a shop on Chestnut Street between Front and Second that had once been the location of a stocking weaver. There was a nice window fronting the street to display goods and a sturdy mahogany door to welcome customers.

I couldn't wait to see it and went over at dusk on Saturday. The shop was cold and bare, but the bones were promising. No fire was lit in the hearth, so our breath made white streams in the air. I huddled into my cloak and stomped my boots on the pine floor. The wide beams looked just like the ones my father had put in our house.

"Come help me with my notice for the newspaper," John said from his perch on an upturned crate as I inspected the empty space. He picked up a pipe and lit it. "I thought of lighting the fire, but I need the chimney sweep in."

I sat on the crate next to him, our legs touching, breathing in the sweet aroma of his tobacco. John put the pipe down and motioned for the paper and quill next to me. "What should I say?"

"What is to be your area of specialty?" I asked. "You will want to advertise what singles you out, makes you special. What about your seat cushions?" I thought he would say furniture upholstery, reflecting the excellence he had in large pieces, or perhaps his work with venetian blinds. Few people in town had blinds. Window coverings were a luxury, even curtains.

"I want to appeal to newcomers. Most people in town already have their favorite upholsterer. They'll be among the clientele at Fleeson's or the Silver Thread or the Royal Bed. Or one of the others. I need to capture the business of new folk and build our customers from the ground up." It was true that Philadelphia's population was shooting up. We had outgrown Boston and New York. Someone had told me that up to ten thousand newcomers came to Pennsylvania, arriving through Philadelphia, each year now, but I didn't know if that was true. Judging by the crowds in the market and how hard it was to get fresh feathers, it often felt like it.

"How about 'John Ross, Upholsterer, purveyor of fine apparel and furniture.' Unless you want a more interesting name, like the Best Cushion or some such."

John chewed on the end of his quill. "Lacks a bit of punch, no? How about, 'all kinds of upholstery done in the neatest and most fashionable manner.' Put the emphasis on the quality of my work. Our work."

"You should add that you'll do it without undue delay," I said. "And with great care. There are some upholsterers on the south side that are churning out terrible work. They're using indentured servants with no experience down in Southwark. A lady came in the other day asking us to fix her mantua. There were gaps in the sewing where the seam was unraveling. At first Webster tried to tell her she would have to go to a seamstress as we don't do garment work, but after he saw the look on her face he reconsidered. They butchered expensive linen. He gave it to me to fix."

"'On the shortest notice, with care and dispatch?'" John said.

"That's it."

John wrote out his notice for the papers while I got up and surveyed where the shelves for the fabric bolts could go. The shop was an average size, the floors slightly worn to a light honey shade by years of feet walking on them already.

"When will you open?" I asked John. "Or more importantly, how long until we marry?"

"I love when you say that," John said fondly.

"How long?"

My long suffering parents. May they forgive me. My mother had stopped asking me about our friendship a long time ago, around the same time as she stopped singing the praises to me of all the single men in the meetinghouse. She and my father had resigned themselves to focusing on the younger children and leaving John and I to ourselves. After my sisters' collective fall from grace, I think they simply didn't want to know. If they suspected John and I may want to marry one day, they gave no sign.

"How long?" I repeated. John thought for a moment, his fingers running through his hair.

"Six months should be long enough," John calculated. "I'd like to open for business in a month, after I've put the shelving up and built up my stock. I've already placed some orders with cloth merchants. Perhaps we could plan on marrying this fall?"

He hesitated. There was something in his face I didn't like. "What? What's the matter? Are you having doubts?"

John laid down the slate and reached for his pipe. "I don't want you to change your mind."

"What on earth do you mean?"

"I know how much your faith means to you. Being Quaker. You should not be asked to give it up. I fear you will resent me for it in time."

"There are many paths to God. If this was not agreeable to me, I would have said no. I love you. Besides, you did not ask me to give it up."

"My mother was a lunatic. It's in the blood."

"Oh, John. Is that what this is about?" I reached out a hand to him, but he looked away, puffing smoke into the cold room. "You're afraid our children will be like your mother?"

"Do you not fear that, Betsy?" he asked urgently. "Marrying the son of a crazed woman?"

"No. I do not."

I couldn't have said why I felt that way. All I knew was that I wholeheartedly chose John. His goodness, his strength, his sense of fun, his reckless and fiery pursuit of justice. His unwavering faith. It was easy to be around his laughter and good spirits. I knew him, really knew him. I did not doubt him. How many brides-to-be could say that, have that level of confidence in their choice of mate?

"We could end up with a child that is not right in the head," John said bitterly.

"John, our child could also die of the pox or be stillborn or face a number of other tragedies. For that matter, advanced age could make either one of us not right in the head."

John picked up my hand and pressed it to his cheek. "I wanted to raise the matter again, to make sure."

I snorted, in a very unladylike fashion. "I have a great number of siblings who all disobeyed my father and the teachings of our faith. One of them even had a baby out of wedlock. Are you sure there is not lunacy in our family as well? None of them seem very sorry." That made him laugh. I continued, "Except maybe for my sister Mary, about the baby, but now she's Mrs. Morgan and happily married to the father of her son, so she seems to have escaped lasting damage."

"Did she ever say why they didn't marry when she fell with child? She was always so particular. She didn't seem like she'd want to wait if she had Thomas then."

"No, but I suspect it was a matter related to Thomas's employment, for they are in Delaware now. Perhaps he was not ready to take a wife for reasons of his employ, and she protected him. It's hard to imagine, but it's possible. Perhaps he had to get settled. I was saddened that she didn't include me in her confidence."

"To think, all those years that we worked with Mary every day. Who would have thought she would do that? Even now, it's hard to imagine the choice she made—what she went through. Plucky lot, you Griscoms are. Actually, it is a shame you're mostly females and your brother George is too young. We could use the Griscom grit in the Sons of Liberty."

The smile died on my face. "You can't tell my father about that."

"I already said I won't. Trust me, Betsy."

I wondered if John was focused on the wrong thing. How could he fear his mother's madness for us, but not his secretive brotherhood that seemed a bit strange during these peaceful days? We were not at war. We had restored our unrest with Britain, hadn't we? In Boston, the Sons of Liberty were aggressive, heavy-handed. Violent when it suited them. I could understand them taking decisive action after the

Stamp Act and the suffocating Townshend measures, not to mention that terrible shooting in the town green that winter, but now? Those days were long gone. It had been three years.

I hoped John would stop being involved with his rebels. Maybe he liked that it was a club full of men, like the St. Andrew's Society or the American Philosophical Society. Perhaps that would be refreshing after working with so many women all the time.

"That frown makes me sorry I made a joke," John said, reaching up to put a cold, tender hand on my neck, his pipe between his teeth.

"John, why are you still involved in the Sons of Liberty?" I blurted. "It puzzles me. There are no new tax laws being passed, are there? No crisis looming? No ships being burned or more troops being sent over?"

John put the pipe down again and took my hand in his. His thumb stroked the top of my hand. He paused to gather his thoughts, and I watched the gentle plume of smoke rise from the pipe where it rested on the crate.

"The way I see it, we've had eight years of tax laws thrown at us, not to mention the troops being sent to stay in Massachusetts. There's no respect. The king doesn't treat us like the rest of his subjects, even though we're supposed to be the same, all of us British subjects. They want to make money from us without including us in decisions. They fill their own pockets at will—which makes them little more than thieves. Where is our liberty?"

I watched him choose his words, intent on telling me his thoughts.

"They'll never be satisfied. If we had a say in it, if we had representation in parliament, it would be different. But we don't. They'll only try to get more from us, then send their men to make sure we agree to everything when their boots are on our necks. You can practically watch the line of money cross over to London—like a ribbon unfurling across the sea. We can't be puppets on a string, Betsy. We should be involved in laws that affect us, otherwise they'll make slaves of us."

He took a puff of his pipe.

"The way Pennsylvania manages trade will mean more in the coming years. For everyone, but especially for you and me. As upholsterers. And merchants of our craft. This is important. It is our own work that we'll be making and selling, and we'll be paying taxes on the materials we use."

Well, yes. I supposed that was true.

I considered this. "I understand what you're saying, but all of this has been going on for years. This is 1773. Nothing has happened for a long time."

"Don't count on that continuing. You know I'm not looking for trouble, but we have to be prepared. Given the last few years, I don't think it will stop. Why would Britain change? The king has made it clear that we are to submit like children."

I remembered the tax collector's beating, that ginger head slamming into the street forever seared into my mind, and shivered. Why would I think of that now, after all the time? All violence made me feel physically sick. What was wrong with men, that they did that to each other?

"I'm looking forward to running our upholstery together," I said, changing the subject. "It will be like old times but different."

John grinned. "I know what you mean. Should I be like Webster and talk about giving Plunket Fleeson a run for his money?"

I groaned. "Please don't. I was hoping to escape Webster's rants after six years of listening to them. We have ten or fifteen other upholsterers to compete with, not just the one."

John laughed. "But Fleeson's the one to beat, or at least measure ourselves against. Who doesn't know the sign of the easy chair? Wouldn't you like to be Plunket-size one day, my love?"

I shook my head. "I'd like you to be extraordinary for being yourself. For being a good man and a fine upholsterer."

"Should we pick a different name? Something catchy, like The Gilded Bed?"

"I like John Ross Upholstery," I said proudly. "One day perhaps we could add '& Sons.'"

"I'd like that," John said, leaning over to kiss me.

I could not wait to be Mrs. John Ross.

Chapter 8

Spring 1773

The shop was not the same when John left. I went there with an easy spirit, though, knowing I would not be at Webster's much longer. I was vibrating with anticipation for the rest of my year.

In the meantime, I got to know the new girl, Emily, who was as capricious as a cat. Her temperament flitted over her like the shifting of the sun. She could be petty and sharp, and then in the blink of an eye be gregarious and generous, as if just the minute before she hadn't been saying something mean. She swung from impish to affable in a breath. She got away with it, I thought, because of her prettiness. Emily was an effortless beauty, that black-violet hair and pale skin combined with her blue eyes made her exotic to anyone who laid eyes on her. I'm sure she'd been complimented on her looks her whole life, and it had wiggled into petulance when the mood took her. It's not that I didn't like her, I did. She was funny and bright and quite kind. I was just uncomfortable with how relaxed she was gossiping. And at her age! I could hear my mother saying. Emily was a few years younger than me, about seventeen. Clearly, she had not been brought up in the Society of Friends, I thought ironically. She had a bold ease about her that comes from not having to censor yourself.

In one of her moods, Emily could just blurt out the most insensible of things, like today, when she went from making fun of one of the other girls for not working with a thimble to focusing her attention on me. Ann King was out with an earache, and Emily took advantage of the lack of supervision to gossip unabashedly.

"Are you and John Ross courting?" Emily asked baldly, the May sky a wispy light blue outside the window. Now what was she up to? I wondered. John and I had kept it to ourselves for a couple of years, and I wasn't about to let Emily in our confidence.

"You're all over the place today, Emily," I said wryly. "From bothering Patsy over there to asking if I'm courting. Why so curious? Are you bored? You could do some of my work if that's so."

"My brother said he's in the same . . . circle . . . as your John." Her eyes narrowed meaningfully as her voice dropped. "I know you're Quaker, so I didn't think it could be true."

The same circle? I could never put John and the Sons of Liberty in Emily's mercurial path. I thought of being coy, saying, *What circle is that?* or *What do you mean?* but that would just invite her to provide all the details she had and force me into a corner. I thought quickly. Luckily for me in this moment, John also had interests that lay outside of the Sons of Liberty.

"John likes the Freemasons," I said breezily. It was true, he did. "He is glad he joined. I did not realize your brother was also a Mason. If that's the case, I hope your brother finds them similarly inspiring. Their work is so good for the community, isn't it? John hasn't been with them very long but he's looking forward to the years ahead."

I needed to leave Webster's for good sooner rather than later if Emily was going to poke about in our business and make remarks to others that cast doubts and suspicion on my future husband.

*

That summer passed as slowly as the ice had melted in the Delaware River in March. One day limped into the next, the flies everywhere, the heat pressing in closely from all sides. I tried to only wear the lightest linen because I was sweating so much.

I was on the brink of my new life, so close I could touch it, feel it, long for it. I couldn't wait to give my notice at Webster's, to marry John, to become a mother. It was all before me, close enough that I could barely stand to wait. Yet I was still tethered to my old life, my life as a girl. How many times had I closed our front door and walked to work at Webster's after he moved the shop to Second Street? How many times had I sat at the same table with Mother and Father, drinking tea and discussing the news of the day, watching my sisters have scandals and leave one by one? How many times did the Quaker women come over and take tea in our parlor? How many times did I go up and down the curved stairs in our house, up and down, up and down? Time seemed to swing in an endless loop. Soon I would be in a new house, at a new table, as a new wife, and yet I couldn't seem to bridge the gap from here to there. I would even be going to an Anglican church with my husband, but I couldn't reveal that, and each week we walked across town to the meetinghouse on Chestnut Street. I was half in my old life and half in my new one, but I belonged to neither. I was in a most peculiar limbo.

My parents were happy with their family now after years of my sisters embarrassing them. The Griscom clan had settled down into respectable marriages and new routines. We saw Deborah, Susannah, and Sarah on a regular basis. Even Mary came up from New Castle to let her little George spend time with his grandparents in the warm days of summertime.

I felt guilty that I would disappoint my parents, who deserved at least one daughter who would marry into the Friends, the faith that meant so much to them and guided their lives. I also knew marrying John was absolutely the right path for me. They had accepted my sisters' husbands, so I had no doubt that eventually they would accept my choice too. When I was nervous, I pushed it out of my mind. I wished I had more guts. Not much longer now, although I still didn't know the details of when and where.

I thought at length about how best to leave the Friends. I wished I didn't have to. I still remember being a small child in the balcony for youth, separated from the boys, feeling my legs dangling from the bench, itching to swing my shoes so that they caught the light. My feet had felt like they were miles above the floor. The meetinghouse was like my North Star, my compass, my comfort, my strength. My extended family.

Some of my sisters had been so afraid to step away that they dragged their disciplinary hearings on for months, hoping their banishment could be avoided or downplayed. I wouldn't do that. I was going to make a clean break. There was no sense in making it worse for everyone. When the elders came, I would be clear about my intention to move on with my life with John. Done. Then I'd be gone.

I rehearsed this speech to myself. I sounded brave, but I was wracked with nerves.

*

In July, Mother decided to host a tea. Mary was still in town, and she wanted all her daughters there. Mother invited several friends from meeting, including a few Friends who were newly arrived in town.

We put tables in the yard under the trees to shield us from the searing sun. We decorated the tables with daisies and snapdragons, and Mother had Rachel make stars out of old broadsheet newspapers to string together as banners from branch to branch. I showed her how to fold the paper to make it easier to cut multiple stars at once.

Father fashioned us a long table from a piece of birch held up on molasses barrels, and we draped a cloth over it to lay the spread. We had four types of tea in four pots: bohea, lapsang souchong, hyson, and congou. Mother loved her tea. My father preferred coffee, but he drank the tea my mother served.

Little George, my nephew, ran around trying to catch dragonflies while my younger brother, big George, tried to keep him busy and out of the way. They ran in circles by the bushes while we laid out lemon bread and lavender cookies and covered the plates with muslin.

The ladies walked into the garden in a sea of cream and ivory and beige until we were sixteen in number. Mrs. Drinker, Mrs. Wharton, Mrs. Pemberton . . . Quaker ladies of standing, in muted colors in calico and loose weave linen. We sat in the late afternoon sun as golden as the orb itself overhead, the children's laughter a pleasant noise in the background.

"Tell me, Betsy," Mrs. Pemberton said. "Are there any young men catching your eye? I understand you had a birthday. Twenty-one now?"

I winced as she spoke, for her words fell into a lull in conversation and everyone present turned their eyes to me.

"There are many fine young men of appeal," I said in jest. "So many I simply can't choose."

Everyone laughed.

"No one special, then?" she asked.

"My sister is sought out," Mary said. "No shortage on that account."

Mary smiled at me. My goodness, I had missed her. We used to spend so much time together. I smiled back.

"Is this tea from your husband's firm, Elizabeth?" Mrs. Wharton asked, sipping delicately from one of mother's best cups.

"Indeed, it is," my mother answered for Elizabeth Drinker. "The firm of Abel & Drinker supplies us the finest teas." She nodded to Mrs. Drinker. "We're grateful to them."

I looked up at the clouds overhead, admiring the thick puffs of white.

"How is your husband, Elizabeth?" asked Mrs. Pemberton. "We've been waiting to come by."

Mrs. Drinker sighed. "Coming along, I suppose. The doctors don't know what they can do for him. They say it just takes time. No broken bones—he was lucky. He had a fall when the scaffolding broke loose at the warehouse."

There were murmurings of sympathy.

"He'll be right enough with some rest, I'd wager," said the widow Thompson. "You mustn't lose heart."

"Kind of you to brew four teas, Rebecca," Mrs. Drinker said. "I do so love the new lapsang souchong. What a smoky flavor. Quite potent, isn't it?"

My mother nodded. "My brother said that one is hard to get. The shipments from China have competition now."

I got up to stretch my legs and wandered over to smell the roses by the gate. How decadent a summer day this was. Behind me, I heard more tea being poured and the clinking of plates when cake was passed.

I was fingering a velvet petal when I felt Mary by my shoulder.

"I have missed you, Betsy," she said. "I don't think I have said that to you. When we see each other, there's always so many others around us."

"I miss you too. I enjoyed our time together at Webster's."

Mary nodded, smiling, gazing over at where the two Georges were sitting by the small fishpond and peering into the water, a twelve-year-old boy and a three-year-old boy side by side.

"It was hard at first, leaving the way I had to. I was so embarrassed. I wouldn't wish that on anyone. But when I look at George now, I can't regret it, Betsy. I cannot imagine not having my son."

I nodded and leaned in to smell the rose. Sweet, so sweet. "You surprised us all. But that's all in the past now, isn't it, lovely Mary? You have a beautiful family. Thomas seems a fine husband to you. Do you truly like living in Delaware?"

"I do. No one there knows what happened. There, I'm just Mrs. Morgan with a young son."

Mary plucked a rose close to the one I was admiring and twirled it in her fingers. "What about you, Betsy?"

Should I lie to her? Mary knew me best.

She looked up at me, eyes questioning when I didn't answer. I hesitated.

"I'm going to elope with John," I whispered finally. "No one knows. No one *can* know."

Mary's eyes widened, and then she smiled. "I'm pleased for you," she said simply, her eyes glistening, and in that moment I loved her terribly.

"I feel guilty about Mama," I whispered.

Mary shrugged. "She has a kind heart once she gets through the shock of it. If the Friends would only revisit the rules . . . Times change. They must move on too."

"Maybe one day they will. You wouldn't believe how many people have been exiled since you left. There have been dozens of youth disowned this year alone for marrying out of the faith. More than I can count. It's been so frustrating, sitting there every week, listening to offense after offense be read out, wishing I could say something."

"Well, you could," Mary offered. "You can."

"I'm not brave like you," I said.

Mary smiled. "I'm not sure it would be that jarring. Aren't you the fifth Griscom daughter to be banished?"

"Don't joke," I whispered. "It's not funny. Father keeps talking about how lucky we are that William Penn freed us from persecution. The other day he said that everyone should be Quaker."

Mary's face turned serious. "I just don't know why a loving marriage has to be such a grievance. You'd think we were committing a crime."

I was glad I'd told her. What a relief to have someone to talk to about what was so close to my heart. I filled her in on the new business on Chestnut Street and where John was looking to find rooms for us to rent close by. Eventually, our conversation tapered off, and we wandered over to the boys.

"Leave the frogs in the water," Mary told her son. "That's their home. That's where they belong."

"We want to catch them," my brother said. "There's lots."

"Look," little George said. He plonked a chubby finger in the water. "We can make them jump!" As if on command, the frog hopped away from the intruding digit near its back. With

George's lack of stealth, I felt fairly certain the frogs would easily elude imminent capture.

"Leave them be," Mary said again. "How about we go fishing tomorrow, my sweet boy? Papa can take you." Her son was not fussed with the idea and ignored her, repeatedly sticking his finger in the water to try and stir one to the surface. He wanted to catch his frog now.

"Watch him, George," she warned our brother. "Don't leave him. In case he falls in."

"'Course," big George said easily.

We turned to wander the yard a little farther, stepping over geese droppings.

"It won't be easy, Betsy," Mary said in a low voice. "You and John. Just know that. Even though you've seen some of your sisters break from tradition, it will always be harder than you imagine. I miss our meetinghouse greatly, and I did not think I would. Sometimes, truthfully, I ache for it. It seems a sad truth in life that you don't know what you have until you lose it. We'll always be Quaker inside—I know that now. No matter where we go, it's who we are. In our blood, isn't it? The way we were raised. Do not think you will change. You can marry and have a different name, but your beliefs are set deep. You'll see."

I thought about this. I would not leave if I were given any other choice. If only John would join the Friends.

"Do you approve of my decision?" I asked her. It suddenly seemed very important that Mary liked what I was going to do. She was the one sister who had sat in Webster's next to me all those years, the only one who truly knew John like I did. Also, even though my other sisters sewed and dabbled in textiles, Mary was the only one who could understand the upholstery world and what John and I were going to try and do together. On our own, in a city full of upholsterers a few blocks from each other.

"John is lovely," she said in a strong voice. "I have no doubts. On any front."

I smiled, happiness settling on me like the summer sunshine that I stood in. I almost laughed out loud when I remembered that I'd thought John had gotten Mary with child. How funny now. I reached down to pick a dandelion fluff and blew it across the yard.

"But be careful," Mary added severely as a starling began to sing. "John has uncles in politics, and that one uncle, if I remember from that day when we were all stuffing mattresses, is one of the lawyers who opposed the Townshend Duties. Didn't John tell us his uncle was wrestling Britain on it? *Outraged* was his word, I recall. Your problems won't be about religion; Father won't want you marrying John just because he's a Ross." She lowered her voice to sound like our father. "'The Griscoms have been loyal subjects of the crown since the 1600s, one of Pennsylvania's oldest families . . .' and so on and so on, just as we've heard a thousand times. You know how our parents are, Betsy. There's a difference between marrying out of the faith and marrying into a family that is rebelling against the government. Have you considered this? That's different than who our sisters married, who I married. In a way, to them it will be far worse."

No, I thought sourly. I had not thought too much about that. I didn't want to think about that. I could not stand all that. I just wanted to have babies and work in our upholstery. A shiver went through me. Mary didn't even know how John really felt about some of what Britain was doing. Didn't know he was a Son of Liberty. Why did men have to get so fiery and political all the time? Governments changed and the world kept moving along. Hadn't it been that way for centuries? I liked being part of the British empire. I shrugged.

"It will be fine," I said, watching a group of little birds chase and dive at a hawk's tail while the hawk was in flight. A red-tailed hawk, it looked like. Magnificent creatures.

"There's a reason I don't mind living in New Castle now," Mary said wryly. "I get to come home for the family affections and then leave again."

I sighed, not pleased to be taken from my happy state of mind. Taxes, taxes, taxes. Disownment, banishment, blame. What a lot of bother. Wearisome. I would take whatever punishment was meted out to me and be done with it. I had literally had years now to think about my course of action and the choice I was going to make. My sisters had survived. I would do the same.

"Let's go have a cup of tea," I said. "You're here with little George, and that's all matters today."

Mary put the rose she'd been holding in my hair. We turned to return to the tea party just in time to see little George lunge for a frog and fall headfirst into the dark water. Almost as quickly, my brother yanked the back of little George's shirt and pulled him out, holding him to his chest and looking to see if he was whole.

"George!" Mary cried, running over to him with a mother's alarm.

Little George shook the water out of his eyes in surprise like a puppy and then started laughing. You'd think a little one would be wailing after a fright like that.

"SPLASH!" he said with delight. "No frog. Where frog go?"

My brother laughed and lifted him higher on his shoulder. "Good man."

Mary yanked her son from our brother and held him tight, but little George just laughed. "Again."

"Definitely not," Mary said.

"You should teach him to swim," my brother offered casually.

Boys. Men. Always finding trouble.

"Betsy," Mrs. Drinker called to me from the table. Some of the women had moved toward the pond but were standing watching when it was clear the toddler was in no danger. "Come see me."

I smiled at her as I sat down. "Is there any tea left in that pot? I'd love a cup. Hyson?"

She obligingly poured a dark brown stream into a teacup the color of a robin's egg. She was in her forties, I guessed, midway through a pregnancy, judging by the slight swell of her belly, the backs of her hands splattered with freckles, as if she did a lot in her garden.

"I have been thinking," Elizabeth Drinker said. "Perhaps you could help with the ladies' meeting in the fall? We could replace Mrs. Stedicorn early. Her baby is due in August, and she'll be glad of a break, I'm sure. I've certainly had my share of babies, and those last few months can be trying. This one isn't due until November, so I have a bit more time. We always try to include a variety of ages to assist and learn from the elders, and of course I thought of you. You would be a wonderful addition, Betsy, so steadfast, and your presence would help us with the younger girls and women. Will you consider it?"

I took my time swallowing my tea. I might be married and in the congregation of Christ Church then.

"I asked your mother," she said. "I know you're twenty-one, but I knew she'd want to be informed. I don't know why we didn't think of it sooner. Perhaps I assumed you'd be married and gone by now. Still, I'm delighted by the thought. You've always had such admirable character. The youth in meeting could benefit from your sensibilities. Especially after the last few years." Her eyes crinkled at the edges when she considered my older sisters.

"What did my mother say?" I asked, watching my mother show off her roses to the ladies.

"She was delighted. Of course."

I reached for a ginger biscuit. How would I get out of this? "The upholstery shop has been busy again," I deferred. "We've had a few people leave, and large orders are coming in. I'm not sure it's the right time to take on anything new. There's a new girl being trained." My excuse sounded weak even to me.

"Oh, don't worry about that. I'll speak with John Webster."

I had no doubt she would. Elizabeth Drinker was used to a world of yes. Her husband co-owned, with my Uncle Abel, one of the city's largest import-export firms, and a couple of years ago the Drinkers had moved into a large three-story house with a yard full of outbuildings and gardens. They were wealthy, and had more influence than many Quaker families in Philadelphia. Elizabeth was respected and equally sought out for her work with healing herbs and physicks. She had an invisible reach across the streets of Philadelphia, beyond the Quaker world, despite her modesty and formal ways.

I blinked, thinking. "Let me consider it. Please. I'd hate for Mr. Webster to think I'm complaining about my work."

"I have a daughter who is good with the needle and is looking for an apprenticeship. Perhaps that would give him an extra pair of hands?"

Oh no. I attempted a smile. "Thank you, Mrs. Drinker, I'll ask Mr. Webster about your daughter. In the meantime, let me consider your request."

She nodded. "I knew you'd be pleased."

"It's an honor."

Chapter 9

October 1773

I heard the noise at the same time my parents did, and we went outside together.

A crowd of people was walking past our house from the wharves and warehouses, marching down Mulberry Street to head toward Market Street and up to the State House.

"What's happening?" My father asked.

"No tea," the crowd chanted. "Reject the tea!"

"We're headed to the green," came the answer. "Kill the Tea Act!"

So it had come to this. In the summer, we'd learned that Britain had passed the Tea Act in May and had sent seven ships packed with crates of East India Company tea to the colonies. The ships were headed to four cities to be unloaded and sold: Boston, New York, Philadelphia, and Charlestown. The new legislation was passed to get rid of a burdensome surplus of tea, which was going moldy in London warehouses and not making any money, and at the same time bail out the East India Company. Parliament thought we wouldn't take exception to the Tea Act because it lowered our tea prices, but the East India Company made revenue from the duty, and its forced sale was a planned effort meant to force our hand—and our purse. It took away our choice on which tea we could buy. Even more damning, the East Indian Company had deliberately chosen a handful of colonial agents that would be the only ones allowed to sell the tea, which ruined trade for other importers who sold Dutch tea, among others.

"It's trickery," John had told me, furious. "Men in the government have shares in the East India Company! They're orchestrating their own riches."

It didn't help that my own uncle's firm of James & Drinker had been chosen as one of the tea agents.

My mother and father and I stood outside our front door and watched the parade of walkers go by, purposefully heading to the State House to oppose the latest in tax schemes by the British.

"Come to the meeting," a man yelled to us. "Tell everyone." He held a pitchfork in his hand, as if he intended to riot.

"Bloody politicians," someone else said. "Telling us what to do."

"Taking away our liberty," his companion agreed. "It's not right."

"No Tea Act," the crowd chanted. "Repeal!"

"Repeal," came the echo.

My father made a show of solidarity, standing calmly by the gate and waving his hand with an amiable expression on his face.

I knew we would not be well liked if the crowd knew the truth. My Uncle James Abel's business meant our family was in, but other families were out. If I knew my uncle, he would be lying low, hoping no one would notice his favor from the British. Some of the men he'd done business with for years had just been undercut and excluded.

"Let us go inside, Sam," my mother whispered after a time. My father motioned us back in the house.

When the door closed, he turned to my mother.

"I have to go, Rebecca. I knew about the meeting. I did not, however, expect to see crowds in the street."

"Don't go," my mother said. "We shouldn't be seen there. Not when my brother is one of the new tea agents."

"We have to know what's being said. Our livelihood depends on knowing who has the money in town, who's in favor and who's not. The workingmen must know the mood of the city. I'll take Betsy."

"Betsy?" My mother cried. "Why?"

"She can be my excuse to leave if it becomes unruly. If they riot. I will keep her safe, Rebecca."

For a long time, I watched from a second-floor window of our house. Dozens of people passed by. Some on horseback, others riding in carriages or chaises, but most on foot. Many of the people were coming from out of town, from Bucks County and north, or from the neighborhoods by the docks. I tried to remember the last time I had seen this many people causing a swell on the street.

I paced the house, moving from room to room on the second floor to peer out the window, tripping over my mother or my siblings. We hung back behind the curtains, watching the crowd pass in front of the red brick wall of the burial grounds, then on past the paper maker's and stationer's. Some of them stopped at the grocer's and purchased fruit or a lemonade.

I saw a few signs. Someone had painted "The tea is poison!" on what looked like a piece of floor plank. Another sign said, "No vote, no tea." Some of the kids held homemade weapons, their fathers carrying muskets. The biggest sign said, "We're not thirsty, you can have it," with a skull and crossbones painted in red.

Finally, it was time for us to leave for the meeting. My father must have known what time it was due to start. It was a warm fall day, windless; I needed no cloak.

My father and I stepped into the crowd.

"Say little," my father said. I nodded.

We joined in the march to the State House, listening to the chatter of those around us, leaves crunching underfoot in bunches of red and gold. Maple, oak, ash, and a few sycamore leaves.

"Philadelphia must lead the campaign against the tea," a man shouted, pushing his tricornered hat back out of his eyes. He stopped and waved his walking stick in the air vigorously to address those hanging out of windows around us on Fifth Street. "Resist! We must resist!"

"Who are they to tell us?" a thin woman agreed. "First tea, what next?"

Tea, I thought to myself. *Such a fuss over tea.* The city had gone mad.

As if reading my mind, or perhaps seeing the confusion in my face, my father said in a low voice, "It's what it stands for, Betsy."

"Governor Penn has done nothing!" a teenage boy called. "Doing nothing is choosing sides! Don't tread on us, Penn!"

We were drawn along with the current of people.

Finally, we reached the State House.

My father and I looked at each other.

There were hundreds—literally hundreds—of people here. I had never seen this large a gathering. I had hoped to meet up with John here, but all I could see were masses of bodies of every size and shape, male and female, stacked dozens deep in all directions, all over the lawns and surging up to the entrance. The crowd looked like it circled the building.

"No tea," the crowd chanted.

"Stay with me," my father hissed into my ear, holding my arm.

I nodded, reaching for his hand.

The crowd was pulsing.

I looked over and thought I saw Charles Thomson making his way to the door of the State House. We were too far away for him to be able to recognize me, even if he had been looking in our direction. I'd met him while John and I were dining with his Uncle George in June. Thomson was openly outspoken about freeing Pennsylvania from what he called "the whims of imperial policy." He was so voluble he scared me.

A short time later the meeting was opened by men with freshly powdered wigs, and the speeches were under way.

I tried to follow what was being said, but it seemed to be the same sentiments over and over again. People thought the Tea Act was sneaky. Reprehensible! One man shouted that if we drank the East India Company tea, we were drinking our way into slavery as Britain would use the colonies at will however they liked. The crowd was clear: all incoming tea shipments would be turned away, by force if necessary. Our very future depended on it!

I studied the people around me. Everyone was there: young and old, rich and poor, gentry and mechanics. I wondered how long it would take England to repeal the Tea Act, like all the others. Wouldn't they know by now it wouldn't work? Soon letters would be on their way back to King George and parliament damning the Tea Act, informing them of the mass protests and unrest.

The speakers tried to yell over the crowd.

My father took my arm. "We've heard enough. We'll go."

We shouldered our way through the crowd behind us. Bodies surged forth into the opening we left. I stepped around a few dogs and small children until we reached the relative quiet of Fifth Street.

"Will Governor Penn do anything?" I asked. He hadn't yet, despite receiving a petition with hundreds of names on it asking for a special meeting of the Pennsylvania assembly.

"He must stop this uprising," my father answered. "If he doesn't, the people will think they can take matters into their own hands."

Quakers did not support unrest. My father and his uncles wouldn't even obey the non-importation rules after the Townshend Duties were passed. They didn't believe in going against the government. The thought gave me chills, for earlier this year, even before news of the passing of the Tea Act had crossed the ocean, I had dined with men that were creating a sense of urgency around opposing Britain. One of those men I was about to marry.

*

"Come for tea," Emily said as we worked cotton into rectangles for bed pillows. "My parents would like to meet you."

"Why?" I asked, wrestling with a corner. Not tea again, I thought.

Emily laughed. "Because I talk about you so often, silly goose! We're friends now, aren't we?"

All of my life my friends were other Quaker girls, from weekly meeting and in our Quaker fold in the city. Quakers kept with Quakers. Not to be exclusionary or snobbish, but because that was my world. It wasn't that I didn't want to spend time with Emily, but it was a peculiar feeling to be making plans with girls out of the faith. But then, I reasoned, I would be married soon, and when I had the shop with John, I would be socializing with all sorts of people from all different walks of life.

"Besides," Emily said, "my mother makes the best candies around. Does that entice you?"

"It does," I agreed. Candy sounded like a lovely treat. I hoped it was candied orange peel, my favorite. Or Turkish Delight.

We went to her house in a fall rainstorm, running all the way with our hoods pulled low. Emily lived in a house by the bridge over the stream that ran through the working-class neighborhood. Her house was small, filled with the smell of burnt sugar and caramel. It was a busy, noisy house, bursting with children and at least three cats. And a dog.

"In the kitchen," her mother called when we arrived. "Making more candy to sell at market."

The center table had been cleared off, and three women were busy making treats, sleeves pushed up. Two of the women glanced up at us and smiled before returning to their candy making.

"You must be Betsy," Emily's mother sang. She was a soft woman, curvy and round like rolled dough, with a smile that beamed. "Betsy has been training Emily at the upholstery," she explained to the other women.

"Pleased to meet you," they said at the same time.

"My sisters," Emily's mother said. "I'm Rose, and this is Daisy and Violet." She nodded at each in turn.

"A flower bouquet," I said. "How nice."

"Indeed," Rose laughed.

"Our mother," Violet said. "She was a Lily, God rest her soul."

"Not that she had a green thumb," Daisy said. "She couldn't keep a plant alive for love nor money. She loved flowers, but everything she touched died, I swear."

Everyone laughed.

"They were all out of flower names by the time I got here," Emily told me. "My sisters all got flower names, though. Not that I mind."

"Well, you were the twelfth, lass," her mother said fondly.

"All girls?" I asked.

Rose nodded proudly. "Until Emily. Thought I'd never have a boy. Well, the joke was on me. My youngest four are boys. All hearty! Blessed are we indeed."

"My poor brothers," Emily said. "Henpecked and coddled at the same time."

"Nonsense," Rose said. "They're lucky to have all their older sisters fussing over them, and have you ever seen any one of them with so much as a hole in their knee? Not going to go hungry either, the way your sisters cook. Not much I can do about the dirt on them, though." She made the last comment cheerfully, with a "boys are boys" shrug, and I could feel the warmth of Emily's family spilling over through Rose.

I was included as part of the clan right from the start. I wiped the rain off my face with a cold hand and felt my shoulders relax. It was nice to not be bent over fabric or worrying about my upcoming inevitable banishment. I'd thought John and I would be married by now, but he was still adjusting to having the shop and needed to save up for our marriage bond.

There was a certain comfort, I thought, of being a child, when the world was small and your choices were made for you.

I felt so comfortable in Emily's mother's kitchen, which was fragrant with spice and scented greenery. Dried flowers sat in pots along the counter; pots hung from hooks on the wall. Candles burned down to the nubs sat in iron holders along the shelves by the window, dried fruits in glass jars in the cabinet. The enticing smells of peppermint and almonds wafted under my nose and made me hungry. Our home was friendly too, but I could tell Emily's family was far more outspoken, and it was this freedom that let her say what she wanted even when she shouldn't.

"Sit," Rose ordered, motioning to the stools over by the hanging herbs. "Take those wet cloaks off and hang them by the door. Emily, get Betsy some of the minted nuts we're making. I'll pour some tea. Heat you girls right up."

What kind of tea? I wanted to ask. The now illicit Dutch tea or the king's tea?

Rose wiped her hands on a towel and let her sisters take over the confection-making as she moved to the hearth to pour out the kettle.

Emily went to the pantry and took out a jar. She lifted the lid and took out a ladle of nuts before plonking mine down on a tin plate in front of me. "Those were made this morning," Rose said.

I ate my mine slowly, savoring the taste of sugar and peppermint coating the pecans and almonds. My mother didn't make sweets very often. She thought it would crack our teeth or teach us to like sweets too much.

"I also made apricot sweetmeats and macaroons," Rose said, approaching us with two cups of steaming tea. "Mind. These are hot. Don't burn your tongue."

I looked at my steaming cup, liquid jostling at the delivery, and added a drop of thick milk from the pitcher that Rose had set down before settling herself on the stool next to us. Emily took tongs and snipped at the sugar cone, brandishing a piece, but I shook my head. The sweet nuts were enough. I took a grateful sip of tea—oh, that first sip after a dash through the rain!— letting the heat slide down my throat and the warmth of my cup remove the chill from my fingers.

"Thank you, Mrs. Spencer," I said. "This is a decadence."

Rose filled her own cup. "There's an awful lot of fuss about tea these days," she said, clanking her spoon against the sides as the milk turned the liquid a light beige color. "Tea should be tea. I couldn't go a day without a cuppa, no I couldn't."

Violet and Daisy murmured agreement.

"Emily has said your family goes to the big meetinghouse," Rose said. "Is there much being said about the tea there? We're Presbyterians ourselves. I usually pay no mind, but my goodness tempers are high! I haven't seen such fuss since '65, when I had my last boy. Funny what sticks in your mind. I just remember being out here with Jacob," she gestured to an imaginary pregnant belly, "watching effigies burned in the street, thinking heads were going to roll. They kept that one bouncing in the tree for—"

"Mother," Emily said.

"Sorry. Emily speaks so highly of you, Elizabeth."

"Please call me Betsy."

"Betsy. I mean no disrespect, but we heard the Quakers are trying to stop the anti-tea movement. That's what they're calling it now, doesn't that sound fancy? *The anti-tea movement.* As sure as I'm sitting here, that's what they said at the bakery. Mr. Lang said that as he was filling orders. I was in the line right at the end, and he said, 'We've got to lead the anti-tea movement and not let the ships land.' Not even lowering his voice, as if he wasn't saying something that might rile people up. And all us in line, all we wanted was our bread and rolls. I suppose that's his right, but if you ask me, you should let folks do what suits them and not get people in a tizzy. I know the Quakers don't want trouble, but some folks that don't like the new tea tax feel like it's their right to make a fuss, just like old Mr. Lang at the bakery. What do you make of it?"

Well, now I knew where Emily got it from, I thought wryly. I struggled to follow her mother's string of words, spoken without any care for the listener, in a quick tumble of sound.

Daisy tutted and poured another bowl of nuts into the sugar mixture in the pan.

I finished chewing and swallowed so I could answer.

"I don't know much," I said carefully. "I don't run a household, so I don't hear what you hear. I think that the Friends in general want to do what is best for everyone, which is what is peaceable. I know Philadelphia is upset about the tea and that some people don't want the tea shipment coming here."

Rose nodded. "Why should the king let some men get fat with profit and others have none? Why did they get to pick the tea agents?"

Hasn't it always been that way? I asked in my head.

"What do you mean, Quakers don't want trouble?" Emily asked her mother.

"After the bakery, I went into the grocer's, and I heard that some of the men are being told off by Quakers. You know, for protesting. The Quakers don't want trouble and are trying to hush people. That's what I heard."

"Well, not my family," I said. "The Griscoms are nice people. We keep to ourselves."

"Yes, dear, of course," Rose said, drinking her tea. "We're just having a chat. Don't give what I'm saying another thought."

"There's another way to think about it," Violet piped up. She was cutting some of the Turkish Delight into neat squares. I heard a low rumble of thunder outside the window as wind sent rain sideways into the glass. "It's us women who decide to buy or not buy. If we want the tea, it will sell, but if we don't, it sits and rots. The men can put up a fuss and carry on, but we women are the ones who decide with our purses."

"Indeed!" Daisy laughed, holding up a knife crusted with syrup. She stepped forward like she was fencing, brandishing the knife with an arc of her arm.

"My sisters, the warriors," Rose said wryly. "Joan of Arc come to life."

"Power of the teacup," Daisy said. "Mark my words, us women have a say in our own way."

Emily yawned, a delicate sound that her small hand flew up to cover. "A month from now, it won't matter. Philadelphia's always in a flap about news from England." She yawned again.

I thought of the surging crowds at the State House and the men who had walked past our house with pitchforks and guns. The papers said three hundred people came out that day to protest the Tea Act, that there had never been that many agitated people at the State House before. I don't know how they came up with the number. The outcome of that meeting had been the formation of a committee that resolved to hold another public meeting when the ship headed to Philadelphia from London arrived. The news of the Tea Act also led to Philadelphia readying itself to fight back. Groups formed with names like the Committee for Tarring and Feathering, which I didn't want to think about. It occurred to me that John had been right all along. He had seen this coming.

"Tell me, Betsy, is my Emily a hard worker?" Rose asked, winking at her daughter.

"Very," I answered. "She is a credit to you. She has a nice touch with the needle."

"Webster is filling the front room with fabrics from India," Emily said. "Even though he can't afford it."

Emily talked too much, but I shared her feelings.

John was busy stocking our shop with fabrics and notions, a little more each week. It was a fine line between too much and not enough. We were going to need the fabrics, especially the wool and cottons from London and Liverpool. If the matter of the tea did not blow over, what would it mean for our new business? New non-importation rules would choke us. We couldn't raise a family on homespun, and more than anything, I wanted our good fortune to continue so I could be a mother.

Chapter 10

November 1773

When I left work on a mild Monday evening, John was waiting outside the Golden Fleece tavern across from Webster's. It was just getting dark, the sky draping thin clouds with streaks of violet. John was lounging against the wall, his coat unbuttoned. I could see the weave of his favorite waistcoat, the way the fabric-covered buttons formed a neat line down his middle. I was used to seeing him in his work apron.

He smiled when he saw me emerge from the upholstery and lifted a finger in greeting.

I crossed the street quickly. "You have proof of the bond?" A bond was required for us to marry, payable to the governor, to ensure John and I would not become charity cases and a burden on the system if our marriage failed. It was common; all couples we required to fulfill this step. We did not actually pay the money, we just had to prove that we could pay the required sum if we got into legal trouble for any reason.

"Not yet." He patted his pocket. "I have the money, though. Finally!"

Tears sprang to my eyes. I'd waited so long. The last year had felt like I was watching for sap to trickle out of a maple tree.

"When would you like to marry me, Miss Griscom?"

"As soon as possible. I've already been waiting too long. When will it suit your friend?"

John picked me up off my feet and buried his face in my neck.

William Hugg, a friend of John's, ran Hugg's Tavern across the river in Gloucester, in New Jersey. He had agreed to help us elope by helping John get a marriage license since we weren't getting married in a church and wouldn't have the banns read. He was also arranging for a minister to marry us in his tavern. I had been there once, with my family on the way to visit the New Jersey Griscoms. We'd stopped in for a meal. It was a beautiful old building, two stories high, with a line of windows running across the front. It was a well-travelled inn and tavern as it was a short walk from the ferry between Gloucester and Philadelphia.

"Please put me down," I said. "People will see." We wouldn't have to hide much longer!

"He said one day this week. How about Thursday? I don't want you to feel rushed. I want to make sure you have time to—"

"John! You can't be serious? I'm ready!" I'd had all the time in the world. It had taken John a year to set up the upholstery and come up with the money we required to marry and rent rooms to live in.

"There's no going back afterwards, Betsy," John said. "Are you certain?"

"Thursday," I repeated. "Thursday it is." Today was the first. Thursday was the fourth. I would be a November bride. Not ideal, but it would have to do. At least the river wasn't yet clogged with ice. I didn't want to wait until the spring just for nice weather and flowering trees. Although I had dreamed of marrying under a magnolia tree in full blossom.

"I'll book the ferry, then," John said.

"Where will we go—after?" I asked. "The night we marry?"

John hesitated. "That depends. We could stay the night at Hugg's Tavern. Or you could come home? I haven't had a chance to tell you. I found rooms for us not far from the shop."

Home. We had a home.

I heard movement in the street behind me, the snuffle of a horses being ridden and the steps of men walking by.

"Let's go home then," I decided. "When can I see our new place?"

"We can go there now, if you'd like."

"Please." I paused. "What if my parents find out before we elope on Thursday?"

"You think they will?"

"No, actually." I did not believe there would be a scene. There was something to be said for having sisters who had already left the house and gone against my parents' wishes. I still would have preferred to have fallen in love with a Quaker man, but that had not happened. I couldn't help that. I would have to ask for forgiveness and trust that my parents would continue to accept me with the same goodwill they'd given my older sisters.

"Are you all right?" John asked, his eyes anxious. "Should I come with you to tell them? They might be angry."

"No. It's best if I tell them alone. I'm fine, I want very much to marry you. You are . . . my life."

"And you mine."

We leaned toward each other so that our foreheads were touching, hidden by the shadows of night.

"I hope you can cook," John joked.

I laughed and swatted his arm. "And I hope you can keep us warm this winter, Mr. Ross. Your wife has standards."

"I shall do my best. What do you say, my love? We'll become man and wife Thursday night?"

"You may be certain of it. I hope it doesn't rain." We had been lucky with the weather this fall. All the days had strung together in a pleasant spate of temperate conditions.

"Are you sure you don't wish to tell them before the day we go to Hugg's Tavern?" John asked.

"I think that will only make it worse. Rachel and George would hear and that will upset them. Rachel is still only eleven. Sometimes my father yells."

"I'll be here when you're finished work on Thursday," John said. "We can go back and get all your things the next day or on Saturday. I will take care of everything else, make all the arrangements."

I nodded, my heart squeezing in my chest. Panic, elation, fear, dread.

"What about Sunday? Do we have to go to church? So soon?" It seemed a bit rushed to show up at a service at Christ Church so quickly after eloping. I wasn't sure I was ready for that.

"It will not hurt us to miss a Sunday and worship at home. That will give us a week to announce our marriage. I will speak with Reverend Peters to prepare him."

I nodded, relieved. I didn't want to walk into Christ Church on John's arm and hear gasps of surprise. Well, I might still hear disapproving clucks, but there was no avoiding that.

"Can we really be doing this?" I asked, my hand reaching for John's. John cupped my cheek with his hand.

"We are indeed, my Mrs. Ross."

A little tear escaped and stayed on my cheek. "I feel like there are a hundred things I have not thought of."

"We'll manage," John said. "I came as soon as I had the money for the bond. As long as we have that and each other, anything else we can work out together."

"How much was the marriage license?" I asked.

"One pound, five shillings. I think you're worth it." He winked at me.

"I'll wear my good brown gown," I decided. John loved the way the lustrous fabric made my blue eyes shine. "I will have to go to work the next day."

"It must be a secret until we're married," John agreed. "For your sake."

"I'll go in on Friday and give my notice to Webster," I said, working through the details. Emily was going to want to smack me. I couldn't have told her; she would not have kept it to herself. She was too impetuous, too childlike. I had the feeling I would be adding her name to a long list of people that did not think me capable of this. Dependable Betsy. Good Betsy. Reasonable Betsy. Cowardly Betsy.

"And then we will be married," John said softly, squeezing my hand. "We can finally be together."

"Finally," I echoed slowly. Weeks, months, days. And slowly, slowly, but then all at once, here we were. Marriage, our own upholstery shop, freedom. I would be relieved from all the Quaker rules and bonds I had known since I was a small child. The thought was a joy and a sharp pain all at the same time.

"Don't change your mind," John said with a smile, but I saw the anxiousness behind the jest.

I threw myself at him in an embrace, forgetting that I didn't want to be seen.

A group of men hooted at us as they walked by, one tipping his hat. I laughed and gave him a wave. Who was this girl on a dark street in the arms of a man who was about to be her husband? *Goodness. Look at me!*

*

To my good fortune, the upholstery was not busy on Thursday, and Webster did not mind when I asked if I could leave at four o'clock. I think I could count on one hand the number of times I had asked to leave early in all my years working there.

"Where are you going?" Emily asked when she saw me put away my scissors.

"I'm meeting someone."

"Who?"

"Emily, don't be nosy. See you tomorrow. I'll tell you then."

I rushed home in the thin autumn daylight, barely noticing the people on the corner arguing over the Thursday paper. *The Pennsylvania Gazette,* Ben Franklin's paper, now run by his partner, was taking every opportunity since the Tea Act passed to ruffle feathers and trumpet indignation. No one was happy with England this year, which helped sell papers, I guessed. All the newspapers were crowing in force. On Monday, my father had been lost in a long article on the tea problem in Dunlap and Claypoole's *American Daily Advertiser.*

I wanted to get home in time to fix my hair and change while it was still light out. As I opened the same door that I had opened for almost ten years, since my father bought the house when I was twelve, I paused, suddenly conscious of the fact that after tonight I would not live here anymore. Unease fluttered through me. Not for the choice I was making, but for the place I was leaving behind.

I found them in the parlor: my mother, Rebecca, Hannah, and Rachel. My mother was lying back on the settee, her face flushed, while Rachel was singing an aria. Hannah was crocheting in the easy chair, Rebecca working on another shell picture. My father had taken George to work with him.

"You're home early," my mother said, sitting up and patting the spot next to her. "We've only just stopped working."

I sat and wiggled my stockinged toes, finally free from the confines of my boots after a long day. I leaned back against the sofa, mimicking her posture.

"Good day?" she asked, turning her head to mine. She leaned in and kissed my temple.

"Good day," I answered, linking my little finger with hers.

It had to be now. My courage was pooling around the floor, and I pulled it up around me like a sack. If I waited it would leave me altogether. I didn't have much to begin with. There was a rushing noise in my ears like a waterfall.

"May I speak with you?" I asked her softly. "Alone? In your chamber?"

My mother raised an eyebrow but got up, and I followed her up the stairs.

She sat on her bed, hands folded in her lap, and waited. I closed the door and leaned back against it.

"I'm going to marry John Ross," I blurted. Those were not the words I had planned to say. I had rehearsed this, and now I couldn't retrieve any of my carefully planned words. "I'm sorry if this disappoints you."

"Oh, Elizabeth. You're with child." It was not a question. She narrowed her eyes, and I realized she must feel that history was repeating itself, only it was me this time and not Mary.

"What? No! Of course not," I babbled. "I wouldn't do that. I mean, no. I love him. I want to marry him. I'm sorry, Mama, I'm so sorry. I wish it was someone from meeting. I did not intend to disappoint you." I waited anxiously for her to respond.

She was silent, her head bent, her hair almost pure white. My mother was fifty-three years old now. The thought surprised me; she was ageless to me. My parents were both still capable in body and mind. My father was as agile and skilled a carpenter as he had been all of my life. They both still worked the long hours they always had.

The silence between us grew.

I glanced down at the floorboards, remembering that it was my father's hands that had nailed them down, this house a labor of love for his growing family. He had purchased the house when it was small and kept adding on to it over the years.

"No." Her voice was hard as a hammer.

I looked up just in time to see her pick up the bolster from the bed and throw it at me. I caught it.

My mother stood up and drew herself to her full height, which wasn't very tall, her fists balled on each side.

"No," she said again. "Not him. Not that family."

"It is too late, Mama. I have decided—"

"*No.*" This time she raised her voice.

I stood and waited, the roar back in my ears. I hadn't expected this. My mother never displayed temper. This couldn't be happening.

"I do not permit it, Elizabeth."

"Mother—"

A silver candlestick slammed into the door by the side of my head. Stunned, I met her eyes. "I know I've surprised you, and it's upsetting," I tried.

"Not you, Betsy. Not you. You were always the one with common sense."

My mother spoke in a tone I had never heard from her. I had never heard her this angry. Her eyes were steel, her face an eerie icy calm.

"What has possessed you?" she hissed. "You can't marry him. I forbid it. Maybe I should have done this with your sisters."

"Perhaps we could sit and talk, Mama," I suggested. "Please? Are you really this shocked? How is this any different than what—"

She threw the brass dish that was on the bedside table. I gasped, tears filling my eyes. "Stop it! I know you're upset, but please! Stop it. Can we talk?"

"You are the one we trusted not to do anything stupid," she said. "You were the sensible one."

Her fists were still clenched with tension, and I wondered if she would strike me. I had never seen her hit anyone, even when my brother was a little terror and he deserved a spanking. This was not my mother. Quakers practiced non-violence.

"Is this why you wouldn't help at women's meeting when Elizabeth Drinker asked you?" she demanded. "You've been running around behind my back making plans?"

I blinked, swallowing.

I was still backed up against the chamber door. In all my wildest imaginings, I had never thought she would react like this, not after Mary and the other three. Why was my leaving for marriage outside of the faith any worse than my sisters? I was suddenly afraid she would try to lock me in the house. It seemed ridiculous, but then I'd never imagined she could throw anything at me either. Ever. My mother was a patient and loving woman. I had broken her.

My mother took a step toward me as if she might throttle me. I whirled toward the door, grabbed at the handle, blinded by tears, and ran out of the room.

"We'll talk another time, Mama," I called over my shoulder. "When you've adjusted to the news." In my mangled delivery, I didn't even think I'd told her that it was tonight I was eloping. A mist of pain engulfed me.

I only stopped to shove my feet in my boots. I didn't stop for my cloak or to retrieve the small bag I had packed and hidden beneath my bed. I had planned on telling Rebecca and Hannah and Rachel in person. Even George. I thought I'd have time to go down to the cellar and get some dried lavender stalks to lace through my hair. I wasn't even wearing my beautiful brown gown. What a mess I'd made of it.

I didn't bother to close the front door behind me. I lurched out to the street, my chest heaving with sobs, then ran down Mulberry toward Second Street. Darkness had fallen. Tears ran down my face unchecked.

I was getting married tonight, one way or the other. *Please, John, be there waiting for me,* I prayed. Then I realized I was an hour too early. He wouldn't be outside the tavern, he would still be at our workshop. Why had we arranged to meet there when I knew I was going home first? I hadn't been thinking.

You are the one we trusted not to do anything stupid echoed in my mind like a bell. Above me, an owl hooted into the darkness.

I turned down Second Street and raced across to Chestnut Street.

Chapter 11

John took me in his arms immediately when I showed up in his —our—upholstery shop in a state.

"She was livid," I hiccupped into his shoulder, still breathless from running. I told him what had happened in a rush of words. "I thought after everything our family has been through that she would understand."

"Shh." He stroked my hair. "It was a shock, that's all. She will come 'round. You know she will."

I stepped back and wiped my nose with the back of my hand. I was gasping, the blubbering of a child. The shop was warm, and John had lit lamps when the sun went down. He'd been working on a bed hanging. He was alone, the men he'd hired to help him gone for the day.

"I want to go now," I said firmly. "Right away. Can we?"

"Take a minute, Betsy. Quiet yourself. We could find you a gown somehow, take some time."

"I want to go."

John nodded. "Me too. You can wear my cloak. My poor love."

"I didn't even get the chance to tell her tonight is the night." I sobbed anew. "I thought—how foolish of me—I even thought they may want to accompany us. I hoped they'd be there, even though I know it isn't possible."

John held me, his arms strong and secure.

"We'll delay no longer," I said, pulling back. "Let's go to the ferry. I'd rather be there than here, even if we must wait at Hugg's Tavern."

I was afraid my mother, in her unsettled state, would send my father to find us. And do what, I did not know, but she wasn't in her right mind. I did not want to chance it in case they tried to stop us. Once we were married, I was no longer beholden to my parents.

"Sit." John pushed me into a Windsor chair that was there for customers. "I'll get you some hot coffee."

I tried to compose myself but couldn't stop crying.

He returned and pushed our marriage license into my hands before he put the kettle on the hearth.

My eyes tried to read through my tears. "By His Excellency, William Franklin, Esq., Captain-General and Governor in Chief in and over His Majesty's Province of New Jersey and Territories, thereon depending in America," the license began. I wiped my eyes and took a breath and kept reading. "To any Protestant Minister or Justice of the Peace. Whereas there is a mutual purpose of marriage between John Ross of the City of Philadelphia of the one party and Elizabeth Griscom of the same place of the other party, of which they have desired by license, and have given bond, upon condition that neither of them have any lawful let or impediment, pre-contract, affinity, or consanguinity to hinder their being joined in the holy bands of matrimony. These are therefore to authorize and empower you to join the said John Ross and Elizabeth Griscom in the holy bands of matrimony and then to pronounce them man and wife."

Man and wife. Through my tears, I smiled.

My eyes fell to the bottom of the page. "Given at Burlington, the fourth day of November in the fourteenth year of the reign of our Sovereign Lord George the Third, by the grace of God, of Great Britain, France, and Ireland, King, Defender of the Faith, Annoque Domini, 1773."

John had got this today.

"We'll need money to pay the justice of the peace," John said. "I just remembered."

"I did not bring my pocket. I left in such a rush."

"No, I have it. Just don't let me forget."

"And the two pence for the ferry," I added.

A short time later John and I left his—our—workshop and walked down to the ferry.

It was almost six by the time we set out. We passed a group of young men coming up from the docks, heading home from unloading ships. One of them was covered in white, and his friends were ribbing him about it.

"What happened, mate? Did you roll in the flour?"

"Next time make it wine," one of his mates guffawed.

I loved to see the ships come up to the wharves, bringing in goods from all over the world, but tonight my mind wasn't on sloops, packets, or brigantines.

"Last chance to turn back," John teased me as we saw the ferry, trying to make me laugh and stop crying. We walked closer toward the river to the ferry dock. "What have you for a dowry, miss?"

I rolled my eyes. "My beauty? My admirable skill with a needle? Not, sadly, immense wealth or any notable family connections."

"I'll take it," he said, putting an arm around my shoulders. "Let's hope our children look just like you. God help them if they look like me."

"Oh, your nose is not so bad. I've gotten used to it."

"Huh? I did not mean—" When he saw me trying to contain a smile, he swatted my arm. "Troublemaker."

"Your nose is actually very regal. No, Roman."

"I am paying you no mind. Now you're just having a go at me."

We were boarding the ferry on foot, but I could see that a rig and two horses were already loaded onto the ferry. A man and two women were standing to the side of their rig, watching the men organize the ferry for the crossing. It was a flat craft with a protruding piece of wood at each end, making it look like a flattened rolling pin. The back end featured the rudder, where the steersman sat and directed our course. The front of the ferry held the oarsmen, who would stand and row us across. I had taken ferries across the river many times—I was a transplanted New Jersey girl after all—but this was my first time crossing with John.

One of the oarsmen reached out a hand to help me step into the ferry as John handed over our coin.

"Lovely night," one of the women said to us.

I nodded back. "Lovely," I echoed.

I must have looked ridiculous with my small form being enveloped by John's voluminous cloak, the ends almost trailing on the ground. My heart clenched when I thought of my wedding outfit hanging inside the wardrobe and the dried flowers in the cellar. Still, I was here. I was grateful for the cover of the darkness as we inched out over the black water, and the bulk of the rig and horses, which kept a distance between us and the other passengers. Every now and then geese squawked above as they slide southbound over our heads.

It wasn't until the ferry nudged onto land again that I stopped holding my breath. Had I been really expecting my father to sneak up on us in the dark with another boat? I couldn't imagine him leaping aboard like a pirate, lunging for John. My imagination was getting the better of me. I couldn't help but fear we would be detained or delayed. I needed to take my marriage vows tonight. After that, the world could erupt at our feet or not. It would not matter.

The ferry came ashore in Gloucester Town, a short way from Hugg's. I huddled in John's cloak until he reached for my hand, and we headed for the tavern, the glow of the lamps in the windows beckoning to us through the dark. At the sign of the ship swaying from the tavern's front, John pulled open the door for us.

After the quiet of the ferry ride across the river, the tavern was crowded and noisy. Several people sat at tables eating their meals and conversing, while another group stood around the bar drinking and talking loudly. Of course it was perfectly normal to see a lot of people at a tavern on a November evening, warming up, filling their bellies, and keeping the night at bay, but I felt like I was undertaking a dangerous operation and didn't welcome the press of strangers. I didn't know why, but I had thought we would slide into the tavern as its only occupants, whispering our vows to the justice of the peace in a quiet room. This felt like arriving fashionably late at a country dance in full swing.

"Help you?" a barmaid said, appearing at my elbow. She had wiry blond hair that was escaping its topknot. "Table for ye?"

"Is Hugg around? I'm John Ross. He's expecting us."

"Aye. Come with me."

She walked us through the tavern to a room at the back. Through the gloom, from the light of the dining room behind us, I could see a candelabra, unlit, on a rectangular table that was covered in small plates of food. A smaller table to the right had been set for eight with cloths and glassware. The barmaid leaned in to light the eight candles of the candelabra, then went to the wall to light both wall sconces.

"There he is!" William Hugg walked in and slapped John hard on the back. John greeted him in kind.

"Martha, luv, get Jim, will you?" William said.

Martha went out, the door closing behind her. The raucous sounds from the main room lowered to a background din.

"Betsy, dear." William Hugg leaned over my hand. "Congratulations to you both. It is indeed a pleasure." I had not met him before, but John had told me all about their friendship over the years.

"We could not have done this without you, old friend," John said. "You have our sincere thanks."

"Pah." William shrugged off the attention. He grinned at me. "Old enough at last, eh, lass? You've kept him waiting."

"I am indeed," I said. "At last."

He winked at me. "You've no idea how much I've heard about you over the years. John's always on about Betsy this and Betsy that. Thank God you're finally here. We're all getting sick of hearing him whinge about waiting until you're twenty-one, needing more Spanish eight to start up his shop, and on and on. It was becoming damned near unbearable to hear him keen like a hound."

John mock swung at him, and William jokingly balled a fist in return.

I looked around me. "Is this for us?" I asked.

"The missus prepared a wee meal," William said. "We couldn't let you two get hitched without a fuss. We'll get you some cider too. Rum in it, if you please."

"That is too kind," I said, feeling a rush of emotion. My mother would have done this for me if I had gotten married in the meetinghouse.

"When Jim gets here, we'll call everyone in and get started," our host said. I had visions of the boisterous people in the tavern tumbling in to witness our vows in liquor-infused gaiety, but William meant his wife and sons.

"Jim is here," announced a man walking in wearing a wig that was slightly askew. He had a florid face and round cheeks. "Good evening to you. I am James Bowman, justice of the peace, at your service. Hello to the happy couple. Shall we begin?"

"Let's not rush, man," William said. "Let the bride take off her cloak and get situated while I call in my family. They've only just come off the ferry."

My cheeks felt warm and flushed, my temperature rising in the warm tavern. I gratefully relinquished John's cloak to the back of a chair and watched as he shrugged off his long coat. Martha put glasses of cider in our hands. I took a sip and then another, savoring the liquid against my dry throat after all my crying. What an emotional afternoon. The ferry crossing had seemed long while I held my breath waiting to arrive at the other side of the Delaware, looking over my shoulder for imaginary pursuers. I felt as dry and crumbly as old scones. I longed for some lotion for my hands and a chance to see myself in a looking glass. Ah, well. What did it matter if I appeared disheveled? John had seen me in many states at work at Webster's over the years, and besides, we still had to take the ferry back home tonight, where the water and wind would just tug at me all over again.

When Mrs. Hugg came back, she was holding a simple wreath made from late fall vines laced with marigolds, a few berries, and leaves that looked like holly.

"For the bride." She held it out to me to see before placing it on my head. I resisted the urge to cry again. This was so much lovelier than dried lavender. I felt like a woodland fairy from an ancient forest.

"I'm Constance," she said. She eyed me closely, hands on hips, and apparently found me lacking.

"Give us a minute," she told her husband. "Betsy, come. Let's go upstairs for a moment. We won't be long, gentlemen. I know you won't mind having a drink or two while you wait. Betsy, let's make you into a bride, shall we? And let's get you a hot drink."

"Just no fecking tea," William Hugg bellowed after his wife. "A toddy I think we can all agree on."

Constance led me up a back staircase. Upstairs in a bedchamber, Constance pointed me toward a porcelain basin filled with warm water and the faint smell of frankincense. "Hands. Face too," she ordered.

After I had dried myself on a towel, she sat me down on a chair and deftly took my hair down, brushed it through, and then twisted it up again and fastened it with a hair comb.

"Do you want to wear one of my wigs?"

"No." I liked my dark hair. "Thank you," I added, feeling overwhelmed by her kindness. That, and my imminent marriage vows. "I like the wreath, thank you. It's . . . very beautiful."

She nodded and put it back on my head, carefully arranging my hair around it.

"You've been crying."

"Perhaps a little."

"Happy tears," she said. "I remember my own day." I did not correct her.

Although I was happy at that moment. I found myself depleted, cried out, and content to let Constance buzz around me while I sat considering myself in the looking glass in the flicker of candlelight. I did not want to talk about the scene with my mother—ever. I was still in disbelief. Would she ever speak to me again? And what would my father say when he found out? I pushed the thoughts away, feeling grief clutch at me. I missed my sister Rachel already. And Hannah, if I was honest. I even missed wily George.

Constance took each of my hands in turn, my fingers rough from working fabric and thread, and rubbed oil into each finger and then onto the palms and tops of my hands. I smelled something musky and rich.

"Now. Rose or orange blossom?" she asked, going to her dressing table. "A little perfume. From Paris."

"Rose."

She dotted my neck with the perfume and smoothed my dress, which unfortunately was my gray work gown.

"For your décolleté," she said, handing me the vial. I obeyed, tucking my fingers behind the fabric at my chest, feeling very suddenly womanly, a rare feeling for me in my mundane life. When I was done, I put the vial back on the dressing table and ran my hands lightly over my cheeks. I had gone from windblown to elegant in a flutter of Constance's capable hands. I was embarrassed by my dress, but that couldn't be helped. Somehow, my wreath transformed me into a goddess of the forest, and the dress faded into a simple piece of fabric that was ethereal in the candlelight.

"There." She laid her hands on my shoulders, standing behind me and watching my reflection in the glass. "Better?"

"Better." I was truly feeling pleased, but I felt like I couldn't speak, dazzled by the shadows and the flickering light and my reflection.

She hesitated, then met my eyes in the looking glass. "One more thing, if I may. Have you thought about timing? Do you wish to have a poultice?"

Puzzled, my brows knitted.

She smiled. "Not all young brides wish to be in the family way so soon. Especially in cases of marrying for love."

Ah. A poultice to prevent a pregnancy. Goodness, she was bold. I admired her. I shook my head. "No, thank you, Constance. John and I have been talking of this day for a long time." I wanted to conceive a child as soon as we could. *Please,* I prayed, *give us a little one right away.*

"There. You look like a woman ready to marry her love."

"You've been very kind," I whispered, my voice a silver thread in the shadows. I jumped when something brushed up against my ankle.

Constance laughed. "Don't mind Tansey."

A cat.

Tansey was black as ink, a smudge of shadow. She jumped up onto the vanity and sat observing us.

"She's a good luck charm for you," Constance said. "Black cats are, you know. Let's go down, hmm? Don't want the boys to get too deep in their cups. Let's get you that toddy."

I rose, lifting the skirts of my coarse gray petticoat like a queen wearing a gown of gold, and floated across the bedchamber and down to where John and our justice of the peace waited. I was filled with tenderness for my husband-to-be and a sudden feeling of profound peace.

Chapter 12

At last, a married woman. Working alongside John in our upholstery felt no different than the years at Webster's, although it was certainly better income. We worked long hours, six days a week, often late into the evening. When a boy stuck his head into our upholstery one day asking for work, we were only too pleased to oblige. We hired Oliver to help both at the shop and at home, with small tasks that needed extra hands and for deliveries and pickups. Ten years old, he was funny and smart, street savvy, and seemed older than his years. His mother appreciated the extra money, and we treated him well.

It was a relief to have Oliver at home with me in the hours when John was still at work. After a lifetime of always being around a crowd of people, both siblings and house help, it was an oddity for me to find myself alone in my little kitchen during those first weeks as Mrs. Ross. I was glad to have the boy's company.

Oliver did a little bit of everything. Soon we fell into a rhythm that worked: I would go home first with Oliver, leaving John to finish up or work late, and Oliver would help build the fires in our small rooms while I set our supper to cook. Sometimes I'd feed the boy before he headed off home.

I took pride in the first home of my own I'd ever had. In the evening, sitting around the hearth, I stitched pillow cases and curtains from fabric that had enough imperfections that prevented the cloth from being transformed into items sold to customers. In the coming weeks, I planned to make thick bed hangings to keep the drafts out and quilt cheerful wall hangings that would add some color and depth to our rough white walls. I added our entwined initials to handkerchiefs and samplers, cleaned the windows and floors, and gathered elephant grass from the meadow to arrange in glass milk bottles for the tables. I added any spare pennies we had to a bowl on my bedside table so we had enough money to get a cradle when the time came. I cherished keeping house for our family of two. Or three, if you counted young Oliver who came and went.

John and I knew each other so well that we were spared the awkwardness that the early days of marriage can bring. Our lives entwined effortlessly. We moved easily from home to work and back again, savoring the time alone in our little rented home, when we could find joy in focusing only on each other. I came to know his body as well as my own. We laughed a lot, and on the harder days we found a calm strength in each other. How lucky I was, to find a joyful partnership for my life, the long years ahead stretching invitingly before us.

I had been worried about leaving Webster's, but Webster was kind when I told him I was leaving. Perhaps he'd known more than he'd let on, and now that I thought about it, it was naive of me to think he wouldn't assume that I would follow John. He had, after all, watched us together for six years. The day after my wedding—I still felt a warmth flutter through me when I thought of it—I had gone to work expecting that day to be my last. Instead, I'd stayed on another two weeks to help finish a commission for the McKean family. I'd always have a fond spot for Webster; I was grateful for the extensive training I had received in his business and the ongoing goodwill he had shown me over the years. I didn't mind staying on a little longer to help him out. Even Emily hadn't been angry with me, claiming she'd known it all along. "I'm so thrilled for you, Bets!" She'd asked if she could knit us a blanket as a wedding gift.

I still, however, had to adjust to my new church.

"We sit here," John had said the first day, leading me to a pew that was halfway down the nave. I had a perfect view of the beautiful Palladian window, its tall arch reaching up to the ceiling and connecting us to the sky without. That I liked. The meetinghouse was dark and dimly lit.

I was nervous. The Friends' meeting had no minister or pastor. We sometimes sat in silence for an hour unless one of the congregation felt moved to say something. We received spiritual nourishment without the preaching of man. Alight from within. Not so here. I wasn't sure I liked being spoken to from a man in a podium intoning above me, but I kept my thoughts to myself. I would have to get used to it.

Christ Church had been founded in 1695 when Philadelphia was not more than a few rough dirt roads. The church's steeple, built in the 1750s, was the highest landmark in the Americas, John said. I thought about that for a moment. Could it be true? It was magnificent, to be sure, a white base sitting on the red brick tower below, rising up through a round section graced with arched windows to a spire that soared into the sky. I'd have to learn the name of the round bit that looked like a balcony. At the top of the spire, a golden weather vane reached toward the heavens.

I'd asked to go early to the service; I didn't want to arrive late and have eyes on us. I'd still wondered if I would be accepted, although John had assured me the congregation would welcome me. We sat in our pew and I tried to feel peaceful. I tried not to compare this place of worship with my Quaker meetinghouse, but how could I not?

My meetinghouse had an earthy feel, somber, the walls painted cream, the pews a warm oak brown. The seats were arranged like the sides of a box, with the pews facing inward so we could all worship together and offer God our silent contemplation. Children under twelve sat in the balcony, girls divided from boys. Quakers had no need for clergy or ostentation. Meeting was comforting and quiet, even though the Fourth Street meetinghouse was a large building with a sizable number of members. We had no steeple or stained glass, no ornamentation, nothing to distract us from our communion.

Here in Christ Church, the interior was grand. The beauty of the striking exterior was reflected within. The congregation could gaze out of beautiful large windows, and admire walls covered with shiny metal plates of memorial and commemoration. The pews were painted glossy white and intricately carved, topped with dark mahogany wood trim. The pew cushions were red velvet. The choice pews, closest to the altar, were more expensive to rent. Shouldn't church be a place for all to be equal in God? Imposing white columns marched neatly down the length of the aisle, reminiscent of the notable architecture of ancient Greece. The clergy were in robes that swept the floor. Everywhere I looked, there was striking color and metals that shone and rich fabrics that were matched by the clothing of the people that had come to worship. It was a great deal to take in.

Even the graves, inside and out, were jarring to me. Quakers were discouraged from headstones and grave markers. They were too ostentatious. Expensive. Everywhere I looked in this church there was some sort of marker or flag, and above us were beautiful ornate chandeliers of brass. The alter felt like a stage. It was just a different way to worship, but the same God, I told myself.

When the organ music began, John had reached out and covered my hand with his, giving me a reassuring squeeze. A woman walked by. I recognize the slender back and straight posture, and my eyes followed her up the aisle. Elizabeth Graeme. We made some tassels for her when I first started working at Webster's. I remembered because she was one of the first customers I helped when I started my apprenticeship there. Her winter home wasn't far from the shop, and she had come in to look at fabrics with a friend.

"Her father died last year," John said. "Dr. Graeme. He was a parishioner here for years. Always in the same pew, even when my father was assistant rector here. Sad to see her here without him."

I nodded.

He leaned closer and whispered, "You'll find that this church is a mingling of everyone who's anyone in town. There's just as many personalities as you would imagine, which makes it fun." He winked at me and I smiled. If John wasn't going to be too serious, I didn't need to be.

The seats filled up around us, and the service began. John was right—no one looked at me twice. To my surprise, I found myself comforted by the hymns and scripture and enjoyed the rhythm of the service.

Afterward, John stopped to speak with Reverend Peters, and I found myself briefly alone under a tree in the churchyard. It was a cold fall day, gray and shivering with the hint of coming rain. I surveyed the bare branches above me, the knobby texture of the naked limbs.

"Hello."

I looked up into the face of the woman who had walked past us in the nave.

"Hello. Miss Graeme, isn't it?" I said. "I used to work at John Webster's upholstery. I don't suppose you recall."

"It's Mrs. Fergusson now," she said warmly. "Actually, yes, I do. That's why I stopped to say hello. I remember you."

She remembered me? I did not recall her getting married, but then I would not have known unless she came into the shop and purchased something with a different name. I had not seen her in a while.

She took a step closer. "I heard you eloped, Mrs. Ross. Your husband is well-known here. He has been in the congregation for almost as long as I have."

Her voice was lovely, cultured, her words round and defined with a sweet lilt to all of the edges. Her sentences sounded like music, and there was a quality about her that made me want to wrap myself in the resonance of her voice. I wondered if she was going to criticize me for not marrying in Christ Church.

"I do not wish to gossip," she continued quietly. "I wanted to tell you that I, too, eloped. Only just last year. We share that, you and I. Currently, my husband is on his way back from Scotland. A family matter."

She was looking at me intently. There was an intensity about her that unnerved me, although her eyes were clear and warm.

"I eloped at another church in town in secrecy. Some people were kind but others were not. I stopped to give you my good wishes. As women, we sometimes make choices that others will not understand. Or appreciate. I wish you much happiness in your marriage, Mrs. Ross. I wanted to tell you are welcome here at Christ Church. I know it's very different from what you're used to. You may consider me a friend, should you desire one."

I smiled, relieved. "Thank you. I do. You may consider me a friend as well, Miss Graeme. Mrs. Fergusson."

"You need not be cowed by this church. We get along as well as any group does." She laughed then, a clear tinkle of mirth that felt like bubbles in soap. I felt so plain next to her, my fingers calloused with work and my pretty dress nowhere near as fine as hers. "They bicker like children at times, the men, but pay that no mind. It changes with the wind. People are people, same as everywhere and in every religious house. Where would we be without a good fight or two along the way?"

"There you are," her friend announced, appearing next to us. "Eliza Stedman," she greeted me with a broad smile.

I murmured hello.

"Just one more thing," Mrs. Fergusson told me. "Forgive my rudeness. I suspect your family may be upset with you regarding your elopement. If that is the case, permit me just this one small piece of counsel: try not to allow your family grievances to separate you, for the grave will take you from each other eventually. I only state the truth, although it sounds like a warning. I lost my father. And my mother. Resolve your differences as best you can. We have such a short time here." She smiled at me.

I nodded, feeling young and tongue-tied. She smiled again, this time with a touch more mischief, and then turned to leave with Eliza.

"Welcome again," she called over her shoulder. "Don't be shy. As I said, I've been at this church all my life."

She and Eliza went down the church path toward Second Street, their laughter floating back to where I stood by the tree.

John appeared next to me. "Making friends?" he asked cheerfully.

"Yes, actually."

I considered Mrs. Fergusson's warning. I decided I would go to my mother. I didn't think she would throw anything at me again this time. Although after last time, who knew?

*

I found my mother in Bell's bookstore a few days later. I'd stopped by the house, and Rachel had told me where she was. It was late in the afternoon, and I'd hurried to get there before she left.

The bookstore had been there, tucked away on Third Street by St. Paul's, since I was a little girl. My older sister Susannah loved books and would take me in to while away an hour holding the latest volumes from England and France. As a child I used to enjoy a good book as well, but now I seldom had time to read, and when I did, I found myself too tired and my eyes too strained from my workday. I would much rather pick up my knitting to relax in the evening, letting my fingers fly without having to pay close attention. My grandmother used to knit like that, without having to look at the line of stitches very often, and I found it curious until I grew older and was amazed when I could do it myself.

I pushed open the bookstore's worn red door and stepped inside. The inside smelled of leather and burnt candle wicks and something more unpleasant. Ah. A dog lay on the floor by the shop window on a piece of tatty bedding. He raised his head and wagged his tail when he saw me walk in, but didn't rise. I bent down to pet him behind the ears. He was definitely old and a little smelly. There were sores on his elbows and patches of dried skin on his back, but he had friendly and expressive eyes. Good old dog. I'm sure in his younger days he leapt up to greet every customer with a nudge from his wet nose and a tail wag. The owner was stacking books behind the counter.

I spotted my mother and stood behind her. I worked through what I could say.

"I am looking for a book for Rachel and George," she said, her fingers flipping through books on the shelf. "I want them to learn French. I should have done that with all of you."

"I thought we tried at one point," I answered. "And failed. Didn't I have a red reader? Verb conjugations? *Je suis, tu es,* that sort of thing?"

"Long gone. Hannah spilled wax on it, do you remember?"

I didn't. "Perhaps Mr. Bell can suggest one?"

"No need. I'm choosing between these two," she held out the books and flipped the pages, considering each. She still hadn't looked at me.

I waited, not sure whether to stay or go. Should I ask her to come outside and talk?

"You aren't surprised to see me," I said into the pause.

"I saw you come in." She glanced up at me, then back down at the books in her hands. "You look well."

"I am."

"This one, I think." With a decisive hand, she put the second book back on the shelf.

"Mama. Can we—"

"Come by the house on Sunday. We'll have a roast." She walked elegantly toward the counter to pay.

"Just me? Or John too?" I said uncertainly to her back.

"A married woman can't very well be separated from her husband during family calls, can she? Of course John as well."

I hesitated. "All right."

"Come for three. Bring turnips, if you have any. Ours are bad."

And that was that.

When we arrived on Sunday, my mother opened the door.

"You were read out of meeting," she said conversationally and took the turnips out of my hand. She held the door wide so we could enter. "Officially. Thanks for these. Ours are soft this year, a bad crop. Too wet, perhaps. Hello, John. Tell me all about your shop."

If it weren't for the dent in the back of her chamber door, it was as if the scene on my wedding day had never happened. She never apologized for throwing the candlestick and a brass dish at my head. I resolved to never again apologize for marrying John.

Chapter 13

December 1773

I knew going there was foolish, but I couldn't help myself.

"Look for the sign of the purple gargoyle," the market woman had said. "That's who you want. Her name's Clarinda."

I slipped through the streets, hurrying past shop signs for a wheelwright, a wood corder, and a whalebone cutter. I stopped to orient myself at a place that looked like it made tools, the yard littered with scrap metal. I rarely strayed to this side of town, the southern streets. Yes, this seemed right so far. I kept going. The end of the route was just as she had described: a strange sharp turn at the sign of the White Horse, past a physician advertising alexipharmic pills, imperial golden drops, and specific purging electuary, then a final turn into a little park, between two buildings. This park was meant to be a garden, it looked like, long neglected, even before winter set in.

The house with the purple gargoyle sign was supposed to be at the end of the park. I looked around, my brow furrowed. Where? I couldn't see a sign. I left the park and turned the corner, thinking perhaps it was on the other side. Just a row of small old homes and a few businesses between them. No sign, no gargoyle.

I found myself in front of a gunsmith's and stood looking around me. These streets on this side of town were rougher, less travelled, not meant for strolling. I shouldn't have come alone, but who could I ask to come with me? I peered in through the gunsmith's window, but only saw guns in wall racks and a bald man bent over his worktable.

I stepped back from the window. It was supposed to be here. Had I made a wrong turn? I would retrace my steps.

I went back to the printer's and began again, ending up in the same place at the gunsmith's. Puzzled, I turned in a slow circle, lifting my hand to shield my eyes from a sharp December sun. I stopped my slow circle with my back to the gunsmith's. Across from me, incongruously, was a wigmaker. In the front window, a large selection of wigs a little worse for wear was on display, for those with less coin. I couldn't imagine a life where I could wear a wig and have a servant do my hair, sitting each day to be dressed and powdered and primped. And idle. I wouldn't like that.

I glanced left. Then right. A wagon passed, spitting out a pebble from underneath as it went. Ah. There, at the corner. A sign so small it could be a page in a book.

When I crossed the street, I could see underneath the tiny sign was an arrow pointing to a side door. No display window, no shopkeeper's bell, just a plain brown door where the paint had cracked. I raised my hand to knock when the door swung open.

"Come in."

A woman in homespun beckoned me in. She was tall and thin, her body all angles and sticks. I had stepped into a room filled with furniture and ornaments to the point of bursting.

"What can I do for you?" she asked.

"Is this the—"

"I'm Clarinda Woodencraft, midwife and purveyor of female health. You were looking for the purple gargoyle? I had a larger sign at one point until I saw the problem. Too many men were seeking a pint, thinking this was a tavern. How do you do. I am Clarinda, and you are?"

I didn't want to give her my name. "I was at the market, and a woman there said you could help me with. . . conceiving a child."

Clarinda motioned me to an upholstered chair that was lodged between two cabinets. I sat. There was not room for another easy chair; she perched on a stool that was touching the bookshelf behind it. My knees were butting up against the low table in front of the chair. The room was filled with paraphernalia, everywhere I looked there were boxes and stacks of papers and books and china figurines.

"Well, that's a change. I'm usually asked to dispense with an unwanted pregnancy or deliver a child. The latter is much more enjoyable than the first. Although they can be slippery."

"I'm married," I said, then thought of my sister Mary and how she had had her son out of wedlock and hated the tone of my words.

"Is there a problem?" Clarinda asked.

She had wise eyes, I thought, peering out from beneath her messy gray hair, free of cap or bonnet. I judged her to be in her sixties, but perhaps she was younger.

"Not really," I said awkwardly. "I guess you could say I'm eager."

"I see. How long have you been trying?"

"It's not that," I said, feeling foolish. "Only a month or two. In truth I am seeking herbs that could encourage general health, including fertility."

I sounded ridiculous.

Clarinda laughed. "No, no, my dear, please do not be embarrassed. We must follow our heart. Why have you come if you are so newly married?"

"Well, I wasn't planning to," I said truthfully. "I was at the market at an herb stall. I thought maybe the right blend brewed up would speed things along, but the stall owner refused to sell to me. She said I must come to you."

"Katharina."

"She would not let me purchase any of her teas or tisanes. Something about the danger of getting it wrong. I was not going to come to you, I told myself I would wait a few months, yet I found myself walking through town. And here I am."

"Katharina is rather bossy," Clarinda acknowledged. "And yet not entirely misguided. Are your courses regular?"

I nodded.

"You eat eggs? The yolks must be runny."

"Yes."

"But you doubt." Clarinda surveyed me from my shoes upward with a long sweep of her gaze.

How much to reveal? Should I mention the dreams I'd been having, waking up groggy with sadness, feeling like I had fallen and was sinking beneath an earth pockmarked with shards of metal? The dreams had started the day after we returned home from Hugg's Tavern.

"Er . . ." I hesitated.

Clarinda suddenly reached behind her and took a pendulum off a shelf. A long chain, a piece of quartz. "Hold out your hand."

"I don't do that," I said defensively, folding my hands together. "No fortune telling."

She reached for my hand and turned it palm side up.

"I'm not a sorceress," she said sharply. "Women are not enchanted. A Quakeress would know that. I don't dabble in witchcraft—too dangerous. This has been in my family for generations. A gift."

Since she was so indignant, I let her have my hand. She mumbled to herself and watched the pendulum shiver over my palm. It seemed to take a long time, for after each mumbled sentence, just lower than my hearing, she waited patiently for the stone to swing and stop. The chain was dull and old, tarnished silver.

Finally, she sat back, but there was no reassurance on her narrow face.

"Elizabeth."

"I never told you my name." Or my faith. Although I was Quaker no more, I must have had mannerisms that gave me away.

"All the more reason for you not to doubt me. You need not worry, you have many healthy children coming to you. Beautiful daughters."

I brightened. "I do?"

She shook her head. "Not, however, for some time. You must be patient. Know this: You will be blessed with a large and loving family. You will see the marks of old age line your face before you leave this earth."

So nature would take its course.

"If there is nothing wrong with me," I protested, "perhaps some herbs to prepare my body? Or a tincture?"

Clarinda shook her head. Her demeanor had changed. She was less airy, more somber.

"No. There is no need. It will be several years," she declared. "It cannot be helped. It is not an issue of the womb."

I felt a crack of disappointment. I knew I should not be in a hurry, but I longed to be a mother. I had worked day in and day out for years, my fingers moving from fabric to fabric and item to item, working diligently to create items that were useful and beautiful for other people. I longed for my fingers to stroke the downy head of our newborn child. I was happy to work as an upholsterer, I had pride in my craft, but it was not meant to be my entire life. I was married now. I didn't want to have to work for years more before we were gifted with a child. I had already given years of my life making furniture and window coverings.

I tried one more time. "Is there a problem with my husband? Some disturbance with him?"

She stood up, knocking the stool, but it was wedged in so tightly there was nowhere for it to fall. "I'm sorry I could not help you more. Good day to you."

"Your payment?" I asked, struggling to stand from where I was wedged in. I reached for my pocket.

"I have done nothing to require payment. And your husband is of no consequence in this matter, I am sorry to say. Your dreams are speaking to you."

I felt a shiver run down my spine. This cheery woman had suddenly become a harbinger of bad omens to me. I wished I had not come.

"I don't understand," I pressed. "If it is not, as you say, an issue of the womb and my husband is healthy, what are you saying?"

She was thoughtful, looking spindly as a tall heron standing there, and I watched her choose her words.

"They say you have changed a great deal, from who you were, and you will change a great deal more still. Your children will have a different father, but you were fated to join with this man. You have work to do before a child comes. Take these words and go, dear girl; they are not from me. I am sorry to disappoint."

"What do you mean? Who is 'they'?"

She didn't answer. She turned and disappeared into a small hall on the right. Before the door clicked closed behind her, I glimpsed the living quarters of a house.

With effort, I dislodged myself from the chair and made my way around the furniture toward a desk. Bunches of dried plants tied with twine lay flat and crowded the surface between glass jars filled with an assortment of teas, according to their labels. Behind these was a line of bottles containing herbal tinctures. I stopped in front of one of the bookcases on my way out. *Toward a Complete New System of Midwifery, Theoretical and Practical* by John Burton. *Culpeper's Complete Herbal* by Nicholas Culpeper. There were dozens of booklets and books.

"Clarinda?" I said, but she was gone.

*

"Why would you do that?" John asked me as I scooped stew into our bowls. "She sounds barmy."

"She knew my name. It was unnerving."

"Every other woman in Philadelphia is an Elizabeth. Or a Margaret. Or a Mary. I would be more bothered if your name was Myrtle or Theodosia and she knew it."

Perhaps, but I was still rattled. "You weren't there, John. She knew things about me."

"Why did you go? Is there something you're not telling me?" There was no censure in his questions, just mild inquiry. John dug into his stew with relish.

"No, of course not," I said, cutting chunks of bread for us. I dropped one on his plate and one on mine. "It started innocently," I explained. "A whim. I was at the market for flour and fresh duck. And then the woman at the market stall was so sure I should go, all because I asked her for herbs. Before I knew it, my feet were leading me on a merry chase. My curiosity got the better of me."

John laughed. "I can't say I blame you. Bit of an adventure, that was."

"You're not bothered?"

"That a strange woman tried to unsettle you with strange sayings? And then you found it *strange*? What is *strange* about that?"

"Well, when you put it like that . . ." I buttered my bread. "It's not strange!"

We both laughed.

"I will keep telling you as long as you need to hear it: no other man but me is going to give you babies." He reached over and patted my thigh suggestively.

"Easy now, husband," I protested halfheartedly. I adored this easy banter; I adored him.

"Clearly, we must remedy this situation so you don't go seeking out strangers in the disreputable part of town again," John said, his eyes glinting. He pushed his chair decisively back from the table.

"What are you doing? You haven't finished."

John dislodged my chair from the table in one strong move. "It can wait."

"What on earth—"

He picked me up and strode the few steps to our bed in the room off the kitchen.

"Practicing," he answered, and when we finally went back to the table, the food was very cold.

*

Outrage over the Tea Act continued to sweep through Philadelphia like a swarm of locusts.

I had been a girl of thirteen when the Stamp Act was passed, but I still remembered how the news had made Philadelphia howl like a dog with a paw caught in a trap. The streets had come to life that year, people flaring with rage over the injustice of it, and our town only slid back into normalcy when the act was repealed a year later. Then the Townshend Duties five years ago had rekindled that anger, with Pennsylvanians beginning to talk about the burden of imperial policy. We had to shake off the chains, people said. Free ourselves from the shackles of tyranny. Britain had no right to put such duties and taxes upon us.

I hadn't paid attention; I was busy growing up and falling in love. Now here we were, three years later, and the men in parliament across the Atlantic had passed yet another act that was as inflammatory as all the others. Would they never learn?

I didn't want to hear about it. I tried to ignore it, caught up in my delight with being newly married and the excitement of having my own home and learning how to have our own business. I turned the other way when I saw sour faces or heard raised voices about town. I especially didn't want to see any more British agents being beaten in the streets. I had waited a long time for this new life of mine. I wanted to protect it and our happiness.

It was really only at church that I came to understand that the matter of the tea was not going to go away. After that public meeting in October, attended by hundreds, the congregation at Christ Church grew increasingly divided and tetchy about taking sides over the tea throughout November. By December, the tension was palpable, and some men were downright belligerent. All of Philadelphia knew a ship filled with the hated East India tea was headed our way, and it was only a matter of days or weeks until it arrived at our docks.

Some folks had no problem with the tea, glad for the low price, while others thundered that if it landed here, there would be no protecting our rights after that. England would push us around forever. Recommendations for how to deal with the insulting tea veered all over the place. What was clear was how great the divide was becoming between those who approved of Britain's actions as simply giving us a set price on tea, and those who thought it was utterly wicked. Some of the men at church said they didn't like that the East India Company stronghold meant that all other sources and suppliers of tea were no longer permitted. An ever tightening leash.

John and I sat in our pew every week and tried to ignore the waves of irritation around us. John wanted to be discreet. He didn't want everyone knowing how deeply vexed he was by British policy, especially as a man who had a new business in town that depended on people liking him, and on imports and exports continuing without interruption. He also had a new wife to feed and keep. I kept to myself because I didn't want to be involved. I disliked conflict intensely. I wanted everyone to get along and for life to be as it had been while I was growing up, when we'd enjoyed peace and prosperity. Instead, we watched as Philadelphia shifted and groaned around us like a frozen lake breaking its ice. The church leaders walked a delicate line, eventually saying they would support opposition to the Tea Act only because they believed in the genuine goodwill and good intentions of England. The commotion was a misunderstanding, that was all. Britain hadn't understood how poorly America would react! It was simply a trade decision that had been badly received.

"Britain does not mean to oppress us," said Reverend Peters confidently, and therefore he could offer his support for resistance measures in rejecting the tea. Many people in the church disagreed with him, including men that wanted to refuse British goods all over again in retaliation, just as we had after the Townshend Acts. John Cadwalader was one of those men. He had been a leader in resisting the Townshend

Acts five years ago. I heard women say that Cadwalader had actively worked to boycott British goods at the very same time that other men in the church were working just as hard to have the boycotts come to an end. The church was divided.

I knew Mr. Cadwalader. He and his wife, Elizabeth, had purchase a fine townhouse on Second Street near Union Street a few years ago. Just last year they had ordered curtains and upholstery for twenty chairs and two sofas from John Webster that I helped make. Webster had been triumphant about this because a few years prior the Cadwaladers had ordered a bed and elaborate coverings for it from the esteemed Mr. Plunket Fleeson himself. Mr. Webster had been humming for days after the Cadwaladers placed their order with him. We'd made the coverings and curtains in beautiful fabrics of blue and yellow damask to match the walls and carpets in their home. The fabrics had been luxurious, particularly the Saxon blue that caught the light with a shimmer.

Mr. Cadwalader did not agree with the church leaders; his face got tight and incredulous every time Reverend Peters said England had no ill intentions toward the colonies. I learned from John that Cadwalader was one of the leaders of a group of men that were going to make sure the tea shipment from the East India Company never made landfall. It was all anyone could talk about: when the tea was going to arrive. All the river pilots were put on high alert. They must have their eyes peeled at all times.

The day the news finally came about the tea ship was a particularly cold day, and the church windows were letting in icy drafts. They were almost fifty years old by then, and the church was trying to raise money to repair the old panes. The members who sat closest to them threatened they would stop coming to church if something wasn't done about the state of the windows. John said we'd need to pay more for our pew next year because the church vestry had decided to increase the pew rental prices in an attempt to get enough money to repair the windows, if they weren't already past the point of repair. John's family had been in pew twelve for a while, and John liked it there. He didn't want to move to a cheaper option. We kept our gloves on and sat closely together to stay warm. Some people brought in coal heaters to warm their pews, but John and I made do.

"Word has it that a shipment of tea will reach Philadelphia soon," I heard a man say in a low voice as I was leaving our pew. He was with three other men who were standing behind one of the columns toward the back of the church. There were only a few people left inside at the front of the church. John had gone up to Reverend Peters to ask about giving a donation to the almshouse.

I listened closely.

The man's companion cocked an eyebrow. "How soon?"

"Month's end. Not longer." They exchanged a knowing look.

I looked around. No one else was close by. I fiddled with the top button on my cloak, then bent to tie my boot. I wanted to hear.

"We need to sound the alarm," the first man said fiercely.

"We must reach the captain early. Bring him down the Delaware alone. We'll force him ashore to hear us out, tell him we're not going to let him land the tea. We can separate him from his ship outside the city."

"I'll spread the word."

"Tell Cadwalader. Tell Thomson. Tell everyone. Let it be known. He won't be able to get close to Philadelphia without a river guide, and no pilot would risk his own neck to bring him in."

They knew I was there but paid me no mind. To them, I was just the quiet Quaker woman who had married John. I had started to call them the Rebel Men in my mind, all of these men who huddled in corners and spoke in heated whispers. Ironically, I was married to one of them whether I liked it or not.

I nodded to the men, but they had already turned away. I was of no interest. I needed to tell John what I heard.

It was only a few hours later that John and I were dining at the Swan, finishing a rare meal out, when a man burst in, red-faced and perspiring, even though snow dusted the paving bricks and the wind hadn't relented.

"Hear ye! Hear ye! Let it be known," he yelled, capturing the attention of the restaurant. "I bring news! The tea has been dumped in Boston. All of it. The whole East India Company shipment. Hundreds of crates to the bottom of the harbor."

A roar went up.

"Who brought this news?" a man yelled back.

"Paul Revere, not an hour ago. Be on your guard!"

The man rushed out again, intent on going door-to-door to break the news.

John and I looked at each other. "The Sons of Liberty," he said with meaning.

A shudder went through me. If it was true, and tea had been dumped, what would the king do? It didn't bode well. All eyes would be on Philadelphia and New York next. And Charlestown.

"They should have let it go back," John said. The papers reported that the three tea ships had sat in Boston for weeks while they fought over what to do with it.

He pushed his chair back. "Let's go to the town square. Maybe Revere is there."

Chapter 14

December 1773

Everyone was abuzz with the shocking news from Boston.

"Revere must have set out right after it happened to get here this fast," John mused. "He rode like the wind if he stopped in New York first like they say he did."

Revere had been sent by Boston's Committee of Correspondence to get support from New York and Philadelphia for what they'd done with the tea.

John and I watched the men leading the tea protest assemble around Revere on the green: Charles Thomson, Thomas Mifflin, John Dickinson, Ben Rush, the doctor, and dozens more.

"Is it true they disguised themselves as Mohawks?" someone shouted. "Or were real Indians involved?"

"Quiet!" another person shouted. "Let him speak!"

"No damage was done to the ships," Revere explained over the din. "Or any private property. The hundred men who boarded the ships destroyed only the tea—nothing else."

They had planned it all, at great length. Revere explained that there had been a fourth ship that ran aground in a storm, near Cape Cod, the week before.

"When the king finds out, they'll hang," a woman shouted. "All of them. Who did this crime?"

"The identity of the men is unknown," Revere said.

"It was the Sons of Liberty!" a man with a deep voice yelled. "I'd stake my life on it. Not the fecking Indians! Were you in on it, Revere? You've got a nose for trouble."

"They must pay for the tea!" a man cried. "We must not condone such lawlessness! There are other ways!"

The crowd booed.

"Boston must have Philadelphia's support," Revere shouted. "We must rise together against tyranny! All of the colonies together!"

The crowd erupted in cheers, and fists pumped the air. A little boy of around six fired an imaginary gun into the air then jumped with excitement.

I looked at John and saw his eyes glimmering with purpose.

"Philadelphia will hold a meeting," Charles Thomson announced. "To draft a letter back to the people of Boston."

"Where's John Penn? Where's our governor? Have Penn call a meeting of the assembly on this matter," my husband shouted. "He can be silent no longer." John's voice was lost in the roar of the people.

I stood, content to be invisible, and watched the crowd yell and cheer, a wave of sound across the dead lawn in the cold December air. It was late in the afternoon, and the sky was fading to a murky charcoal gray. I shifted from one cold foot to the other, looking around me. Would the tea bound for Philadelphia meet the same fate? I had stopped serving tea at home at John's request, but many friends and family were divided about whether such action was necessary. I still felt a bit torn, knowing my Uncle Abel was one of the chosen tea distributors. I had a feeling that would change now. How could he continue to sell the hated tea and act impervious to the roars of injustice rising around us? Suddenly, tea had come to be as inflammatory as spilled oil by a flame.

Eventually, Paul Revere walked away with some of the Rebel Men, deep in conversation, and the crowd slowly dissolved like smoke trailing from a dying bonfire, people drifting away in groups of three or four.

John reached for my hand, and we too turned and walked toward home long after darkness had set.

"That's it, Betsy," he said. "Boston has lit the fuse. They've forced the king's hand. A act like this cannot be ignored."

"Do you really think they have no idea who dumped the tea?" I asked. "He said a hundred men took part. It's hard to believe *someone* wouldn't talk. Most of them would have families or neighbors who must have seen or been suspicious. Especially if they came home painted like Indians."

"Oh they know," John said knowingly. "Trust me, they know. This was pre-planned down to the tools the men carried when they boarded, calculated down to the last crate. This was no last-minute spree. I'm sure Samuel Adams and the Sons were behind it. And think about it, the men who participated are all part of churches and trades and associations in Boston. They'd have to be if they really numbered a hundred able-bodied men. If no one is talking, no one ever will. It means they're being protected."

They were going to get away with it.

"Remember when the mob destroyed the governor's house in Boston over the Stamp Act?" I said. "Didn't they steal and destroy everything until only the bare walls were left? They even ripped out his garden. The Stamp Act didn't last a year. Maybe the dumping of the tea will achieve the same effect without all the violence."

John considered this. "Perhaps. But I doubt it. This is different. They dumped a lot of money into that harbor."

We walked in silence.

"We must order as much fabric as we can afford," John said after a time, his brows furrowed with thought. He was always thinking ahead. "From London. We must save as much money as we can, Betsy. Let's hold off on any new furnishings or extras for the house. We must use the bare minimum of supplies. Just in case."

"Yes of course." I agreed with him, but my mind turned once again to thoughts of a child. A baby would require extra cloths and garments, a cradle, and coin for the midwife or doctor. But a healthy baby was tiny and easily accommodated. Surely we could create room in our lives for a son or daughter, tea crisis or no tea crisis. I knew now wasn't the time to raise the subject again, but I tucked it away for a time when John could consider it.

*

Later that week John and I were headed to the laundress, our sack of laundry over John's shoulder, when a posted sign caught our attention.

"Look at this." John ripped the broadside off the fence and held it up to read.

"What does it say?" I asked.

"It's a warning for the river pilots," John said, his eyes scanning the broadsheet. "A rather grave one."

"Read it aloud."

"To the Delaware pilots. We took the pleasure, some days since, of kindly admonishing you to do your duty; if perchance you should meet with the tea ship Polly, Captain Ayres, a three-decker which is hourly expected . . ." His voice trailed off as he skipped over some of the text. "Much is expected from those lads who meet with the tea ship—there is some talk of a handsome reward for the pilot who gives the first good account of her—"

"What are they planning?" I interrupted. "To just stop the ship from unloading? Or to destroy the tea? Surely they won't vandalize the ship?"

I wondered if Captain Ayres, whoever he was, had any idea what was happening in the colonies while he and the tea sailed unknowingly westward for weeks and weeks. What a thought. To come all the way from London, only to be plucked out of the river heading into Philadelphia.

John continued reading, "All agree that tar and feathers will be his portion, who pilots her into this harbor."

I gasped. "Tar and feather!"

John continued, "And we will answer for ourselves, as an offender against the rights of America, will experience the utmost exertion of our abilities . . ."

Violence. Boiling tar, burned skin. The agony of removing feathers from the melted skin. My father said it was a fifty-fifty chance for survival. If they were threatening to tar and feather the man, the river pilot, who let the *Polly* slip past the watch and dock with its tea cargo in Philadelphia, what else would they do? The reward was a nice touch. Better to be bribed with a payoff than be tortured for letting the *Polly* anchor.

"We can only hope they succeed," John said. "If one of the pilots on the Delaware can reach the ship and stop it while it's still coming up the river, the tea will never reach us. We'll avoid Boston's standoff."

The Delaware was a long river that snaked from the Catskill mountains in New York down through Philadelphia and out to the Atlantic Ocean. Sailing vessels coming up the river to Philadelphia were met by experienced river pilots who guided them into port. Before that, however, there was a hundred miles of river between the ocean and here where boats could be repelled.

"There's a letter too," John said. "Meant for the *Polly's* captain. So that whoever reaches him first can give him this letter. There's no way he can be under any illusions about the impact of his arrival if this letter reaches him."

"Can I see it?" I took the notice and scanned it. "We are informed that you have, imprudently, taken charge of a quantity of tea, which has been sent out by the India Company, under the auspices of the Ministry, as a trial of American virtue and resolution. Now, as your cargo, on your arrival here, will most assuredly bring you into hot water; and as you are perhaps a stranger to these parts, we have concluded to advise you that of the present situation of affairs in Philadelphia . . ."

I stared at John. "This is no joke. They're threatening that they'll set his ship on fire and tar and feather him."

"Keep reading," John said. "It gets worse."

"I'm not sure I want to."

He took the notice back. "Pennsylvanians are passionately fond of freedom, the birthright of Americans. . ."

I read over his shoulder, jumping ahead: "Good grief. . . They sincerely believe no power on the face of the earth has a right to tax them without their consent. The tea in your custody is designed by the Ministry to enforce such a tax, which they will undoubtedly oppose; and in so doing give you every possible obstruction."

What sort of vengeful makeshift justice was this?

John finished: "To our care are committed all offenders against the rights of America, and hapless is he whose evil destiny has doomed him to *suffer at our hands*."

"Wait, there's more," I said.

"All part of the same threat," John said. "For Captain Ayres, his tea cargo equals the destruction of the *Polly* and his own personal suffering. Or death."

This was no different than the beating of the ginger-haired tax officer four years ago, I realized. The men making these threats to Ayres and the *Polly* had no authority from the government or courts. They had no more clout than street urchins. And yet they wouldn't hesitate to carry out the punishments, consequences be damned.

"Is there a chance they won't get to him?" I asked, already worrying about the captain who had spent an untold number of weeks crossing the ocean just to run into an unruly mob.

"Oh, they'll find him," John said grimly. "He's a marked man. If he has sense, he'll listen and turn back. The bigger question is what happens now? It seems the Tea Act has spread a slow poison throughout the colonies."

"Who would want to sign up for the Committee for Tarring and Feathering?" I said. I shuddered. What men could take on such a role? Would do it voluntarily?

"So much has changed in the last few months," John said broodingly.

"Do you know the men who are on the committee? The tarring and feathering men?"

"I do." His eyes met mine. He wasn't going to say anything else. Little hairs rose on the back of my neck.

I thought of my Uncle Abel, one of only four agents consigned to sell the tea here. By extension, these threats were directly impacting my own family. It wasn't lost on me that we were invited to the James' for supper in a few days, to dine with the very uncle who intended to sell the tea that was supposed to be coming in on the *Polly*. If they were threatening to tar and feather Captain Ayres just for arriving with his cargo of tea, they could very well torture my uncle for selling it.

Of course John would know what was going on even if he didn't speak of it to me. In addition to my husband's involvement in the Sons, John's uncle George Ross was still leading the protests. John had mentioned two other uncles that were involved somehow, but I couldn't remember the details. I think he said his uncle Edward Biddle, married to his father's sister Elizabeth, was in politics and on the Committee of Correspondence. I think his other uncle, George Read, was a lawyer who had married another Ross sister, Gertrude. He actively protested the Stamp Act, John told me. All three uncles didn't like the heavy hand of British rule and weren't shy about pushing back.

John crumpled the paper and tossed it behind a street post. "Bradford printed these," he said. "I wonder who paid him."

We were almost at the laundress. We stopped before we crossed to let a couple of chariots pass in the street, pulled by gleaming horses. The Allen family was inside them. Webster had done some chairs for them.

John was making that expression he made when he was about to deliver undesirable news.

"Betsy, new militia companies are forming in the Philadelphia Associators. Men are volunteering by the hundreds. I'm going to sign up. It's my duty but I want to. They've been practicing on the green every day at five."

"I expected it, John. I can stay at the shop when you need to leave, if need be."

"We are fortunate it's still just us," John said. "If we had small children at home, it would be so much harder for me to do what I need to do. For both of us."

"We'd make do," I said firmly. "We would get help at the shop, and I'd be at home." I was still hoping for a child.

To think that only a year ago, we had been at Webster's, courting and making plans. And drinking tea, I thought wryly. Now my husband was going to be a volunteer militiaman drilling in the town square. So much had changed in twelve months.

*

A few days later John and I arrived at the James's residence on our social call.

My uncle greeted us warmly, his wife, Sarah, at his side.

"You scandalous girl," he teased me as he took me in an embrace. "My little niece Betsy, eloping. Upsetting us like that. Mrs. Ross!"

"Abel, stop," Sarah protested. "I'm sure poor Betsy's heard enough of that."

Uncle Abel pumped John's hand. "She seems to have done all right, I'd wager." He grinned at my husband and winked at me before drawing us toward their parlor.

Abel was by far the wealthiest of our extended family and enjoyed a large brick home in the city with no shortage of amenities. They also had a country home in Frankford, about seventeen miles outside of town. I had been there a few times, but not as many as I would have liked. Uncle Abel had always been closer to his other sister than my mother. It wasn't that there was any particular animosity there, he just seemed to have more in common with the other family. Abel had a quick mind, a sharp tongue, and my aunt Lizzie was the same. My mother was more serene, without the wit and humor that Uncle James preferred.

"I like to think I'm worthy of Betsy," John complained rather plaintively to the oil portraits on the wall as we walked down the hall.

"That's a Copley," Sarah said, noticing me admiring a painting. "John Singleton Copley."

"We'd like him to do our family portrait," Abel said. "But there's always a line in front of us."

"Let's go to the library, Abel," Sarah offered. "It's so cold. It's much cozier than the parlor. We never should have bought those new chairs. They're too hard. They hurt my back."

"We could help you there," I said. "John makes fine chair cushions. We made several for Mr. Cadwalader at Webster's, and he was quite complimentary."

"I've heard the Cadwalader furnishings are some of the finest in the city," Sarah said. "What an elegant home they have. And knowing you, Betsy, I'm sure it was your skill with the needle that played a part in the success of that."

"We all contributed," I said modestly. "Although that fringe might be the hardest I've ever done."

"I'll be sure and come by to see about redoing the seat cushions," Abel told John as we gathered in the library in front of a blazing fire. I sank into a chair that had so many feathers inside I was enveloped in a cloud.

I looked at the wall of bookcases around us, awed by the sheer number of books there. I had never had much of an appetite for the novels that so fascinated my sister Hannah. Who had the time? I would much rather read up on a solution for bug bites or a recipe for a cordial to settle the stomach.

"In all seriousness, congratulations on your marriage," Uncle Abel said to us. "We are heartened to know that our niece married a good man. Take care of her, John. We'll have a toast in a minute."

He pulled out a cigar box and offered one to John, who took it. Abel leaned forward to light it before taking another out of the case and lighting his own.

"The best I could find," he told John.

"How did your parents take your elopement?" Sarah asked.

"They are coming around," I said simply. "My mother was upset, but I can hardly blame her. I'm the fifth daughter to be disowned by the Friends."

"My sister can scarcely object," Abel countered. "Rebecca did the exact same with your father. Eloped. She was a dark horse about that back then. And Rebecca was the most obedient of us!"

"Shows you never know," Sarah murmured.

I nodded. "It was the surprise of it, I think. I wouldn't do it that way again. I should have told her how I felt about John years before we eloped."

"Well, dear, it is nice to hear that she is adjusting," Sarah said warmly. "Rebecca is a good woman. Motherhood means aching for our children, unfortunately."

"Have you been formally banished?" Abel asked over a wisp of smoke.

"Officially and completely."

"And unofficially too," John joked. "You Quakers are an unforgiving lot."

I winced. I hoped Abel and Sarah didn't think it was a jab at them.

Uncle Abel nodded without comment. As a Quaker, he took the guidelines seriously, as had I, for many years. For all of my life, until last year.

A maid came in with a tray and set it down next to Sarah. The silver tea service gleamed in the flames of the fire.

We talked amiably for a few minutes of the upholstery business, of the challenges in the import-export world, and of their children.

"Tea?" Sarah asked.

Our slight pause registered with Abel and Sarah, who exchanged a look.

"Oh dear," Sarah said. "I should have sent for coffee. Or chocolate."

"No, no, please," I answered quickly. "I'd love a cup of tea."

John paused. "I can't in good conscience—"

"This is Dutch tea that I purchased at a good price from German traders in the spring," Abel interrupted. "It's not from the East India Company."

"Take it back," Sarah told the maid decisively. "We'll have coffee, please."

The maid disappeared with the tray.

How awkward. I gazed at the greenery laid out on the mantel, boughs of evergreen decorated with pinecones and orange. Someone had crafted little bows from red fabric and fastened them to the boughs of greenery every few inches. The oranges were pierced with whole cloves, scenting the room becomingly.

"Abel, how are you faring in all this tea business?" John asked.

Abel shrugged. "The tea isn't here yet. Henry and I would love to sell it. It's just business for us."

Sarah sighed. "There's been no shortage of nasty notes coming to the house warning us though."

"It's early days," Abel said. "We only learned at the beginning of the month that the *Polly* had sailed from London in September."

My husband considered this. "Yet you were at the meeting in October when news of the Tea Act came. How have you avoided taking a stand? Philadelphia is leading the fight."

We were here on a social call. I knew John liked my uncle, but I didn't feel this was fair of him, to put Abel on the spot. We were family.

"Look," I said, pointing to the window. "It's snowing."

"It's so peaceful, isn't it?" Sarah said, turning to look. "Ah! Celeste! That was quick. Thank you."

The maid set the coffee tray down and withdrew.

I turned to Sarah. "John is too passionate sometimes," I said to her softly. "We didn't come here to peck at you."

She handed me a mug of coffee. "We know that, dear."

"I'll have whiskey," Abel said when his wife offered him coffee. He stood. "John?"

"I'd take a whiskey."

"So far," Sarah said, "for what it's worth, I haven't felt afraid for our safety, you know, on account of the tea."

"Why would you?" Abel scoffed. "I've done nothing wrong. The tea hasn't even arrived yet."

"It will," John said.

"Easy, mate," Abel said mildly, coming back with two glasses and handing one to John. He had my mother's long face, I thought, the high hairline.

"I know you are a moral man," John said to Abel. "I trust you'll make the right decision."

Abel held out his glass to clink with John's. "If only anyone knew at this point what the right decision is. Has anyone even laid eyes on the *Polly*?"

John shook his head. "The ship is days away, I heard. No shortage of pilots with their eyes peeled, hoping for the reward."

I took a sip of my coffee, savoring the strength of it. The snow was coming down harder now, taking away the view outside the window in a thick curtain of white.

Sarah clapped her hands. "Let's take a sleigh ride!"

"Oh, can we?" I asked. "That sounds wonderful!"

John and I hadn't been married long enough or built up enough funds to have a carriage or sleigh or even a simple chaise. John had a rustic wooden cart that he hooked the horse up to for deliveries from the shop. The horse was old and a bit deaf; it was all we could afford.

"Why not?" Abel said affectionately to his wife. He downed his drink. "And the creek is frozen solid. We can easily cross it to the fields beyond."

"Splendid!" Sarah said. "It's been too long."

"One more for the road, John?" Abel offered, reaching for the crystal decanter.

"I'll have a spot of that, please," I said.

"Maybe we should toast to 1774," suggested Uncle Abel. "A little early, but we may not see you again before the new year."

"I'll drink to that," John answered.

*

The *Polly* was stopped on Christmas day on the Delaware River about ten miles from the city. The papers reported that

Ayres's ship carried almost seven hundred crates of tea consigned to the Quaker firm of James and Drinker, my Uncle Abel and Henry Drinker. Captain Ayres had left his ship and crew anchored at Gloucester Point and agreed to be escorted to the city, where two days later some eight thousand Philadelphians showed up to tell him he couldn't land the tea. John and I were in the crowd. I'll never forget it—the surge of bodies crammed in everywhere we looked, all around the State House. To think I'd thought three hundred people protesting news of the Tea Act in October were a lot! We were packed in like trout in a barrel, pressed close and vibrating with the emotions of the crowd. Pennsylvania had never seen anything like it, of that I was sure.

After listening to the crisis being spelled out for him, Ayres went back to his ship, turned it around still filled with tea, and headed back to England. He only stopped to restock his supplies for the journey, the papers said. I suspect he was very relieved to be untarred, unscathed, and still in possession of his vessel.

Philadelphia was drunk with triumph over its victory.

Not everyone felt that way. My parents said it was a sin. Wasteful. My Uncle Abel, his face drawn, was entirely quiet on the matter.

Chapter 15

April 1774

That spring I found myself back at the herb stall in the market. I couldn't say why, but I was drawn to the middle-aged woman with the clear green eyes and hard voice who had steered me to Clarinda. It was April, the uncovered stalls in the middle of the road back again, flanked by lines of horses and carts and carriage traffic on each side. Thin puddles of slush dotted the road. Along the sides, the last of the winter snow clung stubbornly in little gray patches while snowdrops and buttercups pushed through the grass.

"I remember you," the woman said in her thick German accent.

Damnation. I hadn't planned on that.

I lowered my voice. "I would like to purchase herbs. Please. To, er, to encourage fertility."

"I told you to go see—"

"Yes, thank you," I interrupted her. "I did. Unfortunately, the healer would not help me. You are here selling herbs, and I would like to purchase some. I heard you are very good with botanicals. You are known around town, spoken highly of, madam."

She frowned, her dark eyebrows drawing together until they almost touched.

"Clarinda helps everyone," she said accusingly, as if I was guilty of misbehavior. Her manner was very forthright, and I wondered if she was this strict with all of her patrons. I was not used to having to beg people to take my money.

"That may be so," I acknowledged. I did not want to repeat the disturbing conversation I'd had with her in that room last fall. "She did not explain herself to me."

Hard eyes stared at me.

"I assure you I am a married woman," I added, wondering if that was her reticence. "This is only for myself."

She snorted. "Who else would it be for?" she said, as if speaking to a simpleton.

Anything I said irked her. If I waited in silence, perhaps she would relent. I could have gone to another stall; herbs were plentiful across the market, especially after a long winter to dry them. There was something about this woman that appealed to me, though, as if she had ancient knowledge at the ready. It was true that she was known for her expertise. Word on the street was that she always had a cure. That she had a gift.

Katharina Schmidt, her name was. I heard she had arrived two winters ago as a widow with her three sons, all nearly grown. Apparently, she lived on a little piece of land in Germantown, rich with trailing vines and pots of mysterious plants. Quaker women said that even though Frau Schmidt was fairly new to town, she knew as much as most of the town's physicians. People whispered that her garden had grown faster than was normal in only two years.

Frau Schmidt pursed her lips and considered me. "Perhaps you should go to an apothecary. Or see a doctor."

"I would be grateful for your recommendation. You helped my mother's friend when her pregnancy did not hold and she was slow to recover. You stopped the bleeding and restored her strength."

She sniffed. *Oh, for goodness' sake.* I didn't want to have to beg.

"Please," I added. None of my sisters had taken this long to conceive. I could not shake my fear that something was wrong. Clarinda's voice echoed: *Your children will have a different father.* Nonsense, I decided. Utterly ridiculous.

"As you wish." She nodded regally.

Finally.

Frau Schmidt turned away and bent down under the stall to rummage through some bags.

Two women approached the table, talking amongst themselves. They picked up some of the poultices on the table, rifling through them to find what they were looking for.

"Here's calendula," the young blond woman said, holding out the sachet to her companion.

"I thought perhaps holy basil or gentian," her tall friend murmured.

"Stomach pains?" Frau Schmidt demanded.

"My son has worms," the tall woman confessed in a whisper. "His stool has—"

"Myrrh," Frau Schmidt said shortly. She thrust a small bag at the embarrassed woman. "Diarrhea will be the result and the cure. Do you understand? The instructions are written inside. Take no more or no less."

A nod, and then the woman paid and left quickly with her companion.

"Where were we?" Frau Schmidt paused. "Oh yes. My impatient bride."

My patience was indeed wearing thin with this frustrating woman. Perhaps my first trip to the mysterious Clarinda had been ill-timed and presumptive, but I certainly felt no regret about asking for medicinal herbs today. I was about to give up when she handed me a brown glass bottle.

"A tincture?" I had assumed it would be dry leaves to mix in a tea.

"Red clover, wild yam, red raspberry. Angelica. Among others. Take two drops every day, three times a day."

"What are the chances I will conceive?"

"Two moons, perhaps three. Unless."

"Unless?"

"Unless it is not in the cards for you. Is that what Clarinda told you?"

"She said I would have many children, girls, and my face would line with age," I lied, a half-truth.

"Then eat prunes and eggs," Frau Schmidt said. "Not together. Avoid hot baths and horse riding. Your husband can take care of the rest."

"Thank you." I reached for my pocket to pay her.

"Katharina," she said when I turned to go. "Call me Katharina. Come back and tell me how you make out, impatient bride."

I nodded. "Thank you, Katharina. I hope to see you soon with good news."

"I don't care to be called Frau Schmidt," she said conversationally. "I don't wish to be reminded of my husband. He shouldn't have died. He was obstinate even in that regard. Is that the right word? Pig-headed."

What a coarse woman, I thought. Still, I would love to be able to come back again in a few months and let her know her remedies had worked. I thanked her again and tucked the tincture deep in my pocket. I made my way through the market, inhaling deeply and looking around me with the wonder of a child. It was so good to see all the stalls overflowing again. No longer locked by ice, the river was open to ships bringing us goods from all over the world.

The sun on my face felt glorious. I pushed my cap back so I could feel the warmth. Today the sky was a bright cerulean blue, filled with trailing wisps of white cloud, as flirty as a cotton boll, and all around was birdsong. We had spent the winter holding our breath, wondering what Britain would do about Boston and the destruction of their tea and the forced return of Philadelphia's tea, waiting for the weather to turn and the ice to melt so the mail packets could arrive. We'd been waiting a long time.

On my way out, I stopped at a butcher's stall and asked for two chops. A treat for John's birthday. I would marinate them in dill and lavender and leave them in the sun before I roasted them.

A few weeks later I was pregnant.

Chapter 16

May 1774

I couldn't wait to tell John that we were going to have a child. I decided that I would break the news that night when he got home. During the half year we'd been married, I'd kept my habit of going home before John each evening with Oliver to warm the house and make our meal. Sometimes John would arrive home an hour or two later, but just as frequently these days, he headed off to meet up with the Sons or huddle in coffeehouses and taverns about what could be done about Britain.

The men, like John, opposed the Tea Act passionately as an abuse of power. "It's taxation without representation," John complained frequently. Their frustration wasn't about the drink or the duty itself, but that Britain could grant the East India Company a monopoly on a whim, saving their own investors, and then set rules on who could sell the tea in the colonies without consulting us at all. It seemed so overbearing.

After Oliver walked me home and brought water from the well, he was anxious to leave and meet up with a friend, so I gave him bread and jam, and he vanished with his usual youthful speed. I assembled a simple supper: cold chicken and boiled potatoes. I covered it to keep the flies out and sat down to wait, but it grew dark around nine, and John still wasn't home. My eyes were heavy with fatigue. I couldn't seem to stay awake this week. I looked at the clock, debating whether to wait longer, but fatigue won and I retired to bed. I would probably miss him by minutes. Even when John went to his meetings or drilled with his company, he would usually be home by nine and join me by the fire or in bed.

I woke up a few hours later, stretching my legs and knocking the cat at the foot of the bed, who chirped with indignation and leapt off. I knew before I reached for him that John's side of the bed was empty. I sat up and looked around. John hadn't been home.

There must be a simple explanation, I reasoned. I would go back to sleep, and he could tell me about it in the morning.

But the next morning I rose in the dark, and the bed was still half-empty, his side of the sheet cold to the touch. Where was he? John did not drink to the point of being insensible. Something had happened. I thought back to the last thing he had said to me yesterday at work. What was it?

Nothing out of the ordinary. He was going to drill on the green, he'd said. After that, he was going to take a pint in the City Tavern with friends, maybe meet his Uncle George there as well. "See you at home," he'd said.

I lit a candle and reached for my clothes. The cat didn't even raise its head; she had reclaimed her spot at the bottom of the bed. I hadn't wanted a cat but John insisted it was necessary for keeping mice out of our home. "Lucky you, Cora," I said to her. "Lying abed like the queen you are. Go kill something." The cat cracked an eye at my voice and closed it again, unconcerned.

I fumbled with my stays, wincing as they touched my sore breasts. The first of many changes I would have to learn to make peace with. I added my short gown, petticoats, and skirt. Downstairs, I grabbed my shoes and an apple. I glanced out the kitchen window to see a bit of light coming from behind the trees, glowing indigo and dark sapphire out of the darkness. *Good. Daylight.*

Finally clothed, worry knotting my chest, I went out in the morning and headed toward our shop. When I got there, I stopped dead at the light shining in the window in the gloom. Had we been burgled? I drew closer, trying to see in without being seen. Just last year Richard Simms, the pewterer, had been tied up while thieves robbed him and left him there to bleed from his head wounds. He didn't die, but he was never the same after that, half-witted, and his wife had closed the shop and taken them to Canada to live with their son.

I swallowed hard and inched my face closer to the glass. It would have been easier if we had not just added fabric-covered blinds. John had said the blinds would attract customers and show our expertise. He had become skilled at making venetian blinds, and they paid us handsomely. In summer, the wood slats could block out the hot sun, and in winter they helped keep the warmth from seeping out the windows. It was a particular advantage on a hot day; the window could be opened and the blinds could be angled to still block out the sun while at the same time letting in a breeze. The most marvelous invention. I stepped forward, afraid of what I'd see.

John. At the workbench, like usual, nailing the underside of a seat cushion, as if nothing was wrong.

I banged the window, hard. I half expected him to look up with a black eye, but his handsome face looked up in surprise. He opened the door with a thump.

"What are you doing here?" I asked, infuriated. "I was worried sick!"

"Betsy. I can explain." He pulled me inside. "I thought it would frighten you more if I came home."

"Where *were you*?" I scowled, my fear of the last hour sliding into anger. "What happened?"

"My love." He held me for a moment, his arms strong around me, his cheek on the top of my head.

I pulled away to glare at him.

"I can explain," he said quickly. "News finally came from London. The dumping of the tea in Boston made the king lose his mind. Parliament has passed an act to shut down the port of Boston until they pay for the tea."

"I don't see how—"

"Wait. Let me finish. Please. After we drilled, I went to the City Tavern, like I told you I would. I met up with my uncle and my mates, and we were having a pint when the messenger arrived. They're calling it the Boston Port Act, but it's intended to punish Massachusetts until they cry mercy. The messenger had a copy of the Boston paper with him. We passed it around. After that, my uncle got the whole tavern fired up with speeches on how we can push back, and the arguing went until the wee hours of the morning, fueled by drink. I was going to come home, but it was so late I thought you'd think it was a burglary. Instead, I came here and slept. Now that it's morning, it doesn't seem like the best idea, but I'd had a few pints and it was the middle of the night. I'm sorry I frightened you."

I sighed. "Thank God you're all right." I sat in a chair at the table.

"This is staggering news, Betsy. The punishment is severe."

"I wish Hutchinson had just let the tea go back to England," I said. "All of this could have been avoided."

In the months since the dumping of the tea in Boston, we'd learned what really happened. Massachusetts's governor, Thomas Hutchinson, had ordered that the three ships carrying the tea that had arrived in Boston be unloaded and the duty paid. His sons were tea brokers and stood to profit. The Sons of Liberty, however, prevented that from happening, and the ships' captains were stuck. A stalemate. They couldn't leave Boston without signed customs permission papers, which they weren't given, and they also weren't permitted to unload the cargo. The three ships languished at the dock for weeks. A town meeting on December sixteenth attended by thousands failed to change Hutchinson's mind. That was the night the entire tea cargo was dumped in the water. Hutchinson had drawn out the crisis for weeks, and now his people were to suffer.

"That's the point, love, that's exactly the point," John agreed. "England won't bend. How is that liberty and good governing?"

"So what will happen?" I asked.

"They're closing the port of Boston on June first. That means no food going out. Or coming in. No trade. If there's no trade, there's no money coming in. No supplies. People will go hungry. And remember that the port of Boston feeds most of Massachusetts."

I shook my head. "They can't do this."

"They have. They're replacing Hutchinson with a military general. Thomas Gage. French and Indian War hero."

"Good Lord."

"Boston has sent word asking for help. Philadelphia is going to form a committee and decide on a response."

"Can't Boston just pay for the tea and be done with it?" I thought of all the women, children, and elderly people that would suffer there, the sick and infirm as well. It hardly seemed fair.

"It's tyranny. They shouldn't do that."

"Still, to avoid such a harsh punishment. . ."

"Capitulation would be wrong. Nothing will change if they're coerced."

I sighed. Tyranny, tea, punishment. It was exhausting. And what was coming next?

"You must be tired," I said. "Why don't you go home for a few hours? I can manage here. Oliver will be in soon. And the men."

John shook his head. "When the day comes full, the streets will be aflame. I have no desire to be abed when all Philadelphia hears the news."

I reached for my work apron. "Well then, I guess either way you won't get much rest. At least go home to change and eat. You'll feel better."

John refused. He was tense as a coiled spring. "I'll get a beef pie from the cart down the street." He went back to his work.

I picked up the chair cover I had been working on yesterday. My husband was stubborn once he'd set his mind. "How will they enforce it?" I mused.

"Naval blockade. Warships in the harbor."

Wouldn't they have to let some boats dock for supplies and food for the troops?

I threaded my needle. When I glanced up, John was looking at me. "I'm sorry, Betsy. Really I am. I didn't mean to frighten you. It won't happen again."

"I think I might be with child," I blurted out.

John tipped his head back and laughed, a rich, throaty sound that filled our workshop. He let out a whoop, then came to embrace me, lifting me up off my feet. He twirled us. "Why not! Why bloody not!"

"You are hysterical with lack of sleep," I laughed. "Put me down!"

My feet touched the floorboards, and John threw open the front door. "I'm to be a father!" he yelled into the early dawn. "Huzzah!"

I heard a man shout to him in return and the crow of a rooster in the distance.

"John, stop, you madman! It's too early! You'll wake everyone!" It wasn't quite true—this was a mechanics' quarter, full of workingmen who started their days before the sun. There were stirrings all along the street, doors opening and closing, barrels being rolled and hatches opening.

John slammed the front door shut and grinned at me. "I wish I had a drink here!"

"I know you said we should wait. I was a little afraid to tell you."

John did a little jig with his feet like an Irish leprechaun. "Are you certain?"

"My courses are late. We shouldn't say anything until another few weeks have passed. If you can refrain yourself from shouting in the streets from now on."

John laughed. "To the devil with that!"

What a strange day, I thought. What a motley assortment of news all within an hour, after waking to an empty side of the bed. I was glad Clarinda the strange midwife had been wrong.

It was laughable now that I had worried about that.

Chapter 17

June 1774

"Don't be a bore," Emily said, taking my scissors out of my hand. "Old married lady. Come to the fair!"

She had stopped by to visit us. Webster's clientele was almost dead, and there was little work. Emily said he talked about returning to London. I felt bad for him, but I knew Webster's demise was his own doing and had nothing to do with John and I leaving. Apparently, we'd been there for his golden time and I was grateful to him. In the meantime, Emily had time on her hands.

"Emily, I have work to do." I reached to take my scissors from her. "We just got a big order from Benjamin Chew. I can't just prance about anymore."

Emily groaned. "I know, I know, you're a responsible upholsterer," she mimicked in a high society accent, mocking me. I had often said to her that I couldn't drop everything and go out whenever she wanted. The five years between us was showing now.

"Brat," I said cheerfully.

"And just so you know, you never did prance about. That's not the way you are."

She looked over at John, who was putting together a footstool. "Just for an hour?" she pouted, looking at him with big doe eyes. "It's a Saturday. It's June. And it's beautiful out. Please."

"Benjamin Chew!" I said. "Do you understand how important that is to us?" He could have gone to anyone in town. He was rich, and he only wanted the finest. We were delighted. His order made John and I feel that we really could make this work.

"You could use a break," John agreed, winking at me. "A bit of a rest could do you good."

I knew he was referring to my pregnancy, but we were keeping it to ourselves for a while yet. I would rather go home and have a nap—that was my idea of a rest—but the thought of going out in the sunshine and seeing the June festivities appealed to me too.

"All right," I said. "Just for a little while." I shrugged off my work apron and hung it on the peg.

Emily clasped my arm and drew me out of the shop just as George Ross came in. He tipped his hat to both of us and bid us hello.

"That's John's uncle," I said as the door closed behind us.

"He's very handsome," Emily said.

I laughed. "And at least twenty years older than you are. We can find you someone much more appealing."

"And wealthy," Emily added dreamily.

"You're moving in the wrong circles for that. We're all artisans and craftsmen in this quarter."

"And I'm proud to be part of it," Emily said. "What do the rich have that we do not?"

We walked slowly, savoring the sights and smells of Philadelphia in early summer. Someone was cooking over an open fire, and the smells were delicious. The city was alive with flowering trees and green bushes and fresh grass.

"I wonder how I could shoulder my way into getting an invite to an Assembly dance," Emily mused. "That seems to be where all the young men of town are, don't you think?"

"You find a man with a membership and make friends with him. There seem to be several of them at Christ Church, from what I can see."

"That doesn't help me when I'm Presbyterian. Although I guess that's a good reason to swap churches."

"Emily, you're terrible."

"Easy for you to say, you're married."

"As will you be, one day." I stopped to admire a group of three women who were walking toward us on the other side of the street. "That's Italian fabric; I'm sure of it. I did not think we had any in the city. Those gowns look new. Did you see her stomacher? The embroidery?"

Emily shrugged. "No shop talk. We're off the clock. By the way, I don't mind being Presbyterian, even though Philadelphia thinks we're half-mad."

"We're all half-mad these days."

It was not far to the square where the fair was being held. My spirits lifted when I saw the gaiety all around and heard a fiddle playing a lively tune. People of all ages filled the green, laughing and chatting. Paper lanterns had been strung from trees, and the smell of spun sugar and roasting nuts wafted toward us. There were games set up for children, including an archery board, a dunking barrel, and a beanbag toss. Gaming stalls for adults lined the brick wall at the back of the green. On the other side of the square, stalls filled with baked goods and confectionaries beckoned.

"What fun," I said.

"I'll buy you a punch," Emily said, stopping in front of a table with drinks.

We stood under a maple tree, drinking from our cups and watching children fight over a ball being used to try and knock milk bottles off a table for a prize. The fiddle had stopped, and bagpipes sounded through the park.

"What shall we do?" Emily asked. "We could try our hand at the fishing game."

"That's for children," I laughed. "I am enjoying being here with you, listening to the music and seeing the fun. Look at that sky. We have been so lucky with the weather this month. Not a day of rain."

"Look." Emily nodded to a makeshift pen being set up. "Someone brought a litter of puppies to play with."

"To sell, I think you mean. Let's go look."

"Adorable," Emily said as we watched the owner free the tiny dogs from their cage. The puppies tumbled into the makeshift pen, sniffing at the ground and wagging their tails, their bellies almost rubbing against the grass, their legs were so short. "You should get one."

I shook my head. "John would have a fit. We have enough on our hands as it is. They are sweet, though."

We wandered over to a sweets table, and Emily chose a stick of candy to suck on. I shook my head when she offered me one—my stomach was unsettled most of the time.

"I'd like to go listen to the music," I said, motioning to the bagpiper and steering Emily in that direction.

"Not too close," Emily protested. "They're loud."

We settled under an oak tree festooned with ribbons around the trunk, watching paper flags flutter in the air as children walked by holding them on sticks, a rainbow of colors.

The bagpiper played a lively tune. A few small girls were holding hands and dancing in a circle in front of the piper, giggling and going 'round faster and faster until, dizzy, they collapsed on the ground, then jumped up to do it all over again.

"I love a June fair," Emily sighed around her candy stick. "Aren't you glad I dragged you out?"

"I'm thankful you did," I said gratefully. "This is a treat. I used to pine for these outings as a child."

"I want strawberry shortcake too," Emily said. "When strawberries are in season, like they are now, the flavor is so delicious."

"Let me buy you one," a man's voice said from close by.

Emily startled in surprise, and we looked around.

Two men were lounging under a willow tree behind us, and the low-hanging branches half concealed them from us. One of them gave us a jaunty salute when we turned, and his friend grinned. They were both young, around our age, dressed in some sort of military uniform.

"Good day, ladies," one of them said amiably.

"Hello," Emily said, perking up.

"Good day," I said in my best formal and proper voice. All of my mother's warnings about ladies and young men were clear in my mind. "Shall we go look at that fishing game?" I said to Emily.

Emily was having none of it. She turned so she faced the men. I followed suit.

"Why are you dressed like that for a fair?" she asked in her customary bold style. She clearly had not been raised as a Quaker, I thought drily. She was always so outspoken.

"Saturday drilling duty," the man answered. "We've just finished." He was lying on his side on the ground, his head propped up on his hand.

"We're part of the Philadelphia Greens," his companion added. "Pennsylvania Associators. Volunteer militia."

"Oh."

The second man was sitting cross-legged, casual and relaxed, focused on Emily.

He reached out a hand to her. "Edmund. Edmund Worthington. Very pleased to make your acquaintance, Miss. . . ?"

Emily let him kiss the air above her fingers before she withdrew her hand rather haughtily. "Miss Emily Spencer."

"Daniel Welsh," the other man offered. He turned to lie on his back and stare up into the boughs of the tree.

"What brings you to the fair?" Emily asked them. Oh no. This sounded like the start of a social interaction. I wanted to get back to John and all the work that had piled up. But I couldn't leave Emily alone here. She looked like she was enjoying herself and wasn't going to want to leave.

"Clearly, the food," Edmund answered, putting on his hat. He smiled at Emily. "I think we both have a passion for strawberry shortcake. Would you allow me to treat you, Miss Spencer? It would be an honor to get to know you better."

I groaned inside. The two of them were like magnets drawing toward each other.

"I would be very pleased to accept," Emily answered formally, accepting his outstretched hand and letting him pull her up. She smoothed her skirts and touched her hair.

The bagpipes stopped, and the sweet sounds of a simple flute sounded out into the early summer day. The high notes made a dog whine in response, which prompted a group of children to laugh and mimic the dog.

"I think I'd like some shortcake too," I said, getting up. Emily frowned, but I ignored her. "Mr. Welsh?" I asked the other man lying under the tree, to be polite. "Shortcake?"

"Not me," he answered easily. "Come back to me. I'll wait here and have a snooze."

"What do you two ladies do?" Edmund asked as we took our plate of shortcake from the baker.

"We're seamstresses," Emily answered.

"Actually, I'm an upholsterer," I said. "My husband and I recently opened our own shop." I never made garments. That wasn't where my interest lay. I had no intention of ever being a seamstress.

"And they're newly married," Emily added. "I work for an upholsterer too, right now anyway. That's where Betsy and I met. But the sewing I really like to do is when I make clothing. Father set up my apprenticeship at an upholsterer's for my training. I make dresses on the side whenever I can. My dream is to work for Mary Symonds on Chestnut Street. She makes the loveliest clothing in town."

Edmund nodded and smiled at Emily. "I'm sure you will."

"And you?" I asked him. He had a brown smudge on his neck. I thought it was dirt at first and wanted to reach out and wipe it off, but it was a birthmark, coffee colored, about the size and shape of a hazelnut.

"I'm a sailmaker," he answered. "Like my father and grandfather before me. So you and I share a certain type of craftsmanship around fabric," he said to Emily, who was looking at him all soppy and giddy. *Oh please*, I thought.

We returned our tin plates to the dirty pile in the basin on the strawberry table and wandered back to join Daniel under the willow tree, avoiding a race that was taking place between boys who had balanced eggs on spoons.

"Emily, would you walk with me back to the shop?" I asked. "I really need to get back to work."

I smacked at a mosquito that had just taken a hearty bite of the skin above my collar bone. It was a relief when the warmer weather let me wear my simple gowns again, with wider necklines and lighter fabric, but I didn't enjoy being food for the flies and their friends.

Emily frowned again and looked disappointed. "Already?"

"I said an hour, and it's been far longer. It's been wonderful; thank you for bringing me."

We arrived at the willow, and Daniel sat up. When he saw that we weren't going to sit, he stood to join us, his hands in his pockets. He'd had the pox at one time; I could see by his cheeks.

Edmund hesitated. "Perhaps we could all walk Betsy home, and then, Emily, if I may be so bold, after that Daniel and I could walk you home too?" The streets of Philadelphia were all close and walkable. We had not yet grown so much that the town had spread beyond Eighth Street to the west. It was helpful for those of us who weren't wealthy enough to own a chariot or carriage.

"That won't be necessary," I said.

"Thank you, yes," Emily said. "It's a lovely day to walk."

"We don't know them," I protested softly, trying to talk Emily out of it with my eyes. "It wouldn't be proper."

"Quite right," Daniel said smoothly. "How presumptuous of us, Edmund. We'll bid these ladies good day."

I felt foolish against Daniel's slight mocking tone, but stood my ground. I was not concerned by the four of us walking together, but I wasn't going to leave pretty, raven-haired Emily alone with them, no matter how honorable they seemed.

"Yes, all right," Emily acquiesced, not looking very pleased. "Very well, then. Thank you for the cake, Edmund. It was a pleasure to meet you both."

"The pleasure was mine," Edmund said. "Perhaps I'll see you again."

"Good day," Daniel said courteously. I didn't like him, I decided. He was shifty, slick as grease. Edmund, I liked.

I nudged Emily to the street. She looked back over her shoulder at them and flashed a little smile as we walked away.

"He was handsome," she said to me. "Edmund. Didn't you think so?"

"He did not ask to write to you. Or call on you."

"You made sure he could not do so," she snapped. "You were very . . . cold."

I laughed at her. "Don't ruin such a nice afternoon, Em. He will find you if it's meant to be."

She put an arm around me. "Sorry. Let's get you back to work, Old Married Lady."

Truer words were never spoken, and it pleased me greatly.

*

That night there was a banging on the door when John and I were asleep. I opened an eye, groggy, struggling to understand if I were dreaming or if the sound was real.

"God's blood," John muttered, throwing back the covers. He yanked open the bed curtains.

"Another messenger from Boston?" I asked sleepily. We had worked at the shop until well after dark after I'd returned back, at least until ten o'clock. We were tired from the week's labors, and I was doubly tired from the exhaustion I felt.

"A messenger to our home? No. I'm no one of importance." John was curt. "I don't know who it could be."

That jolted me awake. I prayed it wasn't bad news about the health of my mother or father. Or an accident. Or God forbid it was about one of my brothers and sisters. We'd had enough death in the family. It was a relief that no one was under age twelve anymore.

John was halfway down the stairs when I caught up, tying the belt of my robe around me.

He threw open the front door, his pistol in his hand. A man was standing there, his shirtsleeves pushed up to his elbows, holding a rifle.

"John Ross?"

"It is."

I peered out from behind John.

"Mrs. Ross?"

I nodded.

"I am the father of Emily Spencer. Josiah Spencer. It is my understanding that you were with Emily today."

"I was. What's wrong?"

"She did not come home."

"She didn't come home?" I tried to think through what he was saying to me. "Not at all?"

"No."

"How can that be?" I was trying to wake up.

"Come in." John held open the door wider.

Josiah Spencer shook his head like a basset hound. He was a large man, easily over six feet, and his frame filled the doorway. "I must find her." His eyes were wild with panic. He looked frantic but was composing himself with an effort.

"Tell me," I said.

"We were sure she'd be along. My wife said there is something about how a fine summer evening calls people outdoors. We thought at first that she was dallying at a friend's, and then we thought she'd gone to evensong at church. She likes the choir. And sometimes, when the weather is fine, she likes to sit out back and watch the moon and listen to the crickets. Says she doesn't get much quiet with our brood, so we didn't think much of it. Not at first. But she didn't come home. Her bed hasn't been touched. I woke to use the privy, and no one had seen her, not anyone in our house."

I heard the call of a mourning dove in the night and shivered. Where had Emily gone?

"Her sister said Emily was going to ask you to go to the fair by St. Paul's," Mr. Spencer said.

"Yes, she did, and we went," I said quickly. "We were there for about two hours all told. Give or take. She was fine, nothing out of the ordinary. We had a nice time."

"Perhaps if our household wasn't so noisy, we might have noticed quicker," he said.

"We'll find her," John said firmly. "I'll come with you. There has to be an explanation."

"Maybe she stopped at a friend's," I tried helpfully, then realized as soon as I said the words aloud how foolish they sounded. Perhaps she'd fallen ill. But I'd had the cake at the fair too. And the punch. What had happened?

"Let me throw some breeches on, Josiah," John said, running up the stairs. "I'll be right there."

The night air was warm and dry. I stood trying to think of something comforting to say to Emily's father. Emily was brash in temperament, but she was not disobedient. She would not put her parents through unnecessary worry.

"When did you leave the fair?" her father asked me. "Was there anything peculiar in her behavior? Did she seem ill?"

"I would say around three o'clock," I answered. "We walked back together, and then she was just going straight home. She was very well. She was happy. Nothing unusual."

Emily's father thought about this. "Any idea where she could have gone?"

"No, I'm sorry. I have no idea. There's nothing I can think of. We had a nice time and then we left."

"Is there—"

"Oh God."

Emily's father looked at me.

"There were two men. At the fair." A feeling of dread overcame me. "Of course I have no proof. They were friendly enough. But one of them—one of them seemed very interested in Emily."

I tried to remember, tried to think of which direction they'd gone. But they hadn't. They had watched us leave.

"They could have followed us," I said miserably. "Waited until I went inside."

"What men?" Josiah Spencer scowled. His body grew bigger in the doorway, his shoulders stiffening. "Tell me."

John came down and stood next to me, listening. I recounted the afternoon as best as I could.

"They seemed cordial," I said. "I just don't know. We were in the middle of the park, in broad daylight. Lots of people saw us. Dozens. I did think it was odd that the one named Edmund did not ask for Emily's address to come calling, given how smitten he seemed with her. And she with him."

"Let's go," John said to Josiah, stopping to put a knife into his boot shaft.

I described the two men. "One had pocked skin, and the other a birthmark on his neck. On the right side. Small and round, like a hazelnut. It looked like a smudge of mud."

"Right," Josiah said grimly. "We'll start at the docks. You said he was a sailmaker."

"Militia!" I exclaimed, suddenly remembering. "They were in uniform. They'd been training. Philadelphia Greens! Yes, that's it. Philadelphia Greens."

"Associators," John said knowingly. He looked at Henry. "They won't be hard to find. Let's move fast."

He took a lantern off the shelf by the door and lit it, holding it in front of him. Josiah Spencer stepped aside to let him pass and then followed John when he turned left to walk down to the river.

Surely, this was just a coincidence, I thought hopefully. They had seemed like nice men. Well, Edmund had. Would Emily pull a prank? I didn't think so.

"Please find her," I said. "I'll pray for you to find her, Mr. Spencer. And I'll pray for Emily, that she be found safe and well and that there's a reasonable explanation. Go quickly. John, be careful."

When the door finally closed behind them, there were new flies in the house. My teeth worried my lower lip, and I paced the small parlor anxiously. I had not expected to become close to Emily—we were so different—but now that I had spent so much time with her, I liked her very much. She had sass, spunk. I was always so serious, so earnest, and her sense of humor brought me out of myself and made me laugh. Emily had become a good friend to me, and I held a deep affection for her.

My life had changed so much this year, I thought after I picked up the cat and headed back to bed. After John and I married and I left my Quaker world, the rest of the world became much bigger. My friendship with Emily was part of that new, more interesting world I was inhabiting. *Emily, please be all right,* I thought. I put my chin on the cat's head, and we climbed the stairs together, me holding Cora like a doll.

Halfway up, a sharp pain in my belly took my breath away. I dropped the cat, who landed elegantly on the stairs, and reached out a hand to grip the wall.

Oh no. No, no, no. That didn't feel right.

Chapter 18

June 17, 1774

"I wish I had good news." John came into the kitchen alone shortly after dawn.

I was at the table drinking a cup of heated chocolate, trying to talk myself into peeling potatoes to keep in the pot for our supper. I went to the hearth and pulled the kettle away to make him coffee. Other than the bleeding, which was heavy, I felt well enough. At least my body did. My heart was bruised. I wouldn't think about that now.

"What happened?"

"We did not find her," John said, sitting down at the table tiredly.

"Tell me."

"No one knew of any sailmakers by the name of Worthington." John reached for his pipe. "We banged on doors for hours. Josiah was yelling across the docks like a madman. Everyone was sympathetic, but no one knew of a Worthington with a birth mark or a Welsh who was scarred. Didn't you say Worthington was from a family of sailmakers?"

"That's what he said." I put the coffee in front of John. "I'll make you eggs."

He rubbed his eyes with the heels of his palms. "No one had seen her."

"Poor Emily," I whispered, standing with my hand on the back of his chair. I touched his hair, smoothing it. "What about the Philadelphia Greens? They'll know their men."

"No luck so far at first pass," John acknowledged. "We need more information. Had to wait for daybreak."

John leaned his head into my chest, resting on me as I stroked his head and neck.

"Josiah got so frustrated he started firing shots into the air," John said. "I had to get him out of there. He was starting to accuse the sailors of covering for the men. No one seemed to know them."

"Where is he now?"

John straightened and reached for his coffee. "I sent him back home. He'll go door-to-door now that the sun's up. Josiah was going to tell the night watch and gather the neighborhood men. She has to be somewhere."

"I wish I could find her. I want to help." I went to the worktable and reached for the eggs I'd placed there earlier in a brown earthenware bowl. I cracked the eggs against the bowl, not really seeing what I was doing.

"Do you think it was those two men from the fair?" I asked uneasily.

My husband's shoulders lifted and fell. "I don't know. Maybe? It's possible. It's more probable now that we know that a sailmaker named Edmund Worthington most likely does not exist."

"Can I stay at home today?" I asked my husband.

"You did not go back to bed?"

"No. I've been up."

"There's nothing you can do, my love, that the men who are searching for her cannot do. I know how worried you are, and I understand that she's your friend and you're upset, but surely being here thinking on it and worrying will only make your spirits worse."

"I do not feel well," I said. I felt well enough physically. It was my aching heart that was making me feel physically ill. "I am not myself."

"Betsy, if those men followed you back to the shop, they know who you are," John said gravely. "Who we are. A few cunning questions to the other shop owners and they will know where we live. I can't have you here alone. They could come for you, knowing that you are the only one that can identify them if Emily came to harm from their hands."

I added milk and salt to the eggs. A bit too much salt. I wasn't paying attention.

"I don't feel well, John." I paused. I hated to do this to him now, at this moment, but he deserved to know what happened. "I have something I need to tell you."

*

John and I both stayed home that day. It was very rare for us to be away from the shop for any length of time, and I was grateful that John put me first. He only went to the upholstery to put a sign on the door and tell Oliver to spend the day making deliveries. When he came back, we held each other as we mourned the loss of my pregnancy and worried about Emily.

"It wasn't worry that caused this," I told John. "Please don't think that. I've been feeling twinges all week. I thought perhaps it was normal. I wouldn't know." I thought of the brown bottle, the tincture. Had this happened because of what I'd taken? I didn't know. All women lost as many pregnancies as they carried to birth, or at least my mother had, and most of the women in our family, for that matter.

We were having a nap later that morning, lying in bed with the curtains open, air from the open windows shifting over us. Underneath the window, the irises bloomed and daylilies lined the path. I could hear the flowers shift in the breeze. I was dozing when another determined banging began on our door.

"They've found Emily," I said eagerly, sitting up.

"Stay here," John said sharply. "We don't know who it is. It could be anyone. And you need to rest," he added as crossed the room and grabbed his pistol.

I heard the front door open, and John went outside. I got off the bed and stood close to the open window, seeing blackbirds dart in and out of the tree in front of the neighbor's yard. The sky was beautiful, and it annoyed me. On a day like today, it wasn't right to be so lovely.

I listened for good news, then sighed when I heard men talking about resistance measures. This call wasn't about Emily.

"Can you meet tonight, Ross?" a man asked, his voice thick with too much tobacco, low and wheezy. "We must prepare. We'll meet at the Bunch of Grapes tonight."

"I've been dealing with an urgent matter and have not heard the latest," John said. "Tell me what's going on."

The reaction to England's punishment of Boston had been a fever that was increasing daily. The uproar in Philadelphia, and all the colonies, heightened every time a newspaper wrote of the injustices happening in Boston, which they did with glee, hardly letting a day pass between tales of outrage. Parliament thought all the other colonies would not support Boston and that we'd believe their punishment was warranted. Britain counted on re-establishing their authority. Instead, the colonies had banded together to support Boston, deeply disturbed by the town's lengthy suffering.

This time a younger voice spoke, strident with urgency. "The proposed list of men is not the right list, *ja*? The mechanics must have more of a say. And we must have more Germans on the committee. Otherwise, we will not be heard."

I got back on the bed and laid back. There was a small water stain on the ceiling I hadn't noticed before, probably because I was never in bed in the middle of the day when the sun was high. It was an old roof. I clicked my toes together idly. I was worried sick about my friend. I wanted to find Emily, not hear men bicker about the fact that Thomas Wharton shouldn't be included on Philadelphia's committee formed to respond to the Boston situation because he was a tea agent. Or that Dr. Smith should be tossed off the list because he wasn't upset enough about Boston's demise. Smith was rather cool, they said, too calm about what was happening. *Rather suspicious, that one.* I suspected many in Philadelphia agreed with Dr. Smith and were simply wise enough to keep their thoughts to themselves. Many conservative people in town just wanted Boston to pay for the tea they'd dumped and for life to go back to normal. More outspoken personalities, the men with fire in them, said that Boston was suffering for the greater good of all the colonies and that the guns trained on them from the British warships in the harbor represented guns against all of us.

"I suspect the list of forty chosen for the committee is not open to negotiation," John said. "I know how it came about. It was meant to be well rounded."

"We want seven mechanics added. And six Germans," the throaty voice said. "If it comes to non-importation of goods from England again, it's us craftsmen who will be most affected. The workers. We need a frontline position. Those greedy bastards. Messing with the fecking tea! Acting like they're doing us a favor, as if it's not a damned revenue for those greedy-arsed pansies. Piss on 'em."

"Are you with us?" the younger man asked John insistently, almost accusingly, I thought, not caring for his tone of voice. Who were these men, and how could they not know how strongly John felt?

Honestly, I was getting fed up with the whole tea situation. We'd heard of nothing else for a month. It was like an endless cacophony of geese squawking. I would be glad when the summer passed and the crisis faded. It was hard for John to work so tirelessly in our upholstery business, put in so many long hours, and then have to take up the rebel cause. It was like a second job, and he was so fiery about the matter that he could not do half measures or feel that he was not doing all that he could every time a meeting was called.

"You know I'm with you," John said fiercely. "Bunch of Grapes, you said. What time? Know that my wife is under the weather and her health may prevent me from attending, but that would be the only obstacle."

"Saw your sign in the window. We stopped by your shop. Said you're closed for the day?"

There was no answering reply from John, who let the conversation pause without responding to the unspoken question.

"Well, we wish your missus well," drawled the older man when John didn't answer. "Around seven, Ross, if you can."

"We need you," the young and cocky man said. "They're expecting thousands at the meeting tomorrow. We must be prepared."

I doubted it was thousands. More like hundreds. These men seemed like schoolboys hoping for a fistfight, I thought, all puffed up with indignation.

When John came upstairs again, I pre-empted his explanation. "I heard," I said a touch peevishly. "That's fine. You must go."

"It's early yet," John said patiently. "I'll see how you feel by tonight. Of course I won't go if you need me. You're my wife and you come first. Are you sure I can't call for a doctor?"

"No, John. I was newly pregnant. I wasn't far along. I'm not in pain. This is very much like my monthly courses."

John laid down on the bed and ran a slow finger over my shoulder. "Please don't be cross if I go. You know you are the most important thing in my life. More important than any policy crisis."

"I'm not cross," I snapped. "I want our baby!"

I burst into tears.

"Me too," John said and gathered me close.

*

The impact of the loss of the life within me, sadly, was no greater than a leaf falling from a tree and floating down to rest upon the ground. By evening, I felt fine. I changed my rags, had a cup of hot bone broth, and told John he could go to his people with my blessing.

"I still don't plan to leave you here alone," he said, his eyebrows knitting together with concern. "Would it be wrong of me to suggest a visit with your family? I could take you there. Or would the strain of it be too much?"

"I would welcome it," I said, alighting to the idea. "Although I really think I'm fine."

There were times when I missed my old life as a child in a large household, when I had been a happy cog in the wheel and not the entire wheel. I was fast discovering the endless chores involved with running a house, small as our rental was, and being the only woman standing. It was tiring, monotonous without other womankind, and John and I were getting dangerously fond of the restaurant two doors down, a habit we had to curb sooner rather than later due to the expense of it.

"We could ask Oliver to come sit with me. We'd have an evening of cards of jacks. Or whatever boys play. He may be glad of the extra pennies."

"A child? I think not. Has he even fired a gun?"

"I have no idea," I said honestly. "And quite frankly, I hope not. He's very young. Never mind that. Going home to my parents would be a treat. I would like that very much. And it will take my mind off Emily." How I wished I could do something. Waiting to hear was torture. *Please Emily, be all right.*

"Then that's settled," John said. "I will come and collect you when I'm done."

"My father could bring me home in the chaise," I suggested.

"I'll come for you," John repeated. My husband was taking his role as protector seriously, and it felt good to be the jewel that he treasured. I was charmed by him. How lucky I was to be married to this man.

"I'll try not to be too long."

"Can you stop at the Spencers'?" I asked. "Ask about Emily? Find out what's going on. I can't just sit by. Maybe there's something I can do to help."

John nodded. "Of course I will. I had planned to."

*

I had thought my arrival home would be a novelty, but I was wrong. I'd had visions of being welcomed with embraces and cries of "We miss you!" but as usual my hopes were for naught.

My family was in the backyard making the most of the evening sun, and it was as if I had never left. The back of the property had a number of outbuildings my father had erected over the years, including a large carpentry workshop, but they were sitting in the garden behind the house.

"Betsy, can you get the ball for me?" George said unceremoniously when he saw me. "It's right there. Where you're standing." He was already thirteen, his shoulders broadening.

I pulled the ball out of fork in the tree at my eye level and handed it to him.

"Come draw with us," Rachel said.

A few rustic wooden tables were in the backyard, my father's handiwork. He was busy at one of the tables making one of his birdhouses, my mother sewing a doll. I sat with them as they drew and sewed and hammered. This was us as we'd always been: workers, makers, never an idle hand.

"Hello, lovey," my mother said, smiling. "Tea? I have cold tea in the icehouse."

I shook my head. I wanted to tell my parents that Emily was missing and about the child I had lost, but I did not want to do so in front of Rachel, who was still only twelve.

"Where is John?" my father asked as he added the first half of the roof to his miniature house.

"He had a meeting," I explained and admired the doll's face in my mother's hands. She was embroidering on its smile, a sweet pink addition to the black nose and eyes. "You've got the perfect bow on that doll's lip," I said.

"Not a meeting about that Boston matter, I hope," my mother murmured. "Terrible business."

"Is this birdhouse for you, Father?" I asked, wondering if I'd see it in the tree the next time I came.

My father nodded and hammered in a nail. "I thought the public meeting was tomorrow?"

"It is," I said. "John said the mechanics called an emergency meeting tonight as well, to see if they can add some men of their choosing to the committee. Increase their strength. Everything is happening very quickly, and news seems to change all the time."

"What committee?" my mother asked. "I don't think I heard."

"Philadelphia has formed a committee to address what's happening in Boston," my father explained, putting down his hammer and reaching for the other half of the roof.

My father's birdhouses were masterpieces—as sturdy and impressive as the real-life houses he built across town, only in tiny scale. The precise walls, the perfect circle that would serve as the birds' front door, the sharp peak, all spoke of a man who had spent his life crafting beautiful items from wood, a master at his trade.

"That birdhouse is a little bigger than the ones your normally make, isn't it?" I said. "You could sell those at the market. They're so handsome. Remarkable, really."

"Betsy, draw," Rachel ordered. I obediently picked up my charcoal pencil and reached for a piece of paper.

"Too much work. I do it for the enjoyment of it. As I was saying, dear, tomorrow there's a public meeting in the State House," my father continued. "To vote on the resolves from last week."

"Goodness," my mother said. "All this fuss when those men destroyed tea that wasn't even theirs. What a waste. Of course they should pay for it."

"Indeed," my father agreed. "Boston has asked for help, but I'm not sure we need to jump into the fire with them."

"Are you going to the State House to listen?" I asked my father.

"Yes, I'm going to meet Abel and Henry there." I wondered what had happened to their tea when it got all the way back to England aboard the *Polly*.

"So what's the meeting for?" Rachel asked as she added a rose to her drawing. She was looking at the rose on the bush next to her and attempting to recreate it. "What's a resolve and why do you vote on it?"

"A resolve is a written decision announcing how you feel about a situation," my father explained. "A declaration of a sort. You vote so you know the majority of people agree."

"So what's the decision?" my sister asked.

"They're planning to tell Britain that being this cruel to Boston is against the rules," I answered. "They're saying it goes against what government should do to their people. And they're going to ask that all the colonies get together soon and talk about what to do."

"Are they really?" my mother said. "That sounds dramatic. All the colonies? Even the ones far away? It all seems a bit much to me. When they suggested that businesses close here in Philadelphia—in Philadelphia!—on the first of June in sympathy for the closing of Boston, we couldn't help ourselves; we had a bit of a chuckle in our ladies meeting. And then why did they ring the church bells mournfully like that? Too much, I thought. No one has died, for goodness' sake. And we're here in Philadelphia, three hundred miles away from Boston! I could understand doing that there, but why close up the shops and ring the bells *here*?"

I stayed quiet. My parents would never understand, never oppose the British. It wasn't their way, wasn't the Quaker way. It was only then that I realized how far I had married out of their world. The thought sobered me.

"I hope John takes a conservative stance," my father said, picking up his hammer and nails again.

I drew a robin and added a butterfly to my paper.

"Well?" My father eyed me. "Is John staying out of it?"

"My husband is doing what he thinks he must," I answered.

"Now, I'm not saying I agree with the Port Act," my father continued, studying his birdhouse. "It does seem extreme. Yet all this noise about outrage and retaliation is dangerous. John should be cautious and not get too involved. It will be bad for him if he aligns himself with the radicals and then it all blows over. Messy. Too many objections can be seen as treasonous after the fact."

"Mmm," I said noncommittally.

"Betsy, I hope you're listening," my father said. "I'll talk with John."

Dear God, no.

"He knows, Papa," I said gently. "It's all anyone talks about at church. Even the church leaders say we can protest the tea."

I wished I hadn't said that. It was like rubbing salt into the wound, that I had left our meetinghouse for the Church of England.

"Don't get too involved," my father warned again, turning his birdhouse over. "Remember, this will blow over, and you need to protect your good name. Just look at the last ten or twenty years since the Indian war and the Stamp Act. It all comes and goes. Cooler heads will prevail. Don't act. Do nothing."

"I can't tell John what to do," I answered. "I'm a wife now, and I must support my husband."

My father frowned. "We must depend on Great Britain."

"Indeed, we must," my mother said. "All this fighting over tea of all things is absurd. We must put it behind us. Speaking of tea, all this talk has made me thirsty. I'll get the pitcher. We might even have a bit of the last ice block left. Summer is most definitely here."

I stopped drawing and watched her get up and cross the yard. How nice it must be to not have any doubts, to think that there is only one way forward.

Chapter 19

June 1774

"Still no news," John told me grimly when he arrived at my parents' house to get me and saw the question in my eyes.

"Mind how you go," my parents said. My father had not spoken to John privately due to the lateness of the hour.

"I'll come by tomorrow," he said to John. "And we'll talk. Good night."

"Good night," we echoed.

We went into the night, dark and warm, filled with scents of early summer—new grass and Sweet Shrub and animal waste. The temperatures were mild and that was a blessing. As the heat rose in the weeks ahead, the streets would start to stink. The burial ground was across the street from my parents' house, only a four-foot brick wall separating it from its corner location at Mulberry and Fourth Street. The grounds had been given by William Penn to the Quakers, but all types of people threw their dead over the wall. John was amazed when I told him that most Quakers didn't get a headstone or a marker.

"Showy," I explained. "The body is gone. It is the soul that matters." *Ostentatious* was the word the elders used. Pretentious.

We stopped and turned toward each other in the shadow of the burial wall. John described the frantic search going on for Emily, dozens of neighborhood men taking turns at combing the streets and alleys without a trace found. Her mother was beside herself, going from church to church through town to spread the news and see if anyone had seen her.

"Are you all right to walk?" John asked tenderly, placing a hand on the small of my back. "I could borrow your father's horse and bring it back. Do they know?"

"I didn't have a chance to tell them; George and Rachel were with us. But I don't need the horse. I'm fine," I assured him. "I've been sitting for several hours. It's not often I rest. Tell me of your meeting?"

"All huff and puff at this point." John clasped my hand and we headed for home. He set a slow pace, taking his time so I would do the same.

"I thought I could go in to work tomorrow with Oliver and try to work on the Chew order while you're at the State House," I volunteered. "We must be getting close."

John nodded. "It's just the last few curtains now. The bed hangings are done."

"If we finish early enough, I'd like to go to Emily's house. Would you mind? I really want to help. I can't go on like nothing's happened. I can't just go home and fuss in the kitchen. I'm fine, really."

"I'll come with you, if I'm back," John said. "If I'm not, take Oliver with you."

Between us lay the unspeakable. Emily's lifeless body, or worse, an absence that could never be explained. Every now and then a corpse was fished out of the river, bloated and fleshy. Once it had been a woman, but she had been a lady of the night, and little was said about the matter when her identity was revealed. "Syphilitic," people whispered. "Burn the corpse."

"What about the Philadelphia Greens connection?" I asked John as we stepped carefully around manure and food waste in Bread Street in the dim light. The moon was a shell, halfway between a crescent and full bellied, and only partially lit the night. I had seen the moon from the table in my parents' yard as it ascended and the sun descended, the figure in its far away surface hunched over and mottled gray.

"Emily's father was going to Cadwalader's house to see," John said. "He's starting a militia group. He wasn't home when I stopped by. I'll find out what came of that."

"John Cadwalader has a militia?"

"It's new. They're going to call it the Silk Stocking Company on account of Cadwalader recruiting so many gentlemen in town."

As we walked, we passed the back door of a teahouse we noticed had some damage. I knew that teahouse—I had been there several times. It was run by the Widow Farthingham. She was an older lady who liked to feature her cakes in the front window. She had a pet bird in a cage in the corner who would sometimes talk for customers. Someone had painted "tea fussock" on the door leading to the cellar, and there was a hole in one of the windows that had been patched with a board. It looked like it taken the receiving end of a club.

"That doesn't seem fair," I said. "Mrs. Farthingham wouldn't hurt a fly. She's so sweet. She has nothing to do with what's happening with Boston, or the East India Company. She lives upstairs, and she's on her own now that her husband's gone. She must have been terrified."

"Someone decided she was serving the wrong kind of tea," John agreed. "It's a shame."

"I feel like Philadelphia is not the same anymore," I said thoughtfully. "I was young when the Stamp Act was a problem, but I remember my father talking with Uncle Abel and Henry Drinker in the front room and how they spoke of it. This feels different."

"Tense and uptight."

"You feel it too," I noted. "Before, no one would be nasty to an old widow at her tea shop."

"The thought of the British navy surrounding Boston with their guns pointed at the town is impossible to imagine," John said. "I've even been to Boston, and I still can't make sense of it."

"That a country could do that to one of its own?"

"What king does this to his own people? How long can it last? It's warm now, but in winter?"

"I don't know."

"It's an act of war, Betsy," John said, disgust in his voice. "Those warships. Britain means to break them."

"Surely, that's worse than destroying the tea," I said. "It seems like too great a punishment over a shipment of tea leaves."

"That's the iron fist of a ruler who doesn't care."

"Sometimes I wish I could see the future," I said, stopping to look up to the heavens. "Oh, look at the moon now!"

John smiled. "Your face looks like a white rose lifted to the sun. My beautiful wife."

"Is there a flower that lifts its face to the light of the moon?"

He laughed. "I have no idea. A moonflower?"

"Is there such a thing? We are hopeless," I said. "Kiss me, husband."

John stepped close to me, and our lips met. He raised his head and rubbed his nose on mine. "With you, all is right with the world."

There was a snuffling noise behind him, and we laughed as a pig trundled by.

"It's his lucky night—there's a feast in waste for him that we just walked by," I said, thinking of the feces and discarded meat and rotten vegetables we had stepped around.

"How romantic," John drawled sardonically. I laughed.

"Sorry. Let's go back to looking at the moon again. This evening feels like a gift."

"I need to get you home," John said. "We have a long day tomorrow. It's late."

Emily. I felt sick. How could I have forgotten, even for a moment? Emily had been gone just over twenty-four hours; it was still possible there was an explanation. I made a mental note to go to Webster's tomorrow and see if he had heard anything. You never knew.

John was frowning at the sky, lost in his thoughts, which, judging by his face, were dark.

"I love you," I said, trying to draw him back to me.

"I love you too," John said seriously. "Let's go home and go to bed. I'll get you a hot water bottle for your belly, and if you're really lucky, I'll rub your feet until you fall asleep."

"Now there's an idea," I said gratefully. "I knew I married you for a reason."

We walked on again into the night, past an inn that glowed yellow inside, its occupants singing a sea shanty while banging pewter cups.

*

The next morning dawned clear and bright. John dropped me at the shop when he saw Oliver was waiting outside and went on to the State House.

"Are you well today, Oliver?" I asked him as I unlocked the door. I peeled off the makeshift sign that John had put on the glass yesterday morning and crumpled the paper in my hand.

"Couldn't be better, ma'am," he said, following me inside.

"Hungry?" I asked, handing him a bundle. "Fresh biscuits."

He dove in. No matter how much food he consumed, this boy was always going to eat more and be happy about it. I grinned as he shoveled in a second one.

"When you're finished, please go to the stockroom," I told him. "Bring me the red silk. I'm going to finish the Tilghman bed hangings today. You can tidy and stack the fabrics until I'm ready to have you help me package the order."

Oliver wiped his mouth on his sleeve and headed to the back.

Moments later, I heard him shriek.

"Oliver! What's the matter?" I ran to the stock room.

Oliver pointed, his face a mask of horror.

In the corner, a pair of human legs in brown boots was sprawled on the floor. The torso belonging to the body was hidden behind fabric bolts that were leaning against the wall. Skirts covered the legs to below the knees.

"Dear God. Emily." I rushed to move the fabric bolts away from her face and squatted next to her. There was movement. She was alive. "Oliver, go get help."

"Don't. I beg you." Her voice was thin yet fierce.

Oliver stopped, uncertain whether he should listen to me and go, or obey Emily.

What was she doing? Had she been asleep? Anger surged through me. What kind of a prank was this? Emily's long hair was undone and fell over her face, obscuring her features. Her cap was nowhere to be seen. Rather than sitting up, she lay where she was, head pressed into the corner by the baseboard.

"Emily, for the love of God. What the devil do you think you're doing?" I asked. This made no sense.

I felt Oliver behind me, shifting anxiously, hovering.

It was then that I noticed Emily's clothing. She was wearing the same clothing she'd had on at the fair.

The same clothing. Oh no. "Oh, Emily. Let me fetch a doctor."

"No, don't. Why did it take you so long?" she mumbled from beneath the curtain of black hair. "I've been waiting and waiting."

Oh God. Emily had been here the whole time. John had come yesterday morning and only stayed long enough to put up the sign. He hadn't been in the back room.

"Emily, sweetheart, let me help you. Oliver, bring some water."

I reached to brush Emily's hair away from her face, and she flinched and shook her head so it fell back over her eyes again. Had she had some kind of a turn? I thought of John's mother in the hospital all those years ago, insane and out of touch with reality.

"What happened?" I asked when Oliver went to the front room to get the pitcher. "Can you sit up?"

She shook her head. "Please don't touch me."

"I must. We have to get you home and cared for. Tell me what I can do. Shall I send Oliver for your mother?"

"No one can know."

Oliver handed me a glass of water. His little face was pinched with worry as I tried to get Emily to raise her head to take a drink.

"Can you go a few doors down to the grocer," I asked Oliver, my mind searching, "and get me a cabbage?"

"A cabbage?"

"For her headache," I invented.

"All right."

"When you're back, please wait outside the front door by the shop sign. The money for the cabbage is in the box in the drawer—you know where."

It was the fastest way I could think of to divert him. "It won't be long. Don't tell anyone why you're standing there if they ask. For that matter, don't say anything to anyone."

He ran off. I sank to the floor. Emily hadn't moved and wasn't speaking. Realization dawned. I reached out gingerly and lifted Emily's skirts. Blood on her thighs. I gently smoothed her skirts down over her again.

"It was the man from the fair," I said, "wasn't it, lovey? Let's get you help. Will you let me help you, Em?"

She was silent for a time. Then, in a strange voice, she said, "I ate your bowl of apples."

"I do not care about that," I responded. "I'm glad you did."

I felt helpless, wishing John were here to help, wishing I knew what to do. I reached out to stroke Emily's hair, and this time she let me touch her.

"Can you sit up if I help you?"

"Both of them," she finally said in a whisper. "The dark-haired one started it. I didn't know they were there."

I tried to speak, but my voice broke in my throat. I tried again.

"Emily, let me help you. Please."

Philadelphia was a safe town, mostly, where if you avoided the dangerous bits, by the wharves and in the southern Liberties, you could walk safely alone as a woman. Many of the streets in this area were filled with craftsmen and artisans and a sense of bustling commerce and community. There were churches and parks every few streets.

Emily lay motionless. "What if they find me? Come back?"

"Don't worry about that. They'll be whipped. Imprisoned." Drawn and quartered, I hoped. I cleared my throat and made my voice strong and kind. "I know you're hurt. We need to get you help."

"Then people will know what happened," she said darkly. She had been lying here all night and all day yesterday, thinking about this.

"Em, you can't stay here," I said gently. "If you can't sit up, I'll fetch a doctor."

"I can walk," she said. "I just cannot . . . bear it. I can't think of it." Her voice broke. "Betsy, I can't cope."

I reached out and stroked her hair. She looked at me, her face tormented, then looked away. Tears slid from her eyes.

"This is not your shame," I said. I laid down next to her, our heads close together. "You must believe that."

"No one can know," she whispered. "I could not bear it. Please, Betsy. Please."

"I will do as you say, anything, but we must care for you first."

"What a fool I was." Self-hatred laced her voice.

"What beasts they were, to hurt you so," I said tenderly.

I brushed the tears from her cheeks. "We are going to sit up now, together, and have some water. Ready?"

She nodded imperceptibly. I helped her up and propped her against the fabric bolts that she had been using to lie under. She took the glass and drank the water.

I put a thick layer of canvas over her, folded several times, to warm her.

What to do, what to do? My mind whirled. She needed a doctor. If she was still bleeding, time was of the essence. She had already been here more than a day. She must be in pain. If she would not let me call for a doctor, where could I take her? Who could I bring here? Should I send Oliver for her parents? Maybe I should not have even had her sit up. What if she bled out?

My mind worked furiously. Who could I trust? Who would she let me involve? I couldn't lift her, and Oliver was a ten-year-old.

"You need pennyroyal," I said aloud, mostly to myself. "That will prevent a pregnancy."

Emily burst into tears.

I held her while I decided what to do.

"Emily, there's a healer, a midwife I know. She can help, I'm sure she'll help. I'm going to send Oliver to bring her here. She'll know what to do. And she is discreet. If she's home, she'll help you."

Emily looked frightened but did not argue. She drew up her knees and wrapped her arms around them, resting her head on her knees. She was crying silently.

I ran out to the front room and through the upholstery's front door. Oliver jumped.

"Go," I commanded him. "Find the sign of the purple gargoyle on Cox Alley. Across from the gunsmith. Knock and ask for Clarinda. Tell her a woman is in great need and that she'll need her physick bag. Hurry. Run."

I prayed that Clarinda was there and would listen to the boy.

I returned to Emily. "Chew on this," I said, handing her a sassafras stick. "It's for pain." I kept a small stock of medicines in the shop in case of cuts or accidents.

"When Clarinda gets here, I'll sent Oliver to tell your parents you've been found and that you're here. I'll ask them to come after dark."

"I want to see them hang," she sobbed. I wasn't sure her father would let them live long enough for that, but I kept my thoughts to myself.

"John and your father went to the docks, looking for Edmund the sailmaker," I told her, not sure that I should offer the information but wanting her to know the lengths they had gone to. "They couldn't find him or the other man. They're going to talk to the Philadelphia Greens today."

Emily wiped snot and tears on the back of her hand.

"No one can know," she said again. "I must marry well. What life can I have if I do not? You remember what they did to Fanny Bleeker."

I did. The man they'd caught had gone to jail for unlawful carnal knowledge of a woman. That should have ended the matter, but after a month of jeers and hoots, Fanny boarded a ship for Liverpool, never to return. Before she left she tried to cut her wrists.

"Hush," I murmured. "You're safe now. You will heal."

"You weren't here," Emily cried. Strings of snot dripped from her nose. "I panicked. I didn't know what to do. I didn't know where to go. I couldn't go home."

"I'm sorry, sweetheart." The thought of her lying here alone on the floor in the dark all night was appalling. "I'm so sorry I wasn't here."

I'd never been as happy to see anyone as I was when Clarinda walked in behind Oliver, carrying a leather satchel, her face determined.

Chapter 20

I left Clarinda with a bowl of water—cold, unfortunately, since the hearth was ash—and a pile of scrap flannel cut into squares she could use as rags and went to close the door to the back room so they could be alone. I heard Clarinda murmuring to Emily, her voice low and soothing, and glanced back to see Emily relax into her hands. That woman was a vexing mystery, but she seemed to know how to heal.

Oliver and I stood in the front room looking at each other, spent, like soldiers returning from war.

"What's wrong with her?" Oliver inquired with the guile of a child.

"She's sick," I said simply. "She'll be better now."

"I had a bad stomach once," Oliver commiserated. "I had to lie down or I would keep bringing up."

"That's right," I agreed.

"You look worried," he said, his eyes on me, perceptive.

"I'm always worried when a friend isn't well." I shrugged, picking up a cushion and putting it down again. Who cared about cushions and bed hangings and curtains now?

Oliver went back to tidying. I looked out the front window, marveling how life could go on. It was a Sunday, and the street was filling up with people. Horses clomped by outside, noisy and normal, half of the town on their way to church.

"When you're finished with sorting the nails, please sweep and then organize the hardware," I told Oliver, ignoring the cries that were coming from the back room.

Reluctantly, I picked up the curtain fabric and my needle. I had to keep up appearances for Oliver's sake. The thought of Edmund and his fellow thug loose on the streets made my blood boil. I pricked my finger and exclaimed, putting my finger in my mouth to suck the blood. I had been working the needle for so long that rarely ever happened to me.

At long last Clarinda came out to see me. I leapt up, dropping my sewing. She motioned me aside, her face carefully composed.

"Oliver, can you watch the shop for me? I won't be long."

"Oh, I can! I know the shop now!"

I took Clarinda outside, and we walked around to the side of the building and stood in the little alleyway that led to stored fire tools for the Union Fire Company. If fire broke out, the town men would come to retrieve these buckets and tools and rush to the fire. They were all volunteers, but highly organized thanks to Ben Franklin's efforts.

"They abused her well," she said to me in a low voice. "You were right to call for me."

"I was worried there might be bleeding or serious injury," I said. "She wouldn't let me fetch a doctor." I knew a woman after childbirth could die from a bleed. I wasn't sure why or what that involved, but I didn't know how badly Emily was hurt. How strange that we were having such a terrible conversation on a sunny day filled with light and the faraway cries of children playing.

She nodded. "I put a few stitches in for the tear." That explained the sounds I'd heard. They had been that rough in their abuse of her? "I gave her a board to bite on and some whiskey from my bag. I believe she can still have children."

"Did she say what happened?" I asked.

Clarinda leaned back against the brick wall. She shook her head sadly. I didn't know if that meant she didn't know or wasn't going to tell me.

"I much prefer the birthing of babes or the ridding of unwanted pregnancies," she said tiredly. "My heart breaks for her. Such a young girl. Diabolical, what they did. Pure evil."

"Her father and my husband went looking for the men who did this before I found her here," I told her. "Emily and I had been to the spring fair, and we met the two men there. They appeared gentlemanly, but they must have followed her. I feel so terrible, honestly I do. I wish I had known, could have stopped it. If I had thought . . . If I could turn back time . . .

I was unsuspecting. I pray that they're found today and punished."

Clarinda straightened and narrowed her eyes. She set her shoulders. "They won't be found."

"Surely, they will. They wore militia uniforms. Philadelphia Greens. One of them had a—"

Clarinda shrugged. "I've seen it all before. They'll board a sloop, south to the islands or north to Canada, and that will be the end of it."

"I hope not."

Clarinda sighed. "She told me what happened. They must have followed her. There is a house under construction, a few streets away, the workers not there. These men must have known that. Perhaps they'd even been watching beforehand, planning a crime, waiting for the right victim. They pulled her inside the half-built house and abused her. For a long time, I gather, from what she said."

I shuddered. *Poor Emily. God help her.*

"They used both bodily crevices," Clarinda said baldly. I jumped, my eyes widening.

"You mean . . ." I whispered. Disgust filled me. Had I understood her correctly? "Do you mean—"

"Yes. That is what I mean. You are a married woman, so I need not explain."

"I, um, I—"

"You are young. I will not burden you with unnecessary details on the depravities of evil men."

I tried to form words but could not.

"They left her there, she said, between the paint pots and the ladders amongst the drop sheets. When darkness fell, she ran here. She must trust you, Mrs. Ross. I believe you know the rest."

"Tell me how to help her," I said. "We need to get her home. How will we get her home? My husband isn't here today. I told her I'd send for her parents to come after dark, but they're a working family without carriage or chariot. Can she walk? She wouldn't want to be seen on a stretcher."

"She can't walk. It's best that she doesn't because of the stitches. My neighbor is a shoemaker with a very old sedan chair from when he had elderly clients coming from Society Hill. He is quiet, keeps to himself. He'll come if I ask, and between us we can get her home. She's a small girl."

"Thank you, yes. I'll send word to her mother. Oliver can let Mrs. Spencer know we're bringing her home. We'll explain when we get there."

"After dark," Clarinda said.

"Yes."

"And as for her care, nature will take over now. She needs rest, that's the main thing. Her body will heal before her mind. The pennyroyal will make her sick, and too much can be fatal. I'll give her mother herbs and an opium tincture to administer. I'll return in a fortnight to take out the stitches, but of course I'll see her before that. As for you, be a good friend. Don't ask her anything. She will talk or she won't. That's not for us to meddle in."

I took a breath and wrapped my arms around my chest.

"Thank you," I said, searching her eyes. "Thank you. I don't know what I would have done."

Clarinda rubbed her temple. "This is why I do what I do. Women must help other women."

"I want to pay you but I cannot," I said. I thought of her worn sitting room. "We are newly married; we don't have much. I could upholster a chair for you. You could choose the fabric, if you'd like."

"That will do nicely," Clarinda said matter-of-factly, brightening. Her satisfaction surprised me until I wondered if she was usually paid in eggs and honey or promises that weren't fulfilled. Perhaps I was offering her something relatively extravagant. I thought back to that messy room of hers, the furniture crammed together, all of it worn and scratched. Not a lucrative business to be in, birthing and healing.

"I need to go back," I realized. "Oliver is a child. I must go."

"And we've left Emily alone long enough," Clarinda agreed. "She was sleepy when I left her. I made her comfortable."

We had made Emily a makeshift bed out of a mattress we'd been making that was half-stuffed. We covered the shell of it with a sheet and then put blankets over her. Some of the blankets were raw, for horses, and some elaborately and exquisitely embroidered for our wealthy patrons. They looked so incongruous and out of place on the floor, those fancy blankets. To think, those customers would never know how their blankets had been used.

"At dusk, I'll go get my neighbor and the sedan chair," Clarinda said.

"I'll stay with her," I said. "Between Oliver and I, we will manage. Now that you've cared for her."

I stopped under our sign, freshly painted, that said, "J. Ross, Upholsterer," and turned to her.

I hesitated. Now wasn't the time, but I felt compelled to tell her.

"I was with child, Clarinda, but I lost it yesterday. I wasn't very far along." Clarinda and I were connected now, by the tragedy that had happened to Emily, and I inexplicably wanted to let her know what had happened to me.

"I know," Clarinda said, although not glibly. Her silver hair glinted in the sun. "My sympathies," she said earnestly. No *I told you so* or *Why didn't you listen?*

I liked her, I decided. She was queer, perhaps, but kind. Life had made her solid and capable and a little weary from seeing too much suffering—as stalwart as the mermaid figurehead on the bow of a ship.

"Remember, you'll have many children," she said. She did not, however, repeat that it would not be with John, and I was going to pretend it had never been said in the first place. How odd she was, this woman. And how indispensable.

Oliver was standing by a stack of bolts of ticking with a tape measure around his neck, confidently playing the part of shopkeeper.

"I sold a *mattress*," Oliver announced cheerfully, terribly pleased with himself. He beamed. "A man came. He said could I please oblige him as his daughter and son-in-law were in need and he had to go out of town and could we make a mattress for him and he was friends with the Drinkers so he knew you and he didn't think you'd mind," he burbled in a rush. "Is that all right? He left me money." He held out his hand to show me.

"Of course that's all right," I said, my lips curving into a smile. "You'll go far in life, Oliver. Well done. You're a natural."

"I even wrote up a sales slip like I'd seen you do in that black book you keep, and he was ever so pleased. Oh, and when he left, I looked in on that girl, but she was asleep."

*

John found the note on the table at home that I had tasked Oliver with leaving when it got to be midafternoon. I made a mental note to pay Oliver more for today. I'd run him off his feet.

John arrived at our upholstery around nine o'clock, just as the June day was settling into night. I didn't light the candles or a lamp, so the shop looked dark and empty. I told my husband everything, from finding Emily, to Clarinda being a godsend, to the plan to get Emily home undetected within the next hour.

"I should have been here. I would have come."

"We managed," I said. "It was for the best that you weren't here, given the state she was in and that you are . . . male. I would have sent Oliver for you if we needed you. Honestly. I would have."

John looked between me and Oliver, then ran a hand down the back of his neck. "Dear Lord," he said, taking in what I'd told him about Emily's attack.

He shook his head and pinched the bridge of his nose between finger and thumb. I knew his time at the State House had been a scene because of what customers had told us as they came in, but that would have to wait.

"Oliver, you may go home," I said, "now that Mr. Ross is here. I could not have managed without you today. You were a blessing."

"I want to help with the girl," Oliver said, not moving. "With Emily."

"Let him stay," John said. "He wants to see it out."

Oliver grinned. "Can I tell him about the other thing?" Oliver asked me.

"Go ahead."

"I sold a mattress!" Oliver crowed to John. "When Mrs. Ross was out. I knew the price from hearing you last week with that woman."

John gave Oliver a grin. "Well done, my man. Well done. You'll make a mighty fine businessman yourself one day."

Oliver beamed.

The resilience of youth.

"Out where?" John asked me quietly.

"Just outside. I'll explain everything later."

Just then there was a scratching on the front glass. Through the dark, we could see faces and the outline of the sedan chair.

John opened the door, and two men and Clarinda came inside. The men had the sedan chair between them, the older man at the front, holding the posts as he stepped into our shop. John closed and locked the door behind them while I lit a candle to show the way.

"This is my husband and my son," Clarinda said. It had never occurred to me that Clarinda would have a husband or children. She seemed as solitary as an ancient priestess, alone and wizened by knowledge.

"Thank you for coming," I said, taking in the men, one middle-aged and one barely a man but just as tall as his father.

"Stay here," Clarinda instructed the men. "We'll tell you when."

Emily was groggy. Clarinda must have given her something—laudanum maybe. Clarinda and I roused her from sleep and straightened her clothes. We called for John, who carried Emily to the front room and gently placed her, whimpering, in the sedan.

"Sorry, love," Clarinda soothed, "there's no room to lie you down. Home soon."

I blew out the candle, and we left the shop. I locked the door behind me, noticing that the street had quieted after sundown. There was a serenity to the night, the air still.

Clarinda's husband held the front of the sedan chair again, his shirtsleeves rolled back to reveal ropy brown arms, muscles catching the moonlight. John replaced Clarinda's son at the rear but made room for Oliver to help him. Clarinda and her son and I walked a few steps behind the sedan chair and off to the side. No one looked at us twice.

At Emily's house, Clarinda spoke in a low tone to Emily's mother and father before they took her in the house, both openly crying. I turned to thank Clarinda again but she and her husband disappeared into the night with the empty sedan chair, their son in tow.

John and I turned away.

"Thank God you are unharmed," John said fiercely, thinking it could have been me. "I'll teach Oliver to use the shop pistol."

"John, no. He's a boy."

"He is old enough."

"We should check with his family. He's not our child."

"I'll speak with his father, then, but I doubt he'll protest. As soon as possible."

We turned onto Front Street, which was alive with taverns and coffeehouses.

"Fancy a drink?" John asked me.

I almost sagged in relief. "I certainly do." This day had been a month long, at least.

We chose a quiet tavern in the front room of an old house with an arched door and settled into a table that overlooked the street. Only two tables were taken, and no one had looked up when we entered. The owner had propped the door open, letting the summer air in.

Our drinks arrived.

"To you," John said. "My wife."

No wine tonight for me. I took a long swallow of rum and shuddered at the burning taste at the back of my throat.

"Tell me about your day," I said. "Tell me about the meeting. I heard people say it was fiery."

"Are you sure you want to hear it? Why don't I tell you tomorrow? You've had a long day. Your poor friend. We'll hunt those men down, Betsy, I promise you."

"I don't want to think about what they did to Emily. If it had happened to me, I don't know how I could go on. I'm just not that brave. I would be so afraid all the time, always looking over my shoulder. So please tell me about your day. I need to think about something else."

John held my hand, his finger caressing the top of a fly bite I had picked into a scab.

"I have to think about where to start. I've never seen anything like it, and I've lived in Philadelphia all my life. Thousands of people came. Not hundreds, Betsy, thousands. More than those who came to protest the tea landing. So many people poured into the State House yard that they couldn't hold the meeting inside. I think it even surprised the committeemen."

"Oh my." I could not picture it, and yet I could. Every customer that had stopped by the shop spoke of the melee that was taking over the State House.

"People were shouting, yelling to be heard. The crowd was—I wish you could have been there—*alive*, like a swarm of bees. And not just men. Women too, and their families. Rejecting the tea has begun to stand for freedom, that became clear. If there ever was a question about that, there isn't any doubt now. Philadelphia sees the Tea Act and the East India Company tea as symbols of outright oppression."

"What about the people who want the tea?" I asked. "The people who support Britain? The Tories. Surely, they had a say there too."

"Not as much as you'd think. Maybe they were just not as loud."

"So what happened?"

"By the end of the day, the resolves from last week were agreed to. Pennsylvania has formally declared the Boston Port Act to be wrong. Unacceptable. Word will be sent back to Boston in support."

My Quaker bones were shivering like the leaves of a tree turning upside down, warning of an incoming storm.

"They decided a congress is in order, and it looks like it will be held here in Philadelphia. A continental congress, they're calling it. Representatives from every colony are going to come. Apparently, it was Virginia's idea."

My husband's hand was curved loosely around his cup, but his fingers drummed the side restlessly.

"When?" I asked.

"The date has not been set. I would guess September or October, to give time for news to reach everyone and for the worst of the summer heat to pass. The delegates will need time to travel. Pennsylvania has to decide which men will represent us at the congress."

"Perhaps England will back down now to prevent this," I suggested.

John shook his head. "I doubt it. They're set on watching their punishment play out in Massachusetts. What sort of government do we have, that they would throw their own citizens into hunger and despair over the actions of a hundred men?"

"There is strength in numbers," I considered. "If this . . . continental congress . . . does take place. Word will get back to the king."

John grinned. "The king won't see this coming. That's for sure. He thought the colonies would agree with the punishment of Boston. As a kick to lawlessness."

"And I don't suppose Governor Penn will do anything," I said. "He still hasn't."

"By not taking a stand one way or the other, John Penn has allowed Pennsylvania to fester," John said. "He's done nothing. Our governor was supposed to lead us."

"Was there fighting at the meeting today?" I asked. "Tempers out of hand?"

John shook his head. "Surprisingly, no. Plenty of boos and jeers. The speakers called for peaceable discussion. By the end, a committee of forty-three was agreed upon to respond to Boston's call for help. It's going to be a long summer."

My mind was spinning. How could anyone know what to make of this? A proposed congress with men coming to Pennsylvania from all thirteen colonies, violence over tea, crowds in the State House yard. Boston harbor still shut down and under military guard.

"I'll tell you one thing, Betsy," John said. "The tradesmen aren't pleased about today. They're pushing hard for non-importation with Britain again to force them into a corner and get the situation resolved as quickly as possible. The mechanics weren't having any of it."

"That will hurt us," I said, thinking of what Webster had gone through during the year we weren't importing goods from Britain in 1769.

"The leaders want to negotiate with Britain," John finished. "It's only a matter of time until the king realizes that punishing Boston has only brought all the colonies together. That's never happened before. Not like this."

I took another sip of rum and made a face as its heat seared my throat. A sudden giggle escaped me. Here I was, a former Quaker girl, sitting in a tavern, sucking back rum and listening to my husband talk of how our city was going to organize against the crown. If my father could see this, he'd have an apoplexy. I almost snorted with laughter, the thought was so funny to me.

"What?" John said, half smiling as if he had missed the joke.

I shook my head. "Nothing, my love. Long day. I'm a bit punchy."

I wanted this summer of discontent to end. My life was finally as I wished it to be. I should have been sitting here as a married woman, happy, with no more in my head than what to make for supper or sewing a baby gown. A year ago, I had been planning my marriage. Our happiness and union had been hard earned over several years, and I had hurt many people at home and in the meetinghouse to be with the man I loved. Now that happiness was being threatened with all this strife. To the devil with 1774!

"Are you well?" my husband asked me, concerned. "You're making a strange face. We'll go home now. Forgive me for keeping you out so late in your weak condition."

"I'm well," I said, and I meant it. It felt like a balm to be sitting here, not sewing or working or tending house. Or caring for the victim of a rape. "I was just thinking that it grieves me to see what's happening. In two months, we've gone to hearing about the troubles in Boston to organizing committees and militia companies. How is it possible? I was hoping to be happy newlyweds."

John finished his drink. "We are happy newlyweds."

"I want to turn back the clock. Can we go back in time to before the Tea Act, before our baby passed, before . . . Emily. . . got hurt."

John reached out a hand and cupped my cheek like he often did. "If only."

"Philadelphia seems crazed." The city was spitting people out like embers thrust from a fire. How had we become a rebel city so quickly?

"Come, love. Let us be done with this day."

I didn't want the congress to take place. All those men could stay in their own towns. I wanted another baby to take root within me, burrowing in my flesh until I could hold her in my arms and keep her safe. I wanted John to stop meeting with the Sons and getting fired up by his ranting uncles.

"Take me home." Despair was poking me gently, a bony finger in my side, warning me to listen. A sound, barely there, but rising.

Go away. I was overwrought, and yet I felt afraid.

Afraid of what? I asked myself. *Just go home and go to bed. All will be well.*

John's arm was around me, and the summer air closed in on us like damp linen as we headed for home.

Chapter 21

July 1774

I did not see Emily for almost a month. I worried about her constantly and thought about her every day with my head bent over my sewing. I sent messages to the house and little gifts here and there: a summer pie, a crate of berries, a new tablecloth I'd embroidered. I wanted to call at the house to speak to her mother, but I was reluctant to intrude upon their privacy.

They had not caught the men who had abused her. The jackets they were wearing had been stolen to encourage trust. Everything about them had been false, a staged work of trickery and deceit. They weren't seen around town. I couldn't help my eyes straying to every man's neck for the telltale birthmark, but it was largely assumed that, as Clarinda had predicted, they had skipped town.

For weeks, I waited to hear until finally one day I knocked on Clarinda's door, begging for news of Emily.

"She is recovering," Clarinda told me with her usual calm. "Let her come to you. In her own time."

"I pray that she will," I said. "I do not wish her to feel embarrassed to see me. To equate me only with that day. I thought she would send word, or her family would."

Clarinda eyed me coolly. "You are an anxious one, aren't you? It wasn't your fault. If you must do something, pray for her. I think you will find her to be healing well. She is young and strong. Emily just needs time, and the strength of those who love her around her."

I nodded, turning to go, satisfied that Emily was recovering. Then I remembered the time I had sought out Clarinda for help conceiving a child. I should ask again. "Could I have a tincture—" I began.

She shook her head. "I think not. No. The fates have spoken. I'm sorry, Betsy."

She smiled and closed the door on me, leaving me no chance for further conversation.

I resigned myself to carrying on as before, even though it felt as though I couldn't turn back the clock to what our lives had been before this summer. My days had a cadence to them, home to the shop and back again. We worked long days with the windows and door propped open against the heat and close air, hoping for any breeze that would offer a reprieve.

The streets began to stink in earnest when the rain stayed away and garbage lay rotting undisturbed. Although I wasn't usually one for envy, on the hottest days I couldn't help but long to be one of the ladies who glided into the shop in their thin linen and muslin, their smooth white hands sorting through fabric samples to place orders before they left for their summer homes in the country. I pictured them lounging by a cool river or sleeping with the windows flung open to sweet country air that wasn't marred by the stink of shit and piss, both human and animal. I imagined long strolls through manicured gardens during the golden hour, the sun casting a sweet yellow glow on its way to bed. How nice it would be, I thought, to have servants who would cook and clean and prepare ice cream for you as you awoke from an afternoon nap that escaped the worst of the day's sun. My hands were bronzed from bargaining in the market, my skin covered in fly bites, bug scars speckling my skin like stars scattered against the sky. Although I wore my bonnets religiously when I was outside, freckles marched over the bridge of my nose, and I looked very much like the worker I was. I didn't mind that so much; I was proud to have a trade, proud of our artistry. It was the heat I couldn't abide.

"Your freckles are sweet," John had said, tracing a finger over my nose, connecting the brown dots. "They give you an impish air. Sprite-like."

230 • Wendy Long Stanley

I'd laughed and swatted his hand away. "They remind me of measles. I think if I grew a second head, you would find it endearing."

That July we had the most orders since we'd opened our doors. Philadelphia was hosting a provincial congress on the twenty-first in order to choose the delegates for the continental congress, among other matters, and the city was alive with summer visitors. Customers from out of town shopped for sheets and bedspreads and the latest in window dressings.

I was happiest in the evenings, treasuring time alone with John. Sometimes we stayed home; other times we wandered through town seeking a meal or a cold drink or visiting friends and family. These were the times I had longed for at Webster's before we married, when we could only stare at each other over our work in the workshop full of people or steal a word outside by the privy. Even now, living together, working together, we never ran out of things to talk about. He could make me laugh. We were always deep in conversation or chuckling over a funny story.

"I thought I'd ask my Uncle George round tonight," John said late one afternoon after the provincial congress had ended. "He's in town from Lancaster, and I'd like to see him. He may be glad of company. And a meal."

"You just want to learn all the gossip," I teased him. There was never a shortage of good conversation when we saw George. He had impressed me when I met him at the wood-chopping contest. I had liked his wife, Ann, too, when I met her, before she'd died last year. George and John seemed more like brothers than uncle and nephew, they were so alike, and I often forgot that more than twenty years separated them by age, such was the strength of the rapport between them. They shared political viewpoints, which was interesting to listen to.

"I'll make a fish loaf," I said. "Unless you think he'd prefer a cold plate—meats and pickled beets. The heat, you know."

"Fish," John said and kissed me. "I'm going to swing by the State House and invite him. They should be getting out soon. Do you mind closing up? Oliver can help you. I sent him to deliver the window valances to the Reinholds, but he'll return soon."

"I won't need to stay late. We've finished most of what we needed to do today."

Oliver dropped me off at my house, and I gave him a couple of molasses cakes for his trouble. I didn't think I needed a chaperone. It seemed so silly on these bright summer days, but after what had happened to Emily, I did not argue. It made John feel better.

I made the fish loaf and hung it over the hearth to cook. A short while later I went outside to hang the quilt. I had spot-cleaned a few marks on it that the cat had made coughing up a hairball and thought I'd air it out on the line to dry.

"Hello," Emily said.

"Emily!" I jumped. "You gave me a fright!"

I put the clothes pegs down and turned to her.

"My brother is out front," she said.

"Does he want to come in? Will you have a chocolate with me?"

She shook her head. "I can't stay long."

Tension hung between us, that terrible day we found her injured at the upholstery.

"I'm happy you're here," I said, pushing the dark thoughts away, wanting her to feel comfortable and welcome. "I have thought of you so often."

"Thank you for everything you sent to the house. Mother told me."

I nodded, searching her face. What could I say? "I'm so sorry that I didn't—that day—"

Emily's face closed, a lid on a chest banging down, and she dropped her eyes. "I'm back at work now. At Webster's."

"Oh. You are?"

"He's still not doing well, though. It's not like it used to be. Father's going to help me look for work as a seamstress."

"How fine." I smiled at her. "You deserve the chance to make lovely clothes. That's what you've always wanted."

"Even if I wanted to stay there, which I don't, Webster doesn't have a lot of work coming in. He's talking about closing up again. This time I think it will happen."

"I'm sorry to hear that," I said sincerely. "He was good to me, to us. John and I cut our teeth there, learned our trade." It had been the best training possible, really. We were fortunate.

Emily shrugged again.

"John's uncle is coming for supper," I said. I wiped beads of sweat from my forehead. Even now in late afternoon, the sun was merciless. "You could stay too. And your brother?"

She shook her head. "I don't want Mother to worry."

"You could come back, and we could embroider together? Or go have a look in the shops?"

"Maybe." Emily looked at me. There was something impenetrable in her eyes.

I felt my heart beating above my stays in the pause while I waited for her to speak.

"I'm so glad you came," I said again. "I hope you do not feel—"

"Mother's having a ladies' circle next Sunday evening. Why don't you come?" Ah. She was welcoming me back into her life.

"I will," I said quickly. I knew she did not want to speak of what happened. I could not blame her. I wouldn't speak of it, either.

She nodded and left, her back straight and shoulders stiff. Good, I thought, good. Better to fight than to crumble. She would be all right, or as all right as possible after enduring what she had.

I picked up my pegs and secured the quilt on the line. The sun was still plenty strong enough to help dry the spots I'd scrubbed by nightfall. Suddenly, the sky crackled overhead and there was a resounding boom far away. A late day thunderstorm was moving in, as happened so frequently during these hot summer days. The sun had made a liar out of the sky.

I took the pegs off again and loaded the quilt into my arms to lug it back inside. I'd hang it over a door for a few hours. If the entire thing got wet it in the rain, it would be a sodden mess.

*

"Betsy, you've outdone yourself," Uncle George said as he finished off the meal.

"You are too kind," I said. "It's just humble fare. But thank you, Uncle George. Will you have stewed apples and cream?"

He shook his head. "I must watch my girlish figure," he said, patting his stomach with a grin. He had undone the bottom buttons of his waistcoat, as was the custom now, and his shirt peaked out from beneath.

I took the plates and dumped them in the wash bowl for later. It was raining hard, the water hitting the window with force. Lightning split the sky over and over again between booms of thunder. The temperature had dropped when the storm moved in, and with it a new patch of air that wasn't nearly as heavy and choking.

"Mother Nature giving us a good one," Uncle George said as the window rattled.

"How is your family?" I asked him. They must miss Ann terribly.

"Well," he said, "although I cannot match my children's wit or energy," he added wryly.

"We look forward to having those troubles of our own one day," John said. "The rain has thwarted my plan to sit outside, so shall we go to the front room?" John had recently picked up some secondhand chairs and reupholstered them in a nice cheerful floral. Slowly, we were piecing together a comfortable home in our little rented rooms.

"I'll bring coffee in," I told them.

"Did you hear the latest from Boston?" John asked his uncle.

"Barbarous," Uncle George was saying as I walked in with the tray laid out with cups and cream. "All of it. They won't get away with their brutality. We're right to protest the Intolerable Acts. We won't stop."

"What news from the provincial gathering?" John asked.

"Ah, now that is the question." Uncle George reached for the cup I'd placed in front of him, waving off an offer of cream. "Talk of the coming congress, of course. Mostly, there is talk of how to convince Britain to be fair. And the question of how hard to push back." He crossed his legs and took a swallow of coffee, closing his eyes briefly as he inhaled the aroma.

"How do we do that?" John asked.

"There's talk of a letter to the king. That's what I'm hoping will happen in September at the continental congress. A discussion of terms to agree to remain united in the empire."

"You're a delegate, then?" John said. "That's official?"

George nodded. "I'm pleased to say I am. Pennsylvania has elected seven of us to represent."

"This is marvelous news!" John's hand thumped his leg.

"Edward Biddle as well. And George Read will be representing Delaware. You have three uncles that will be in the continental congress."

I knew John was relieved to have family members who would be present during the historic session.

"Will delegates really travel all the way to Philadelphia from all thirteen colonies?" I sat down with my own coffee. "It's such a long way for the men from New Hampshire or South Carolina. Or anywhere, really, outside of Pennsylvania. Except maybe just across the river in New Jersey."

"We've done similar gatherings before," George said. "In 1765, to respond to the Stamp Act—"

"And twenty years ago, to deal with the Indians," John finished. "In Albany."

"Although not all colonies came," George mused. "This will be different. Too much is at stake. Imagine if all the colonies send representatives to Philadelphia!"

"Thank God we set up the Committees of Correspondence when we did," John said.

"Indispensable now," George agreed.

"Perhaps," I said, rising, taking my cup with me, "I will leave you two to it."

"Forgive us the talk of men," George said. "How boring for you, my dear."

"No, no," I said. "I simply don't wish to be in the way. Pay me no mind. I'll get the dishes sorted."

They were deep in their politics again before I even reached the door.

"What the Intolerable Acts have done is make compromise more difficult," George told John. "The king has shown his hand. The closing of the port was one thing. But then the additional measures . . . unconscionable."

"Hard to reason with that," John said. "An appeal seems a stretch."

"He'll show no mercy, I predict."

In the other room, I poured water in the kettle and set it to boil to warm the water to clean the dishes. Long after I finished cleaning up and darning a stocking of John's, I still heard the men in the other room, their voices intent, talking heatedly late into the evening as the rain lashed the window. Never a lull in the conversation. I wasn't listening until I heard John ask his uncle if he thought the British would target Philadelphia.

I had a sudden image of warships pinning us in from the Delaware River, cannons pointed at our long line of bustling docks and soaring church spires.

No, that wouldn't happen. Or was that what Boston had thought too?

Chapter 22

September 1774

When I got to Emily's house, the yard was empty. The sky was overcast, as dark as pewter. The sparse amount of sun that day had spared Philadelphia the searing heat of late summer, and the untethered animals of the city were sharing their gratitude by wandering lazily through the roads instead of lying panting in what shade they could find. I passed a goat munching on the low branches of a yew tree.

I knocked on the door, noticing all the detail Emily's mother had added to the home. A carved wooden bear by the door, bunches of chrysanthemums in bottles on the step. A mobile of paper doves danced from the eves like a flock of seagulls, spinning and dipping in the air. There were children's toys on the ground by the step.

"You came," Emily said, stepping aside to let me in.

"Well, of course I did," I said, untying the strings of my cap and putting it on the coat tree by the door. "It seems a bit quiet. Did you say—"

"Unfortunately, Mother came down with a beastly headache that took away her vision and put her in bed. The ladies' circle has been postponed."

"Oh, I'll go," I said quickly, reaching for my cap. "Let her rest."

"No, please." Emily stopped me. "Betsy, truly. My mother sleeps like the dead. The house could be on fire and she would need a bucket of water in her face to wake. Father says it's how she has survived all us children in the house all these years. I would have sent word if I didn't want you to come."

"If you're sure," I said.

"I would love your help, actually," Emily said, leading me to the back room where the family crafted. "I'm making stays, you see, and I'm trying to work out how many ribbon holes I need at the front."

We settled in at the table pushed to the side of the room, a large rectangle of walnut, lightened in parts by use, scratched with wear.

"Father took the young'uns to the river," she said when she saw me looking around. "A month from now, it will be too cold to swim. Gave Mother some peace."

I nodded, reaching for the fabrics on the table. "These are very finely woven," I said, fingering the fabric. They had been cut to the pattern pieces already and looked ready to assemble.

"The brown linen is for the front," Emily explained. "The white linen is for the lining." She held up thin pieces of whalebone and a heavy cotton buckram.

"Are these for you?" I asked.

She nodded. "I've made them before, but I want to make a change to the front." She showed me the back, where the two pieces of cut fabric would join together, ten holes on either side. When together, they would lace closed with a sturdy ribbon.

"These look good so far," I commented. "I haven't made stays myself, but they're well crafted. I have my clothes made so I can focus on upholstering, although sometimes my mother will make me something."

"The last time I made stays the front tie was decorative," Emily explained. "I want to see if I can make the front laces functional. I'd like to be able to put them on without undoing the back."

I picked up the front sections and placed them together as they would be when worn.

"Four holes on either side?" Emily asked, pointing to the top center.

I shook my head. "No, two per side. You want a concentrated spot to close them. If you have too many holes, it will be more complicated and not as easy to secure."

She nodded. "I see. I knew you'd know."

"Flattery will get you everywhere," I said. "But I draw the line at working with whalebone."

"When you're not in your shop toiling away."

"Exactly," I laughed.

Emily began adding the holes to the front of her stays, two on each side, as I'd said, and I helped rim them in eyelet thread so they would be secure when closed with ribbon. They had to be strong enough to withstand multiple wears.

After that, I sat and watched her work. Emily was different with this work than she had been at Webster's, her face intent and almost reverent. It seemed to bring a quiet joy to her. I could see why she wanted to craft ladies' garments and told her so.

"Oh, let me show you!" she said, jumping up. "I made sketches of a formal dress for when I go to a ball or fancy party. Or maybe for my wedding day."

She came back with a sketch. "This is what I'd like to make."

"What color?" I asked, looking at the charcoal drawing.

Emily sighed happily. "The petticoat is white silk. The overskirt is blue satin, a robin's egg blue. A most stunning blue."

She turned the paper over. "Ta da! And the back is a sacque back! Look at the flow of fabric from the back of the neckline."

Her sketch was extraordinary. Every detail was there, exquisitely completed by the finest pencil stroke. I could see the line of flounces that ran down each side, the careful ruching the elaborate design would require. Elbow length sleeves, falling in flounces to a curtain of lace that ended at the forearm.

"It's superb, but sacque back is a little dated now," I said. "Don't you think?"

"I don't care, I think it's beautiful. It's also lined with white linen and white mohair," Emily explained dreamily.

"And the stomacher?" I inquired.

"A matching shade of blue but slightly darker, with silver embroidery."

"Emily, it's absolutely celestial," I said. "This is exquisite. You must make this and wear it one day."

"I'll need a hair ornament," Emily agreed. "Or a headdress. Something that catches the light and complements the dress."

"Exquisite," I said again. It truly was. She would be a vision in it, with her dark hair and alabaster skin.

She held the sketch out, looking at it, and I was surprised to see a little wet spot on the paper. A tear.

"Thank you," Emily whispered, not looking up from the sketch. "For what you did for me."

"Of course." My voice caught in my throat. "You would have done the same. I just wish that I had sensed that those men were—"

"Please stop saying that. You couldn't have known. But remember: no one must ever know what happened."

"And no one will."

"Sometimes I worry," she whispered, swiping her eye with a fist. "That they'll come back."

"Please do not think that. They are hunted men. Between John and your father, they wouldn't stand a chance. I believe that." I prayed that it was true. Philadelphia had mostly petty crimes—thievery and random brawls. What she had endured, the carnal abuse, was rare, and it would have shocked the city had anyone been permitted to know that two rapists were on the loose.

"I do not think I've ever had a friend like you," Emily said, raising her eyes to mine. "I'll not forget what you did for me."

"Please do," I said. "Forget it all. Take it from your mind."

"I would do anything for you. I want you to know that. Anything." Emily paused. She cleared her throat. "That is the last time I will speak of this."

She was giving me her loyalty, placing a crown on my head and her sword at my feet. I felt the weight of her pledge, saw her conviction that she would defend me always. I had not done anything that any caring person would not have done to try and help her. I wanted no laurel upon my head. We were all connected to God; we all had access to the same light.

"Clarinda says you are healing well," I said.

Emily nodded. "I have healed, yes. She says I should be able to have children. I will have to pray that my husband never suspects."

"Surely, you do not intend to deceive the man you marry," I said, taken aback. "You should be able to trust—"

Emily turned away, and her faced slammed closed.

"I'll show you a trick I learned for managing the whalebone placement," she said in a pleasant voice.

I blinked at the sudden change of conversation.

That was exactly what she intended. We weren't going to discuss it.

*

In spite of myself, I had to admit the congress was good for Philadelphia. My town had never been more popular, it seemed, and it was an exciting time. Philadelphia was humming with activity.

The streets were filled with people. Although there were only fifty or sixty men who had traveled to town for the congress, news of the gathering was widespread, and we seemed to be swollen with spectators, newspapermen, families of some of the delegates, and an increase in visitors who were anxious to be part of what was happening. The increase in bodies was matched by an increase in horses and carriages rattling through the streets. I swore even the bugs and flies rose in number as a supporting cast.

As the proceedings got underway, many people waited outside Carpenters' Hall for news of what was being said in the large assembly room inside. But the delegates had taken a vote of confidence and revealed nothing about what was going on behind the shuttered windows. When they adjourned for the day, town gossips would follow them about, harassing them for details on what was being decided in the sultry interior, but Carpenters' Hall was shut up like a fortress every day despite the stifling heat, and when the men spilled out at the end of the long days, their lips were firmly sealed. Week after week they revealed nothing, a bond of secrecy meant to discourage public uproar.

When the men weren't in session, they were about town, eating and drinking in the city's establishments, or shopping, or adding bodies to the city's church pews on Sundays. In addition to the men attending from twelve colonies—Georgia's royal governor had prevented the election of delegates—many other men in authority came to town as the weeks wore on to join in the conversations in the taverns.

To my surprise, the bell on our upholstery door chimed repeatedly as newcomers entered seeking some of the fine upholstered Philadelphia goods they had heard about. We had never been busier, so much so that John took to making extra trips down to the warehouses to try and bargain for cloth as soon as ships were arriving.

"Part of me feels sorry for those men in there," I told John as we walked to church one day at the end of September, noticing the cupola of Carpenters' Hall framed against the sky like a domed cake. "They're boxed in like cigars in this heat. The air must be so unbearably close and sticky."

"My uncle hasn't complained," John responded. "We'll have to ask him how they're faring."

Congress wasn't in session today since it was Sunday. "Maybe we'll see him at church," I said.

I stared at the pleasing shape of Carpenters' Hall as we drew closer. My father had been one of the men who'd helped build the hall and had purchased shares in it. It was only a few years old, everything inside new but rough and not completely finished. My father complained bitterly that they had run out of money to do the final treatments throughout, and indeed only a rough wooden step led the delegates from the street to inside. Still, the outside was striking, a two-story red brick building, with, according to my father, ten-foot cutouts at each corner, the walls thirteen inches thick. Carpenters' Hall featured one of the largest assembly rooms in the city after the State House. My father kept telling us how impressive the structure was, rhyming off numbers about trusses and tenon joints and the right mortise. Ben Franklin had even advised them on fireproofing the second floor.

The congress had met every day for three weeks. George Ross said there was no end in sight. John and I had assumed it would be over in a week or two.

"What do you think is taking so long?" I asked John as we got closer to Christ Church.

"Disagreement. Half the delegates support Britain and want things to be the way they were, and the others want a different way, demanding radical change."

"And you? What do you want? I know you don't like what's happening, but what if Britain softens?"

John considered this. "I'm not sure going backward is possible, not with the Intolerable Acts in place. If they can kick one colony hard, what's stopping them from doing it to the other twelve on a whim or at the slightest provocation? I'd rather see them finally give us representation over taxation. And trade rights."

Colonists called the Coercive Acts the Intolerable Acts. The Intolerable Acts forbade town meetings in Massachusetts without British approval, replaced the Massachusetts government with one appointed by parliament, and gave extra power to their royal governor. Power was being stripped from Massachusetts. By the severity of his actions and retaliation, the king had unwittingly united all of the colonies in a sweeping desire for reform.

"Talk about poking the bear with a stick," my father had said when news of all four of the Coercive Acts reached us. "Are they asking for war?"

We arrived to church a little early and stood outside lingering on the walkway.

"John." A man's voice, familiar. We looked up to see John's uncle walking up the path toward us with another man.

"This is my nephew, John Ross, and his wife, Betsy," George Ross said. "I'd like to introduce you to my friend George Washington, one of the delegates from Virginia."

"A pleasure," John said as I dipped in acknowledgment. "Since you're both George, you'll forgive me if I address you as Washington and Ross."

"That will be fine," Washington said, his voice tinged with humor. "We have no shortages of Johns either. Come to think of it, we've got several in congress: John Hancock, John Dickinson, John Adams, to name a few. I think there are six or seven Johns in all."

"What can I say? We're biblical," John quipped. "Gives us a higher standing."

"And funny enough, I have a half-brother also named John Ross," Uncle George told Washington. "Confusing but true. So there are two of them in the family."

"A good strong name," Washington said amiably.

He towered over me, this man from Virginia. I felt diminutive beside him and had to tilt back my head to see his face. There was a warmth about him, something calm and generally good-humored. The angle of my neck pushed my hat back, and the stark September sun hit my eyes. Squinting, I lowered my gaze to my feet. I was standing next to a gravestone, laid in the earth longways against the red brick of the church. Ann Graeme, I read. Died 1765.

"I wanted you two to meet," Uncle George told Washington. "Despite his young age, my nephew is one of the finest upholsterers in Philadelphia. He's done work for the Tilghmans, the Cadwaladers, the Shippens, the Chews. You two should speak." He lowered his voice. "And his alliances lie with ours."

Addressing my husband, George said, "John, Washington is in search of bed hangings for his wife. Their home is on the Potomac River in Virginia, a country estate."

Washington nodded. "I promised Mrs. Washington I would look for what she wants while I'm in Philadelphia. She's set on chintz. I've been married long enough to know better than to question her."

"We have both Indian and English," I offered, feeling shy. "The Indian chintz has a bold pattern that is hard to find, a distinctive black-and-white floral. You might find it agreeable if Mrs. Washington wishes to have something unusual. Although the English chintzes are striking as well."

"Why don't you come by the shop?" John said. "We're on Chestnut Street between First and Second Street. No shortage of chintzes or any other fabric you may wish to see. I keep a good stock."

Washington nodded. "Indeed, I will. Mrs. Washington won't be pleased if I return home without placing an order. Three sets, she said."

My husband looked pleased. Our business was doing well.

Uncle George stretched slightly, his hand at his lower back. "This is one time I'm glad for the velvet cushions on the pew," he said with a groan.

Washington laughed, a low, rich sound that reminded me of wood smoke. "Those damnable chairs, eh," he quipped. "Long hours."

"I'll never look at a Windsor chair again the same way," Uncle George said, referring to the wooden chairs in Carpenters' Hall, where the delegates were spending their days in heated discussion and elevated temperatures.

"Try being my height," Washington added wryly. "I'm folded in like a praying mantis."

They both laughed.

"We'll give you a cushion," John said cheerfully.

The church bells started ringing, and we turned to go inside.

*

It turned out that the delegates of the continental congress would not be released from those wooden chairs until the twenty-sixth of October. They had been meeting for so many weeks that the weather had turned from the heated days of late summer to the crisp mornings of fall by the time it was finally over. And I had finished sewing Washington's bed hangings by then, some of the finest work I'd done, including a sumptuous double drapery effect that would leave any woman breathless at its artisanship.

All of Pennsylvania held its breath—indeed all of the colonies—to hear the results of what had taken place at the congress in Carpenters' Hall, the building my father's hands had helped to construct. New terms were being used freely now: Tory and Whig. Pennsylvania was now divided between both, between the loyalists and the rebels. People either supported the king or they supported the Patriot cause. That's what everyone called it now. The cause.

When the news finally came of what had happened in the congress, it was extraordinary.

We were walking home from work, autumn leaves crunching underfoot, as John read from the pamphlet handed out all over town. This was the result of congress's six weeks of work. In addition to establishing an army, a navy, a post office and issuing currency, John read off something called the Suffolk Resolves as he held the brochure. There were more than a dozen items. I listened, trying to pick out the words that meant something. And there was more.

I think I heard that what was happening in Boston was deemed so unacceptable by all the colonies that Massachusetts was encouraged to stockpile military supplies, operate an independent government, refuse British goods, and give no allegiance to a king who failed to consider their wishes and their welfare.

The overbearing actions of the British must stop. A letter had been sent to George III, swearing our undying loyalty if he would withdraw the Intolerable Acts and restore the colonies to their previous rights.

A continental association had been formed that would refuse all goods from Britain as of March 1, 1775, and stop all exports to Britain the following September 1, 1775.

A second continental congress would be held here in Philadelphia again next May if the king did not respond favorably to the American requests for redress.

"Interestingly," John said, "the date for the second congress implies that they expect to be disappointed. Sadly, I don't think they're expecting much from our king."

I suddenly felt it again, that bony finger of despair poking me.

Careful, careful.

Chapter 23

February 1775

"I'm still not with child," I complained to my mother as we stood folding sheets in her bedchamber. We doubled the sheet over in sequence, stepping toward each other, the bundle getting smaller and smaller until she took the folded sheet from me and sat on her bed. I tried not to remember the last time she had sat there, in that very spot, pitching objects at my head. I stole a furtive look at the door: the dent was still there.

I moved to sit beside her, enjoying our effortless visits and conversation. It was much easier being a married woman visiting home than a girl trying to marry the wrong man.

"It's been a year now," she said thoughtfully. I realized with a pang of guilt that she did not know I had lost a child last year. It seemed too long ago to bring up now.

"More than a year," I said. "I have faith. I just wish it would happen soon." My mother had birthed seventeen children. My married sisters didn't seem to be struggling either.

"You've always dreamed of having children of your own," she said. "Always so helpful and patient with the little ones who came after you. You were a great help to me, Betsy. You still are a great help."

She put a hand over mine. "Try not to let your mind weigh heavily on it, for that cannot possibly do any good. Do you have any reason to believe there is a problem?"

I shook my head, "No. I don't think so. John has been so anxious and distracted by the imperial crisis. And we've been working so hard in the shop. Maybe that's it."

I glanced up at my parents' upholstered headboard and then down at the matching bedcover. Much had changed in ten years. My father was doing well as a carpenter and in the union. We had seldom had fabrics this fine when I was a child. When we moved into this house, I was twelve, and all our beds were basic and dressed with simple inexpensive fabrics. I still remember the day we moved in. My sister Deborah loved the name of the street, Mulberry, but Mary was upset because she wanted to be closer to the river. I smiled thinking of it. They were both a long way from Mulberry Street now, as was I, even though I was just a stone's throw away across town.

It had been an achievement for my father to move his burgeoning family from New Jersey into Philadelphia and have the opportunity to own and expand this house. Certainly, all of the initial investment had gone into the bones, the curving staircase, the spacious front room by the street, the milk-glass windows and large cellar. Over time, they had added more expensive furnishings to it. My mother's latest acquisition was a set of lion-clawed chairs in the dining room, stained to match her grandfather's high dresser behind them.

"How's the shop doing?" my mother asked me, standing up to dust the window frames.

"We've been busy with bed hangings and cushions," I told her. "Items that can travel. Some of the men who were in town for the congress in the fall placed orders with us. We are feeling very fortunate. No shortage of work."

My mother frowned at the mention of the congress. Our ease with each other seemed to rely on not speaking about politicking, or Christ Church and being Episcopalian, or any of John's opinions.

"You're not getting involved in any of that, I hope," my mother said. "The protests and such."

I hesitated. "John's uncle George was a delegate at the congress. He's been an assemblyman for years so he has seen the conflict unfold. I think you knew that? I told you he was a delegate, I remember. He has very strong views and a tongue that could convince anyone of anything; he's so good with his words. He's a lawyer out in Lancaster, and he must be good at it since he speaks so convincingly. Anyway, all of John's family is very involved in the cause, not just George. John as well."

"The cause?" she said.

"That's what they call it now. Mama, I don't want to upset you. Let's not speak of it. Shall we go down and get something hot to drink? It's so cold today."

The snow was gusting against the row of brick homes and piling high in the streets where there was a space between houses. The wind made a keening noise and pushed the snow out and over the clearing.

My mother came back and sat on the bed again. She laid a hand on my knee and patted me. "Loyalty to king and country," she said simply. "God is in the silence. Do not forget that, Elizabeth."

I looked at her, at her pretty, aging facing that was so dear to me. Why would I try to convince her of the soundness of the argument if she could never hear it?

John and Uncle George had spent the last five months organizing and leading attempts to ward off any possible altercations or military engagements with Britain. I wasn't sure what silence had to do with any of that or how it would help. This was the problem with the Society of Friends, I thought. When surrounded by people that did not value or cultivate peace, what help was it for Quakers to preach peace? It seemed like trying to persuade a hungry wolf that they should just be friends with the hare and go eat some berries instead.

I knew the Quaker annual meeting a few months ago had published strict edicts on not getting involved in the controversy with Britain. My father had dropped by the house to leave me a copy. Fathers would be fathers, and he hoped he could appeal to the old part of me. Maybe he hoped I'd always be a Quaker girl, disguised as a wife in a Church of England pew. My Uncle Abel told us that some Quakers were pulling away from meetinghouse rules, retreating from the assumption that we could continue on the same path we'd been on. I wished my parents were among them.

At Christ Church, the church ministry was divided as well. John and I saw them walking on eggshells. As a house of worship for the Church of England, Christ Church could not openly criticize the crown. Nor could they afford to lose parishioners who were upset by Britain's heavy hand. Each week the church leadership walked a precarious line between not supporting the protesters or rebels too much while at the same time voicing support for people of Massachusetts who suffered at the hands of the British.

"I wish none of this were happening," I said to my mother. I leaned my head on her shoulder. She smelled of cloves and anise seed. She laid her head on top of mine. I caught sight of the toe of my shoe and stuck my leg out to see the whole foot. Worn. I needed to visit the shoemaker. I couldn't remember the last time I had ordered new shoes. I'd shed my winter boots downstairs and put on the house shoes I'd brought with me to ward off the chill of the cold floorboards.

"John wants me to do more for the cause," I confessed. "Be more involved, more outspoken. But the truth is I'm not a rebel. I detest the haranguing, the arguments, the hate. I should be holding babies in my arms, not holding protest meetings in our house. I'm not brave like he is."

My mother smiled against my hair. "You are my sweet Quaker girl. You must remember that."

"That I'm not brave?" I joked. "Or that I'm your Quaker girl?"

"That you're committed to the truth."

Her truth, she meant. The Quaker truth of not taking up arms or going against parliament or protesting. No matter if laws were being passed to make money from us, and all the other insulting slaps, as John would say. How long had it been since Boston was placed under siege? Years, really, because even before the Boston Port Act, there had been standing armies in Boston since 1768 trying to control the folks who resisted the Townshend Acts. The soldiers of the

British army were much hated there. You didn't have to read the newspapers to know that. Folks talked.

"The truth shall set us free," my mother added piously.

"I hope so, Mama."

"The babies will come, Betsy," she said comfortingly. "Mark my word."

*

John was outside clearing snow from our door when I trudged home through the snow. I stopped next to him, waiting for him to see me.

"My parents say hello," I said when he looked up. He grunted absently, his face tense.

"What?"

"There's news," John said. "Word has come. I heard in the coffeehouse today."

"Tell me."

John wiped the sweat on his brow with the arm of his coat and leaned on his shovel. "We've learned that the king made a speech to parliament at the end of November. He says the colonies are obstructing the due process of law and misbehaving. He called the situation criminal. That's the word he used: criminal."

"Oh." I lowered my hood from my cloak.

John banged the shovel, snowflakes gathering on his eyelashes. "We'll talk inside. This changes everything, Betsy. There can be no misunderstanding the situation we're in now."

"What does that mean?"

"I can't see how we can avoid war."

"I'll put the kettle on," I said resignedly. "And heat some chocolate."

*

March 1775

It was the first time I could remember being truly angry with my husband.

I thought when John joined the Freemasons it would satisfy his need to have more connection during these turbulent times, a need that couldn't be met by working with his wife, a child, and the temporary hired men in our upholstery shop. I understood that he needed more male company, more involvement with the resistance. I knew it was frustrating for John to have heated conversations with his Uncle George, a member of congress, or Edward Biddle, the new speaker in the assembly, and then have to spend hours in our small shop hammering venetian blinds or speaking with customers about whether the Indian block prints would be too overpowering on a curtain for their dining room.

I was not allowed to know what went on in the secretive male world of the Masons, but I had been told that the organization was about men coming together in the Freemason brotherhood to promote moral discipline and carry out acts of charity. Many customers I had met at Webster's, men I respected, were Masons, and I knew that John's membership would lead him further into the resistance with other like-minded men.

So I had celebrated with him when his membership with the Masons was approved and even helped him sew his gift of cushions for the lodge. I suspected many of the men involved in the resistance efforts were Freemasons, although I had no proof. Masons seemed to draw that type of men, like my husband, who strained toward the attainment of more in their lives, men that worked for justice, increased intellectual satisfaction, and a greater morality.

John seemed to be content with being a Mason. Then I learned that wasn't all he was doing.

I was at the washstand with a wet cloth on my face when he appeared behind me. He embraced me from behind and dropped a kiss on my ear.

"I'm going out, love. I'll be back this afternoon," he told me.

"Where are you going?" I asked from behind my cloth. He knew I didn't like it when he went to the gaming tables or cockfights. Thankfully, he only went there occasionally in the company of friends who insisted. I did not mind the horse races as much, they didn't seem to be as seedy.

"My militia company is drilling again. And then I have other meetings."

"What other meetings?" I paused, looking at him. "John, no."

I didn't know how I knew. Maybe it was the tone of his voice when he said "meetings," deliberately nonchalant to avoid discussion, or the way he'd come to tell me when I was covered in soap. Maybe it was the inflection of his words, an attempt to sound light when it was anything but. Or maybe I just knew him as well as I knew myself from having worked alongside him since I was fifteen years old and loving him as I did.

"John, what are you up to?" I said very slowly, drying my face, giving each word with the same inflection.

"Maybe it's best that you—"

"If you are about to tell me I should not know, I'm going to smack you," I said with uncharacteristic force, surprising us both. When I lowered my towel, John was still there, staring at me, but I did not apologize.

I had had enough of being told what to do, receiving unsolicited advice every which way I turned. My parents were repeatedly instructing me to avoid any and all resistance activity and warning John not to join any of the network of committees that had sprung up since October, after the delegates had ridden out of town when the congress ended. There were so many committees, springing up like wild strawberries everywhere. After the March deadline came for not importing goods from Britain, every ship's captain that docked in Philadelphia had to come into the London Coffee House by noon the next day to meet with committeemen who made sure their cargo wasn't illegal. Most goods that came into Pennsylvania by boat went through Philadelphia, the largest port, and the new committee made sure no one was going to slip illegal goods into land that had become the heart of the resistance against Britain.

I turned to John and put my hands on my hips. "John." I used my sternest voice. If my husband thought he could pat me on the head and disappear, he was sadly mistaken.

I thought I saw a smile tug at the corners of John's mouth, but he hid it quickly.

"I'm part of the ammunition and artillery committee under Robert Morris. We need to stockpile weapons, gather ammunition. We need to teach more men how to make saltpeter," he confessed.

"For God's sake."

"Betsy, it's not a game. If Britain decides to attack us, we need to be armed and supplied. We need to be able to defend ourselves."

"You seriously think they will attack us?"

"Everyone knows Philadelphia is the leader of the resistance. There could be armed conflict with the British, even if they don't take Philadelphia."

"Charles Thomson," I blurted out. "You're working with Charles Thomson too." How could I forget? Thomson was the man who owned an iron forge at Batsto in New Jersey. John told me that before we married. Thomson was now the lead voice in Philadelphia antagonizing the British, and a known Son of Liberty. He'd also been the secretary for the congress in the fall. His role had expanded rapidly in the last two years. Every protest in Philadelphia had Charles Thomson attached to it.

"For your safety, I don't want to talk of this with you. I don't want to have secrets from you, but if anything happens and you're forced to talk about me, my actions, it will protect you." John tried to hold me but I wiggled away. John was part of weapons gathering?

I drew the line at John on a weapons committee. Working for the cause, drilling on the green in a volunteer company, joining the Freemasons, that all seemed reasonable, given the suffering in Boston. But my husband actively acquiring explosives? No. He didn't need to be part of that. Someone else could do that job.

"No," I said to him, furious. "I don't want you doing that."

The silence grew between us as we stared each other down. John looked determined but desperate, and it was then that I realized he was afraid. My husband's love for me was butting up against his need to serve. The conflict was killing him; I could see it in his face.

"It's necessary," he said, worry in his eyes. "Betsy, I swear. I wouldn't do anything that would hurt us."

I sighed, softening. What good could come of me standing in his way? His duty was going to guide him anyway.

"All right," I said softly. "All right."

His eyes searched mine, doubtful, checking to see if I was still angry.

"Truly," I said. "Go. I know your heart. But please, John, please. Be careful."

He drew me hard into his chest, cradling me there. "I do not do this carelessly."

"The saltpeter is for powder production?" I asked. "What else are they stockpiling? Muskets, rifles? Bullets?"

"All of it," he said softly, striding away. "I'll be back for supper."

"Cannons?" I added mockingly, wanting to poke at him.

"If we're lucky," he called back.

When the door closed behind him, anger rushed in. What was happening to us? And why did my husband have to volunteer to lead the charge? I felt a sudden grief for our plans, for the life that I envisioned for us vanishing before my eyes. I'd thought our first son or daughter would have been here by now. I'd thought John and I would be making friends with other couples, growing in our stature in the upholstery circles, enjoying our social reach. I wanted to be on the same level as Plunket Fleeson and Thomas Weyburn, John's name said in the same breath as the best upholsterers in Philadelphia. More than that, I wanted peace.

*

I had let my husband go to his meeting with my blessing, but I was still fuming about him being on a weapons committee when my sisters stopped by to ask me to go sledding with them. Rachel stood there on my doorstep chewing a mitten while Hannah held our old wooden sled under her arm. Rachel was thirteen now, as short as our mother and me, Hannah nineteen and taller.

"Are you mad?" I demanded. "I'm not a child. How did Rebecca get out of this?"

Rachel shrugged. "Mama said we should come get you. Father ran into John and said you'd be in a state. Because of him going somewhere and doing something. I don't remember. Or maybe he didn't say. Anyway, we're here, so let's go."

"I have work to do."

"Mama said you'd say that," Hannah said. "We have orders to take you out. Besides, it's Saturday afternoon, and if John's not at home and you don't have to be at the shop with him, you can come out with us, yes?"

I could see that I was not going to avoid this.

"Can I collect a friend?" I asked. If I had been roped into this, maybe Emily would come too. "Her house isn't far."

Emily was delighted by the idea and brought along two of her brothers as well as a sled of their own. We would have made a festive group of six if my heart had been in it.

We walked past the hospital and up to a large hill that descended into a cemetery. Emily and I stood and watched as our younger siblings doubled up and took off on the sleds with shrieks of laughter.

Emily dropped to her back on the ground and made a snow angel.

"You look just as you must have as a little girl," I said, amused.

She patted the snow next to her, "Come on! Don't be a dullard."

Last month I had turned twenty-three. I did not feel like lowering myself into the snow and getting cold. Surely, part of the perks of being an adult meant you could be dignified when you wanted to. I shook my head. If I could avoid my turn on the sled, I'd do that as well. I didn't like winter, wasn't fond of snow, couldn't stand being cold and wet.

"Why so pouty?" Emily teased.

"For heaven's sake, I am not pouting. I could be warm by my fire at home. My sisters ambushed me."

Emily leapt up again and brushed off the snow. "You look like you're ill-tempered."

I shook my head, sighed, and watched the girls reach the bottom of the hill. The outing had not improved my mood, even though the snow glistened like diamonds where the sun shone on it and the sky beamed with silver light.

"Well, I for one am glad to be outdoors in the fresh air after the smoke of the fires all week," Emily said. "Winter makes my lungs ache."

"I should be at home preparing supper," I said. "And I've got the hearth to sweep out. The ashes are going to be as high as my knees."

"Why don't I come and help you? You said John will be out for a few hours. I'll do the dirty work and sweep the hearth. You can make the meal."

"That's kind of you," I said sincerely. "I accept."

I was grateful. Emily had been a good friend over the past few months. Her attack had made her older beyond her years, and she did not often resort to the capriciousness she had displayed when we were together at Webster's, but she was slowly returning to her happier self. I often forgot there was five years of age between us until days like this and she seemed much younger than I. She had become very attached to me, which I supposed was because we shared what happened that day of the fair. I knew Emily and her family were loyal to the British and didn't believe in the resistance movement, but that was the way it was with all our friends and family: we had fallen onto sides. Some people climbed from one side to the other and then back again.

"But honestly, Betsy," Emily said. "Why don't you get help? You seem to have found your footing at the shop. A kitchen girl or a maid? You and John are doing well enough now."

We were, but I couldn't say how non-importation and non-consumption would affect us over the coming year. Upholstery was a business for the well-to-do. The poor didn't order fine tassels or tailored curtains or thick mattresses stuffed with the best curled hair or feathers. If the city's merchants, importers, and shopkeepers had reduced income, that would spread across our neighborhoods to all trade in Philadelphia and impact all us craftsmen.

"Maybe soon," I said noncommittally. We still had sweet Oliver working with us. If I could only get him to do women's work. *Ha.*

Emily laughed when she saw her two brothers fall off the sled at the bottom of the hill. My own sisters seemed to be taking pleasure diving from the sled like acrobats. What a treat that must be after long hours at the Quaker School for Girls sitting in a desk. Rachel was still there, and Hannah was helping as an assistant.

"I don't think we'll be here long," I said, seeing the girls start trudging up the long sloping hill. They'd already been up and down a few times, and they were getting slower with each walk up to the top. "They're tiring pretty quickly."

"Oh, I just remembered!" Emily said. "I haven't told you. I have a new job at the millinery as a seamstress! With Mary Symonds. Well, an apprenticeship again, but still, it's a start."

"Oh, Em, that's wonderful. I'm happy for you!"

I wondered how that would go when women stopped being able to get all the fabrics they wanted from England.

Chapter 24

April 1775

If we thought 1774 was unruly, it was nothing compared to the mess that 1775 was becoming.

John and I managed to hang on at the upholstery and had work every day even as the city spiraled into chaos around us. All incoming boats in the Delaware River were viewed with suspicion, all cargo from Britain turned back. Rejected. We were glad we had stocked up when we did. We were far less busy at the upholstery, but we still had enough essential work to get by.

Philadelphia lurched from calamity to calamity, confused by the whiplashing of power, not understanding how the conflict would play out for any of us, especially us mechanics who worked the trades and were far down the line of decision-making. It was difficult to have a day without inflammatory news blanketing the city like a spray of red embers, searing on contact and threatening to light us ablaze.

After word reached the colonies of King George's refusal to acknowledge or respond to the petition so carefully crafted to him at the congress, a hard, invisible line became evident, carving Pennsylvania into sides. Our neighbors hissed accusations to both sides. *He's a Tory! He's a Patriot!* People on England's side were loyalists firm in their beliefs that the rebellion was wrong. Those who believed in the cause, and were against Britain, were zealous Patriots convinced change was needed. Quakers claimed not to have a side. Others fell back and forth between camps. There was great emotion in the streets. Whispered conversations under hats worn low. We couldn't keep track of the bursts of activity in the committees steering the resistance. People fought constantly.

Despite not wanting to get involved, even the Quakers couldn't remain neutral. John commented that the Friends had suddenly begun fundraising campaigns in order to send money to suffering families in Boston and that there were as many armed Quakers in uniform now as non-Quakers. "Whole companies, Betsy," John exclaimed, incredulous. "Of Quakers. Drilling!" I knew my father would not be among them. He was not alone; there were many Quakers who held the line and would not go against the laws of Pennsylvania, who saw themselves as peaceful and non-violent, first and foremost. Their ancestors had come to Pennsylvania to avoid being persecuted and had been assured of the safety of future generations of religious tolerance by William Penn. Military conflict was a direct pain to their souls.

Uncle George, Uncle Biddle, and Uncle George Read were frequent visitors to Philadelphia and could be found in our front room, huddled with my husband, sometimes over maps. John would disappear for hours at a time to go out to meet them in a tavern or coffeehouse. There was so much to-ing and fro-ing over resistance activities that I wondered how the men were getting any work done that brought their families an income. How was George Ross managing his law practice? How was George Read managing his? What about Edward Biddle in government?

Through it all, I tried to stay focused on what I could control so my imagination would not get the best of me. I still hoped that we would resolve the problems and reclaim a tenuous peace. Now that my time was less spoken for at the upholstery, John and I could often get our work done in half a day, and I would visit family and friends. I rekindled a few of my Quaker friendships with the girls I had gone to school with years before, enjoying the company of women.

If I was home alone when John was with his militia unit, or coming and going at odd times in his quest to arm Pennsylvania, I stitched a baby quilt to occupy my hours. Emily would come keep me company a few times a week, and I was grateful for her cheerful chatter. Made easier, I told myself, by her young age and not having to hear of politics and conflict. Sometimes her mood was grim, and I let her silence settle over us without trying to cheer her. Her mother had whispered to me that Emily had nightmares sometimes, night terrors that woke her screaming for mercy, and had asked for a lock on her bedchamber door. It may have helped Emily to unburden herself of her misery by speaking of her troubles with me, but she would not. As far as Emily was concerned, that night last September never happened. I learned to gauge her mood; I knew when I could jest with her and when she had retreated to a dark corner of herself. My concern lessened when those moments seemed to be fewer and fewer. Emily's ongoing recovery may have been the only positive step forward that spring.

I longed for some good news, any good news. Winter had been dark, long, and anxious. At some point between the deep freeze of Christmas and the thaws of March, I had convinced myself I could go visit the herb lady in the market again. Her herbs had worked once, why couldn't they work a second time?

"How do you know that wasn't what caused you to lose the babe?" John had asked me once. "What was in the tincture she gave you? Just give it time, love."

I didn't want to give it time. My hope for a child was the only thing I had to look forward to so far in 1775. The world was spiraling into madness.

I decided I would ask Clarinda before I went back to Frau Schmidt. Katharina. I hadn't really asked her specifically about medicinals and why she was making those dire predictions about my future children, or lack thereof, with John. She knew me better now, and I wasn't as cowed by her. Clarinda knew women and their bodies; she would know what herbs could cause harm. If she chose to spew nonsense, I would ask her to educate me on women's herbs. She was a woman of iron will—surely, she would respect a similar stance in another if I held firm.

I headed for the shops late Monday afternoon, intent on my mission but dallying over my weekly food purchases. I was relaxed, luxuriating in the feel of an hour away from work and hearth. I would go see Clarinda after my shopping.

"Mrs. Ross."

A lyrical voice pulled me out of my reverie. I was standing outside a stationer's, admiring the creamy paper displayed in the window.

"Mrs. Fergusson," I said, startled.

"How delightful to see you," she said, her voice warm and husky. "The weather is indeed a gift, is it not? Springtime is a salve to the soul. Even the smells are so fresh, all the tender shoots and blossoms. I saw you there and had to say good day." She was ten years older than me, at least, but her skin was as smooth and clear as new skin on a white plum.

"I have not seen you since that day at church," I said. "How are you, Mrs. Fergusson?"

Her pew had been empty for months, but word around town indicated that she was staying year-round at her estate in Horshamtowne now that means were reduced. At the church social after the service at Christmas, her husband, Henry, had been loudly denouncing the decisions of the new congress, mocking the delegates even, and John had made us leave, his eyes dark with anger.

She smiled, a little wistful half twist.

"I find myself rather ensconced in domestic concerns," she said enigmatically.

"Unavoidable for all of us," I sympathized. "You and Mr. Fergusson are well?"

"Yes, thank you."

I expected her to bid me good day and leave, but she lingered, and I searched for something to say.

"I saw in the paper that Graeme Park is for sale," I said finally. I had actually seen the advertisement when I was using the newspaper to insulate the side window from the cold draft whistling through, not reading it.

"We are not farmers," she agreed wryly. "The land has found the absence of my parents trying. We thought selling might be the right thing to do, although in this time of uncertainty, we cannot seem to find a buyer."

"Perhaps in the nicer weather," I murmured. "After the unrest settles down."

"Yes. Perhaps. It would be nice to be in town again. I miss it."

"I'm sure you do." I had heard about her glittering parties when she was a spinster.

She watched a little dog wander through the stalls, sniffing the ground hopefully.

"I must get on," I said awkwardly. "I do hope to see you at church when you're in town. How nice to run into you!"

Mrs. Fergusson smiled farewell, and we parted ways. I watched her walk away, elegant and self-contained, slim and straight-backed. Our husbands could not be further apart in their beliefs toward the troubles, I thought, which was a shame, as I very much liked her, but I thought her husband was a clodpate.

I had stopped to buy beans when a commotion in the road made me look up.

"What is happening?" I called up to a man on horseback who was motioning the crowd forward.

"News from New England!"

I pressed in, struggling to see around the taller people in front of me.

I could only catch every second or third word from where I was at the back.

"Lexington . . . Concord . . . shots."

Had I heard correctly? An armed conflict between the Massachusetts militiamen and the British army?

"The British have opened fire on their own," a man said grimly to his wife.

*

Something changed in me that day. I, who had been so sure of my beliefs, so convinced I was right to not get involved, began to squirm. Anger grew in me like tangled roots around my heart.

I rushed home and burst into the house to find John shaving at the basin. The cat was curled up in furry ball on top of the washstand. John was as stunned by the news as I was.

I tried to tell him what I heard.

"Wait, Betsy," he interrupted me, drying his hands. "Say that again. What happened?"

"An express rider," I fought for my breath. "He said Wednesday the British opened fire and dozens of Patriots were killed."

"God's bones," John muttered, hastily wiping his face off and reaching for his shirt. "Five days. I must go to the Sons."

"I want to help," I blurted. "I can't believe they fired at will. I can't imagine. . ."

He let me babble on, telling him what people were saying, what I'd heard, and that I knew now what could happen. I finally understood what my husband had been trying to warn me about all along.

He threw on his coat and walked past me.

"I want to help," I said again.

"Are you willing to make musket cartridges?" he asked, stopping at the top of the stairs to look back at me.

"Yes."

"Betsy, listen to me." He searched for words, his eyes piercing mine. "What we're doing, it's very dangerous. I need you to know that, to truly understand it. To feel it in your bones. If I get caught, if we get caught, if this ends badly, we may have to face the highest penalties."

He let the sober implications hang between us.

I nodded, strangely unemotional. I felt like my eyes were finally open, that I could see what he had seen all this time, right from the early days when the Massachusetts government would not let the tea cargo sail back home and then Britain had begun a strange dance of control and punishment of its people.

"Yes," I said simply. "I know."

"My little rebel," John said with great emotion. Were those tears in his eyes? In that moment, I understood how hard it had been for him when I was so removed from his efforts for so long. Even if I had meant to support him, my detachment made it impossible for him to be able to rely on me as a confidante.

I leaned forward to kiss him.

John stopped me. "Have you considered your parents? When you were neutral, they could look the other way, but if they know you have started working for the cause, you may find yourself estranged from them."

I nodded. I couldn't help that. "Today changes everything." I could imagine the blood and the screams of the fallen men.

"And if they disown you?" John insisted. "They might refuse to see you and not soften with time. It would cause you pain." My husband would do anything to prevent me from pain.

"I know that," I said calmly. "I am a good daughter. I cannot control what others will do or say, including my mother and father."

"I saw how upset you were when we wed. I would not want you to suffer that again." How like him to protect me, warn me, when I was finally in a position to fully support him.

"This is different," I said. "*I* am different. How do I learn how to make musket cartridges?"

"We'll teach you."

I had never been so sure. If we got caught and they hanged him, they would have to hang both of us. I would volunteer to swing next to him.

But my preference would be not to get caught.

Men had died last week in Lexington and Concord, dozens on both sides, according to the messenger. Men who had been fathers and husbands. Brothers. Sons. The king had not responded to pleas for accommodation over the troubles, and instead his army was killing his own people. It was a matter that should have been set to rights with compromise and talk but instead had come to the firing of guns, and death.

When I saw my father the next day he tried to argue that it had been warranted, that the Patriots were stockpiling illegal weapons and ammunition against the crown. The king was dealing with an insurgency that must be quelled.

I was unconvinced.

All my life I had been surrounded by peaceable intent, the surety of the rightness of non-violence. I had been raised by those rules, believed them. Yet look at what was happening now, all around us. What rules were the British following? What assurance had we that we, too, would not bleed should they suppress Philadelphia for protesting a tax or policy? What future had we with Britain now if they were so bent on physical punishment? Aggression. They had every advantage, every vote, every law on their side. Empire. Navy. Power. Instead, they had shot at their own men.

Chapter 25

May 1775

I was sure that the new feelings inside me would show up like a mark upon my forehead, garnering a reaction from everyone who saw me. But of course that was fanciful. After a few days of feeling nervous, secretive, afraid of being caught out, I stopped holding my breath and realized that only John and I knew that I had become a full-fledged member of the resistance, burning inside. Strangely, my life went on as usual, and no one looked at me twice, not even those closest to me who knew me well. Even Emily did not think me different, although of course I did not ask her.

The day after the news of what happened at Lexington and Concord reached Philadelphia, thousands of people assembled, stunned, in the State House yard on Tuesday to ask what to do. John and I were among them. John and I stood listening when the decision was reached. The crowd was instructed "to associate for the purpose of defending, with arms, our property, liberty, and lives."

John and I stared at each other. We were now preparing for war—war against our own country. We were to take up arms. Goosebumps ran down my arms. I looked around at the crowd. Many people had disbelief on their faces, the same question unspoken through the crowd: How had it come to this? We were all in shock. Pennsylvania was asking for a military budget, for congress to grant supplies, for paper money to be issued and bills of credit written.

That spring was one I wouldn't forget. The rebel forces took control of Philadelphia, forming an extralegal government, declaring anyone not in support of the new government to be a traitor to the cause. The Patriots got louder, and the people who supported Britain became quieter. The second continental congress was going to start in a few days, and it was only a matter of time before the delegates began arriving again. Strangely, it had become dangerous to live in Philadelphia and want to be loyal to the crown.

John and his uncles were in the resistance efforts up to their necks. George Ross was still an elected delegate to congress, as was Edward Biddle. John met with them frequently when they came to town from Lancaster and Reading.

*

"Betsy, did you hear what I said?"

Emily poked a spoon in my direction. We were having lunch at the Blue Duck tavern. John had sent us out of the shop because he was expecting a delivery that I suspected wasn't related to upholstery. He had also sent Oliver out to pick up horsehair.

"Sorry, no. What did you say?"

"I met someone. A gentleman." She was glowing, I realized.

"You did? Who?"

"His name is Gilbert Barkly." Emily beamed at me. "I think it will become serious rather quickly. I'm quite taken with him already!"

"Who is Gilbert Barkly, and where did you meet him? Why is this the first I'm hearing of this?" I took a bite of my biscuit.

"Ah, now I have your attention," Emily said. "I met him at the theater on Saturday. Someone gave my father tickets to thank him for fixing their wagon wheel on short notice, and he gave them to Mother and me. I had never been to the theater. It was a wonderful play! Have you seen—"

"Emily, I don't care about the play! Don't keep me in suspense. Tell me about Gilbert Barkly."

Emily smiled. "We were standing there at intermission, and he said I looked very fetching, and Mother gave him the side-eye. He apologized for his impropriety and introduced himself, and then we started talking. We had so much in common! Mother told him he could come by the house to call on Sunday if he'd like, and he did! That's when I got to know him, and we realized we get along really well. He asked if he could write to me until the next time we see each other. Oh, Betsy, he's who I've been waiting for! I know it."

"Is he a local? Or from out of town?"

"Gilbert has lived here a while. He came from England a few years ago."

"Well, this is unexpected!" I said. "What does this Mr. Barkly do?"

Emily took a breath. "He's involved in imports. Believe it or not, he was on the *Polly*. Remember the ship that brought the tea and was turned back to England?"

Of course I remembered. That was the beginning of the mess we were in now, with my husband helping gather weapons and stockpiling gunpowder.

"Then he's an agent for the East India Company?" I asked.

"I don't know. He didn't say. Why would you ask that?"

"Sorry, tell me what you like about him."

"He's smart, Betsy. And he's a real man. I mean, he's older. Not a silly boy. He spoke to me with such respect. How refreshing! I can tell he's a man of honor."

"How much older?"

"He's in his forties," Emily admitted.

"Oh, Emily." I hoped this Gilbert Barkly was as honorable as Emily believed him to be, but I couldn't help but wonder if she was jumping at the first fish on the line. I didn't want her to marry just so she could block out what happened to her.

"What do you mean, 'Oh, Emily'?" she asked, anger streaking her face. I bit my lip. I had upset her. "Why do you think the worst?" she demanded.

"I did not mean to. I care about you like a sister."

"You do not think my mother would exercise care?"

I sighed. "I know she would. Please let me try again. I am happy for you. Tell me more about him."

It was too late. Emily's mood had turned sour, and she stabbed her bread pudding. She was frustrated with me for not swooning along with her.

"Why do you have black under your fingernails?" she asked, noticing my hands.

My heart skipped a beat, and I tried to compose my face. I would make a lousy spy. "I was cleaning. Trying to get some tar off John's boots. He must have stepped in it down by the docks, picking up another shipment of block prints from India."

My fingernails bore the marks of my efforts at forming musket cartridges, which was delicate, time-consuming work. I was increasing my speed each time, but it was laborious and painstaking. I measured the paper just so, six inches on one side and five and a half down the other, which was the easy part, but wrapping it around the dowel to create the tube was exacting work. After the paper created a cylinder to hold the musket ball, I tied the end off, securing the lead ball inside. After that, I had to remove the dowel, measure just the right amount of powder from the horn, and pour the powder into the cartridge I had just created. Another twist and a bit of twine secured the other end. The work was slow going, and my fingers were taking a beating. I worried about spilling the powder, wasting it, or worse, that the cartridge would be faulty just when a man needed it in his musket. Working with thread, fabric, and lace was so much gentler on my hands than gunpowder.

"Hmm," Emily grunted, annoyed with me, her eyes still on my cuticles and fingernails.

Now was as good a time as any to issue the invitation that I was sitting on. "Do you remember when John and I did that order for the Cadwaladers?"

"Not really," she sniffed.

"Well, John and Elizabeth Cadwalader are having a dance, and they invited John and I. They told us we could invite another couple. Would you like to come with us? You and your Gilbert Barkly?"

"Why would they invite you?" she asked pointedly.

Craftsmen and artists normally did not get invited to customer balls, it was true. "Cadwalader is a cousin of John Dickinson's, who is a Mason," I explained. "My John became better acquainted with John Dickinson in the Masonic lodge. They invited us through the Freemason connection, not because we upholstered their chairs."

Emily looked up from her pudding. "When is it?"

"Saturday next."

"I'm not sure." She was still miffed, and I wished I had been more enthusiastic about Gilbert, but the significant age difference had taken me off-balance. Especially with Emily being so vulnerable.

"Gilbert made noises that he does not care for dancing. I do not know if he'll want to go."

"Perhaps you could ask. I'll understand if he would rather spend time with you another way."

*

Emily came into the upholstery as if she were floating on air.

"Good morning," I said. "Isn't Mrs. Symonds keeping you busy as a seamstress?"

"Oh yes," Emily sighed, sitting on a stool.

I was adding lace to the edges of a bedcover.

"You should see the gowns we're making for Mrs. McKean. Stomachers of embroidered gold and skirts of the most luxurious tiered silk. I came here now because Mrs. Symond's daughter is in childbirth, and she closed up early."

"I'm pleased that you're finally getting a chance to do the work you wanted."

"Is the Cadwalader dance fancy?" Emily asked. "I was thinking I might try and make something new. I could make something for you too, if you'd like." She had accepted my invitation quite readily after speaking with Gilbert.

"Oh, Em, I need to talk to you about that. John is quite ill. He's at home. I'm afraid we cannot go. Even if John's better by then, he will be too weak."

Emily's face fell. "I'm sorry for John. Do you think we could we still go, Gilbert and I?"

"Why? You've never met them."

I did not even want to ask the Cadwaladers or send a note of introduction. It was unusual enough that John and I had been invited. Emily was unknown to the Cadwaladers, and I had never met her Gilbert Barkly beau. How could I possibly send them to the grand Cadwalader house if John and I weren't there as well, to smooth the introductions?

"I love dancing," Emily said persuasively. "I don't get to go to many balls."

"I'm sorry," I said. "It wouldn't be right."

"Well, Gilbert would like to meet them," she wheedled. "He's trying to meet more people in town."

"It doesn't sit well with me. It would be awkward if John and I weren't there when we were the ones invited in the first place. You don't know the Cadwaladers."

As I thought about it, I remembered that Cadwalader was colonel of the Third Battalion now. John said Cadwalader's responsibilities in the cause had increased dramatically since Lexington and Concord. While I had no reason to be suspicious of Emily's new love interest, I didn't want to send someone I did not know to a commander's house.

"Gilbert was so looking forward to it." Emily had an odd expression on her face.

"I would love to meet your Gilbert Barkly," I said. "John and I both. It has been weeks now that you've been getting to know each other, hasn't it? Why not come for tea when John is better? Dutch tea." I'd managed to find some in Hannah Lithgow's shop one day after I left my parents' house, half-buried on a shelf in the back. I think she'd forgotten she had it.

"Very well." Emily sighed.

Chapter 26

June 1775

John was still sick in bed, and his mood was foul.

"Leave me be," he said, brushing off the cold cloth I was trying to place on his forehead. He pushed back the covers and attempted to get up. I did not even need to try and stop him; he immediately fell backward with a *wump* on the bed and reached for his head, dizzy.

"That will teach you," I said cheerfully.

"I cannot be ill," he growled.

"And yet you are." I moved his pillows to make him more comfortable.

"Send for the doctor," John ordered.

"He's already been," I said. "Dr. Rush was here. You weren't awake. I'm happy to report he says you are on the mend."

"Mend! I cannot get out of this bloody bed!"

"It takes time," I soothed. "Give it another few days."

John had been ill for more than a week. Dr. Rush had said it was common, a fever that brought people to their knees and then weak as they slowly recovered. Not much to be done but wait it out.

John balled his fists in frustration. "I am never sick. There are matters I need to attend to. I must get back to work."

"The world will go on without you, John," I said gently. "Just for a little while."

"Betsy, I—" He muttered an expletive and then closed his eyes, exhausted.

Thank goodness. At least he was himself today. When his fever was high, he'd been insensible.

When I voiced my fear, Dr. Rush had laid a hand on my arm and said the brain reacted poorly when a fever went too high. "Have patience," the doctor had counseled. "I have seen worse."

When John was finally well enough, I would have to tell him that there had been a terrible battle in Massachusetts, a thousand-fold worse than the shootings at Lexington and Concord in April. Accounts coming from Breed's Hill said it was a battle that two armies of men had fought, with hundreds dead and wounded, both Patriot and British, although the British had fared far worse. I was going to wait as long as I could to tell him, for I knew he would bolt out of bed and try to head down to the river to the munitions store there, or seek out the Sons.

As it was, there had been men coming by the house looking for him and growing more impatient by the day. Some of them had brought me more supplies for the musket cartridges: powder and lead balls. I set up a table in the corner of our bedchamber in front of the window over the street where the light was good and I could keep one eye on my husband as he recovered. A few weeks ago, John had carved a hole in the wall behind a picture of the king so we could hastily put supplies in a sack and deposit it there if Tories came to the house.

I watched John fall asleep, and when he didn't stir for a few minutes, I decided to make more cartridges. My needlework had long since been abandoned now that my hands could be used to help the cause. I went to the table and moved the aloe plant and the lace doily from underneath it, putting them on the corner of my dresser. At the wall, I took down King George, reaching into the open hole for the sack. I took it to my table.

I laid out my supplies carefully: paper, twine, powder horn, wooden dowel. I had gotten competent enough to make twenty or thirty an hour once I'd learned to cut the paper in bulk so I had a stack to reach for without having to stop to cut a new paper each time.

A knock on the front door surprised me. It was a quiet Tuesday morning, and we were expecting no one. Sometimes a farmer's cart would go door-to-door, the farmer seeking to sell the rest of his produce before heading back up to Bucks County. My mind calculated. It was June, and I thought I'd just heard the rhythm of a horse's hooves. Strawberries and rhubarb were in season. Fresh strawberries would be so refreshing, I thought, my mouth already anticipating the sweetness. And they'd be good for John if I mushed them with some cream. I was sure it was a farmer. It sounded like his rig.

I wiped my hands on my apron and hesitated. Should I put the cartridge materials away? I cocked an ear. I did not hear voices. I peeked out the window, but the street was quiet, no patrolling units or constables. With a glance at John, who was sleeping soundly, I went downstairs and opened the door.

My mother and father stood on the step.

"We came to ask after John," my mother said. She held up a basket. "How is he faring? I brought him bone broth. And fried liver."

I accepted her basket, moving it to hold it behind my back. They made to step forward, but I did not move to allow them entry.

"How kind of you to come," I said. "John was awake for a time but is still unwell and has just fallen back asleep. I had best not invite you in lest we wake him."

"We'll be very quiet," my mother said, pushing past me. "We won't stay long, dear."

My father followed her, and they sat on the sofa John had just recently recovered when a customer was threatening to throw it out.

I sat on the stuffed chair, the basket on the floor by my feet. I burrowed my hands in my skirts. I didn't know if there were stains on them—I'd been getting better at handling the powder, more deft with securing the cartridges—but I wasn't sure.

"Has the doctor been?" my father asked, concerned.

I nodded. "Dr. Rush, yes. John is getting better. Slowly."

"He bled him?" my mother asked.

"No. Not yet. He'll come again tonight and see if he's improving. He may bleed him then." I had delayed it as long as I could. I didn't agree with bloodletting. I'd had better results curing sickness through the years with herbs than calling for a doctor and letting them do that.

"If you need to move to the house for a while, we have plenty of room," my father offered.

"You know we would be pleased to help him recover," my mother added.

"For family, you put aside your differences," my father said firmly.

I thought of my worktable just at the top of the narrow stairs, if I tilted my head, I could almost see it through the open door to the bedroom: powder horn full, cartridges in a line on the table, the very cartridges that would be thrust down the muskets of soldiers that were training in the companies gathering strength in number. I had been sloppy. I had to be more careful.

"Yes, and I'm grateful for you," I agreed.

"Terrible news out of New England, isn't it?" my father said conversationally. "Breed's Hill."

"Let's go, Samuel," my mother said. "Betsy doesn't want to hear any of that while John's abed sick."

I felt a surge of love for them both as they rose and gave me advice on sickness. They had always been wonderful parents. Why must life be so complicated?

"Cut an onion and leave it next to his bedside," my mother advised. "Garlic cloves under the pillow."

"I always found the fastest recovery was through a stiff drink or two," my father said. "Not watered down."

"Everyone knows that doesn't work," my mother said scornfully. "You don't even drink, Samuel."

"Whiskey definitely works for me, Rebecca," my father teased her, even though I rarely saw him drink.

I walked them to the door and put a hand on the doorframe to lean out and say goodbye. It was their horse I'd heard; Fred stood tethered to the front tree. My father leaned in to kiss my cheek, and his eyes strayed to my hand on the doorframe.

I removed my hand hastily, but I saw in his eyes that he'd seen. *Damnation.*

Guilt lurched through me, but not regret. Not an ounce of regret. I only wished I did not have to hurt my family.

*

July 1775

A month later, in July, John was finally better, although it was a long time before he had his normal energy.

Much had changed in the weeks he had been bedridden. George Washington had been appointed to lead the new continental militia at the second congress. I still was flummoxed by that one, that the distinguished man from Virginia that I'd met at church, and had sewn bed hangings for, was now in Massachusetts as head of the new army. How strange life was.

If Philadelphia had been at a slow boil over the troubles with Britain, we were now at full flame. The general feeling coursing through the streets was that Great Britain had wronged us terribly. People who disagreed with the growing rebellion were now being openly shunned and punished. You did not even have to be a Tory, it was just enough not to support the Patriots. I was afraid for my parents. Quakers used to be respected for their peaceable ways, but now people accused them of being self-righteous and obstructing justice. John said it wasn't long before even the Quaker men would be forced to join a militia company or pay a fine if they wouldn't volunteer for the cause. After Breed's Hill, all men between the ages of sixteen and sixty were expected to join the militia. All of them were to serve and bear arms, no matter their religion.

The Pennsylvania assembly had done something startling and had appointed twenty-five men to form a Committee of Safety to coordinate defense and protection, which meant that Pennsylvania was now ruled by two systems. I did not fully understand it, but it seemed that while the assembly was still the legal government, the Committee of Safety had great power on its own terms and was tasked with enforcing the new rules. It was a momentous decision, for it meant that the long accepted established order in Pennsylvania was rapidly disintegrating.

The Tories were now the disaffected. Their ability to say what they liked, and to print what they wanted, was disappearing. In Philadelphia, it was a Whig agenda. The rebellion came at a price: trade was grinding to a halt, prices were rising, and smuggling was rampant. The city was struggling.

John and I began taking slow walks along Chestnut Street in the morning and evening to strengthen him. When no one was around, he spoke to me in a low voice of the difficulties of funding a war. While the continental army was growing under Washington, they had not nearly enough guns, ammunition, supplies, clothing, and uniforms.

"What can be done?" I asked. "There must be something we can do."

"I admire you, Betsy," John said. "I am proud you're my wife."

We walked past Mary Symonds' millinery, Emily's new workplace, and stopped to admire the impressive display in the window. A beautiful assortment of lace from Brussels and Buckinghamshire, furs and fringes, leather gloves and even beaver and raccoon skins. Gold and silver knee garters, brass cloak pins, gilt buttons. The entire window was filled with loveliness. Somehow she had managed to hang on to being able to sell luxury items through the troubles.

"The cause has become important to me," I told John as we continued up Chestnut Street. The city of my youth had been full of people that were proud to be loyal subjects. We had toasted the king and hung his picture. No longer. Now we had all seen the extravagant price of the greed of a few powerful men.

"Sometimes I worry that I am not being a good husband, putting you in harm's way. The future is uncertain. We're in a mad world." John scowled, frustrated.

"I choose to put myself in harm's way. I am steadfast now. Besides, even if we were the most enthusiastic Tories in Philadelphia, toasting the king, we'd still be in danger. Look what they're doing to anyone who's not with the Patriots. It has become dangerous to follow the old ways." Loyalists had their windows smashed and were the target of abuse.

John laughed, but it sounded bitter. "I hope you're not doing this for me. I wouldn't want that. Promise me this isn't for me."

I put my hand through his and squeezed tight. "It is not for you, my love. Let me put your mind at rest."

"Sometimes it's easy to forget that we could lose. This could all be for nothing."

"Don't think like that."

"It's true. I can't help but worry. Congress is sending another appeal to the king to avoid war. He could accept to end the war and retain power."

We both considered that.

"Up until now, the resistance effort was about getting Britain to take the chains from our necks," John said. "To respond to our concerns and involve us. But those days are gone. There may come a day when I have to go and fight and I won't be here to take care of you. Can you manage without me?"

"Please don't die. I could not bear that. You're not allowed to die, John. But of course I could manage without you for a time, if you promise to come back."

"I won't die," John said firmly. "I know I won't. I can feel it in my marrow. The men in my family are survivors. It's what we're known for. There are enough aging Ross family reverends and lawyers to form a line to Canada and back. There probably always will be."

"I hope so," I said. "Maybe some of them will be our sons one day."

"I'm counting on it." John said. His face was thoughtful. "You'll have to run the shop while I'm gone."

"It only makes me more determined to help in any way I can. I don't want to be alone longer than I have to. No matter how many muskets cartridges I have to make."

"My little rebel," John said, his voice rich with love. That was his nickname for me now.

"I just remembered. My parents dropped by when you were sick," I told him. "My father saw the powder stains on my hands. I wasn't sure if I should say anything to him."

"Did he comment?"

"No."

"Then say nothing. He may not have noticed. We have to go on as usual. Be as normal as we can. Don't put them in a position that could make it harder for them if they're forced to reveal knowledge one day."

Go on as usual. How did one do that? What was normal now?

"Well, in that case, speaking of trying to be normal, we are to go to tea with Emily and Gilbert. My idea. Dutch tea, of course. I was going to invite them here but they want to meet at Swenson's Teahouse."

"Who's Gilbert?"

"Exactly," I said smartly and steered him into a baker's shop. The smell of freshly baked bread calling to me was irresistible.

Chapter 27

August 1775

Gilbert Barkly was very charming, with offhand court jester mannerisms, and I liked him very much. He was like a male version of Emily, bold and effusive.

We were at a table in the backyard of the teahouse under a canopy of ash trees. The August sun was peeking out in bursts behind a white cloud, dappling the leaves above with light. Two bluebirds were darting in and out of the branches.

Gilbert told us he was the son of a prosperous farmer and had begun life as a merchant. He had entered the import business after that with intentions of seeing more of the world. Although he was in his forties, he had a sanguine temperament and seemed boyish and easygoing. He was sandy haired and hazel eyed, his face made darker by time in the summer sun. He gazed at Emily with open affection, often pausing to make eye contact with her while he was speaking and treating her with deference.

"I hear you are a tea merchant," John said with his customary directness.

"Was," Gilbert corrected. "No one in their right mind could be in that employ these days, could they? At least not for the East India Company."

John chuckled. "Glad to hear it. Not many men will get to have the distinction of saying they were actually on the infamous *Polly* that day. One for the history books, my man."

"Imagine our surprise after eight weeks at sea to be pulled over like that," Gilbert said drily. "Not the welcome we envisaged."

We all laughed, although the drama of that day a year and a half ago was still fresh in our minds, perhaps always would be, for that had been the earnest beginning of the rebellion.

Boston had sent their tea to the fish. We had sent our tea
back, with great fanfare. New York had also sent the tea back
to Britain. In Charlestown, the tea had been left to rot at the
docks. If Boston had not tossed those crates of tea, enraging
the king, would we be where we were today, preparing for
war? How different the eighteen months could have been.

There was a little twist in my belly when I thought of the
life for us I had imagined on my wedding night at Hugg's
Tavern. Philadelphia could have been thriving, heaving with
the bounty of incoming goods, bustling with industry, filled
with happy people. Instead, we were drawn with worry and
watching each other with suspicion, an extralegal
government in place overseeing a new continental army, at
war with Britain. All unthinkable until now.

"I trust you were made true by the Company," John said,
"and did not suffer a personal financial loss."

John and I were craftspeople; we knew the painstaking
value of every piece of silver lost and gained.

Gilbert shrugged. "In this business, we adapt. If it's not
tea, it's the rising price of molasses or squabbling over the
quality of tobacco."

"I would love to see what you've seen," Emily said, taking
a sip of her tea. "I've never been out of Philadelphia County."

"Would you go to England?" Gilbert asked her.

"With you, I would. If you were to ask." She blushed then,
embarrassed by her outspokenness. I was amused by this.
Emily never blushed.

"I understand you go back and forth between London and
here?" I asked him, raising my teacup, which was pink. "Do
you have a preference for either side of the ocean?"

"America is a place of great opportunity," Gilbert said.
"One would be foolish to underestimate it."

"Very much so," John agreed. "Betsy and I had the good
fortune to open our own upholstery. For years, we only
dreamed of it when we were in the employ of another. There
are many other upholsterers in town, so our venture was not

assured, but we have had a good measure of success and are thankful. In this city, hard work pays off."

"And talent," Emily chimed in, smiling at me. How encouraging she always was. A good friend was worth more than a pound in gold.

"Then you are blessed indeed, and the envy of many, I'm sure." Gilbert said. "How are you managing the non-importation rules? I have noticed that they are strictly observed."

"So far we are staying afloat. Doing well enough. It goes without saying that we would prefer the restrictions were not in place. It's not good for business but they're necessary."

"Ah yes. We must do what is best for the future," Gilbert said.

The talk turned to what Gilbert should do with Emily during the nice weather, such as riding out to the rich farms of Lancaster or seeing the rolling hills inhabited by the Moravians in Bethlehem. Perhaps the waterfall at Passyunk.

"If you are a fan of the arts, you cannot go wrong with a concert or play in town too," I added.

"Men usually prefer the horse races or salon game tables," John said. "Cards."

"Dancing," Emily said. "I love to dance. Perhaps you could come to like it more, Gilbert."

"It would be my honor to take you," Gilbert said smoothly. "I'm a bit rusty. I'll have to practice."

The serving woman came and added hot water to our teapot, taking away the empty plates full of crumbs. I watched squirrels leap in the bushes that lined the yard. What a pretty tea garden, I thought, full of flowers and little creatures.

I looked at Emily and Gilbert, drawing toward each other. I was happy for her. This was what she wanted, and this man, this Gilbert Barkly, importer of goods, seemed to be kind and steady. They would make a good union. He did not say whether he had been married before, or widowed, although he gave off the impression that he had been too busy with his work to settle down until now.

"I heard your uncle is in the new congress," Gilbert said to John.

"Three of them," John answered. "I have three uncles in congress, George Ross, Edward Biddle, and George Read. Edward and George Read married sisters of my father's. All Patriots."

"Any chance of an introduction? I'd hate to be so green that I embarrass myself. I'd like to do more for the cause. It would be an honor to be introduced to Cadwalader and Dickinson too. And Ben Franklin's back in Philadelphia now, isn't he?"

"Are you a Mason?" John asked.

"No."

"Let me see what I can do," John said. "This summer men have little time for socializing, on account of the troubles. You would have to prove yourself devoted to the pursuit of liberty."

"Of course. I am still a stranger. That's understandable."

"No," said Emily, putting her cup down on the saucer with a clang, "no more talk of revolution. That's taken up too much of our time as it is, Gilbert. Enough. Besides, not all of us are of the same beliefs."

I glanced at John, but his face was relaxed. Emily's viewpoint was reflective of many in town. We could not castigate everyone who expressed sympathy with the crown. We could leave that for the men. They at least could vote. I believed John thought of Emily as a girl, and he would always humor her because of what she had been through. That, and because of her devotion to me. Emily had become my shadow over the last year.

Gilbert laughed and reached for her hand, bringing it to his lips. "I can see I have work to do to show you my admiration. I would not want you to think me inattentive, for that would be a crime, knowing how ardently I feel for you."

"You'll have to bring Emily over to our side, Gilbert," John said good-naturedly, teasing her. "Show her what America could be without British interference."

"Indeed," Gilbert said, smiling at Emily. She ignored John and was gazing with open affection at the man at her side, her face soft and happy. She looked positively radiant.

*

John and I prepared for bed that night with the windows open, the humidity of the day dissipating in a light rain shower. I sat on the side of the bed and fanned myself with my old white fan before setting it down. My shift was made from the thinnest linen, barely there, and yet it felt clammy against my skin.

"Sleep without it," John told me when he saw me pulling at the neck of my shift. "I'll do the same."

"I haven't seen you in your shift," I teased. "Have you a lace one?"

We pushed the covers back to the end of the bed, a single sheet and light quilt for summer, and laid together on the bottom sheet, his hand lightly fanning the bare skin of my back.

"Oh stop, no touching—I'm too hot," I moaned. I reached for the fan from my bedside table and fanned both our faces.

"Gilbert seems keen on Emily," I said.

"I liked him," John mused. "They should marry."

"And be quick about it," I agreed. "It would be good for her, and maybe we would all worry less about her."

"You worry?"

"Of course I do. My father had a dog once when I was a little girl that couldn't be out of his sight. A stray. Queenie was her name. When he was gone long hours, Queenie whined at the door continually. Eventually, my father started taking the dog with him on jobs; it was just easier that way. And honestly, my mother had had enough. I care for Emily, but I feel I'm responsible for her. I don't mean to be unkind, but sometimes I feel like my mother felt when she was burdened with that hound. Not that I would ever compare Emily to a dog. I'm only trying to convey the feeling. She wants to be with me all the time."

"Gilbert came along at the right time, then."

I shrugged and snuggled into my husband. I heard an owl hoot outside the window and listened to the rain patter on the cedar shingles.

"What happens now?" I asked, just as he was falling asleep. "Now that the king has rejected the colonies' plea?"

"More," John mumbled. "We do more."

"I want to come with you to the arsenal," I told him. "Wherever it is that you go by the river. I want to see it."

There was no response; he was asleep.

I tried again the next day. "Take me to the arsenal by the river."

"Absolutely not."

"Why? I've made hundreds of musket cartridges. Don't I deserve to see what's there? I think I do."

"Betsy, this isn't for women. I can't have you seen there. It's not a game."

"Take me there," I insisted. "I'm not just anyone."

"Why do you want to see it? I keep telling you, it's dangerous. It's an ammunitions storehouse. That's all it is. Guarded by militiamen, taking turns."

"I just want to see it," I said. "I feel like I'm missing out on part of your world. I just want a glimpse. Even from afar."

"I will not do that," John said, unmoved.

"Please."

"No."

I hounded him relentlessly. I don't know why I wanted to see it. I just did.

Finally, after several weeks, I pressured him into agreeing. "Just from afar," he said irritably. "After the sun goes down."

We waited until there was enough of a moon, not quite full but close enough, that we could see without a torch or lantern.

We walked all the way down to the little jagged streets by the river. With a glance over his shoulder, John veered off onto a path behind a shipbuilder's, then up and around a warehouse until the river met us, a dark glint of ribbon under the moon.

John pointed down the side of the Delaware River.

I could see two militiamen outside, patrolling, a smudge of dark against the opening of a cave. There wasn't really anything to see. Two shadows in the dark. I turned to step away.

"What's in there?" I whispered as we picked our way through debris behind an old smithy site.

"Powder, muskets, bullets, bayonets, swords. Pistols. Crates and kegs stacked up. Not enough. Most of it old, given by people. A lot of rusty pieces from the French and Indian War. But it's a start."

I nodded. Another reminder of the reality that bloodshed could happen here too.

We climbed up the riverbank.

"George Washington plans to get more powder in production locally," John explained. "Congress has plans to buy arms and powder from foreign dealers. And steal as much from the British as we can." It sounded like he'd been getting information from his uncles again.

"Is there more I can do besides musket cartridges?"

"Field tents, if we can afford it. Or help sew uniforms. The Committee of Safety is starting to draw up uniform regulations for units."

The Committee of Safety was starting to punish anyone in Philadelphia who was seen as a traitor to the cause. Loyalists were now leaving the city in droves. The thought reminded me of the Fergussons.

"That reminds me. I saw Elizabeth Fergusson at the market," I told my husband. "I forgot to tell you."

"Who?"

"Elizabeth Graeme. Remember? From church."

"Ah. And?"

"She looked sad to me. Lonely, perhaps. Her husband is a Tory, but I don't think she is."

"That idiot of a husband of hers is back in Scotland now. Jacob Duché told me. That might save his life."

"I feel bad for her," I said. "She had such a melancholy way about her."

We emerged from the docks and found ourselves at the bottom of Sassafras Street.

"Betsy, I do not say this often enough." John stopped me. "Not many women would do what you're doing. Your fortitude is admirable. These aren't easy times. You make me proud."

"I could say the same of you, husband."

"The fact that you're my wife still astonishes me. How lucky I am. I know nothing has been the way you wanted it these two years since we wed, and I'm sorry for that."

"Thank you, love," I said, and we held hands as we slipped home through the darkness. "Correction, if you please. One thing was the way I wanted it. You."

*

We spent the next three months taking social outings with Emily and her Mr. Barkly. They were a reprieve, a diversion, in a city smoldering with hostilities and unexpected skirmishes.

"We can't work every waking moment," I admonished my husband whenever he complained that we didn't have the time to go out socially with them again.

We needed the fun, the fresh air, the companionship in another couple without talking of work or politics for a few hours. While we—and all of Philadelphia—anxiously waited to hear the king's response to the plea for clemency sent in July, we boated down the Schuylkill, watching the leaves dazzle us with gold and red in a perfect symphony overhead, went to fall parties and danced outside while fiddles played a jig and drummers drummed, and attended casual dinners at taverns and inns.

John and Gilbert found good company in each other. Talk was easy between them. Gilbert seemed eager to meet his friends, and John gladly introduced him to his coterie of men all over town.

Emily confessed to me that she was waiting for Gilbert to ask for her hand and was sewing the blue dress she had shown me in the sketch to wear as her best dress when the day came that she married.

"Mrs. Symonds must be treating you well," I commented, knowing how much the silk cost and how much fabric that dress would require. All the flounces and folded pleats, not to mention the expensive gilded thread the embroidery would take. I knew that Emily was giving her small wages to her family. Times were becoming increasingly tough, the restrictions in trade a tightening belt.

"It was a gift from Gilbert," she confessed, her color rising. "He gave me the fabric and all the notions. Even the buttons and ribbons. He said a beautiful girl should have a beautiful dress."

I raised an eyebrow. "How generous."

Was it usual for a man to gift a woman so extravagantly after such a short time? I didn't know; my own love story had unfolded slowly over several years. Perhaps it was thoughtful of Gilbert, so that she could wear the dress of her dreams at their wedding.

Chapter 28

November 1775

I was summoned to my parents' house. When I arrived, the front room was full of women. In addition to my mother, the parlor was bursting with the elders from the ladies' meeting at the meetinghouse. Some of them I had not seen in two years. They sat like a line of bottles at a shooting range, stiff and linear in shades of brown and gray.

"Hello," I said, surprised, when I walked in. "Am I still in trouble after all this time?"

I tried to joke, not understanding the tension in the air. My attempt at humor fell short.

"Betsy, sit, please," my mother said solemnly. "There are matters we must discuss."

I walked in gingerly, perching on the only empty chair. I realized it had been left vacant in the center of the room for me.

"Let's get right to it," Mrs. Tomas said. She motioned to the woman in my mother's rocking chair.

"Mrs. Ross," Mrs. Wharton said, her face as crumpled as a raisin and without an ounce of levity in her expression. "You married outside of Quaker faith. We asked you to make amends and stay. When you would not, we wished you well in your choice to leave us. This you know. That is in the past. We are here today at the request of your mother, who fears for you."

"Mama?" I turned to her. "What is this? What's going on?"

My mother sat stiffly on one of the chairs pulled in from the other room. The lion's claw feet were hard and intractable on the worn floorboards. "There is talk of actions you are taking that are of concern."

"Mrs. Ross," said Mrs. Tomas. "We come as friends."

I gazed around at the faces in the room. Not a smile to be seen.

"I don't know what you are referring to," I said finally. "I'm an upholsterer who works with my husband."

"Please, Betsy," my mother said. "Do not dally with us."

"Of course we wish you would return to the Quaker fold," said Mrs. Wharton. "We have prayed for God to guide you back to us. We would welcome you back with open arms, please know that, if you want to return. Whenever you wish. But that is not why we are here."

"Today we beg you to consider your actions," Mrs. Tomas cut in eagerly. She was younger, with gravelly skin and a slightly crooked nose.

"What might those be?" I said, my back stiffening.

"You have been seen with people who are plotting against the king."

I stood up. "Ladies, how nice to see you again after such a long time. I thank you for your concern, which is unwarranted. You'll forgive me if I wish to depart. I'm a grown woman, after all, and I believe we finished with witch hunts in Salem or shortly thereafter."

"We have come to help!" Mrs. Wharton exclaimed. "You may not know the seriousness of your actions, especially in the current mood of the city. Many are deceived."

There were other ladies in my mother's sitting room who were silently watching. They sat alert, hands folded on their laps.

"Thank you for your concern," I said evenly and turned to go.

My mother followed me out.

"Won't you at least listen, Betsy? These women could help you. They are older, wiser. They could—"

"Come," I hissed and led her swiftly up the stairs. "What is the meaning of this? Could you not have spoken to me directly?"

"If I believed you would listen, I would have. I thought if the elders were here—"

"How could you!"

"There is a marked difference between being a bystander, even through marriage, and taking a deliberate stand against the king—"

"It's none of your concern."

"I am your mother! You are my blood! Of course it's my concern!"

"Whatever you think you know, you just made it so much worse for me," I said sadly. "I have a right to choose for myself."

"If you hadn't married John—"

"Do not! Don't you dare!"

"Have you forgotten England gave us Quakers refuge? Our ancestors—"

I ran down the stairs. My mother caught my arm at the bottom and pulled me in to her.

"Do you know what they will do to you?" she said urgently. "Or John? They made Marta's husband ride the fence for less than what John has done. She said he will be quite useless from now on, his private parts mangled beyond—"

"Stop," I hissed. "Both sides are engaged in those torments now. How can you not know that? Even Quakers aren't safe anymore. Especially Quakers! Loyalists are in danger. This is a Patriot city now."

"My love for you is what you cannot see," my mother cried. I could hear the shuffle of feet in the front room. I heard someone on my mother's couch say briskly, "Shameful. The people who go against the king are deluded."

"I have love for you also," I said, breathing hard. "We disagree on matters. Please do not get involved, Mama. I made my choices with open eyes. Now please let me go, and I will endeavor to forget this humiliation."

"Then go. But remember this: when these troubles are over, you will be a marked woman."

"And still your daughter."

"Be careful."

I laughed, a harsh sound without humor. "You've just made sure it got much harder to be. What did you tell them?"

Her face shuttered, and she turned away, her countenance sad.

*

I ran without stopping out of my parents' house and all the way down Mulberry Street to Second Street and then onto Chestnut. I burst into the shop. Oliver and John were bent over a bed frame.

"I need to talk to you," I told my husband, tears flowing down my face.

John shooed Oliver away, into the back room, alarmed by my appearance. Somewhere during my charge through the streets, I had lost my bonnet and my hair was loose and wild.

"My mother asked me to the house to confront me. The elders from the ladies meeting were there. I think they hoped to convert me back. They tried to corner me."

"God's blood," John muttered. "Fools."

"I think they meant well," I began and then stopped. Why was I still doing that, still being kind to those who weren't kind in return? "The British is cannoning the coastline of Massachusetts, and still my mother defends them."

"What do they know?"

I shook my head. "I don't know. You may assume we do not have many secrets now. We have been betrayed. Outed. There were eight women from the ladies meeting. One of them is a known gossip. She has been censured for her tongue by the Society of Friends in the past. She will talk."

"Even if she doesn't, one of the others will, or their husbands. We are no longer safe." John heaved a great sigh and went to stand in front of the window, staring blankly out. For two years, John had managed to work away in obscurity, first to protest taxes, then British dominance, and finally to help with the resistance, only to find himself being raked over the coals by elder Quaker ladies.

My mother had unwittingly thrown us to the wolves. If I was one of the king's men looking for a rebel to crush, I could easily follow a trail leading to us: John was both a Freemason, an organization known for its sympathies with the cause, and he was a militia man. John and I belonged to Christ Church, the largest church in Philadelphia, which was full of Patriots, including Francis Hopkinson and Dr. Benjamin Rush, among many others. We dined with—and had created goods for— John Cadwalader, one of Pennsylvania's new rising star colonels in the continental army. John's uncles were leaders in the rebellion, and deeply embedded in the works of the rebel congress, which was fast becoming the government in Pennsylvania that held power. I could go on. My mother could have discouraged suspicion, held the Quaker leaders at a distance, but she did not.

John began to pace back and forth.

"It's my fault," I cried. "I should have been more careful."

John put up a hand.

"We are among thousands in Philadelphia now who are working for the cause. The Tories can't come for all of us at once."

"But what the king said in August! Have you forgotten? He told everyone that is loyal to him to *do everything they can* to stop us. It was an invitation to hunt us all. We're going to be caught. You know how wicked people have become in recent weeks, John."

John ran a harried hand through his hair, trying to think. "It is in our favor that the bulk of the British army is in Boston."

"How does that help us a month from now? In six months? There are more British troops on the way. Surely, there is a difference between giving lip service to the cause and stuffing musket cartridges. Or collecting guns meant to shoot the king's soldiers!"

My mother hadn't understood the consequences of her actions. She thought she was saving me, begging me to reconsider. She didn't realize she had unintentionally made John and I easy targets.

"Your safety is most important," John said with intensity. "I will take you to my father in Delaware. Give me time to think."

"No." I shook my head and took a deep breath. I was starting to see through the fog of emotions that had gripped me as I ran from my parents' house. "No. I told you I would not have regrets. We knew this might happen. I'm not going to flee like a fugitive into the night. I'm no damsel in distress. I'm staying here with you. If the king is sending men to hang Patriots, we will need more musket cartridges and weapons than ever. More grapeshot, more powder, more people like you and me fighting."

John took up pacing again. "If I am sent away to soldier, sending you back to live with your parents while I'm gone may no longer be an option. And I can't leave you all alone at home. I cannot. I won't."

"Maybe I can stay with Emily's family. Pretend neutrality. Or a change of heart. They would shelter me."

I knew my parents would take me in if I asked. They had good hearts and a deep regard for all their children, no matter what. They would not turn me away, but I was equally clear that I did not wish to live under their roof. Their feelings on the troubles with Britain seemed to be driven by habit, by the rules that had governed them all their lives, not by the events of the past few years. The king had been offered many chances for reconciliation and seemed intent only on punishment. Malevolence.

I too abhorred violence. I too would always be a Quaker in my heart, doing my best to connect with God and care for others. I too craved peace. Yet what good could come of ignoring what was so unjust?

John strode across our workshop and took me tightly in his arms. "Together," he murmured.

"Always," I said.

"No regrets?" He pulled back to search my eyes anxiously. "My little rebel," he added with tenderness, his thumbing caressing my lips.

"None." I meant it.

For the first time in my life, I was not being driven by the opinions of others, anxiously trying to please. Even when we had eloped, I had been fearful and shaky about those who I would disappoint and how I could make amends. Now I felt my spine a little straighter, my jaw a little steadier. I had pride in my work as an upholsterer, but this felt of greater weight, of something I could wrap around myself for a long time, far beyond a well-turned cushion or curtain. This work felt as if it mattered beyond John and I.

"We will be living cautiously for a while," he said. "The days may be long and trying."

"Maybe I should learn to shoot."

*

Emily arrived in my kitchen while I was cooking pork that evening. John was at the hearth, cleaning his gun and muttering about the lack of iron forges in the area.

"Good grief, Emily! Whatever is the matter?"

Her eyes were swollen and red, her face a tableau of misery. I'd certainly shed enough tears of my own earlier. Apparently, today was a bad day for more than just me.

"Gilbert said his feelings have changed."

"What are you talking about? Come in. Sit down."

She sat stiffly in front of the onions I'd been chopping, their skins scattered across the worn pine of my table. I had apples boiling in my cooking pot, spiced with cinnamon and nutmeg and a touch of ginger. The smell was making me hungry.

"His feelings have changed for me. He doesn't want me."

"Of course he does," I said. "All couples have disagreements. What happened?"

"I did not hear from him for days. Days! Then he said he had to go to New York but that he didn't think I was the one for him and we likely won't see each other when he returns." At this, she let out a choked wail. She was flicking her fingers nervously, pulling at the tips of the nails.

"New York? Why?" I was trying to sort out her report, sure that she was mistaken. I heard the clicks of John's gun going back together and the clink of a glass when he poured himself a drink.

"Business, he said. You should have seen his face. It was stiff and formal, as if we were strangers. He wouldn't come in. He stood on the doorstep like he was the debt collector. By the time my mother came to the door to see who I was talking to, he was gone."

I glanced at John. He lifted his shoulders and spread his hands. *Don't look at me. I know nothing. Women's troubles.*

"Oh no. I'm sure there's an explanation. That doesn't sound like Gilbert."

I tried to reassure her, but even to me, something wasn't right. Gilbert had spent months fawning over her; much of his adoration I'd seen with my own eyes. He had bought her new shoes in the French style. Confectionaries from the most expensive shop in town. The costly silk fabric for her dress. He'd carted her around town in his carriage and had taken her to concerts and the opera. I added up the time in my mind: six months. That was a long time to spend in close quarters with a young woman seeking marriage and then suddenly cut ties. Had he met someone else? Was this why he was still a bachelor? Could he never commit?

A thought struck me, and with it a terrible feeling, as if someone had immersed me in a bucket of ice water. Did he find out about Emily's attack? Who had told him?

Emily's face told me she was thinking the same thing.

I shook my head. "No. It's not possible, Em. Don't think like that. That's not it."

*

I was awoken from a deep sleep a few hours later by a loud boom that came from the direction of the river.

I sat up, groggy, wondering if it had been thunder I'd heard. I pushed back the bed curtain and looked to the window. It was snowing, the first snow of November. My head was thick, and I shook it a little, rubbing my eyes. Surely, we had only just fallen asleep? John and I had laid in bed, talking long into the night, trying to figure out how to avoid capture by the British if the time came, until exhaustion claimed us and we drifted into sleep with our feet touching.

I turned to John. "Did you hear that?"

His side of the bed was empty. I reached out a hand: cold.

The cat leaped on the bed and brushed its tail against my arm with a small chirp. I scratched her head and laid back down again, drawing the wool blankets close under my chin. Cora stepped delicately onto me and laid on my legs, seeking warmth. John coming and going was not unusual. I was asleep again within minutes.

In the morning, there was a persistent banging at the door. The sun was barely in the sky, lavender mist sleek behind the lacy reach of the black limbed trees. I groaned. Good sleep was something that I dearly missed.

I reached out a hand to poke John to go down but found only a cold sheet again. Frowning, I wrapped my robe around me and trekked unwillingly downstairs.

A man stood there, his face apologetic and somber in the crack of light I allowed between myself and his muddy greatcoat.

"There has been an accident, Mrs. Ross. I was sent to let you know they're bringing your husband home."

Chapter 29

November 1775

"What happened?" Dr. Rush asked me, shrugging off his coat and bending over John, who had been placed in our bed. Drops of my husband's blood left a trail in the fresh snow leading up to our home. They had used an old door from the warehouse next to the arsenal to cart him through the streets leading from the river before bringing him to the house and up to our chamber. "Any information you can give me may help me treat him."

"They told me there was an explosion," I said, my voice husky. I stared at John, his boots still on, willing him to wake up and speak to us.

"Help me remove his clothes," Rush instructed me. "I'll cut, and you pull the cloth away."

I did as he said then sat back down in a chair by the bed.

"John was one of the militiamen guarding the arsenal by the river . . ." I whispered, my words like ash in my dry mouth. Dr. Rush was a member of the resistance, so I knew I could trust him. He was one of the men who was fighting to arm the continental army, and he had been a loud voice for refusing the tea.

Rush nodded grimly, rummaging through his medical bag.

Rush found what he was looking for, a pair of metal tongs and a smaller tool that looked like pliers. He laid cloth out on the table that I had been using to make cartridges, pulling the little table close to the bed so he could work. Deftly, he began at the top of my husband and worked his way down, pulling tiny shards of metal and debris out of my husband's flesh. He used a bottle of spirits to wash each section as he went along, and then again afterward to wash off the gravel.

There were pieces of metal stuck to my husband's skin like the burnt pieces of seared beef. I barely recognized John. Dr. Rush was bandaging him almost everywhere, save for his head, and the left side of his face and neck was marred with damaged skin and mysterious textures.

I sat quietly in a state of shock. A long time passed as Dr. Rush rhythmically removed shards of metal and dirt from my husband with a practiced hand. He had brought a woman with him, and she was quietly coming and going, carrying out a series of tasks. She moved deftly, her feet light and sure. She did not address me, walking past me in succession: a bowl of steaming water, a handful of wet cloths, a stack of bandages, an armload of firewood, my water pitcher. Back and forth she went, not once asking me for directions on where to find something in my cupboards or if I could help. I watched her without seeing her, not able to move. My mind whirled, struggled to grasp something solid, then swirled again like the snow outside.

"He was with me when we went to bed," I told Dr. Rush. "And then he wasn't there."

The doctor looked up at me, his features soft with sympathy. "I am sorry, Mrs. Ross," he said gently.

"I did not know he had gone out," I said. "He often did, you see, but he always came home. I didn't know he wasn't there. He always comes back. Well, one time he was at the upholstery, but that was unusual. You see, I went to the shop and I found him. . . " I let my voice trail off.

Dr. Rush eyed me. "You've had a shock," he said soothingly.

"He was just here," I said, remembering our feet wrapped together under the covers only hours ago. "How can this be happening? We were sleeping. I didn't know this would happen." Nothing was making sense to me.

"Mrs. Ross, no one can expect a tragedy."

"Why is he not moving? Can he feel that?"

Dr. Rush didn't answer right away, continued to fish for pieces in my husband's skin. "We do not yet know the gravity of John's injuries. It is better that he rests like this. Sleep will bring healing, and for now he is spared the pain that he will encounter when he wakes. I've given him quite a lot of opium tincture."

"He will wake, though?" I asked anxiously.

"I believe your husband will wake, yes. Injuries like this take a long time to heal. You must steel yourself for weeks of recuperation."

"What injuries?"

"A broken femur. Two ribs. His skin has suffered burns and, as you can see, invasive penetration. We are limited in knowing the bruising or damage he has suffered on the inside until he can talk to us when he wakes. His heart is steady. He breathes without labor. All good signs. Have faith, Mrs. Ross."

I nodded. That seemed not so dire. A broken leg and two broken ribs. His left side had taken the brunt of the impact, but Dr. Rush expected him to recover. He would be disfigured on his face, but he would mend. He was young. Strong.

"You will need help to care for him," Dr. Rush said, finally putting his tools down and washing John's skin with the bottle of spirits. "I will send carers. You won't be alone."

"Was he there alone?" I whispered. "Do you know? I forgot to ask."

Dr. Rush shook his head. "The other man died."

"You were there?"

"No. They came to get me."

I sent up a fervent grateful prayer for John, and another for the man who was gone, and sank back against the hard chair, my mind far away, far outside of myself and this chamber.

Dr. Rush continued to work while the woman came and went. It was hours later when he left. "I will come in the morning," he said, squeezing my shoulder. "Hilda will stay."

Over the following days, a rotation of women arrived to care for him, shadows sliding past us from where I lay next to John in the night, then blurs of white aprons going past my chair where I sat brooding during the day. When food was placed in my hands, I tried to eat, but mostly I sat with John and talked to him, willing him to get better. The stream of women coming and going did not expect anything of me, and for that I was grateful.

The only time I left the house was to place a sign on the shop door: *Temporarily closed due to family illness.* I dispatched Oliver to deliver any items we had finished and sent messages to those who had just placed orders notifying them of the delay. Items were delivered to the house, but I paid no attention: a chicken newly killed, a tin of gingerbread, a jar of pears. Then the next week: a sack of nuts, a blanket embroidered with hearts and doves, a jar of pickled cabbage. I did not ask who had come. Someone even left a wooden flute one day, which I reached for with curious hands. How smooth it was. I took it back upstairs and whistled into it, trying to play, hoping it would bring John back from his long journey through the other side.

Dr. Rush came every day, applying salves and changing bandages. He made sure John was keep comfortable with laudanum, administering it slowly through a bottle dropper.

I could tell what time of day it was by how low the rectangle of yellow from the sun through the window was on the wall. I watched each day as it slid down the wall in increments, shining on the bumps in the white wash, the crack by the door, its clarity or dullness speaking for the brightness of the day outside. The caregivers kept the fire piled high, the floor swept, John's wounds cleaned. Dr. Rush gave him more laudanum.

On the fifth day after the accident, as the rectangle of light on the wall slid into a dull gray, the floorboards creaked and someone entered. I did not look up.

The person who entered stopped by the side of my chair. I was holding the flute, looking into the holes, trying to see how it was made. Perhaps it was Hilda again, here to light the wall sconce. I could barely see in the deep dusk. I had thought of getting up to light it myself, but the movement required too much effort. I couldn't move. Willing John to get better took all I had.

"Could you light the lamp, please?" I said when there was no strike of flint.

"Elizabeth."

Mother.

She stepped close and took me in her arms, pulling me close.

I turned to her and buried my face into her chest. I began to sob.

She stroked my hair, standing over me, letting me melt into her.

"Sweet child," she murmured, holding me tight.

*

When John finally regained consciousness, he was not himself. He would rage and cry out and then descend into sleep again. Occasionally, he was calm, his eyes blank. As the days passed and he was awake for longer periods, his emotions were those of a child. Petulant, angry, wheedling, joyful. Eventually, when he recovered enough to sit up, he wanted mostly to hold the cat and asked to have his leather pouch of marbles returned. In the nine years I'd known John, he had never mentioned a bag of marbles.

"Does he know you?" Dr. Rush asked me.

"No," I said, my voice broken. "Tell me he will get better."

"I hoped this would not be the case. I did not wish to frighten you with speculation. Mrs. Ross, with injuries of the head . . ."

I stopped listening, my heart a dull rock in my chest, black obsidian, barely moving. I knew he was gone. I knew because the bony finger of despair was poking me again, begging me to listen. His body was here, and he was alive, but my husband was gone. This man in the bed was not the man I married.

"What now?" I said. "His physical body recovers while his mind does not."

"We could take him into the hospital," Dr. Rush began. "Treatment for him there would be good for his recovery."

"I went to the hospital," I said, "years ago. I've seen what the hospital does to people not in their right mind. John's mother was there for many years before she died."

"I'm doing my best to change that," he said. "It is deplorable, I agree. Real change takes time, especially in the medical field. I am one of the doctors who is trying to alter the treatment of the insane. But all that aside, I do not intend to place your husband in the ward for the insane. We could find a bed for him on the second floor with the men that need long recovery times for more serious injuries."

I shook my head. "I want to keep him at home."

"And when his body has healed? He may not be able to be left alone."

How would I earn our keep? Perhaps I could sew in the front room, minor jobs, work that did not include lifting chairs and sofas or making mattresses or heavy blinds that had to be lugged about and delivered. Our house was rented, but perhaps the landlord would not mind if I made cushions and curtains and bedspreads. Soft small items whose creation would not annoy the neighbors. I was an upholsterer, and I would continue to work my trade. I would find a way to make it work and care for John.

"I will deal with that when the time comes," I said.

Dr. Rush looked at me. "You are a strong woman, Mrs. Ross, like my Julia. Admirable."

"Can you find a job for Oliver?" I asked.

"Oliver? The boy?"

"Yes. He's a fine boy, dependable. Very hardworking. He had been good to us. His family needs his wage."

"I will see that he's cared for."

*

John died in January, his death wholly unexpected. No infection, no fever, no frantic calls for the doctor. He simply fell asleep and did not wake. I knew instinctively it was his gift: both to me and himself. John would not have wished to live so impaired. His death was also his way of protecting me, as he had always sworn he would, right to the end of his days. John knew, I was sure he knew, that his exit from this earthly life freed me and at the same time anchored us together. If he had lived and been so unwell, his survival would have yoked me to a life of hardship and suffering. Instead, my husband's death meant I could carry on with my life and our work for the cause. I would need to figure out what that would look like, whom I could trust, what I could do. I knew that when I did, I would feel John's spirit alongside me.

We buried my husband of a little more than two years at Christ Church, near his mother, at the end of January. When they laid him in his coffin, I tucked two pieces of thread in his waistcoat, one black that looked like the sky on our wedding night, when we had sat grinning at each other as our ferry lurched toward the Jersey shore. The other was dark blue, the color of the new continental army uniform. I knotted the two together in the pocket over his heart.

I asked his father, Reverend Aeneas Ross, to come from Delaware to conduct the ceremony, which he did willingly. After the service, which I had kept small, discouraging people from coming—I could hear John saying, *Security, Betsy, do not call attention to yourself*—we gathered at his graveyard on a windy day, the temperature unseasonably warm. Emily looked pale and wan next to me, my parents solemn, my sisters and brother unusually quiet, a select few other friends sad and pensive.

John's death ended the months-long stupor I had been in. I had been sitting for weeks, my mind and body in separate orbs. Now, purposeful and focused, I began to move into action, pushing away my sorrow to attend to the matters at hand. I had much business to do. I gave notice to our landlord, packed up the contents of our house, and moved back to my parents' home on Mulberry Street, the home I had spent almost ten years in as a girl. It would be temporary. There was comfort in returning home to the street I knew so well and being embraced back into the family fold, just for a few weeks until I could get on my feet. To think six months ago I had thought I could never live here again.

A short time later, I rented the house next door to my parents that used to belong Daniel Niles the shoemaker while I was growing up. I used the front parlor as my showroom, taking advantage of the window facing Mulberry Street. The light was better there, and street traffic would attract business into the shop until I was more known in that location. I did the bulk of the messy sewing and construction work in the tiny room at the top of a short staircase around from the parlor. I had a sign made and hung it outside: "Elizabeth Ross Upholsterer."

"I need new cushions, madam," my mother announced, walking in the day I officially hung up my sign and declared myself open for business. "Only the finest will do. Don't try to give me cheap fabric, Mrs. Ross. I insist on quality. Nothing from England, of course. We obey the rules."

I laughed, dashing away the tear that had escaped. "I will not take your needs lightly, Mrs. Griscom."

How complicated it all was. Love and war, all together in a jumble.

I forgave her what she had done that day with the elders. She was only trying to save me. How could I fault her for that, when half of her children had already died? In my dark moments, I wondered if that was the reason John was dead, if someone had talked and the explosion hadn't been an accident.

But that was absurd.

Chapter 30

February 1776

I am a widow. I am a widow. No matter how many times the words repeated in my mind as I sewed, I could not fully comprehend that John was never coming back.

I had turned twenty-four years old at the beginning of January as John laid in our bed raving about red moons and spies on the water, his face scabbed and cracked, bits of bandage sticking to the deeper spots that struggled to heal. The day of my birthday, I had to take our bed curtains down. He would grab them and pull, convinced they were the incoming masts of a British warship.

And now he was gone. Loneliness followed me like a shadow as I tried to continue on without him, the raw slap of solitude always one step away, even on the better days. Still, one could only look forward. I had to make peace with the pain, the feeling of being dangled over a cliff. *This too shall pass*, I told myself. I was fortunate—my return to the neighborhood of my youth meant upholstery orders were flowing to me at a steady pace. I even hired two neighborhood girls to help me and had them do some of the basic stitching so I could focus on the more painstaking and advanced work. I planned to marry again eventually if I could. I knew John would want that for me. Thoughts of being a mother one day helped me get through the worst days of winter, especially when frost clung to my window and snow was flung from the sky.

No one had approached me yet to help with musket cartridges or standards for military units, but I would say yes when they did. A period of grieving had been allotted to me, it seemed. I was not afraid anymore of being caught by the British. What could they do to me? I had already lost the only thing that mattered to me. Anything else I was reasonably confident I could live through. And if I didn't, so be it. I'd be with John.

I talked to the cat as I sewed and waited for the longer, sunnier days of spring so my candles were fewer and my mood brighter. I took meals with my family next door, although I did not return to the meetinghouse. Friends came to visit; I had no shortage of company, although there was one person who I did not see very often: Emily. I attributed her absence to her melancholy over Gilbert Barkly, who had not returned to her. I knew Emily would resurface when her spirits were better. Her mother, when I saw her in town, looked drawn and worried about her troubled daughter. Poor Emily. I wondered what Emily was going to do with her blue dress or if she'd finished it. I resolved to visit her when the snows melted and I could better stomach the thought of walking through town.

Somehow, the days passed. When he was in Philadelphia, George Ross would visit. One day toward the end of March, he arrived bringing me food gifts and an order for tassels.

"Tassels?" I repeated, puzzled.

"Tassels." He winked at me. "For our curtains."

"Which curtains? What color?"

"Er, gold?"

I laughed and shook my head. How kind of him.

"If you're not too busy," he added politely.

"Despite my vast popularity, I can always fit family in," I teased him.

"Your customers must have high regard for your work. John certainly sang your praises."

"My customers are all still stunned by Common Sense," I said, referring to the new booklet that dared to advocate for independence from Britain. "That's all anyone wishes to discuss these days. Even the women."

"'The cause of America is in a great measure the cause of all mankind,'" George quoted. "Ah yes. Masterful."

"Is it possible? Independence?"

"Possible? Yes. At what cost? That is the question. Would men want it enough to die for it?"

I was silent, pulling my needle through the bolster I was making. My husband already had.

*

In May, people began to leave Philadelphia, saying the British were coming to invade us, the result of a terrifying exchange of cannon fire between a British frigate and Pennsylvanian ships on the Delaware River. The cannon fire exchange lasted so long that thousands of people lined the river to watch before the ships finally turned away from each other. The smoke from the cannon fire drifted slowly up the river until it curled around Philadelphia's waterfront like the tail of a snake.

I was not leaving Philadelphia, and my family was not leaving Philadelphia. The wealthy could go to their summer homes, but where could we go? All we had were our houses and our shops. Our hands were calloused and strained by work. There was no carriage pulling up to whisk us away to a retreat in the woods or the safe sanctuary of a country home. I wasn't going anywhere even if I wanted to, which I did not.

The new crisis and talk of war at our doorstep again made me realize I needed to see Emily. She had stopped by in April, a cursory visit to say hello, but she was with her mother and her sisters and I couldn't read her feelings. It had been three months since I had last seen her, which was at John's funeral. I knew my new status of pitiable widow gave me leave to withdraw and grieve, but the time had come to seek her out.

I went to her house on the Sunday afternoon after the cannon fight on the river. There were tulips blooming in the garden, honeysuckle climbing the arch by the gate. The yard bloomed with spring, rabbits jumping about on the lawn. I stepped around the cow patties and knocked on the door.

"Betsy, what a shame, you just missed her," Mrs. Spencer said, looking pleased to see me. "I sent them into town to the cheese shop. Won't you come in?"

I told her I would try and catch up to Emily and her sisters on Second Street.

"Perhaps you can cheer her," Mrs. Spencer called after me. I turned back. "She might listen to you. She has been so aloof this winter, brooding and spending time by herself. At first I understood it, but now I don't know." She shook her head and raised her hands in a gesture of defeat.

"I will try, Mrs. Spencer," I promised.

"I have no right to ask it, you in your grievous situation and all. . ." she fretted.

I put my lips together in what I hoped was a smile and bid her good day. I set off toward the shops.

Emily and her sisters weren't hard to find. They were grouped in front of a window, three figures with their noses almost pressed to the glass at a jewelry shop.

"Betsy!" Emily exclaimed. "I meant to. . . I was going to come by. . . How are you?"

"We're going ahead to the chocolate maker's next to the cheese shop," her sister Louisa told her. "Meet us there."

"Look at these lovely rings," I said, motioning to the window. "The gold is filigree."

I tried to make conversation, but Emily was quiet.

"I have missed you," I offered finally.

"Thank you," Emily said after a pause, which I found was a strange thing to say, adding too late, "And I you."

"Are you well, Emily?" I asked, looking into her eyes. "Your mother is worried about you. I'm worried about you." We had spent so much time together until John's death. Her absence had been jarring.

"I am well," she said, but her eyes strayed over my shoulder, and I sensed that she wanted to leave. "I'm fine."

"Perhaps we could go for walks now that spring is here? Every so often. Would you like that? Fresh air can be quite restorative. For both of us. We've both lost men we loved."

She murmured some platitudes and excuses, and eventually, frustrated, I made my leave of her. I was halfway down the street and had stopped to admire a basket of tulips outside a flower shop when a rush of feet made me turn. Emily pulled me over to the side.

"I'm the reason John is dead," she said, putting a hand to her mouth, her eyes wild. She choked on a sob. "I would die so that he could live again, I truly would. I'm sorry, Betsy, I'm so sorry."

"What are you saying?" I asked, confused.

"I didn't understand at first," she explained in a rush, her voice barely above a whisper. "Gilbert wanted to meet everyone that I knew, and then he started asking me to introduce him to specific people. When I didn't want to, he wouldn't stop pressing me. Then he started buying me things, beautiful things, and I thought they were for me because he held me in his affections, but then I realized he bought me things to get me to do things for him. I should have refused to see him when I started having doubts, but I thought he loved me." She hung her head in shame.

"Having doubts about what?"

"I think he was working for the British." She whispered this.

Memories came flooding back. *I heard your uncle is in congress,* Gilbert had said to John that day at the teahouse. *Any chance of an invite?* Dear Lord in heaven. Gilbert Barkly was a spy?

"I told myself I was imagining it, that it couldn't be true. I know now that I didn't want it to be true. I'm so sorry."

"Go on."

"He was sending letters. I wasn't supposed to know. One day he fell asleep in the carriage on the way home from a party, nodded off. Probably the drink. I saw something sticking out of his boot, a piece of white. It was a letter. I think Gilbert intended to hand it off to a man at the party who wasn't there. He always wanted us to go out, get invited to dinners and salons, and sometimes he'd disappear with someone. A man. Different men. All of it was planned. I know that now."

I stared at her.

"He kept taking me for walks down by the river near the battery. One day we were walking, and he asked me about John. I told him . . ." She faltered.

"You told him what?"

"That you had gunpowder stains on your fingers. That John had joined the militia and was . . ." She swallowed, looking miserable. "I told him that you said John would come and go at night. That you were both suddenly very busy and had become a little secretive after that first shooting thing up north."

Lexington and Concord.

"Oh God, Emily. You didn't. Tell me you didn't."

"I think Gilbert followed John there one night. I don't have any proof, but I just do. After that, after he saw it, Gilbert didn't want to get together with you and John as much. It was a marked difference from one day to the next."

"No," I said, horrified. "*No.*"

"I think that accident . . . wasn't an accident," Emily whispered. "I think Gilbert told someone who made sure to blow it up."

Rage surged through me. Emily was crying openly, tears streaming down her face. I stared at her in disbelief. My husband was dead because of Gilbert Barkly?

"I would take it back, I would, I would. I'm sorry, I'm so sorry." She was openly crying.

Gilbert had gone to New York in November, I recalled. Was that to give his reports to British General William Howe who was there? John had told me he thought the British would try to occupy New York, to cut off Canada and separate the northern and southern colonies.

"So you see," Emily moaned, "that's why I can't be your friend. You will hate me now."

"Where is he?" I asked her, still reeling. I couldn't see her face in front of me, only the dark smudge of Gilbert Barkly following my husband down to the river in the dark. "Gilbert? Where is he?"

"I don't know. I swear I don't. I haven't seen him since he left for New York in October. He was using me the whole time. I made it easier for him for get into dances and dinners, a woman on his arm."

Yes, I could see that. Few people would suspect him next to Emily, dazzling and beautiful and painfully young.

"I didn't know, Betsy, really, I didn't know," Emily cried. "I'm sorry, I'm so sorry."

"Please stop saying that," I said wearily. "I don't hate you." She was horsewhipping herself enough for all of Philadelphia. I closed my eyes and leaned my forehead on the brick wall of the flower shop. In my mind, I saw Emily the day after the attack, on the floor in a heap of her skirts; Emily at the shop, smiling as she helped us stuff mattresses; Emily next to me for months, as faithful and devoted as my father's stray years ago.

"Please leave me," I said. I could not comfort her, could not take away her guilt.

"You should know I overheard him tell someone that Lord North sent him," Emily said. "In a hallway at the Shippens'. That's why he came back from London. I didn't want to know. I hate myself for that now. I told myself I just hadn't heard him correctly."

She had betrayed us for the prospect of marriage. Bile rose in my throat. I would forgive her one day, but not now.

"Please go."

*

One day early in June we were finishing up for the day, the girls and I, when the bell tinkled and three men walked in.

I looked up in surprise. It was rare to see more than a man with his wife or a solitary man who had come alone to place an order.

"Uncle George," I said, standing up. I knew George Ross was in town for congress again, but he had just been by a few days ago to pick up the tassels and take me for a meal. He had confided in me that congress had assigned a committee of eight to start working on a formal declaration of independence, his eyes flashing with excitement. I so wished John could be here for this, could know this.

Uncle George was with George Washington and Robert Morris, John's munitions man, who also worshipped at Christ Church.

"Mr. Washington," I said, flustered. "Er, Colonel Washington. General Washington." I struggled to find the right greeting.

Washington smiled at me and looked at ease. "Mrs. Washington has expressed great satisfaction with the bed hangings and has asked me to convey her appreciation for your impressive handiwork. The Indian chintz, in particular, is well admired in our home and my granddaughter is well pleased. The black and white print is in her bedchamber."

I nodded my thanks.

"I am sorry for your loss," Washington added, his charming Virginia voice sincere. "Your husband was a fine man who served the cause well."

"Betsy, do you know Robert Morris?" George Ross asked.

I nodded. I heard John's voice in my head, *I'm part of the ammunition and artillery committee under Robert Morris.*

"Good day. Won't you come in?" I said, motioning to the best chairs for customers. "This is a surprise."

The girls lingered in the background, then sat down again to bow their heads over their sewing.

"We are in need of a standard," Washington said, "a flag, to represent an independent America." He reached in his pocket and took out a piece of paper.

It was a square flag, a small rendering. There were stripes on the right. The upper left had stars floating across a large square.

"The stripes are red and white," Uncle Ross said. "The square is blue, the stars white."

"Can you sew a full-sized version of this?" Washington asked.

"Is that from Hopkinson?" Morris asked. "Wasn't he working on a few designs?"

"He's too precious about it," muttered Uncle George. "We need a robust supply, not the prance and foppery of an artist. He's treating it like that song he wrote."

I took the paper sample from him and looked at it closely. The three men watched me, the room absent of idle chatter. The clock on the wall ticked, and a dog barked somewhere outside.

"The stars," I said, "are complicated. Unnecessarily so. You see how they have six points?"

I pointed to one of the stars. "These are difficult to cut. To craft a star in this manner requires effort for each star. If you plan to make this flag many times, it will be time consuming and cumbersome to create. There is greater room for error in getting each star to be symmetrical. It is expensive in labor."

I got up and went to my stash of leftover fabrics. I ruffled through them until I found a square of broadcloth in brown and reached for my sharpest scissors. "Let me show you."

I folded the fabric square in half, and then again with the point on an angle. My hands worked quickly, I knew this shape well from other jobs. In one continuous motion I made a decisive cut. I put the scissors down and opened the fabric to reveal a five-pointed star that was weighted equally on both sides, symmetrical, the points satisfyingly even.

"Look at that," Morris said, impressed. "Remarkable."

"And I recommend your flag be a rectangle," I said. "It will better catch the wind than a square."

"I told you she was capable," Uncle George said pointedly, as if he'd been accused of pity patronage. *A struggling widow?*

George Washington held out his hand, and I placed the star in it. "You did that quickly," he said, examining the points closely to see if they were weighted or shaped differently. "I would not have thought it possible in one cut."

The men passed the star I had done between them, considering it.

"Is there a reason we need each star to have six points?" Morris asked. "Will five suffice?"

Uncle George shook his head. "A star is a star, is it not?"

"Can you make this flag?" Washington asked me. "In full size?"

"I think so," I answered. I had not made a flag before. "I can try."

I looked at his sample and considered the rash of stars.

"I wonder," I said slowly, "if it would not be a better idea to have the stars in a circle, rather than scattered across the blue square like that."

Washington raised an eyebrow. I tried not to notice his teeth, which looked yellowed and unwell. What a shame, the rest of him was so handsome. Imposing even, in the best way. His height, the strong brow, those piercing eyes. My aunt Sarah, the stay maker, had struggled with her teeth to the point where she wanted them pulled, saying the pain was incalculable.

"You see," I explained, "when you intend to reproduce an item in large quantity, such as a flag or a military banner for multiple companies, you must be able to get the proportions correct over and over again. The stars in this field, numbering only thirteen, must be aligned just so, at all the edges—top, bottom, left, right. And the spaces between the stars too, aligned just so. Measured and measured again. Laborious because of the number of stars. But if you transform the stars into a circle, it's much easier to construct. There's less fussing. And a circle is a much stronger symbol to look at, it seems to me, as if we are all connected in the same struggle and cannot break apart. A circle of togetherness."

Washington looked at Uncle George and Morris, who both nodded.

"Yes, Mr. Washington, I can make this flag. I would be happy to."

There was some going back and forth between the men about cost and construction and circles versus free-flowing stars, and then rather quickly they reached a consensus. The men stood up. I stood up too, feeling pleased and eager. *Can you see this, John?*

Morris began to speak to me of payment when Uncle George interrupted.

"Betsy, it would be downright wrong of us to not point out that getting caught for making a flag for an independent America—"

"Is treason," I finished for him.

"Punishable by imprisonment, torture. Burning." He watched me closely, his face grave.

We stood there, the June sun streaming through the window from Mulberry Street, its golden light falling into my sewing room like a banner. The men looked at me expectantly, as if I was going to say more. In the silence was all that I knew: that America may not win, probably would not win against the biggest empire in the world, evidenced by the day-long cannon fire between a British warship and an American frigate on the Delaware River just a month ago. John had warned at length about how America was unarmed and unprepared, how important supplies and weapons were to winning, and how great the deficit currently was in the colonies for the continental army. That knowledge, that fear, had driven his trips down to the stockpile by the river.

"So be it," I said in a clear voice. Perhaps if I saw Francis Hopkinson at church, we could confer privately on the final design. I liked Mr. Hopkinson.

"You are brave, my dear," Uncle George said.

Tears pricked my eyes. *Brave. Finally.*

Yes, I thought, *I am now. For this.*

"Perhaps we could agree not to mention my name," I said, thinking of my parents. If I went to prison, if I were hanged, I could at least spare them that, after all they'd been through.

"An agreement between us. Nothing on paper. No acknowledgment."

"We give you our word," Washington said firmly.

"I'll begin right away," I said, remembering that Uncle George said there were men just a few streets from here who were busy writing a declaration of independence.

"To the cause," I said. "I wish you luck, gentlemen."

Epilogue

1835

My world is dark now. After more than seventy years of sewing, my sight has left me. Blindness is not a torment, for my days are waning and my pleasures are simple: the smell of my daughter's roses through the window, the softness of my silky pillows, the taste of sweet cherries, my grandchildren and great-grandchildren in my arms. I am at peace, and my hands, finally, are at rest.

That day of the hanging in 1777 seems as if it were this afternoon. The girl's screams. My father's fear. James Molesworth's body dangling and lifeless, the guard blandly reading his confession. I was not deterred: Two months later I received a large order from the continental Navy to make ship's colors. I sewed those flags with relish. And then I kept going. I made flag after flag for the government and its various branches for fifty years. My father never accepted it, but time takes care of many things. After the war ended in 1783, we simply didn't speak of it.

Sometimes my grandchildren ask me, *Weren't you afraid? Was it dangerous?* Yes, I was afraid, and I was frightened because it was very dangerous—what treason isn't?—but I believed in what I was doing. I was willing to take the risk. Although when the British invaded Philadelphia in the fall of 1777 and wrecked the city, I often wished I was just a seamstress making ladies garments. Especially when troops were quartered in my house—what an awful time that was. I was very worried then, especially after I heard what they did to female spies. I still kept secretly sewing for the cause. I did it for my John, too. That was the longest nine months of my life, when the soldiers were in the house. What a relief when they finally left the city.

Old age has been a surprise. I never expected to grow this old. My parents were killed by the yellow fever outbreak in 1793, along with my sister Deborah and, shortly thereafter, my dear Mary. My sister Rebecca died in the almshouse, too addled with drink to look after herself. She never married. Susannah, Sarah, George, even Rachel, they're gone too. It's just me and Hannah left now. We got along fine after she grew up.

I stayed in the house in Mulberry Street for almost ten years. Years later, long after I moved out, I walked by it every so often, even when there was no one left who remembered that it hadn't always been called Arch Street. The beautiful big tree is still out front. I would stare at the window and remember the day the flag committee came to see me.

Some days I have trouble believing it's been sixty years since the colonies declared their independence. I have outlived all three of my husbands. Although I was never blessed with John Ross's children, I had seven children in my next two marriages, all girls. Five lived beyond infancy. After Joseph's sad death in prison at the hands of the British, I found the comfort and joy of a long marriage with my third husband, John Claypoole, and we had more than thirty happy years together. After he died, my daughter Clarissa and I ran the upholstery business together. She carried it on after my sight failed and is stitching flags even now. I'm so proud.

My children have been a gift. When they were growing up, I told my daughters all about that day in '76 when George Washington came to the house with Uncle George and Robert Morris and we worked on the first American flag. It was so exciting. I only wish I had kept that paper sample flag he'd brought as a keepsake. I never dreamed for a minute that one day General Washington would be president. Before they left, they gave me instructions to buy all the bunting I could find to make the flags, as many as I could. If I could have that day back, I wouldn't ask to be invisible.

Francis Hopkinson claims he made the first star-spangled banner. That's the way of men, even the good ones. He certainly had many achievements, that's true, but not that first flag. It wasn't that simple. It may be wrong of me, but I'm glad Congress didn't pay him when he asked. They knew that carrying the war effort took many of us, and they told him as much. The need was great; there were so many new military units forming that needed banners and pennants and standards, not to mention all the boats the navy was organizing—they all needed ship's colors too. I was one of many upholsterers, and at least three other women, that were sewing flags and tents and shirts during the revolutionary war.

Except for that one day. That one special day in 1776 when those men came to my workshop with General Washington, and I showed them a five-pointed star, turned the square into a rectangle, and sewed that flag. That day is mine.

Author's Note

My goal is to bring interesting women from history back to life. As a historian, my commitment is to the truth. I'm passionate about getting the facts right and spend a lot of time combing through primary sources to uncover the historical detail that creates accuracy in my writing. Understanding the past as it actually occurred is so important. On the flip side, as a novelist, I am driven to tell a good story that will hold a reader's attention. Here's the tricky part: sometimes, when you're writing about people who lived two or three hundred years ago, you're faced with gaps in the written record. There's just . . . nothing. White space and silence. Or worse, you find conflicting information. That's when the fun begins: trying to bridge the gap in a meaningful way, digging for the truth, reimagining a life, and telling that person's story as you believe it may have happened. In *The Treason of Betsy Ross*, throughout my research and writing, I juggled the truth against the myth.

I first became interested in Betsy Ross in a meaningful way while doing my graduate degree in Public History at La Salle University. In an evening class one day in January 2020, a few of the other students suggested that the story wasn't true, that Betsy Ross hadn't sewn the first American flag, and that the Betsy Ross House was merely a Philadelphia tourist trap. I was intrigued. I needed to find out more.

I visited the Betsy Ross House and took the audio tour. That was my second time there; I had first visited in 2012 as a tourist with our two young daughters after we moved to the United States from Canada in 2008. The house itself is a wonderful time capsule spanning three centuries and well worth the visit—the front section was built in the 1740s—

making it one of Philadelphia's oldest structures. If you get a chance, please visit. There are many architectural details throughout the property that have withstood time, backed by a fascinating story of the people who first saved the house in the 1890s and then promoted her legend for many years after. (I was really thrilled to be able to do my graduate internship at the Betsy Ross House in 2022 for two months. Many thanks to Director Lisa Acker-Moulder for having me and for sharing her love of Betsy.)

I quickly learned that Betsy Ross was worth writing a novel about. Even if she had not made the first American flag, her story alone called to me. How did a young Philadelphia woman go from obedient Quaker girl to making musket cartridges for the revolutionary war effort? What a frightening, confusing, and exhilarating time to be alive. More than anything, I wanted to uncover the real Betsy Ross as she was in the years leading up to the American Revolution, when the streets of Philadelphia were filled with chaos and violence. I was interested in the real flesh-and-blood twenty-four-year-old girl behind the myth, the woman who walked the streets of revolutionary Philadelphia and chose to marry a militia man.

The woman we know as Betsy Ross only had that name for two years and two months of her long eighty-four-year life. She was Betsy Griscom, Betsy Ashburn, and Betsy Claypoole far longer than she was ever Betsy Ross. She was married to John Ross from November 1773 until he died in January 1776, and it was as his widow that she began making flags and actively engaging in treason. She not only sewed flags to earn an income, she voluntarily made musket cartridges to help the continental army fight the British.

Betsy Ross as a historical figure is controversial. Did she sew the first flag? Historians will point to the lack of evidence. Congress officially approved the design of the first US flag on June 14, 1777, and yet Betsy's daughters claimed their mother was clear that the meeting with Washington, Morris, and Ross took place a month before independence was declared, in 1776—a full year earlier. Critics point out that if Betsy Ross did sew the first flag, what happened in the year that followed? Why is there no record of the meeting that day, or of Congress's acceptance of the flag with Betsy's five-pointed stars? We'll never really know. Betsy had been raised in a Quaker environment that promoted humility and deliberately avoided notoriety. She lost her husband and became a widow because of John Ross's involvement in the revolution. These were dangerous times. During the war, she may have felt secrecy was necessary, and after the war she may not have had a mechanism to announce her role, other than to tell her children and grandchildren. It's important to remember there were many secret committees during the revolutionary war and espionage rings under Washington that much has been written about. They were trying to overthrow the government, and losing the war to the British was a real possibility. Through the first years of the American Revolution, the continental army continually struggled, and they lost more battles than they won.

Years after Betsy died, her daughter Clarissa, as an old woman, asked one of Betsy's grandsons, William Canby, to take notes while she told him what her mother had told her about making the first flag. Years later, William Canby presented his grandmother's story to the Pennsylvania Historical Society in 1870. As part of an effort to prevent Betsy Ross and her flag-making from fading into obscurity, no less than twenty-one of Betsy's family members and descendants, including her daughter Rachael, recorded their testimonies, which were notarized by a public notary and thus turned into legal documents. Why would so many people go to the trouble to do that unless they honestly felt they were preserving the truth?

Wrote Rachael Fletcher (one of Betsy's daughters with John Claypoole) in 1870 in Affidavit #3,

"I remember having heard my mother, Elizabeth Claypoole, say frequently that she with her own hands (while she was the widow of John Ross) made the first Star Spangled Banner that ever was made. I remember to have heard her also say that it was made on order of a committee, of whom Colonel Ross was one, and that Robert Morris was also one of the committee. That General Washington, acting in conference with the committee called with them at her house. This house was on the north side of Arch street a few doors below Third street, above Bread street, a two-story house with an attic and dormer window, now standing, the only one of the row left, the old number being 89. [. . .] That it was in the month of June 1776, or shortly before the Declaration of Independence that the committee called on her. That the member of the committee named Ross was an uncle of her deceased husband. That she was previously acquainted with Washington, and he had often been in her house on friendly visits, as well as on business."

A granddaughter and niece provided similar testimony, both of whom had actually worked for years with Betsy making flags in the family business. What reason would they have to lie? There is no indication that they profited from their statements.

I'm sure readers will ask me if I believe Betsy Ross really met with George Washington, Robert Morris, and George Ross that day in June 1776. The answer is: I do.

Philadelphia in 1776 was a city of about 30,000, and relationships were as interconnected, and intricate, as a large spider's web. George Ross and his nephew John Ross had worked closely together during the resistance. George Ross signed the Declaration of Independence and had been a member of the first congress. He was also a colonel in the continental army. When John Ross was killed (according to the family testimony, from injuries sustained by a gunpowder explosion), it's reasonable to assume that George Ross, in the time before social security nets, wanted to give his nephew's young widow work. He also knew they could trust her. It would not have been a hard sell for Colonel Ross: George Washington knew Betsy from Christ Church, where he would attend services when he was in town. In addition, Washington liked John and Betsy Ross well enough, or at least their upholstery work, to ask them to make three sets of bed hangings for him in September 1774 when he was in town. Proof of this can be found in the archives at Mount Vernon.

Do I believe Betsy Ross sewed the first American flag? I do. Her family's testimonials are earnest and detailed. You can read them for yourself in Oliver Randolph Parry's 1909 book, referenced in the 'Further Reading' section.

As to whether Betsy Ross designed the flag, I suspect not. Family memories say that Washington brought a paper sample of a square flag with them that Betsy improved upon. I believe Betsy Ross did suggest using five-pointed stars instead of six-pointed stars and that she may have suggested the stars be in a circle. What's extraordinary to me is that when Betsy Ross sewed that flag, she was a young woman in her early twenties deliberately going against the current legal government, consequences be damned, even though she had been raised as a law-abiding Quaker. The American Revolution was in its infancy, the prospects for victory no more than a candle in the wind. Betsy did not stop with sewing the American flag in 1776, she sewed flags for the new US Navy from 1777 onward. After the US became an independent nation, Betsy continued to make flags for many decades.

Those of you who know your American history will know that Francis Hopkinson (founding father and signer of the

328 • Author's Note

Declaration of Independence) claimed that he designed the US flag, as well as a seal for the US navy, and other items. In 1780, he wrote to the government seeking payment for this work. (The text of the letter exists today.) Congress refused to pay him, saying there were too many others who could make the same claim, and that it had been an effort of many rather than one. What if it had been Hopkinson who sketched out the paper sample that Washington brought to Betsy Ross that day?

Did Betsy Ross and Francis Hopkinson know each other? I like to think they did. They were both parishioners at Christ Church at various times and Hopkinson played the organ there. They must have known each other at some level. During the time that Betsy and John worked at Webster's upholstery, Francis Hopkinson sold fabric from his dry goods store on Walnut Street, between Fifth and Sixth Street, in Philadelphia. He was serious about his fabrics and advertised in several issues of *The Pennsylvania Gazette* to make sure everyone knew he sold the finest available. They 1772 tax record for Philadelphia lists five male upholsterers. One of them was John Webster, where John and Betsy were still working prior to marrying and setting up their own upholstery. There was a small enough number that it's likely that Hopkinson would have had a general idea who the Rosses were when they opened their own shop the following year. Or perhaps they only knew of each other from a distance. If that's the case, I think he and Betsy would have liked each other. Francis Hopkinson was known for being a fiery Patriot, just like Betsy.

Betsy Griscom Ross Ashburn Claypoole outlived Francis Hopkinson by forty-five years. Her body was moved three times, and she now rests outside the Betsy Ross House on Arch Street in Philadelphia. You won't find her story in any serious history book on women in the American Revolution.

Further Reading

If you have a fondness for the American Revolution, you may enjoy reading any of the titles in the list below. These are some of the books I read in order to really understand what was happening in Philadelphia at a detailed level through Betsy's youth from 1765 through 1779. I wanted to immerse myself in what Betsy Ross was seeing and experiencing. I am especially grateful for the scholarship of Anne Ousterhout, Mary Beth Norton, and Marla Miller, which gave me a rich landscape to draw from.

I would love to hear from you. Feel free to reach out to me through my website **www.wendystanley.com** or by email at **wendylongstanley@gmail.com**.

Atkinson, Rick. *The British Are Coming: The War for America, Lexington to Princeton, 1775-1777.* New York, Henry Holt and Company, 2019.

Boudreau, George W. *Independence: A Guide to Historic Philadelphia.* Yardley, Westholme Publishing, 2012.

Brands, H.W. *Our First Civil War: Patriots and Loyalists in the American Revolution.* New York, Doubleday, 2021.

Ellis, Joseph J. *The Cause: The American Revolution and Its Discontents, 1773-1783.* New York, Liveright Publishing Corporation, 2021.

Hagist, Don N. *Noble Volunteers: The British Soldiers Who Fought the American Revolution.* Yardley, Westholme Publishing, 2020.

Hoock, Holger. *Scars of Independence: American's Violent Birth*. New York, Broadway Books, 2017.

Miller, Marla R. *Betsy Ross and the Making of America*. New York, Henry Holt and Company, 2010.

Norton, Mary Beth. *1774: The Long Year of Revolution*. New York, Alfred A. Knopf, 2020.

Ober, Barbara B, ed. *Women in the American Revolution: Gender, Politics, and the Domestic World*. Charlottesville and London, University of Virginia Press, 2019.

Ousterhout, Anne M. *A State Divided: Opposition in Pennsylvania to the American Revolution*. New York, Greenwood Press, 1987.

Parry, Oliver Randolph. *Betsy Ross and the United States Flag: Philadelphia Woman Maker of the First Standard*. Doylestown, The Bucks County Historical Society, 1909.

Ryerson, Richard Alan. *The Revolution is Now Begun: The Radical Committees of Philadelphia, 1765-1776*. Toronto, University of Pennsylvania Press, 1978.

Slaughter, Thomas P. *Independence: The Tangled Roots of the American Revolution*. New York, Hill and Wang, 2014.

Smith, Robert F. *Manufacturing Independence: Industrial Innovation in the American Revolution*. Yardley, Westholme Publishing, 2016.

Wood, Gordon S. *The American Revolution: A History*. New York, Modern Library, 2002.